W9-DDF-919

HARLEQUIN SMALL TOWN CHRISTMAS COLLECTION

It's a wonderful time of year! A time when friends and family gather to celebrate the joy of the season with good food and beautiful gifts.

And where better to meet than in a small town? The warmth of community adds extra delight to Christmas. Even the hardest of hearts is warmed by the sight of Main Street wearing its festive finery. Seeing the town square decked out in bows, lights and holly brings a smile to every face.

There is even the possibility of romance for the unsuspecting beneath those sprigs of mistletoe!

So join us in this special 2-in-1 collection as we bring romance and good cheer to this special holiday.

If you enjoy these two classic stories, be sure to look for more books set in small towns in Harlequin Special Edition and Harlequin Superromance.

KATHLEEN O'BRIEN

is a former feature writer and TV critic who's written more than thirty-five novels. She's a five-time finalist for the Romance Writers of America RITA® Award and a multiple nominee for *RT Book Reviews* Awards. Though her books range from warmly witty to suspenseful, they all focus on strong characters and thrilling romantic relationships. They reflect her deep love of family, home and community, and her empathy for the challenges faced by women as they juggle today's complex lives.
Visit her online at kathleenobrien.com, facebook.com/kathleenobrienauthor, or twitter.com/kobrienromance.

Be sure to look for other books by Kathleen O'Brien in Harlequin Superromance—the ultimate destination for more story, more romance! There are new Harlequin Superromance titles available every month. Check one out today!

Kathleen O'Brien
and
Karen Templeton

A CHRISTMAS HOMECOMING

HARLEQUIN®SMALL TOWN CHRISTMAS

If you purchased this book without a cover you should be aware that this book is stolen property. It was reported as "unsold and destroyed" to the publisher, and neither the author nor the publisher has received any payment for this "stripped book."

Recycling programs
for this product may
not exist in your area.

ISBN-13: 978-0-373-60965-9

A Christmas Homecoming

Copyright © 2014 by Harlequin Books S.A.

The publisher acknowledges the copyright holders of the individual works as follows:

Christmas in Hawthorn Bay
Copyright © 2006 by Kathleen O'Brien

Husband Under Construction
Copyright © 2011 by Karen Templeton-Berger

All rights reserved. Except for use in any review, the reproduction or utilization of this work in whole or in part in any form by any electronic, mechanical or other means, now known or hereinafter invented, including xerography, photocopying and recording, or in any information storage or retrieval system, is forbidden without the written permission of the publisher, Harlequin Enterprises Limited, 225 Duncan Mill Road, Don Mills, Ontario, Canada, M3B 3K9.

This is a work of fiction. Names, characters, places and incidents are either the product of the author's imagination or are used fictitiously, and any resemblance to actual persons, living or dead, business establishments, events or locales is entirely coincidental.

This edition published by arrangement with Harlequin Books S.A.

For questions and comments about the quality of this book, please contact us at CustomerService@Harlequin.com.

® and TM are trademarks of the publisher. Trademarks indicated with ® are registered in the United States Patent and Trademark Office, the Canadian Intellectual Property Office and in other countries.

Printed in U.S.A.

CONTENTS

CHRISTMAS IN
HAWTHORN BAY

Kathleen O'Brien

CHAPTER ONE

NORA CARSON HAD ALWAYS found it hard to say no to Maggie, even when she knew that her bullheaded best friend was being stupid. Though Nora, at nineteen, was only three months older than Maggie, the younger girl had a way of making Nora's common sense sound pathetically boring.

And if making Nora feel like a fuddy-duddy didn't work, Maggie had big sad eyes and a killer pout, a little-girl-lost look that turned Nora—and just about everyone else—straight to mush.

This late-autumn Saturday, Maggie's nineteenth birthday, was no exception. Maggie, who was eight months pregnant, woke up with a hankering to go sailing. Nora knew it was a rotten idea, and so did Dr. Ethan Jacobs, the young obstetrician who had begun as Maggie's doctor when they'd arrived in town three months ago—and ended up more like a love slave with a stethoscope.

But neither of them could resist Maggie in a Mood.

So here they were, halfway to nowhere, with the Maine coast receding as Ethan's sails filled with crisp, clean wind. The cooler at their feet bulged with fried chicken, egg-salad sandwiches and bottled water. Ethan had caved in to Maggie's pressure first, and admitted that he knew a tiny island Maggie would love. Just a couple of miles wide, it had everything, he said—a green forest, a cliff, a small white waterfall.

Best of all, it was completely uninhabited. The perfect place to make the world go away for an afternoon.

They'd been on Ethan's tiny day sailer for almost an hour—the island was about ten miles offshore—when suddenly Maggie hopped up onto her cushioned seat and let out an exhilarated squeal.

"This is the best birthday *ever!* Oh, my God, I *love* this day!"

Nora, who was sitting at the back of the boat, couldn't help smiling. Maggie's spiky brown hair stood straight up in the wind, and her pregnant stomach looked as rounded and full of energetic purpose as the sails above her.

Maggie's moods were always infectious. If she was depressed, everyone around her suffered. But if she was happy…

"And I love *you!*" Maggie climbed down and wrapped Nora in a bear hug. She turned to Ethan, who was angling the tiller, and, taking his face in her hands, covered his parted lips with a loud, smacking kiss. "And you, my dashing seafarer!"

Then she whirled away, and, with a contented sigh, leaned over to drag her fingers in the green current that rushed along the side of the boat.

Nora caught Ethan's gaze. Behind his wire-rimmed glasses, he looked stunned, as if he'd never been this close to anything as dazzling as Maggie. The sails began to luff, as Ethan forgot to steer, but he corrected the mistake and shrugged sheepishly, his cheeks pink.

Just last night, he had confessed to Nora that he was in love with Maggie. When Ethan had finished rubbing Maggie's feet, which had been sore after a long day waiting tables at the lobster shack, she had stumbled off to bed, leaving Nora and Ethan alone together.

He had flushed the entire time he spoke. He knew it was inappropriate, he said, given that Maggie was his patient, but he couldn't help it. She'd made her way into his blood, and he was going to ask her to marry him.

What did Nora think? Would Maggie say yes?

Nora wasn't sure. For all her childlike displays of emotion, Maggie kept her deepest truths in darkest secret. That's how you knew something really mattered to her—the bubbling stream of chatter suddenly dried up to dust.

Though they'd been best friends since they'd eaten paste together in kindergarten, Nora had accepted that there were things she'd never learn, no matter how many times she asked.

Like where Maggie got that old-fashioned gold ring she wore on a chain around her neck.

Or who was the father of her baby.

"Land ahoy!" Maggie leaned way out this time, pointing east. "I see it!"

"Maggie," Ethan said sharply, "don't lean out so far! You could fall overboard!"

"Stop being such a worrywart." Maggie cast a sour look at Ethan, then went back to dragging her hand in the water. "Even if I did fall over, I know how to swim."

Nora gave Ethan a look, too. She tried to signal that bossing Maggie around was not a good idea. Maggie hated domineering, patriarchal men—probably because her father was one of the worst. Nora knew that Mr. Nicholson had hit Maggie, at least twice, and she often wondered what else might have happened that Maggie didn't confide.

But Ethan wasn't paying any attention to Nora. He was still watching Maggie, and his mouth was set in an anxious line. Nora looked over at her friend, too. Maggie had both hands on her belly, and her face was gripped in a sudden, strange tension.

"What is it?" Nora leaned forward. "Is something wrong?"

"I'm fine. Carry on."

Ethan's dark brows pulled together. "Are you having contractions?"

"I'm *fine,* sailor." Maggie waved her hand nonchalantly, clearly trying to lighten the mood. Nora couldn't blame her. Ethan did hover a bit. "Colin was just giving me one of his Morse code messages. You know, punch-punch-jab-poke. I think he said something about *nappy turfday.*"

Nora smiled. Maggie always called the baby Colin, though the ultrasound had been inconclusive as to sex. She'd decided it was a boy, and, as usual, the facts didn't really concern her.

But Ethan wasn't buying it. He reached out with a doctor's instinctive authority and put his hand on Maggie's stomach. "I don't like it. You sure he's not saying something about going into labor?"

Maggie stood up and moved beyond Ethan's reach. "My Morse code is pretty rusty, but I think I could tell the difference between 'Happy birthday, Mom,' and 'Look out, here I come!'"

"Could you?"

She glared at him. "Colin is fine. I said *carry on.*" It always frustrated her when the universe didn't fall right in line with her plans. "Look, not only is this my birthday, but this may be the last completely free day I have for—oh, say eighteen years? So don't you two go all smothery and cheat me out of it, okay?"

Ethan adjusted his glasses. "But in the third trimester—"

Maggie stood on the seat, stepped one foot up onto the gunwale and pointed her hands over her head in the classic diving position. "I'm going to that island," she said, "if I have to swim the rest of the way."

Ethan laughed nervously. "Get down, you dork. Do you want to slip?"

He wasn't really concerned that she'd jump. But Nora knew Maggie better than he did. She glanced quickly toward the island, calculating the distance. Only about a hundred yards. Maggie could swim it. And, if he didn't back off, she just might.

"Ethan, don't piss me off." Maggie wasn't laughing. "You're not my father."

"No, I'm your *doctor*. I simply can't allow you to take foolish risks—"

Nora groaned. Too bossy. He even sounded a little like Maggie's father. Maggie despised her father.

She dove into the ocean with an emphatic splash.

Ethan lurched. "For God's sake, *Maggie!*"

She ignored him, her arms cutting through the water with a brisk freestyle. Her feet churned up little green-white whirlpools, and soon she was moving faster than the boat.

"She's a great swimmer," Nora said when Ethan turned around to give her a horrified, open-mouthed stare. "At home, we swim all the time."

"But she's eight months pregnant! She has no idea how dangerous that is."

He looked down at the water, and Nora knew he was thinking of diving in after Maggie.

"Bad idea," she said. "You know how stubborn she is. She'll fight you till you both drown."

Though his adoration made him act silly sometimes, Ethan wasn't stupid. He knew when he was outmaneuvered. Obviously the only thing they could do right now was stay close to Maggie, and get to the island as fast as possible.

He sat, wiped his water-speckled glasses on his shirt, and then grabbed hold of the tiller. It took several seconds, but he adjusted the sails until they caught the wind.

They were only a few yards behind Maggie, just a few feet to her left—Ethan was steering as close to the wind as he could, so that they wouldn't separate much. Her small white face kept turning toward them every other stroke. Once, Nora could have sworn Maggie stuck out her tongue at them.

"Little brat," Ethan murmured. But Nora saw that he was smiling—and, in spite of her annoyance with Maggie, she felt happy for her. How great to have someone love you so much they even found your flaws adorable.

Back in high school, Maggie's edgy personality had scared off most of the guys. She'd had only one boyfriend, as far as Nora knew—a short, dumb fling with Mr. Jenkins, their senior biology teacher who shortly afterward had married the English lit teacher and had moved out of town. Nora assumed Mr. J. must be the father of the baby, though of course Maggie wouldn't discuss it.

But perhaps Mr. Jenkins had been a sign. Maggie needed someone a little older, a lot wiser.

Yes. Nice, honest, loyal and *unmarried* Ethan would be good for Maggie.

If only she'd have him.

The wind had shifted, so Ethan had to tack. Maggie beat them to the beach by at least five minutes, and they were coming in several yards west of her.

All they could do was watch as she climbed out of the surf, little bits of foam clinging to her bare legs. She shook water from her ears and ran her fingers through her hair to spike it back up where it belonged. Finally, she assumed a pose of exaggerated boredom, as if they were taking forever.

And then, abruptly, she doubled over, gripping her stomach with both hands.

Ethan made a skeptical sound. "Faker," he said. "I'm not falling for that one."

Was it just a joke? If so, it wasn't one bit funny—it was actually damned scary. Would Maggie really be such a jerk? Nora frowned and moved to the other side of the boat, hoping to make out the details of Maggie's face.

But her chin was tucked down against her breastbone. Her shoulders were hunched, and her hands were still hanging on to her stomach, fingers widespread and curved, like stiff claws.

"No," Nora said through suddenly cold lips. "No, she's not faking. You know how she is. She never pretends to be weak. She always pretends to be strong."

Ethan frowned. They had almost made land. A shrill cry reached them, knifing through the crisp autumn silence. It sounded like a gull, but it was Maggie.

"Oh, my God," he said. His knuckles were stark white around the tiller.

As they watched, Maggie swayed from side to side, as if she were wrestling with something inside her. And then she sank to her knees in the sand.

The sailboat was only fifteen feet from shore. Without thinking, Nora jumped out and waded through the cold, chest-high water as fast as her trembling legs would take her. Behind her, she heard Ethan jump out, too.

Her feet were clumsy on the grainy sand, but she ran as fast as she could. She reached Maggie just as she toppled over onto her side, her hands still wrapped around her stomach.

"Honey, honey, what's wrong?" Nora dropped to her knees beside the moaning girl. "Is it the baby? Is the baby coming?"

"I don't know." Maggie's face was coated with sand. Her voice sounded high, half-strangled with either pain or fear. "Maybe, but...but it's too soon. And it hurts. I think something's wrong."

"How exactly does it feel?"

Maggie turned her face toward the sand. "It hurts."

"Did your water break?" It might be hard to tell, Nora thought, given that Maggie was soaking wet all over.

For the first time, Nora looked down at Maggie's legs. They were streaming with pale, watery blood.

The comforting words Nora had been about to say died away. This wasn't right. This wasn't what she'd been told to expect. She'd been to the birthing classes, and it had all sounded so organized. Step one, step two, step three...

No one had said anything about pale, quivering legs

laced in blood that grew a brighter red with every passing second.

She didn't know what to do. But even if she had known, she wouldn't have been able to do it. She was going to faint.

Why, why had she listened to Maggie? Why had they come out here, to the end of the world, all alone? And before that…why hadn't she insisted that they go home to Hawthorn Bay and tell Maggie's parents about the baby? Maggie should have delivered her baby in the little hospital by the bridge, with a dozen brave, experienced adults to see it through.

But Nora had never been able to make Maggie do anything. Maggie was the strong one, the defiant one—she didn't care what anyone thought of her. She didn't need anyone, she always said. Not even Nora.

And maybe she didn't. Maybe she would have been just fine alone. But, though Nora was almost painfully homesick to be back in Hawthorn Bay, back in her own little yellow bedroom at Heron Hill, she hadn't been able to leave Maggie behind.

Under all that defiance, there was something…something tragic and vulnerable about Maggie. Nora had decided to stay with her, at least until the baby was born.

After that they'd decide what to do next.

Ethan was still thigh-deep in the water, trudging toward them, pulling the small sailboat along by a tug line. Intellectually, Nora knew he was right to take the time—they couldn't afford to let the boat drift away. No one knew where they were. Even Ethan's father, who was also a doctor, just thought they were having a picnic in the park.

But emotionally she wanted him to just drop the line

and race over here. He was one of the brave, experienced adults they needed. She was only a teenager, and she wasn't ready for this.

Maggie had begun to weep. "It hurts," she said again, and she reached out for Nora's hand.

Ethan finally dragged the boat onto the sand. A couple of gulls landed near it, obviously hoping for dinner. Ethan reached into the cockpit and extracted their beach towels and his cell phone.

Oh, God, hurry.

He punched numbers into the phone as he ran toward them. He listened, then clicked off and started over.

It was like watching a mime. Even from this distance, Nora could read the significance of that wordless message. They had no phone signal. They were officially in the middle of nowhere.

And they were officially alone.

When he reached them, Nora focused on his eyes—she knew the truth would be there. She'd known him only a few months, but she had already learned that he was a terrible liar.

For just a second, when he saw the blood, his eyes went black. For that same second, so did Nora's heart.

She felt an irrational spurt of fury toward him, as if by confirming her fears he had somehow betrayed Maggie. She turned resolutely away from his anguished gaze.

"You're going to be okay, honey," she said, but she heard the note of rising panic in her voice and wished she hadn't spoken.

Maggie stared at her with wild eyes. "There shouldn't be blood," she said. "There shouldn't be blood."

Ethan touched Maggie's shoulder gently. "We have to

see what's causing it. And we need to see what's going on with the baby. I need to know if you're dilated."

Maggie moaned in response.

"Nora," he said without looking at her. "Please get the water bottles out of the cooler." He held out the phone. "And take this. I don't think it's going to work, but keep trying."

She clutched the phone and started to run, her sodden tennis shoes squishing with every step, making mud of the sand. Though there were no bars on the cell phone's display, indicating they had no service, her fingers kept hitting 911 over and over.

By the time she had gathered the little plastic bottles in her arms and run back to the others, she'd tried 911 a dozen times.

Nothing.

While she'd been gone, Ethan had somehow spread out the towels, arranged Maggie on them, and removed her shorts and shoes.

Nora didn't look at anything below Maggie's face. She couldn't allow herself to see how much blood there was. She couldn't even think about how the baby might be coming. Here, in this empty place. A full month too early...

She gave Ethan the water, and then she took her place at Maggie's shoulder.

Maggie rolled her face toward Nora, and the whites of her eyes were so huge that for a minute she looked like a frightened colt.

"Ethan will take care of everything," Nora said numbly as she took Maggie's hand. She felt like the recording of a person, programmed to speak words she didn't even understand, much less believe.

Maggie's face was so white. Was that what happened when you lost too much blood? Nora wanted to ask Ethan, but she didn't want Maggie to hear the answer.

She didn't want to hear the answer, either.

Ethan had positioned himself between Maggie's knees. He'd opened some of the water, and poured it onto a small towel. He must have been hurting her, because Maggie's grip on Nora's hand kept tightening, until she thought the bones might break.

"Ethan will fix it." She realized she was speaking as much to Ethan as to Maggie, telling him that he had no choice, he had to make this right. "Ethan won't let anything happen to you."

"I don't care about me," Maggie said, shutting her eyes and squeezing her fingers again. "Just be sure the baby is all right, that's all that matters."

Nora nodded. "Yes. Of course the baby—both of you will be fine."

"You've got to relax, Maggie." Ethan shook his head. "I need you to relax so I can find out what's going on." He glanced at Nora, the consummate doctor now, all business and no emotion. "Talk to her," he said.

About what? About the blood? About the cell phone that was no more useful than a lump of scrap metal? About the miles of ocean that stretched out all the way to the horizon?

Over by the boat, more gulls were arriving, screaming overhead and diving for crumbs, like vultures.

She swallowed, her mind casting about. "Did you ever tell Ethan why you call the baby Colin, Maggie? Did you ever tell him about Cornwall?"

Amazingly, she seemed to have hit on the right subject. Maggie seemed to be trying to smile. "We were happy in Cornwall," she whispered.

"Yes." Nora nodded. It had been a lovely summer—and it was, she thought, the only time she'd ever seen Maggie completely relax. It was the only time the underlying vulnerability had seemed to vanish.

"You tell him, Nora." Maggie nudged her hand. "Tell Ethan about Colin."

Ethan wasn't listening, Nora knew, but it wouldn't hurt to talk. It was a good memory, and it would at least distract Maggie for a minute or two.

"When we graduated last spring, my parents gave us a trip to England," she began awkwardly. She smiled down at Maggie. "Four whole months abroad, just the two of us. We couldn't believe our luck."

Maggie shut her eyes. "And all thanks to Jack," she said with a hint of her normal dry sarcasm.

Nora let that part go. Ethan didn't need to hear about Jack Killian. But it was true—the trip had been partly to celebrate their high-school graduation, and partly, Nora's parents hoped, to help Nora get over the broken heart handed her by Black Jack Killian.

"We liked London," she went on. "But we really fell in love with Cornwall, didn't we, Maggie?"

Maggie's eyes were still shut, but she nodded, just a fraction of an inch, and she once again tried to smile. It had shocked Nora to see Maggie, whose punk sassiness seemed much better suited to the London club scene, bloom like an English rose among the brutal cliffs, stoic stone houses and secret, windswept gardens of Cornwall.

But from their first night in the West Country, which they'd spent in a tiny fishing village that echoed with the cries of cormorants and the strange, musical accents of the locals, Maggie had clearly been at *home*.

"We met Colin Trenwith in Cornwall," Nora said. "I think it was love at first sight for Maggie."

Finally, Ethan looked up. Nora knew he'd always thought Colin might be the name of the baby's father.

She smiled. "Or at least we met his ghost," she added. "Maggie found his tombstone. He was a pirate who died in the 1700s. I think she fell in love with that name, right from the start."

Ethan blinked behind his glasses, then returned to his work.

Nora tried not to see what he was doing. Instead she pictured Maggie, kneeling in front of the tilted tombstone in that half-forgotten cemetery overlooking the Atlantic.

"Nora, listen," she'd called out excitedly. "Colin Trenwith, 1756–1775. Once a Pirate, Twice a Father, Now at Rest with his Lord." She'd run her fingers over the carving. "Isn't that the most poetic epitaph you've ever heard?"

Maggie hadn't been able to tear herself away. She'd begged Nora to linger another week in Cornwall, and then another. They'd changed their tickets, and, cloaked and hooded against the wind, they'd hiked every day to the graveyard.

While Nora read, Maggie used Colin's stone as a backrest and invented romantic stories about the boy who had packed so much life into his nineteen short years.

It was there, in that cemetery, that Nora had realized her parents were right—a new perspective had been just what she needed. Jack Killian had hurt her, yes, but her heartache was neither as immense as the Atlantic beside these ancient tombstones, nor as permanent as the deaths recorded on them.

And it was there, in that cemetery, breaking off impulsively in the middle of a tragic tale, that Maggie had first confessed her secret.

She was pregnant.

She was going to name her son Colin.

And she was never going home to Hawthorn Bay again.

So far, she hadn't. Though they'd left England, having run out of money, they hadn't gone home. They'd taken a bus from New York's airport to small-town Maine and found menial jobs here, so that Maggie could have her baby in secret. Nora had called her parents, to let them know they were all right, though for Maggie's sake she couldn't tell them exactly where they were.

Maggie hadn't called her family at all.

"We have to get back to the mainland," Ethan interrupted tersely. "Right away. We have to get her back on the boat."

Maggie cried out and her body jackknifed, as if someone had stabbed her from the inside.

"No," she said, her voice tortured. "No. Do it here. The baby's coming, Ethan. It's too late to go back."

Nora balanced herself with one hand on the wet sand. "Is it true? Is the baby coming?"

He nodded. "She's already seven centimeters." He gazed down at Maggie. "You must have been having contractions all morning, you little fool."

Maggie shifted her head on the beach towel, grimacing. "Just twinges. Braxton-Hicks, I thought."

Nora knew what that meant. When she'd agreed to

stay in Maine with Maggie until the baby was born, she'd agreed to be her labor coach. Braxton-Hicks. False labour. Not uncommon in the weeks prior to delivery.

Maggie looked at Nora, as if she needed absolution for the sin of such dangerous foolishness. "Honestly, I didn't think— Everyone says it takes so long the first time—"

"Well, it's not going to take long for you." Ethan sounded tense. "We have to get you back on the boat. Even if the baby is born there, we have to do it."

Nora twitched her brows together, silently asking the question. Why? Why did they have to take such a risk? Surely it was safer here, where they at least had solid ground under their feet. *Why go?*

For answer, Ethan simply held up his hand. It was covered in blood, from fingertip to wrist, like a red rubber glove.

Nora felt the beach tilt. She thought for a minute she might pass out. It wasn't just the baby coming early, then. Maggie was in real trouble. She was losing too much blood.

Maggie must have seen Ethan's hand, too, though they both thought her eyes had been closed. Her whole body clenched, and then once again she reached for Nora's fingers.

"Nora. Listen to me. If anything happens, I want you to take the baby."

Nora pulled back instinctively, as if the words had burned her. Her heart was beating triple time, and her flesh felt cold.

"Don't talk like that, Megs," she said. She forced a teasing note into her voice. "It's absurd. I know you love melodrama, but this isn't the time. You need to focus on your breathing."

"Not yet." Maggie's gaze bore into hers. "If it's absurd, we'll all have a good laugh about it later. But just in case. I want you to promise me that you'll take the baby."

Ethan was wrapping the towels around her. He must have done something that hurt. Maggie cried out, and her legs stiffened.

"I'm sorry," he whispered. Nora saw a bead of sweat make its way down his hairline and mingle with a smear of blood on his cheek.

"Promise me, Nora."

"Okay," Nora said as she began to shiver. "Okay, Maggie, I promise. Now please. Focus."

"And you must never let my parents know. About Colin. They can't have him. My father—"

Maggie bent over again, making a sound like a small animal.

Ethan cleared his throat. "Nora, you have to help me carry her."

When had Ethan stood up? Nora felt confused. This was a nightmare, where things happened in confusing, nonsequential jerks. But she had her part to play in the nightmare, too, so she struggled to her feet, though she no could longer feel them or trust that they were rigid enough to carry her own weight, let alone a bleeding woman and an unborn baby.

Maggie was so light, though, frighteningly light, as if part of her had bled away into the beach. They tried not to jostle her, but once or twice she seemed to pass out, then come back to consciousness with a groan.

Ethan cradled her in his arms while Nora made a

pallet out of blood-soaked beach towels on the floor of the cockpit. As they placed her on it, Maggie seemed to rally a little. With one hand that, though it shook, seemed surprisingly strong, she pulled off the chain that held the mysterious gold ring.

She held it out to Nora.

"For you," she said. Her voice seemed slurred. "For Colin."

Nora took it, and her first tear fell.

Colin Trenwith.

Once a pirate, twice a father, now at rest with his Lord.

While Ethan towed the boat out to deeper water, Nora chanted the epitaph silently, over and over, like a prayer.

And then, with the words still circling through her mind, like a slender chain wrapping its fractured pieces together, Nora watched Ethan climb into the little boat, and the three of them set sail for home.

CHAPTER TWO

Eleven years later

MOTHERHOOD, NORA CARSON decided as she retreated to the kitchen, leaving her eleven-year-old son pouting in the living room, was not for the faint of heart.

Nora had three jobs—mayor of Hawthorn Bay, co-owner of Heron Hill Preserves and mom to Colin Trenwith Carson.

Of the three, being Colin's mom was by far the toughest.

At least it was *this* week. Last week, when the Hawthorn Bay City Council had been sued by a recently fired male secretary claiming sexual discrimination, *mayor* had been at the top of Nora's tough list.

Luckily, Nora had kept some of the secretary's letters, all of which began *Deer Sir.* She produced them at her deposition, explaining that she didn't give a hoot whether their secretaries were male, female or Martian, as long as they could spell.

The lawyers withdrew the suit the next day.

Now if only she could make this problem with Colin go away as easily. But she had a sinking feeling that it was going to prove much thornier.

She put the blackberries and pectin on to boil—she had orders piled up through next Easter, so she couldn't afford a full day off. She read the letter from Colin's teacher while she stirred.

Cheating.

Fighting.

Completely unrepentant.

These weren't words she ordinarily heard in connection with Colin. He wasn't perfect, not by a long shot. He was a mischievous rascal and too smart for his own good. But he wasn't *bad*.

This time, though—

"Nora, thank heaven you're home!" Stacy Holtsinger knocked on the back door and opened it at the same time. She was practically family, after eight years as business partner and best friend, and she didn't bother with ceremony much anymore.

Nora folded the letter and slid it into the pocket of the World's Greatest Mom apron Colin had given her for her birthday. "Where else would I be, with all these orders to fill? Out dancing?"

Stacy, a tall brunette with a chunky pair of tortoise-shell glasses that she alternately used as a headband, a pointer or a chew toy, but never as glasses, went straight to the refrigerator and got herself a bottled water. She wanted to lose ten pounds by Christmas and was convinced she could flood them out on a tidal wave of H2O.

Nora thought privately that Stacy would look emaciated if she lost any more weight, but the water sure did give her olive skin a gorgeous glow. She wondered if Stacy had her eye on a new man. She hoped so.

"Well," Stacy said, raking her glasses back through her hair as she slipped onto a stool, "you could be down at city hall, I guess, trying to knock sense into those Neanderthals. Which would be disastrous right now, because I need you to make an executive decision about the new labels."

Nora groaned as she added the sugar to the blackberries. Her mind was already packed to popping with decisions to make. What to do about the latest city-council idiocy—trying to claim eminent domain over Sweet Tides, the old Killian estate by the water? What to do about that crack in her living-room wall, which might be the foundation settling, something she could not afford to fix right now?

And, hanging over everything, like a big fat thundercloud—what to do about Colin?

"Labels are your side of the business." The berries were just about ready. Nora pulled out the tablespoon she'd kept waiting in a glass of cold water, and dropped a dollop of the jam on it. *Rats.* Not quite thick enough.

"Come on, Nora. Please?"

Nora looked over her shoulder. "Stacy, do I consult you about whether to buy Cherokee or Brazos? What to do if the jam's too runny? No. I make the product, you figure out how to sell it, remember?"

"Yeah, but—" Stacy held up a proof sheet. "This is a really big change. And I drew the artwork myself. I'm sorry. I'm weak. I need reassurance."

Nora put the spoon down. It was probably true. Stacy was one of the most attractive and capable women Nora knew, but her self-esteem had flatlined about five years ago when her husband had left her, hypnotized by the dirigible-shaped breasts of their twenty-year-old housekeeper.

Zach was a fool—although rumor had it he was a happy fool, having discovered that The Dirigible was into threesomes with her best friend, whom Stacy had dubbed The Hindenburg.

"Okay." Nora wiped her hands. "Show me."

Nora would have said she loved it no matter what, but luckily the new label was gorgeous. Done in an appropriate palette of plums, purples, roses and blues—all the best berry colors—it showed a young beauty on a tree swing, with a house in the background that was the home of everyone's fantasies—wide, sunny porch, rose-twined columns and lace curtains fluttering at cheerful windows.

Everyone wished they'd grown up in that house.

But Nora really had.

She looked up at Stacy. "You used the real Heron Hill?"

The other woman nodded. "You don't mind, do you? I changed it a little, so that no one could sue or anything. But it is the ultimate dream house, don't you think? It was our business name before you sold the house, and we've worked that out legally with the new owners, so—" She broke off, fidgeting with her glasses. "I mean…you really don't mind, do you?"

"Of course not." Nora smiled. She'd been born at Heron Hill. And Colin had spent his first few years there. It had indeed been the dream house. But when her father had died, and Nora discovered that the Carson fortune was somewhat overrated, she and her mother had decided to sell it.

Heron Hill was now a very popular local bed-and-breakfast. Nora's mother had moved to Florida last year, so she didn't have to pine over the loss. It stung Nora, though, sometimes, when she passed it and spotted a stranger standing at the window of her old bedroom.

But whenever that happened, she just reminded herself of the big fat trust fund they'd set up for Colin with the proceeds from the house, and she'd walk on by, with her chin up and no regret.

"The label is gorgeous," she said. "It will sell so well I won't be able to keep up with the demand."

"Great. I'll tell the printers today." Stacy tucked the proof back into its protective folder and gazed happily up at Nora. "Now, can I return the favor? I haven't a clue whether Cherokee or Brazos blackberries taste better, but I do have a breakdown of their sales figures for the past three years, which might—"

Nora laughed. "No, no, I've got that part covered. But I—I could use some advice about Colin. He's gotten himself into some trouble, and I'm not sure how to handle it."

Stacy raised one eyebrow. "Colin's in trouble? Trouble he can't charm his way out of? I didn't know there was such a thing."

Nora knew that wasn't just empty flattery. With his curly black hair, big blue eyes and dimpled smile, Colin was already so handsome and winning that most adults couldn't stay mad, no matter what he did. He'd get caught right in the act of something devilish, like the time he'd learned the signs for several off-color words and had the class rolling out of their seats with laughter while his poor teacher tried to figure out what the joke was. Or the time he and a few friends had fiddled with the school's front marquee and changed the phrase We Love Our Students to We Love Our Stud Nest.

Both times, Colin had apologized so humbly—even, in a nice touch, using the sign for *ashamed*—that the principal had ended up praising his honesty instead of kicking him out of class.

"I know, but this time it's different," Nora said. The jam was ready, and she began to pour it into the sterilized jars she had lined up on the central island. This little house, which she'd bought after selling Heron Hill, wasn't much to look at, but it had a fantastic kitchen.

"Different how?"

Nora sighed. "They say he and Mickey Dickson cheated on their math test."

Stacy raised her brows. "What? He hates Mickey Dickson. Heck, I hate Mickey Dickson. Sorry, I know he's some kind of cousin of yours, but the kid is a brat. And an idiot. I take it Mickey cheated off Colin's paper, not vice versa?"

"Yes, but Colin let him. He said he knew Mickey had been doing it for months, so this time he made it easy...and he deliberately answered all the questions wrong, so that Mickey would get caught. He said he didn't mind going down, as long as he brought Mickey down with him."

"Yikes." Stacy shook her head. "That's gutsy. Dumb, but gutsy."

"Yeah, and that's not all. After school he and Mickey had a fistfight on the softball field. Tom called about an hour ago. He and Mickey just got back from the emergency room. They thought his nose might be broken, but apparently not, thank God."

Stacy twirled her glasses thoughtfully and let out a low whistle. "Wow. It does sound as if Colin has slipped off the leash. What are you going to do?"

"I have no idea. He starts his Christmas break soon, which is both good and bad. Good, because he won't have to see Mickey, but bad because he'll have way too much spare time. Colin and 'free time' are a recipe for disaster."

"Maybe you can get him to help you with the jams."

Nora laughed as she screwed the lid onto the first of the filled jars. "No way. He's a bull in a china shop. Last time he helped, he broke a gross of jars and ate more berries than he canned. We'd be out of business by New Year's."

Stacy laughed, too, but she kept twirling her glasses, which meant she took the problem seriously.

"Besides," Nora went on. "Hanging out here with me is too easy. We'd have fun. I want to give him some chore that really hurts. Something he'll hate so much he won't even think about getting in trouble again."

Stacy scrunched up her brow, thinking hard. "Man, I don't know. What did your parents do when you got in trouble?"

Nora tilted her head and cocked one side of her mouth up wryly.

"Oh, that's right," Stacy said, laughing. "I forgot you were the reigning Miss Perfect for a couple of decades there."

"Miss Boring is more like it." Nora began wiping down the countertop, though she hadn't spilled much. "My friend Maggie used to say that if she weren't around to keep things stirred up I would probably turn to stone."

"I wish I could have met her," Stacy said. "You always make her sound like a human stick of dynamite. I'll bet she'd know how to handle Colin."

Nora's eyes stung suddenly. She turned around so

that Stacy couldn't read her face too easily. "Yes," she agreed. "She probably would."

"Well, okay, let's think. I wasn't exactly dynamite, but I wasn't Miss Perfect, either. I remember one summer, when I was about sixteen, and I'd just met Zach. I stayed out until dawn. I thought my dad was going to kill Zach, but my mom held him back. They made me spend the rest of my summer volunteering every night at the local nursing home."

"Oh, yeah? How did that go?"

"It was hell. I wanted to be wrapped in Zach's manly arms, and instead I was reading the sports section to an old guy who hacked up phlegm into his plastic cup every few sentences and kept yelling, *'Nothin' but net!'* every time I mentioned the Gamecocks."

Nora laughed.

"It's not funny," Stacy said, though there was a twinkle in her eye. "It could have scarred me for life. To this day, whenever I see a basketball, I twitch."

"Okay, then, I won't send Colin to the nursing home just yet. I'll reserve that for the day he comes home at dawn smelling of Chanel."

She looked toward the living room, which was suspiciously quiet. "Right now he's in there stuffing candy canes into the goody bags for the Christmas party. Even that little punishment annoyed him. He seemed to think nearly breaking Mickey's nose was a gift to mankind, something to be applauded."

"In there?" Stacy pointed with her tortoiseshell glasses. "Sorry, but I don't think so. I'm pretty sure I saw him climbing the tree when I came in."

Nora frowned, then, without stopping to say a word, reached for the latch. She yanked the door open and, pulling her sweater closed against the blast of December wind, took the steps down to ground level quickly.

Oh, good grief. Stacy was right. Colin wasn't indoors, working through his punishment. He was about six feet up the leafless maple tree, hanging by his knees from a large, spreading branch. His sweater nearly smothered his face, leaving his skinny rib cage exposed and probably freezing.

Beneath him, his friend Brad Butterfield squatted in the middle of about two dozen scattered candy canes, some broken to bits inside their plastic wrappers. Both Brad and Colin were eating candy canes themselves, letting them dangle from their lips like red-striped cigarettes.

"Come on, Colin, you're only hitting like thirty percent. Let me try. It'll take us all day to do these damn bags at this rate."

"Shut up, butt-head," Colin said, his voice muffled under folds of wool. "You're the boat, and I'm the bomber. That's the deal. Now…target ready?"

With a heavy sigh of irritation, Brad began moving the paper bag slowly across the winter-brown grass. When he was directly under Colin's head, a candy cane came sailing down. It fell squarely into the bag, and both Colin and Brad made triumphant booming sounds.

Stacy, who now stood at Nora's shoulder, chuckled softly. "Well, what a coincidence," she said. "Nothing but net."

MOST PEOPLE IN Hawthorn Bay said the Killian men had an unhealthy obsession with gold. A Civil War Killian ancestor supposedly buried his fortune in small caches all over the Sweet Tides acreage, and no Killian since had been able to drag himself away from the house, no matter how hard the community tried to run them off.

But Jack Killian, who hadn't set foot in Hawthorn Bay for twelve years and therefore had a more objective perspective, didn't think their problem was the gold.

It was the water.

Living in the South Carolina lowlands meant your feet weren't ever quite dry. Thousands of acres of spartina marshland, endless blue miles of Atlantic coastline, haunted black swamps and twisting ribbons of tea-colored rivers—that was what Jack saw when he dreamed of home, not the antebellum columns and jasmine-scented porches of Sweet Tides.

And certainly not the gold.

Almost every major incident in his life was tied to the water. He'd been four the day they'd dragged his grandmother out of the river behind Sweet Tides, where she'd unsuccessfully tried to drown herself. He'd been nine the day he'd broken his fibula learning to waterski behind their new boat—Killian luck never lasted long, and that boat had been sold, dime on the dollar, before the cast had come off Jack's leg. He'd been sixteen the day his mother, lying on the floor in a pool of her own blood, had sent him to find his father, who'd been drinking malt liquor at a shanty on the edge of Big Mosquito Swamp. It was the first time Jack had driven a car alone.

And, of course, he had won Nora Carson on the water—the day they'd wandered away from a high school science trip to a loblolly pine hammock, and he'd kissed her beside a cluster of yellow water lilies.

He'd lost her on the water, too, the day he'd taken her filthy cousin Tom out to a deserted spoil island, beat the crap out of him and left him there to swim home on his own. He hadn't realized that he'd broken Tom's arm, rendering the jerk unable to swim an inch, but the cops had decided ignorance was no excuse.

Jack had escaped an attempted-murder charge by the skin of his teeth, and by a timely enlistment in the United States Army.

He hadn't been home since. Until today.

He drove his Jaguar around back, between the house and the river. In Jack's lifetime, no one but the sheriff had ever entered Sweet Tides from the fancy front, where gray, peeling Doric columns guarded the portico like ghosts from a long-lost world.

Yeah, the front of Sweet Tides was pure Greek tragedy, but the back was merely pleasantly ragged, with mossy oaks, leggy camellias, crooked steps and weathered paint that all needed a lot more tending than they ever got.

Jack's brother, Sean, stood at the back porch. When Jack killed his engine, Sean loped down the uneven steps, arms open, a huge grin on the face that looked so eerily like Jack's own.

"You made it! I thought surely the minute you hit the marsh flats you'd break out in hives and make a U-turn back to Kansas City!"

Jack folded Sean in with one arm and ruffled his unkempt black curls with the other. They both still wore their hair a little longer than other men—it was Jack's one rebellion against the establishment. But while Sean clearly still cut his own with the kitchen scissors, Jack paid a small fortune to someone named Ambrosia, who knew how to keep the uptown-edgy-lawyer look from revealing its roots as backwoods bad boy.

"I thought about it," he admitted. "But curiosity got the better of me."

Sean raised one eyebrow into a high, skeptical arch, a favorite Killian trick. "You managed to keep your curiosity under control for twelve long years."

"Yeah, but this time you sweetened the pot. I couldn't pass up the chance to thwart the evil plans of that low-life Tom Dickson and his cronies." Jack popped the trunk, exposing a suitcase and a garment bag. "Give me a hand with these, okay? I brought some extra suits, in case the bastard puts up a fight."

Sean smiled. "Oh, he'll fight, especially once he realizes you're his opponent. Somehow I don't think he's ever forgiven you for trying to kill him."

Jack hoisted one of the black leather cases and extended the other to his brother. He held on to the handle an extra second.

"Just for the record. If I'd ever tried to kill Tom Dickson, he'd be dead."

"Point taken." Sean chuckled as he led the way into the house. "Though I'm not sure that logic will cut much ice with Tom."

Given the dilapidated state of the exterior, Jack was surprised to see how neat and clean—if somewhat Spartan—the interior of the mansion had been kept. The rooms had all been painted recently enough to shine a little, and the heart-of-pine floors were freshly varnished.

There wasn't much furniture. Their dad—Crazy Kelly, his friends called him—had sold all the antiques years ago, in his attempt to set the world record for butt-stupid poker playing. He'd lost the grand piano betting on a pair of tens.

But the few pieces Sean had scattered around were sensible and high quality. Even Kelly Killian hadn't found a way to sell the marble off the walls, or the carvings off the cornices, so the interior still made quite an impression.

As they walked past the elaborate painted-brick archway that led to the living room, Jack realized he was tensing up instinctively. Their mother had kept her collection of miniature glass unicorns in there, and it still made Jack cringe to remember how he and Sean had occasionally joined in their father's mocking laughter. "Unicorns! Are you daft in the head, Bridey, or just a goddamn fool?"

When she'd fallen that day, she'd hit the case and broken every one. Jack didn't look into the living room as they passed, but out of the corner of his eye he imagined he still saw the twinkle and glitter of shattered glass.

So, he thought. Not all the ghosts had moved out.

But overall, the place had definitely changed for the better. It didn't smell damp and defeated anymore, as if it stood in a stagnant bog of booze and tears.

"I put you in your old room," Sean said. "But let's have a drink first, okay? There's some stuff I probably ought to fill you in on."

They dropped the cases at the foot of the wide, curving staircase and headed toward the smoking room, where the liquor cabinet had always been kept. Jack didn't wonder, even for a second, what kind of drink Sean intended to offer him. Neither of them had ever drunk liquor in their lives—except for that one night, the night before Jack had joined the Army. Jack had gotten plastered that night, and it had scared the tar out of him. There was no nightmare more terrifying than the fear that they'd turn into their father.

"Soda? Or iced tea?" Sean had obviously tossed out the cherry-inlaid liquor cabinet, with its front scarred from Kelly's fury when Bridey had dared to try to lock him out. Instead, Sean had installed a handsome modern marble wet bar. "I've got water in six flavors. The chicks love it."

"I'll take a Coke," Jack said. He parked himself on one of the bar stools and looked around the mostly bare room. "I have to tell you, buddy. For a junk dealer, you have remarkably little *junk*."

Sean handed over the cold can and shrugged. "Yeah, well, I buy to sell. I don't keep. I don't care much about stuff, you know? All these people, they accumulate these expensive trinkets, hoping the stuff will define them, or save them, or…whatever. Bull. If material things had any power, then Mom…"

He didn't finish the sentence. He didn't need to. A hundred crystal unicorns, and not enough magic in the lot to stop a single tear from falling.

Jack's apartment in Kansas City was equally spare.

"Anyhow," Jack said to cover the silence. "Fill me in. You said that the city council has let you know they want to buy Sweet Tides. And that they've hinted that, if you don't sell willingly, they'll find a way to claim eminent domain. Somebody wants to put up a shopping plaza or condo complex or something like that, right?"

"Yeah. They brought it up earlier this year, but I thought they were just trying to rattle my chains, you know? I thought they'd back off, because it's such a stupid idea. Unless they can claim that Sweet Tides is a blight, it's going to be hella hard to assert eminent domain. But they haven't let go of the idea. They've already tried, informally, of course, to talk numbers with me."

"And what kind of number did they suggest?" Jack knew that, unfortunately, the people displaced by eminent domain often ended up taking less than their property was worth, just because they didn't have the savvy to know how to fight back. "Was it even in the ballpark?"

"That's what made me nervous. They offered top dollar. Does that make sense to you?"

Jack shook his head slowly. "Not as a first offer. They have to know they need bargaining room."

"That's what I thought."

"So what's going on? You know these people better than I do. Do they really want to put a shopping plaza out here that bad? Didn't look to me as if the commercial area had spread out this far yet anyhow."

"It hasn't. And no, they don't want that blasted shopping center. They couldn't. The one they built last year doesn't have full occupancy yet."

Jack sighed. "So. Can I assume this is just a new case of Killian fever? Someone has decided that the trashy Killians can't be allowed to live this close to decent folk?"

"Maybe." Sean looked thoughtful. He came out from behind the bar and stood at the picture window, which looked out toward the river. "Or maybe it's a different kind of fever. Maybe it's the gold."

"Oh, for God's sake, Sean. No one really believes that anymore. Everyone knows that, if there had been gold on this property, dad would have found it and bet it all on a pair of tens."

Sean was quiet a long time, just staring out the window, as if he was hypnotized by the moss swaying from the oaks. Finally he turned around.

"But what if there is? We used to think we'd find it, remember, Jack?"

Of course he remembered. The two of them had sneaked out almost every night for a year, right after their mother had gotten sick, and had dug holes until they'd been so tired and dirty all they could do was lie on their backs and stare at the stars. And whisper about what they'd do with the gold when they found it.

Sean, who was two years older and much nicer, had always listed a detox center for their dad first. Jack had called him a moron. Betting that Kelly Killian could get off the bottle? You might as well throw the whole treasure away on a pair of tens.

"I remember," Jack said. "That's about a thousand hours of our lives we'll never get back, huh?"

Sean shrugged. "Another piece washed up last month. We got six inches of rain in two hours. When it stopped, there was a Confederate coin out on the South Forty."

Jake wasn't impressed. Coins had washed up at odd intervals for the past hundred and fifty years. Just enough to keep the rumor alive. Never enough to make anybody rich.

"So, look, Sean, what exactly do you want me to do? I can try to get an injunction against the city council, preventing them from pursuing the eminent domain claim. But it'll only slow it down. If they're determined, they just might win in the end. The Supreme Court has ruled that this sort of thing, to bring in necessary revenues, is legal."

"Slowing them down is enough." Sean looked tired, Jack suddenly realized. "Truth is, Jack, I don't really care about the house. I'm ready to let go of it. Too many memories, I guess. I've done everything short of an exorcism, but the damn place is still haunted, you know?"

Jack nodded. He'd never understood why Sean stayed in the first place. Their only living relative was their grandfather, Patrick, who had once been a strong force in their lives, but who now resided in the local nursing home.

A major stroke had brought him down—no one was sure how clear his mind was now, Sean had explained when he'd called Jack after the stroke. Patrick had almost complete loss of motor control on his left side. He couldn't even leave his bed, unless the nurses hoisted him into a wheelchair and strapped him in.

Surely he could be moved to another nursing home, in some other city, if Sean really wanted to get away.

Jack certainly had wanted to. Once Nora Carson had made it clear she never wanted to see Jack again, Hawthorn Bay had held nothing for him. He was sick of fighting the Killian reputation—even if he had contributed plenty to it himself.

And he wouldn't have lived in this house for all the gold in the world.

"Okay. But if you don't want to save Sweet Tides, why did you need to import a big-shot Kansas City lawyer like me?"

Finally Sean smiled. "To slow them down, like you said. I want time, Jack. I want time to find the gold. And I want you to help me."

Jack hesitated. Then he laughed. "You sure you haven't taken up the bottle? You're talking crazy now."

"No, I'm not. A friend of mine, a woman named Stacy Holtsinger, she's found something. You don't know her, she came here after you'd already left. But she's doing a master's in history, and she's going through a lot of the old Killian letters for her thesis. She found one that seems to talk about the gold."

"Everyone talks about the gold," Jack said irritably. "Words are cheap."

"She's got the letter now, but I'll show it to you tonight. I think you'll see what I mean. It feels important. It feels real."

"Sean, look, you told me you needed a lawyer, not a treasure hunter. I'm afraid I left my metal detector at home. Besides, I've got a job. I've got cases in Kansas City that—"

"A month. That's all I'm asking. Every big shot can get at least a month off, can't they? It'll mean we have Christmas together. And you can see Grandfather."

That would be nice. He and his grandfather had been close when Jack was little. Patrick had provided the only affectionate "fathering" Jack had ever gotten. Some of his happiest memories were of walking through the marshes with his grandfather, bending over to inspect the bugs and butterflies Patrick pointed out.

When Patrick and Jack's dad had fought for the last time, Patrick and Jack's grandmother Ginny had moved away. Through the years, he'd visited them often—glad that he didn't have to return to Hawthorn Bay to do it.

But he hadn't seen Patrick since his grandmother's funeral last year. He hadn't seen him since the stroke. He had to admit, it was tempting.

"And hey," Sean said, "we can clear out the rest of

the stuff in the attic while you're here. So even if we find nothing, the time won't be a waste."

Sean put his tea down on the bar and shoved his hands into the pockets of his jeans. He stared at Jack, and his face had that mulish look that all Killians got when they weren't planning to back down, come hell or Union soldiers.

"Come on, Jack. I haven't asked for a damn thing in twelve years. Can't you give me one month?"

Jack couldn't say no. He'd started out tough, and the Army and the law had only made him tougher. But not tough enough to say no to Sean when he sounded like this.

Besides, Jack was already here. That had been the biggest hurdle. Now he might as well look around. And if Sweet Tides was going to get bulldozed to make room for Slice O'Pizza and Yuppies R Us, he might as well stick around long enough to say a proper goodbye.

He'd say goodbye to old Patrick, too.

He stood. "Okay. I'll stay till after Christmas. Meanwhile, I'll go talk to the city attorney and see what this band of weasels is planning. I'll pretend we're going to fight tooth and nail. I'll see if I can buy you some time."

"Thanks, Jack. Really, thanks a lot." Sean looked pleased, but still, oddly, a little uncomfortable. "I— Well, if you're going right now I guess there's one other thing I probably should tell you."

"Yeah?" Jack raised the Killian brow. "What's that?"

"Know how I told you Tom Dickson is on the city council?"

"Of course. That's how you got me to come, remember?" Jack grinned. "Actually, I could probably have guessed that anywhere there's a band of weasels, Tom

Dickson will be nearby. What else is there? Have I got some other old friends on the council?"

"Sort of. Not exactly a friend, and not exactly a councilman. You see, it's the mayor."

"Okay. Tell me. Who is mayor these days?"

Sean paused.

"I'm sorry, Jack. It's Nora Carson."

CHAPTER THREE

1862

JOE KILLIAN WASHED UP in the river, though the December air was frigid. He was too covered in dirt and sweat to use the basin in the bedroom. Julia slept lightly on her perfumed sheets, and the stink of wet earth would wake her.

His shoulders ached. He'd worked hard all his life, but only with his mind, not with his arms and legs. Though he had inherited Sweet Tides and the one thousand acres of rice fields all around it, he'd never planted anything with his own hands.

Until tonight.

Tonight he had planted the crop that would, he prayed, secure his future. Billings and Pringle were arriving in the morning. They would take his gold for the Cause, and in return they'd give him piles and piles of Confederate paper.

Joe was a Southerner by birth, and his father before him. But Joe had married a Philadelphia woman, and he'd visited there many times. He knew facts, hard realities about the differences between the two places. He knew things that these naive Hawthorn Bay zealots—men who thought the South Carolina state line was the edge of the civilized world—couldn't even imagine.

He knew that, unless God intervened with a miracle, Confederate paper would be worthless within the year.

And he knew that Julia, with her divided loyalties and her love of all things graceful and easy, would despise him for a fool. She had already hinted that, if foodstuff were to be rationed any further, she might have to make her way home to Daddy.

Joe wasn't afraid to live without coffee and sugar and meat. He wasn't even afraid to die, although that didn't seem likely, since, bowing to Julia's charming entreaties, Dr. Hartnett had certified him unfit for fighting.

But Joe couldn't live without Julia.

And so he had buried the gold. Dozens of heavy bars, hundreds of elegant coins, all gleaming dully under the cloudy moonlight, their fire winking out as he shoveled the black dirt over them, spade by spade. When Billings and Pringle came tomorrow, Joe would toss them a few bars, like scraps to the hogs. They'd be surprised, maybe even suspicious, but what could they do?

Julia would know, of course. She was as clever as she was lovely. She would give Joe one long look, and then she'd bewitch Billings and Pringle until they forgot to be suspicious.

When he was through, Joe made his way to the bedroom quickly. He'd begun to shake from the cold and the exhaustion of his limbs. As he climbed into bed, a shaft of moonlight fell on Julia's ivory face, and he told himself it would be all right.

But, in spite of the perfumed sheets, in spite of Julia's warmth beside him, the sleep that finally came to him was thick with dreams.

He dreamed of dead men bursting from black-sod

graves. They rose and, like an army, marched slowly toward Sweet Tides to avenge their terrible deaths.

They had no skin, no flesh to soften their skulls, no eyeballs to gentle their pitiless stares. But their bones shone in the moonlight.

Bones made entirely of gold.

WHEN JACK SAW the bustle in the town square, with the Santa in the band shell and the Christmas tree in the center, he wasn't a bit surprised.

Like most little towns, Hawthorn Bay loved a good festival. Without the museums and theaters and operas and bars of a big city, the good people of the community had to break their boredom other ways. So they held parades and picnics and rodeos, carnivals and cook-offs and white elephant jumbles. Any excuse to string the town square with fairy lights would do.

Jack had actually liked the festivals, back in high school. As the reigning community leaders, "Boss" Carson and his society wife, Angela, had always been in the thick of things, busy with committees and volunteers, organizing the dances and pouring the lemonade. Which had given Jack the perfect chance to sneak away with Nora.

Back then, he'd always been burning up with the need to touch her. With a girl like Nora, you had to go slow, but over the six months of their romance he had been claiming her, inch by tormenting inch. He'd already owned her soft, sunshine-golden hair, her lips, her cheeks, her ears, her eyelids. He had left his mark on her neck, her collarbone, the inside of her elbow, her swelling, rose-tipped breasts.

He'd win her all someday, he'd been sure of that. The

fire lay so deep inside her that it didn't often show on the outside, but he knew it was there. He could taste it in the heat of her lips. He could hear it in the trapped-butterfly beat of her heart.

And then, one day, in a black Killian temper, he'd put the fire out for good.

But that was ancient history. He gave himself an internal shake and put the memories back in cold storage.

It had been late afternoon when he'd left Sean at Sweet Tides, and by the time he got to City Hall, though it was only about four thirty, the offices were closed. At The Christmas Jubilee, the sign on the door read.

He left his car by the municipal complex and walked back to the town square. It was growing colder, and the trees were already casting long shadows on the sidewalk. The sun would probably go down in about an hour or so—he could tell by the light on the river behind City Hall, which was morphing from dark blue to dirty pink.

The sky was a little busier, too, as the birds made their last-minute flights back to their nests.

Funny how quickly he could fall back into the rhythms of coastal life. He might have been gone for only twelve days, instead of twelve years.

He stood at the edge of the square for several minutes, just absorbing the scene. They'd gone all out for this particular festival. Main Street was lined with life-size, blow-up snowmen, which would have been right at home in the Macy's parade. Every tree, large and small, twinkled with colored lights. At the south edge of the square, an ornate merry-go-round in which every horse was a reindeer twirled to the tinkling sounds of "Jingle Bells."

But most of the activity was concentrated at the north

end, up by the band shell. That was where Santa was holding court, enthroned in red velvet under the bright lights that usually illuminated the Hawthorn Barbershop Quartet. A long line of children wound down the band shell stairs and out into the square, waiting to sit on Santa's lap.

Boss Carson used to do the Santa bit, but Jack knew that Nora's dad had died quite a few years ago. He wondered who had taken over. He moved up a few yards, to the edge of the bank of folding chairs, to get a better look.

Well, how about that? It was Farley Hastert. Talk about casting against type. Farley had been the tallest, skinniest boy in Blackberry High. A couple of years older than Jack, he'd been a basketball jock and a straight-A student, on top of having a very nice, very rich father. Naturally, Farley was never without a gorgeous girl on his skinny arm.

Jack had been so jealous of Farley Hastert, he hadn't been able to see straight. Once, Nora had let Farley give her a ride home from school, and Jack had gone caveman, getting up close into Farley's long, hound-dog face and ordering him to stay away from his girl, or something equally Neanderthal.

Nora had broken up with Jack on the spot, and the week before she forgave him had been pure hell.

True to form, Farley still had a gorgeous girl with him. Santa had a sexy elf helper this year, dressed in a tight-fitting, very short red satin mini-dress trimmed in white fur. Red tights set off fantastic legs, and a perky red cap perched on top of bouncing blond curls.

Jack stood up straighter.

That was no elf. That was Nora.

"Well, knock me down with a feather! If it isn't Black Jack Killian himself, all dressed up like a banker!"

Jack turned. It took him a minute to place the face, which looked like the much-older version of someone he once knew. The red hair was a clue, and finally he made the connection.

"Amy!" He gave her a hug, hoping his face didn't register surprise. Amy Grantham was actually two years younger than he was—maybe twenty-nine or so? But she looked forty-five and exhausted. "I didn't know you were back in Hawthorn Bay."

"It sucked me back," she said with a dry smile. "I married Eddie Folger, he's got a charter boat business. We...we don't have any kids yet, but we're still trying. We do all right."

"I'm glad," he said, but it hurt to see her so drawn and discouraged. He had hoped her life had improved.

They'd met at an Al-Anon meeting his first year of high school. Amy's father had been an alcoholic, too. And they'd both been poor. That had been enough to make them friends. Secretly, they'd bonded against all the happy families in Hawthorn Bay—*secretly* because Amy hadn't wanted anyone to guess how much being an alcoholic's child could define you.

Jack had already accepted his fate as an outcast— what was the point, after five generations of Killian hatred, in fighting it?—but Amy was still pretending she was just like everyone else.

They still exchanged Christmas cards sometimes... or at least his firm used to send his. He tried to remember whether they'd started to bounce back, after she'd moved. He was ashamed to realize he had no idea.

"What about you?" She smiled at him. "What are you doing here? Don't tell me this place has got hold of you again, too?"

He shuddered inwardly at the thought. "Nope. I'm just here to see Sean. He's in a tangle with the city council, and he needed some legal advice."

Amy rolled her eyes. "*Them!* Yeah, I heard about them wanting Sweet Tides. They're just a bunch of vultures, the lot of them. But they've got the power, just like they always did. Tom Dickson is one of them, did you know that?"

Jack smiled. "Sure. That's the icing on the cake. Made the whole trip down here worthwhile."

Amy glanced at the band-shell stage. "And *she's* one of them. In fact, she's the head buzzard. I guess you knew that, too."

"Yeah."

"Have you seen her yet? I mean, to talk to her? Does she know you're in town?"

"Not yet." He watched Nora lead a little girl up and lift her into Santa's lap. The little girl began to cry, so Nora knelt beside her, soothing her tears. "I don't think she'll exactly be thrilled to see me."

"You two never made up, then?" Amy's pursed mouth moved nervously. "You never—explained things to her?"

He put his hand on the woman's arm. It was painfully thin. Amy had been anorexic back in high school. He wondered if she still was. Her neck was stringy, like an old woman's.

"I promised you I'd never tell anyone about all that," he said. Had she carried this fear around with her for the past twelve years? "I meant it."

"But…" Amy's eyes looked watery and pale. "She never forgave you for what you did to Tom, did she? Surely you were tempted to explain—"

"Explaining wouldn't change anything," he said. "Nora didn't want the kind of man who would try to murder anyone."

"But—"

"And I didn't want a woman who thought I was that kind of man."

Amy gazed at him a long moment, then nodded slowly. "I guess I can see that," she said. She drew herself up a little straighter. "I should be getting on home. Eddie will be docking soon, and he'll want dinner."

They hugged goodbye, and Jack watched her go. Even from the back she looked like a tired, middle-aged woman. He couldn't help comparing her to Nora. In that ridiculous but strangely seductive elf suit, Nora could have been mistaken for a teenager.

He looked at the stage again. There seemed to be some kind of commotion. Nora was talking to a group of kids, and Santa was walking slowly down the stairs. As soon as she herded the kids back to the line, she posted a sign that said Santa Will Be Back In Five Minutes. Then she turned quickly and followed the man in the red suit.

Looked as if they were taking a break.

If Jack wanted to talk to her, now was the time.

But did he? What did they have to say, after more than a decade? Wouldn't it just open up a wound that had healed nicely over the years, hardly giving him so much as a twinge anymore?

The questions were purely rhetorical. Jack was already moving toward the stage.

NORA HADN'T EVER BEEN in a men's restroom before. And if she never went into another one, that would be fine with her.

But this time she'd had no choice. The minute she'd realized Farley was drunk, she'd had to do something. The kids had been crushed, of course, and a couple of parents were annoyed, but she'd explained in her best elf voice that Santa had an emergency call from the North Pole, and he'd be right back.

She'd managed to get him in here before he started vomiting. But unfortunately, she hadn't pulled his beard off in time. When he was finished groaning into the bowl, she unhooked the elastic carefully, and deposited the beard in the trash can.

As an afterthought, she covered it over with paper towels. No point shocking innocent kids.

"Thank you, darlin'," Farley said in a little boy voice as she wiped his face with a cool paper towel. "I think you saved my life. My lunch must have disagreed with me."

Nora felt too grumpy to participate in the charade. "More likely the bottle of wine you drank *with* lunch, don't you think?" She scrubbed at his white fur collar, which wasn't quite white anymore. "Look at you. What are we going to do about that line of kids waiting to see Santa?"

"Tell them Santa's been distracted." He reached up and caught Nora's hand. "Tell them Santa's fallen in love with his beautiful little elf."

"Gross." She batted his fingers away unemotionally. "I'm not kidding, Farley. There are at least fifty kids out there. You'd better call one of your friends and get them to take over."

"Whatever you say." He smiled. He might have thought the smile was sexy, but he was wrong. Farley had been sexy in high school, and even in college, but from the time he'd started drinking heavily a couple of years ago, all that had disappeared like smoke in the wind.

"I'll call Mac," he said. "But only if you give me a kiss."

Nora turned away and tossed the paper towel into the trash. "Your mouth smells like a toilet, Farley. Nobody's going to be kissing you tonight. I'll go stall the kids. You stay here and make that call."

She would have thought he was too wobbly even to stand up. But she had just exited the men's room when she felt him wrap his gloved hand around her waist.

"I'm serious, Nora," he whispered in her ear. She nearly vomited, too, as she recognized the odor of half-digested seafood. "I think I love you."

"Farley Hastert," she said through gritted teeth. She kept her voice low, in case any children were nearby. "Let go of me."

"But Nora—" He brought his other hand up to her waist and began trying to spin her around to face him. "Nora, you're so beautiful."

"Goddamn it, Farley." She put the heel of her hand on his chin and shoved his face up, so that at least he wasn't exhaling rotten food into her nose. "Get a grip."

He was so tall, and though he was as thin as a stick he was pretty strong, from all those years playing basketball. Her arm was failing. His face was getting closer and closer.

Oh, hell. She brought her left knee up hard.

Farley made a sound somewhere between a curse and

a kitten's mew, and then he slid to the ground, clutching his red velvet-covered crotch.

She looked down at him, just to be sure he hadn't cracked his head on the sidewalk. Nope, he was fine. She felt kind of sorry for him, but not sorry enough to stay and face the wrath when he recovered. She brushed the front of her elf dress, in case he'd left anything disgusting there, then turned to go back to the band shell.

She'd have to think of something to tell the kids. *Santa's a drunken letch* probably wasn't the right approach.

But she never made it to the stage.

She got only about ten feet, and then, there on the path, clearly watching the whole thing with a broad grin on his face, stood a man she hadn't seen for a dozen years. A man she'd hoped never to see again.

Jack Killian.

Her heart raced painfully—from normal to breathless in less than a second. She had a sudden, mindless urge to knee him in the groin, too, and make her escape.

She couldn't do this right now. She couldn't do this *ever*.

But he wouldn't be as easy to subdue as Farley. Farley was basically a spoiled man-boy who thought the world was his box of candy. Jack Killian had been a street fighter from the day he was born. He didn't expect life to be simple or sweet.

And he didn't know how to lose.

She had loved that about him once. Before she'd realized the twisted things it had done to his soul.

"Hello, Nora," he said with a maddening composure. "Been explaining to Santa that all you want for Christmas is to be left the hell alone?"

She smiled in spite of herself. "Something like that,"

she said. She adjusted her elf hat, which had slipped sideways, and tried to look semi-dignified. "It's nice to see you, Jack. I didn't know you were in town."

How stupid she'd been not to consider this possibility. She knew that he and Sean were still close. Through the years Sean had traveled to Kansas City frequently to visit Jack, but the only time Jack had come back here was for his mother's funeral, which had been held while Nora had been in Europe.

She had naively assumed she was safe.

Why hadn't it occurred to her that the council's bid to confiscate Sweet Tides would be the one battle he'd be willing to fight in person?

"Is it, Nora?"

"Is it what?"

"Nice to see me."

She willed herself not to flush. But, as she looked at him standing there with his curly black hair and his piercing blue eyes, a dizzy confusion swept over her. For just a moment, she was transported back a dozen years, to a cold Christmas dawn rising over the water in wisps of blue and gold. Jack's lips had tasted like the chocolate he'd stolen from her stocking, and his arms had been hotter than the bonfire they'd built on the beach.

In another instant the memory dissolved. All that was left was the awkward present.

"Of course it's nice," she said. She would not give him the satisfaction of knowing how easily her composure could unravel right now. She had to keep it distant, keep it professional. "I know we're going to be on opposite sides of the eminent domain issue, but still…I'm glad to see you looking so well. Apparently the Army agreed with you."

"Not really, but getting out of it did. And I enjoy practicing law. It's a relief to be on the right side of it for a change."

She laughed politely. "I can imagine."

God, who were these two people? Years ago, they'd sat in this very park, in a twilight much like this one. They'd shared a cold park bench, and she'd laid her head in his lap. He had hummed a love song—he had a beautiful baritone—and had lifted her long curls to his lips, the gesture so sexy it had burned her scalp.

"I should go," she said. "The children—"

"Yes." He stepped out of the way. "I'll look after Santa for you."

"Thanks." She paused, a sudden anxiety passing through her. Jack's temper. If he'd seen Farley pawing her, grabbing her against her will…

"He's been punished enough," she said carefully, hoping Jack would get her meaning. "He drinks a little too much, but he's not a bad guy."

Jack understood her alright.

His familiar blue eyes narrowed briefly, and then he raised one eyebrow high. Oh, God, she thought. She knew that expression. She knew it so well it took her breath away.

"I think I can control myself, Nora. After all, I have no reason to hurt him, do I? He hasn't messed with anything that belongs to me."

"No." She felt like an idiot. The man who stood here, with his expensive suit and his expensive haircut and his sardonic voice…he wasn't going to get in a brawl over some woman he'd forgotten a decade ago.

He didn't lust after Nora Carson's body anymore, or her heart, for that matter.

But that didn't mean she was safe.

She might still have something he wanted. Something he'd battle for. Something that would bring out the bare-knuckled street fighter she used to know. Just thinking of it made her racing heart come to a dead standstill.

She just might have his son.

CHAPTER FOUR

"I'M OUT," THE MAN in the camel-hair suit said, slapping his cards facedown on the game table set up in the gun room of Sweet Tides. "My wife will kill me if I lose any more. You're too damn lucky this week, Killian."

"He's too lucky every week," the older man across from him, who had a strangely bouffant set of gray curls, grumbled around his unlit cigar.

"What can I say?" Sean laughed. "The angels love me. You in or out, Curly?"

"In, damn it. I'm not afraid of you." Curly held on to his cards, but he kept rearranging them nervously while his cigar bobbed up and down.

Jack, who had spent the past hour sitting by the window reading through some eminent domain research, could see even from this distance that Curly's knuckles were white with tension.

Jack smiled, bending his head back to the boring papers. Damn if Sean wasn't going to take this hand, too.

It had been the same all night. One by one, the yellow and blue mother-of-pearl chips had marched their way across the green felt, as if under military orders, to stand in neat piles at Sean's elbow.

Frankly, Jack had been shocked to hear that Sean even had a regular poker game. Like drinking, gambling had always been something the brothers avoided. Too much like dear old dad.

But, just before his friends had arrived, Sean had given Jack the quick rundown. About five years ago, Sean had decided to give cards a try, and he'd discovered that, unlike Crazy Kelly, he was pretty good.

Jack couldn't bring himself to join in the game— technically, it was illegal, and he knew there were people in this town who would love any excuse to put a Killian behind bars, even if it was just for jaywalking or quarter stakes in a friendly neighborhood game.

But he'd enjoyed watching. He'd learned a lot about his brother. Sure, they'd spent plenty of time together on Sean's trips out to Kansas City, but this was different. Like observing a very clever wild animal in its natural habitat.

He'd also learned a lot about the pretty brunette grad student Stacy Holtsinger, the one Sean had mentioned earlier. Stacy had climbed down from the attic about an hour ago, brushed the dust from her hair and had immediately started refilling glasses and peanut bowls.

Apparently Stacy had been studying Sweet Tides history long enough to become the unofficial hostess of the Saturday-night game.

And what else, Jack wondered?

Curly grudgingly tossed a couple of blue chips into the pile. "Okay, big shot. Show me."

Sean smiled. He had a Killian smile, equal parts cocky bastard and pure good humor. The cocky part had made people around here yearn to tar and feather Killian men for generations. The good-humored part had kept them from doing it. Usually.

Sean splayed out his cards on the table. "Straight. King high."

The other man took a deep breath. "Crap."

Chuckling, Sean started picking up his winnings. As if on cue, Stacy appeared at his shoulder, grinning happily, and refilled his sweet tea.

"More beer, anyone?" She tore her gaze from Sean—reluctantly, Jack thought with a new twinge of curiosity—and she scanned the table. "Or is it time to switch to coffee?"

The other men began looking at their watches, as Stacy had no doubt intended they should. As the big winner, Sean couldn't suggest quitting, so obviously she'd stepped in with the gentle hint. Within minutes, everyone had cashed out. Then they pulled on their overcoats and headed for the door.

After seeing the men out together like an old married couple, Sean and Stacy came back into the gun room, still grinning. He high-fived Jack, then went over to the game table and flicked the first stack of chips. It fell sideways, knocking down the next stack, then the next, like dominos. Apparently Sean had won often enough to have perfected his technique.

"Okay, I'm impressed," Jack said. "What's your secret? Marked cards?"

"Hell, no." Sean tilted his head back and finished off his tea in a long swig. "Why would I need to cheat? Poker's not exactly rocket science. I just have three unbreakable rules."

"Yeah? What are they?"

Jack noticed that Stacy was already smiling. She knew the rules, obviously. She knew a lot, for someone who supposedly was only interested in dead Killians.

"One, I never bet big when I'm broke, tired, pissed off or in love. Two, I never bet big unless I'm holding something better than a pair of tens. Three, I never bet big, period."

He held up four five-dollar bills. "My total winnings tonight."

Jack laughed. "In other words, you're the anti-Kelly."

"Pretty much." Sean put his hand out and stopped Stacy, who had begun to clear away the beer bottles and peanuts. "Leave this stuff. I'll get it in the morning. I want you to show Jack the letter."

She hesitated, but then, with one last look at Sean, she went over to the mantel, an ornate marble affair carved with a hunting scene, and picked up a plastic sleeve into which a yellowed document had been slipped.

She brought it over to where Jack had been reading. She twisted the knob on the desk lamp, increasing the wattage.

"It's from 1864," she said, holding it out for him to take. She looked uncertain, as if she thought he might reject it. He wondered what she'd heard about him—from Sean, and from everyone else in Hawthorn Bay. Probably the attempted-murder story had grown claws and fangs over the past twelve years.

"Who wrote it?" He took the letter, even though he still believed the whole thing was a wild goose chase. Every now and then, someone would heat up the search for the gold. Sometimes it was greedy treasure-hunters. More often it was someone young and naive, like this woman. Either way, it always ended in disappointment.

Because there *was* no gold. There was only a harvest of dreams, lying tender on the ground, ready to be stomped flat by reality.

Even worse, he had a feeling that finding the gold wasn't Stacy Holtsinger's only dream. If he were a betting man, he'd bet that she had a thing for Sean.

Jack felt vaguely sorry for the woman, who seemed very nice but innocent, younger than the thirty or so Sean had said she was. And needy. Definitely needy.

He wondered if he should give her a heads-up.

Her boyish figure, her tortoiseshell glasses and her baggy jeans and sweater were the wrong recipe for snagging Sean's attention. Sean had no interest in settling down with a refined, well-educated woman. He liked his females lusty, busty and loud.

Or at least he used to. Of course, he also used to say he had no interest in following their dad down the poker trail, too, so maybe Jack didn't know as much as he thought he did.

He turned his attention to the letter, deciding it would be premature to nudge poor Stacy Holtsinger toward contact lenses and implants just yet.

"It was written by Joe Killian," Stacy said. She cleared her throat. "It was written to his wife, Julia. She seems to have left him, a year or two before, ostensibly to wait out the war with her family back in Philadelphia. But this letter makes it sound as if she left because of a quarrel."

"Okay." He glanced at the faded handwriting, which crisscrossed the page in both directions. "And? I'm sure this letter has been looked at a million times through the years. If it had confirmed the existence of the gold—"

"That's just it," she said. Her voice sounded a little more confident. She was clearly sure of her ground on this topic. "I'm sure it has been 'looked at,' but I'm not sure it's really been read. Not all the way through."

"She's right," Sean said, as he tossed himself onto the leather sofa. "I tried to read it myself, the day Stacy found it. I just couldn't. It's this endless regurgitation of love-mush. Julia is more beautiful than the gold of twilight, the pearl of dawn. He'll become a living ghost if she doesn't return to him."

Sean shook his head. "Disgusting. The man needed a spine implant, that's for sure."

"So…?"

"Well, you have to get past that stuff," Stacy said, shooting a stern look at Sean. "And then his words seem more pertinent. He tells her that if she comes back—"

Stacy held out a hand for the plastic sheet, which Jack relinquished willingly. She turned it over and squinted at the back. "Let me find it, so I can really… Here it is! He writes, 'For you, I have dirtied my hands and stood in my own grave. If you will come back to me, I will unearth the golden love, the priceless happiness we once had. Come home, my treasure, and you shall want for nothing.'"

Stacy's voice lowered on the last words, as if old Joe's begging had moved her. She blinked, cleared her throat, and then looked up at Jack.

"He must be referring to the gold," she said. "He buried it rather than turn it over to the Confederacy, just as the rumor always said he did. He's promising her that, if she comes home, he'll dig it up and give it all to her."

"That's one way to read it. But who knows? He sounds like a windbag. In love with his metaphors, don't you think?"

Clearly she didn't think. She lowered her brows and

held the letter against her chest, as if to protect it from his cynicism.

"Come on, Jack, don't be such a buzz kill." Sean was tossing a blue poker chip up and down, catching it with first one hand, then the other. "Treasure, dirt, unearth, golden. Those are some pretty pointed images, if you ask me. Maybe he buried it up on the cemetery hill."

Was Sean really buying this? Jack couldn't tell. Sean might just be trying to make Stacy feel good about her discovery.

"Even if you're right, what happened then? Julia came home, didn't she? My family history is a little hazy, but I'm pretty sure their son was born after the war. So why didn't old Joe dig up the gold and shower her in gifts, as he promised?"

"I don't know." Stacy bit her lower lip. "Maybe when Julia returned, she told her husband she loved him with or without the treasure."

"Sure," Jack said with a laugh. "And maybe tomorrow it'll snow sugar and rain roses."

Stacy flushed. "I should have known you were too cynical to take any of this seriously. Nora told me about you. She told me you were—"

She stopped herself abruptly, clearly aware that she'd been about to cross an invisible but electrically charged line.

"I was what?"

She glanced anxiously at Sean, but Sean didn't look disturbed.

"Stacy and Nora are best friends," he explained to Jack. "Partners, too. They're in the jam business."

So that was why Stacy had been subtly hostile ever since she'd laid eyes on him. As Nora Carson's best buddy, she'd probably taken a blood oath to despise Jack Killian sight unseen.

He could easily imagine what Nora had said about him. Still, some perversity made him push. "So…she said I was *what?*"

"She… I… Just—" The woman swallowed. "She said you were cynical. And…unkind."

"Unkind?" Sean laughed out loud. "Damn. That's probably the least offensive thing that's been said about a Killian in two hundred years."

"I suspect that's the edited version." Jack shrugged. "But she was right, Stacy. If *cynical* means I don't believe the Killians have been squatting on a fortune in gold like mindless brood hens ever since the Civil War, then I'm cynical. If *unkind* means that I won't pretend I do believe, just to make you two dreamers feel good, then okay. I'm unkind."

Stacy narrowed her eyes. Something he'd said had struck a nerve. He wondered if it might have been the "dreamer" comment. Perhaps she'd been called that before.

"Yes. Well. The unedited version? She also said you were *dangerous.*"

Jack took a breath. Stacy couldn't know what a direct hit that was.

He tried not to hear Nora's soft voice saying the word, wrapped in shock and tears. *They all warned me about you, Jack. They told me you would break my heart. They told me you were dangerous.*

He pushed the voice away. Dangerous? You bet he was.

Somehow, he found the customary Killian smile.

"Right again," he said.

"Nora, slow down. I have to talk to you about the god-damn Killians."

Nora looked around. Bill Freeman, Hawthorn Bay's white-haired, sixty-something city attorney, chugged up behind her on the sidewalk in front of the hospital.

Nora frowned, tilting her head at Colin, who had joined her for the ribbon-cutting at the hospital's new cardiac wing. Bill grimaced, mouthing an *oops* as apology for the profanity. He shifted his battered briefcase from one hand to the other as he caught up.

"Gawd, I'm out of shape," he complained. Though it was only about forty-five degrees outside, he was sweating. He pinched his upper lip to get rid of the perspiration. "Teresa says I've got to either give up the pecan pie or take out more life insurance. Says if she has to be a widow, she wants to be a rich one."

Nora was well aware that Teresa Freeman adored her husband and had no intentions of being any kind of widow. She'd probably subbed in a low-calorie version of that pecan-pie recipe years ago. She'd been secretly ordering sugar-free jam from Nora ever since Bill's sixtieth birthday.

Nora slowed down just a little. "What about the Killians?"

"I had a visit from Jack this morning. That boy certainly has changed. Have you seen him since he got back to town?"

Nora checked Colin out of the corner of her eye. Good—he was still absorbed in his video game. You couldn't ever be sure what kind of dumb comment Bill might make. He knew all about Nora's high-school romance with Jack. Almost everyone in Hawthorn Bay did.

That was one of the reasons she hadn't returned, at first. She didn't want to answer a million questions from people who would take it for granted that Colin was Jack's illegitimate son.

Even more importantly, she hadn't dared to return as long as Maggie's parents had been alive. But, when Colin had been only about eighteen months old, they had died in a car crash, hit by a drunk driver going over the Hawthorn Bay Bridge.

And then, gossip or no gossip, Nora had made a beeline for home. Single motherhood was hard. She'd wanted to be with her own mother, the only person, other than Ethan, who knew the truth. Nora had known that her charming, dignified mother could handle the curiosity of friends and neighbors. She could even handle Nora's father, Boss.

It had worked. Though Boss had probably been disappointed in his daughter for bringing home a fatherless baby he'd never shown it—to her, or to anyone else.

The Carson family, once united, had presented a formidable front. No one had dared to probe.

As the years had passed, it had become a nonissue. Nora was a model mom—and people admired her work, first on the city council, and now as mayor. Jack had never returned, and his brother, Sean, had never shown any particular interest in the boy, so most people had lost interest.

"I said, have you seen him?" Bill looked curious, and Nora realized that she'd let her thoughts get away with her.

"Yes. I ran into him at the tree-lighting ceremony."

"Quite a transformation, isn't it?"

Nora actually thought most of Jack's changes were

superficial. Behind that suave suit and lazy poise, he still hummed with the edgy energy of a wild animal. And behind those eyes, the fire was merely banked, not extinguished.

"Yes," she agreed blandly. "So how did the meeting go? I assume he wanted to discuss the city's bid to buy Sweet Tides."

They had reached Nora's car. Bill leaned against it, dropping his briefcase as if it were loaded with lead, and pulled out his handkerchief to wipe his face.

Colin glanced at the older man. He obviously understood that Mom was detained again, so with a dramatic sigh he hoisted himself onto the hood of the car and bent over his video game. He kicked the side of the car with his sneakers, until Nora reached out and stilled them.

"Well, now, I wouldn't exactly call it a discussion," Bill said with a smile. "Jack's become a lawyer, you know. And the boy knows his stuff. He doesn't appear to have inherited his father's slacker gene, even if he did get the—"

He broke off awkwardly.

"The *mean* gene," Nora supplied. "So what did he say?"

"He said that they had no intention of selling at any price, and that as the city had no legitimate grounds for condemnation, he assumed that would be the end of it. But he wanted us to know that, if we decided to pursue eminent domain on any grounds, he had already drawn up an action challenging the condemner's right to take."

Nora widened her eyes. "Wow," she said. "He doesn't waste time."

"Nope. And he's right, of course. Any pretext we

could trump up for claiming eminent domain would be as phony as a stripper's—"

"Bill."

"Oops," he said again. "Well, you know what I mean. These days, in spite of the Supreme Court ruling, any economic-development takings are risky as hell—*oops*. And though the mansion could stand a new coat of paint, it would be pretty hard to prove it's a blight."

Nora agreed, of course. Both she and Bill had argued all these points to the city council for hours when the eminent domain issue had first come up. But unfortunately, in Hawthorn Bay, the charter had created a "weak" mayor position, which meant she had only one vote, like every other councilman.

She couldn't veto anything, even something as stupid as this.

And, on this issue, Tom Dickson was like a dog with a bone. For whatever reason, fair or foul, he wanted that new retail development to go in on Sweet Tides property, and he wasn't giving up the idea just because it was incredibly venal and unfair.

"Anyhow," Bill went on, "Jack plans to fight, and apparently he knows how. For us to win in court, we'd have to find a judge who literally eats out of Tom Dickson's hand."

"Unfortunately, that wouldn't be all that hard, would it?"

Though she'd been fond of Tom when they'd been teenagers, Nora had learned a lot about her cousin through the years. He knew how to work the system, and had no ethics to prevent him sinking as low as he needed to go. His boot-licking and back-scratching with the other lawyers and judges might not legally constitute bribery, but it sure didn't smell right.

And the stink rubbed off on the whole city council, which she resented.

Bill sighed. "I don't know how many judges he owns, and I don't want to find out. I just want the whole thing to go away. I heard Tom say he's planning to raise the offer. I hope to God the Killian boys will decide to take it."

Though she knew it was completely selfish, she half hoped they would, too. It would make her life so much easier if Jack would just go back to Kansas City.

It wasn't just that his arrival had set all the old emotions bubbling. She was a strong woman, and she could handle a little leftover yearning and angst. She had an old scar on her knee, from the chaos that day on the boat with Maggie. That scar hurt sometimes, too. She took an aspirin and went on with her life.

No, the serious issue was Colin. How long could she keep Jack from running into the boy? And once he saw him, once he saw an eleven-year-old kid with curly black hair and eyes that sparkled with a color she had always called *Killian-blue*...

Ironically, it had taken Nora a few years to figure out the truth. Thanks to the loving cocoon her parents had raised her in, she'd always been ridiculously naive, almost childish when it came to the real world.

Besides, she'd been at a disadvantage. She would never in a million years have suspected that Maggie, her best friend, might have slept with Jack. With the man Nora had loved.

Even after Colin's features had begun to take shape, Nora had innocently assumed it must have been a coincidence. Then she'd tried to tell herself it must have been Sean. But Sean, a couple of years older than Jack, had been away at college that spring.

Finally she couldn't deny the truth any longer. Maggie and Jack must have…

Betrayed her.

Nora wondered, sometimes, what Sean thought when he looked at Colin. At first, she'd been afraid that he might tell Jack, but that fear had subsided, little by little, as the months, then years, had passed without incident. She always had her story ready, though. The whirlwind romance in Cornwall, the black-haired charmer who had broken her heart.

But no one had ever asked.

Still, if Jack saw Colin…

He already possessed one of the key pieces of the puzzle. He already knew that he'd betrayed Nora with Maggie.

How long would it be before he put the whole sordid picture together? About five minutes?

And what would he do then?

Oh, yes, she wanted him to take the money and run. But she knew how selfish that was. Sweet Tides had been the Killian family home for almost three hundred years. It was Sean's home still.

So she tried to push the thought away. This wasn't about her. It was about justice. She'd have to talk to Tom again, and try to make him see reason. If the council would just drop the issue, that would accomplish the same thing.

Jack would go back where he belonged.

And she and Colin would be safe.

She glanced toward her son, who was using the

windshield as a backrest while he punched buttons on the small display. Over his head, the metallic Christmas garland wrapped around the streetlight cable swayed in the wind, casting flashes of green across his ivory wool sweater.

He sensed her attention. He looked up with wide blue eyes and smiled angelically.

That set off her baloney meter. Why was he accepting this delay so patiently? Ordinarily, he hated ribbon-cuttings and groundbreakings and speechifying and couldn't wait to get back home where he could play with his friends.

And then she remembered. Their next stop was the nursing home, where Colin had been doing volunteer work reading books and newspapers to the residents.

He hadn't seemed to hate it as much lately, but still, he'd probably welcome a reprieve. If they were delayed here a hundred years, he wouldn't utter a syllable of complaint.

She shook her head. *The rascal.* It was disgusting how much she loved him. She had the most spineless impulse to go ruffle those silky curls and tell him he didn't have to do it today, not if he really didn't want to.

But she put her hands in her sweater pockets and looked away. She had to stay strong. He mustn't be allowed to believe that he could get off without paying for his sins.

Nobody could, in the end.

CHAPTER FIVE

WHEN JACK WALKED INTO the Bayside Assisted Living Facility, he was glad to see what a nice place it was. Cheerful, clean and brightly decorated for Christmas, it looked more like a condo than an institution.

Still, he found it difficult to believe that Patrick Killian was here. Could he really have become one of these frail old people?

Standing about six-five, Patrick had always looked more like a lumberjack than the accountant he was. His physical and moral strength, frequently put to the test by his wife, who had what today would probably be diagnosed as a bipolar disorder, had been legendary in Hawthorn Bay.

Even people who disliked the Killians on principle made an exception for Patrick. *He's a saint,* they'd say. What they meant, of course, was how did he stand it, living with a trashy son, a crazy wife and those two grandsons who were clearly doomed to be hooligans just like their dad?

Jack scanned the white-haired gentlemen who sat in wheelchairs by the window of the reception area. It gave him a strangely hollow feeling to realize that his tough grandfather might lose this last fight.

"May I help you, sir?" An attractive middle-aged woman stood behind the volunteer desk. She wore a lapel pin in the shape of a reindeer with a blinking red nose. "Are you looking for someone?"

"Yes. Patrick Killian. Room twelve, I think."

"Oh, yes." She smiled at him. "You must be his other grandson. How nice. Just turn right at the next corridor, and you can't miss it. He'll be so happy to see you."

Not half as happy as Jack would be to see him. Patrick had always been the one sane center of Jack's dangerous childhood universe. He still made Jack feel just slightly more balanced, and since seeing Nora the other day, Jack needed a little of that.

The door to number twelve was standing open, and when Jack was still two rooms away he could hear the noises emanating from it. A boy's voice shouted odd words, alternated with a guttural grunt from an old man.

"Thundering apoplexy!" The child was trying to imitate an adult's voice, his tones artificially deep and rounded. "I tell you, Silver, lay down your sword or meet your end!"

Jack reached the door just as the boy finished this odd speech. The old man's voice began to holler a response with a string of excited syllables that didn't quite make words at all.

Curious, Jack entered the room.

His grandfather lay in the bed. Jack's heart loosened a little, just to see how essentially *himself* the old man still looked. His silver hair was still thickly curling, and still had streaks of the old black. His arrogant profile was pure Killian, and it was turned now toward the window. In his right hand, he held a cane, waving it wildly at shoulder level.

This must be the sword the boy had ordered him to

lay down. Obviously, in true Killian fashion, he had refused to surrender.

The boy knelt on a small footstool that sat in front of the window. The light was bright, so Jack saw the child only in silhouette, but he was pretty damn sure the kid was pointing the television remote control at Patrick, as if it were a gun.

At that moment, the kid turned his head and saw Jack. The remote control froze in place.

Patrick was slower to realize that they had a witness. He was still waving the cane and shouting.

The boy lowered the black box slowly. He looked back at Patrick. "Hey, Mr. Killian," he said. "It's okay. Time out. Time out."

Patrick stopped gabbling and frowned at the boy.

"Somebody's here." The boy eased himself off the footstool. "We'll finish the game later, Mr. Killian." He pointed to Jack. "See? Somebody's come to visit you."

Patrick, who apparently could still understand words, though he could no longer speak them, rotated his face slowly toward the door with a fierce scowl clearly designed to terrify whoever had dared to interrupt the game.

Jack almost laughed. He knew that look so well. He'd seen it a million times, whenever he or Sean had stepped out of line.

Suddenly, his throat was as tight as if someone were choking him.

"Hi, Grandfather," he said. That was pretty much all he was capable of right now.

The old man didn't move a muscle. The cane still pointed skyward.

"Grandfather?" Jack moved farther into the room.

He took the cane out of the old man's hand, resisting the urge to hold on to the cool, papery fingers. "It's me. It's Jack."

"He's okay," the boy said. "I think he's just surprised, and he always has trouble talking anyhow. We were just playing a game. We've been reading *Treasure Island,* and we decided to have a sword fight. But we only had one sword, so I had to use a blunderbuss, and—"

The boy halted his own stream of words, as if he realized they were silly. He laid the remote control on the metal table that fit over the hospital bed. Then he straightened and faced Jack squarely.

"It was just a game, honest. He likes it."

For the first time, now that the boy had moved out of the sunlight, Jack could really see his features. His full lower lip, his pointed chin. The highly arched brows, and the intense blue eyes beneath.

What the hell?

Jack frowned. "Who are you?"

The question came out more harshly than he'd intended, and immediately the boy's conciliatory expression vanished. He drew his dark eyebrows together over those startling blue eyes, clearly disliking Jack's preemptory tone.

"I'm Colin," he said with an edge of defiance. "I read to Mr. Killian every day." He lifted his pointed chin. "Who are *you?*"

Jack felt the strangest need to sit down. "I'm Jack," he said. "Jack Killian. Mr. Killian is my grandfather."

Colin narrowed his eyes. "I've never seen you here before. Sean is Mr. Killian's grandson, and he's here all the time."

How incredible was this? Jack was getting the third

degree from this kid—how old was he, maybe thir-
teen? He was as long and stiffly skinny as uncooked
linguini, so he could have been older…but his face was
still young, vaguely unformed. Jack revised his estimate
down. Maybe only eleven or twelve.

But as determined and self-confident as an adult.
Jack was staring, he knew that. The kid just stared back.
He clearly saw himself as Patrick's guardian, at least for
the moment, and he didn't intend to flinch first.

"Sean comes more often because he lives right here
in Hawthorn Bay. I don't. I live in Kansas City." Jack
held out his hand. "I didn't mean to be rude. I was just…
surprised to see you. It's nice to meet you, Colin…"

He let the sentence drift off, giving Colin the chance
to supply a last name.

But the kid obviously hadn't forgiven Jack for being
so curt. Though he put out his hand politely, he volunteered nothing further.

"Nice to meet you, too, Mr. Killian."

He let go of Jack's hand quickly, and moved to the
edge of Patrick's bed. The old man had been watching the interchange in complete silence. Jack wondered
what he was thinking. Had he noticed, too? Had he
looked into the kid's blue eyes and thought…

But maybe Jack was imagining things. Lots of people in this world—even in this town—had bright blue
eyes, dark, curly hair and a pointed chin that squared
off belligerently when they were angry.

Jack took a breath. Damn, he was getting as delu-
sional as his grandmother, who, when she'd been in a
manic phase, used to accuse Patrick of fathering half
the children in town. Every pair of blue eyes Ginny

Killian saw, whether they belonged to the pretty waitress's daughter or the high-school vice principal's brand new twins, were cause for suspicion and tears.

"Mr. Killian, I have to go now," Colin said, touching the pillow. "My mom is going to be here soon. But I want to be sure…are you up to having visitors? Is it okay if your grandson Jack stays here when I'm gone?"

The old man's eyes, their blue unfaded, moved from Colin to Jack, then back again. He raised his right hand about six inches above the mattress.

Colin turned to Jack. "His neck's stiff, so that's his way of saying yes. When he wants to say no, he shakes his hand sideways."

"Okay," Jack said, though the whole thing felt surreal. He wondered what he would have done if Colin had reported that Patrick's answer was no. Would Colin really have tried to send Jack away?

That would have been quite a feat. But it was sort of amusing to watch the kid play guard dog.

Jack glanced around the large, pleasant room. Not as big as the rooms at Sweet Tides, but more homey, with blue walls and white curtains at the window, and a small Christmas tree on the corner table. A very pricey place, as Jack already knew from the size of the check he wrote each month.

Still. Jack realized how Patrick must hate this. How he must wish he could go back to his own home.

There was a comfortable chair next to the table, but Jack wanted something closer. He reached out to drag a straight chair up to the edge of the bed.

As he did, his gaze fell on the nightstand, where an assortment of pills, water glasses, Christmas cards and pictures had been piled together. One of the pictures was of Patrick himself, as a young man in the Navy.

Jack knew that photo—it had been taken right after Patrick's only son, Kelly, had been born. Patrick looked so proud and strong at that moment, in the first flush of fatherhood, in the pride of his uniform, unaware of the disappointments that were to come.

Jack stepped back two paces, so that the tableau in front of him encompassed all three—the old man in the bed, the boy beside him and the young father in the photograph.

Good God.

He might as well have been looking at three stages of the same man.

"Oh, shoot, there's my mom." Colin glanced out the window, then spun into action, grabbing a well-worn black corduroy jacket and tossing it over his shoulder. "I'll see you tomorrow, Mr. Killian."

He gave Jack a polite, rather chilly nod as he passed, but Jack hardly saw it. He was crossing the room quickly, heading for the window. Though his mind had instinctively formed a picture of Colin's mother, he had to be sure. He might be wrong.

He wasn't.

As he watched, Colin came barreling around the side of the building, smiling at his mother, who had just started to get out of her car.

Jack spoke the word aloud without meaning to. *"Nora."*

Behind him, he heard Patrick make a noise. It could have been an awkward laugh—or a smothered cry.

Numbly, Jack turned to face the old man. Patrick's eyes were bright and fixed on Jack. With effort, Patrick raised his good right hand and pointed a shaky finger toward the window.

"Killian," he said, as clear as day.

SEAN DID MOST of his junk dealing out of the stable, which had been built in the late 1800s, after the old stable had burned down. All the horses had been lost in that fire, so, though the structure had been rebuilt bigger and better than ever, just to show the townspeople the Killians hadn't been beaten, no one had ever had the heart to fill it with animals again.

Through the years, the empty stable had been used alternately as a servant's quarters, garage, storehouse and lover's tryst. Like the rest of Sweet Tides, it looked run-down now, and tired, the white paint peeling down to pure pine, and the roof stained with mildew and oak pollen.

In the lavender light of early evening, though, with the windows glowing a warm honey-yellow, the stable looked better. Almost inviting. Jack moved through the black shadows of the oak trees, his eye on the bright squares. He could see Sean's silhouette moving back and forth, busy and efficient.

Jack hardly knew what he was going to say when he got there. The questions that had burned through him all the way back from the nursing home seemed almost crazy now.

He knocked at the stable door, though he knew Sean never locked it. Knocking seemed more polite, more restrained. Less like a madman barging in to hurl accusations that might well be insane.

"It's open," Sean called. "Whoever you are, I hope

you brought a big bucket of greasy fried chicken, because I'm starving."

Jack shut the door firmly behind him. The stable had a window heater that didn't work particularly well, and the place was already chilly enough without letting in more of the outside air. Tonight's forecast called for a soft freeze.

"Sorry," Jack said. "I've got nothing. I didn't know you hadn't eaten."

Sean tilted up a painting he'd been studying. "This is crap," he said with a sigh, pointing to the wild tangle of colors that appeared to have been flung at the canvas. "I had hoped it might be valuable crap, but no. Just everyday what-were-you-thinking-when-you-bought-this crap. I'll be lucky to get five dollars for the frame."

He let the painting fall back onto the scarred wooden table. "Have you?"

"What? Eaten?" Jack realized suddenly that he hadn't had a meal all day. "No. I've been at the nursing home."

Sean nodded sympathetically. "That could take your appetite away, all right. It's a damn shame, isn't it? A man like Grandfather, and he can't speak a single coherent word, or get himself out of bed."

But Patrick *had* said one word. One word that had damn near cut Jack's knees out from under him.

He couldn't start there, though. He had to start more slowly, with...

With what?

"Sean," he said. His voice sounded funny. Even he could hear that. "Sean, I need to ask you something."

Sean tilted his head quizzically. He slapped the dust from his hands, then swept the dangling curls of black hair behind both ears.

"Okay," he said. He pulled up a chair, flipped it around and sat down backward. "Ask."

"I met Nora Carson's son today. I met Colin."

"Oh." Sean raised one eyebrow. "Technically, that's not a question." Pausing, he picked up a stray Phillips head screwdriver and tapped it on the edge of the table. "But, come to think of it, it might be an answer."

"An answer to what?"

"To the question of why you came busting in here as tense as a kite string in a hurricane."

"I'm sorry." Jack took a breath. "It's just— He's so— I mean, you've gotta admit the kid looks—"

"Like a Killian."

"Yeah. So I'm not crazy? You see it, too?"

"Definitely. I first noticed it a couple of years ago. Before that he was just a blob, you know. The way kids are."

Jack waited. There was no good way to ask what he wanted to know. He hoped Sean wouldn't make him say the words out loud.

Sean tapped the screwdriver in an irregular rhythm, a light calpyso beat. His smile looked lazy and amused.

"Sean," Jack began. "Damn it."

"Okay, okay." Sean dropped the screwdriver. "I ought to make you sweat it out, just for being such an idiot. But I can't really blame you. Those eyes… Anyhow, you want to know if the kid is mine, right? You want to know if, after you left for the Army, I came home from college and comforted your brokenhearted girlfriend. Comforted her all the way into my bed."

"Something like that." Jack could feel the pulse beating in his neck. "So. Did you?"

"Nope."

Jack slowly lowered himself onto the edge of the table. He wiped his hand across his face.

"Okay." He was amazed at how much better he felt, just knowing that. It would have been—impossible. "Then what—"

"Frankly," Sean broke in, "at first I figured the kid had to be yours. Remember a couple of years ago I called you and asked you whether, back in the old days, you'd ever, even once, managed to make the Ice Queen open up?"

Jack had forgotten about that, but he remembered it now. The call had come out of the blue, and Jack had wondered, at the time, what had prompted it. He'd even wondered whether Sean might have developed an interest in Nora himself and was putting out feelers to see if Jack still considered her marked territory.

Jack had assured him that the Ice Queen hadn't ever come close to a meltdown, not even once, in spite of the fact that Jack had applied heat like a blowtorch for two long years.

In fact, he'd warned Sean that there might not even *be* a flesh-and-blood woman under all that ice. The night before he'd left Hawthorn Bay, he'd called her phone number like a madman. He'd been in the park by the river, alternately using the pay phone and dangling on one of the kids' swings with a bottle of vodka in the dirt at his feet, abandoning pride as he got drunker and drunker.

He'd begged her to trust him. To forgive him. To sneak out and come to him. To let him explain. To let him say goodbye.

Nothing. In desperation, he'd sent her best friend Maggie to intercede.

Even Maggie had clearly been shocked by Nora's answer. *No. Never. She never wanted to see him again.* Maggie had had tears in her eyes as she delivered it.

Like the drunken fool he was, Jack had exploded. He'd shouted. He'd called Nora all kinds of barroom names. He'd thrown things. He was pretty sure he'd broken the swing. He had, in fact, confirmed every ugly thing people thought about him. He was difficult, violent, dangerous.

In the end, he'd even scared Maggie away. The last thing he remembered about that night was hearing Maggie's sandals slapping on the sidewalk as she'd run to her car, and then the sound of her tires squealing as she'd peeled off, unable to get away from him fast enough.

He'd puked then, inevitably, into the bushes. As he'd hunched there, heaving, he'd wished he could puke out every last bit of feeling he'd ever had for Nora.

And maybe he had. When he'd woken up, dew had glistened like shards of glass on the grass where he'd lain. And his heart had been as cold and hard as the puny gray moon that had been fading away in the early morning sky.

Sean was watching him now. "You said you'd never made it into her pretty panties. I believed you. You don't want to change the story now, do you?"

Jack shook his head. "No. I dreamed about it a thousand times, you know how it is to be eighteen. But in real life, never. She was locked up tighter than Fort Knox."

Sean nodded. "I figured as much. That's one of the reasons I never even tried. You know I don't like to work that hard. I like women who think sex is a one-way ticket to heaven, not hell."

Jack knew that was true. And Sean had never suffered any shortage of willing women. It was weird how many women were turned on by a bad boy.

Just Jack's luck to fall for the one woman in town who wasn't.

"Okay," Jack said. "So where did the kid get those eyes? And that hair? Were you ever curious enough to snoop around and find out?"

Sean shook his head. "Honestly, I already knew it wasn't me, so when I made sure it wasn't you I just stopped worrying about it. Obviously the lady likes men with dark hair and blue eyes. It's her type. And though it may prick our pride to face it, we're not the only men in the world who have those things."

"Yeah, but—" Jack tried to find the hole in the logic. "The boy looks about eleven, which means she would have had to—"

"Find a new pair of blue eyes pretty quickly after you left? I know." Sean shrugged. "Sorry, Jack, but I'm not sure she nursed that broken heart very long."

Jack reached out and took hold of the junk painting. He scraped it toward him across the table and stared down into its chaotic depths. The longer he looked, the easier it was to make out the pattern. Though it looked like a mess, it was actually a bouquet of flowers.

Maybe Sean was right—maybe the explanation was really that simple. Nora liked tall, thin men with blue eyes and black hair. She'd slept with one. End of story.

So why did it feel so wrong?

Sean cleared his throat. "She went abroad, you know, not long after you enlisted. I know they went to England. Maybe they went to Ireland, too. We get our coloring from our Black Irish forefathers, right?

Maybe, when she got over there, she found herself the real thing."

Jack looked up. It made sense, but…

Damn it. He felt hot, suddenly, and pissed off. "Do you really believe that? After two years with me…this…this *stranger* just happened to have the key to Fort Knox in his hip pocket?"

Sean's eyes were gentle, which inexplicably just made Jack feel even madder.

"Maybe…" Sean said softly. "Maybe she was just tired of saying no."

CHAPTER SIX

COLIN'S MOM WAS cooking dinner while he did a sheet of practice math that she'd assigned him as part of his punishment. He didn't really mind because he liked math. He was good at all kinds of puzzles, and that's what math was, really. Puzzles they graded you on, instead of puzzles you did for fun.

This page was full of "negative integers" problems that she'd downloaded from the Internet. He had finished about half, but he was hungry and his attention was wandering.

He'd started making anagrams with the words *negative integers,* and he was already up to twenty-five. Most of them were easy words, like *egg* and *ten,* but some of them were really good, hard words, like *revenge* and *senate.*

"So how was it at the nursing home?"

He looked up. His mom had her back to him. She was making stir-fry chicken, which smelled so good his stomach was rumbling.

He considered his answer carefully. He knew better than to sound enthusiastic. Once she got the idea that he liked the nursing home, she'd think it wasn't a bad enough punishment anymore, and who knew what she'd come up with next.

"Boring," he lied. Well, not a complete lie. Some of

the old people just sat and stared, no matter what he said, and that part *was* boring. But a lot of them did crazy things, like Mr. Pettigrain, who would be real quiet, and then he'd all of a sudden yell, "Turkey bollocks!" The nurses would look at each other and pretend not to be giggling.

And there was Mrs. Ingraham, who would be walking down the hall, making that shuffling sound, looking all innocent. But when she saw Colin she'd get this sneaky smile and she'd open up her hand, and in there would be a bright green, sweaty rabbit's foot. She'd say "Shh," as if they were spies or something, and then she'd close her hand again.

Some of them told him stories about the old days, and Colin knew they exaggerated, but still it was cool. The old people weren't very different from anyone else, really. They just wanted life to be more fun than it was.

He liked Mr. Killian the best. They understood each other. Colin always knew when Mr. Killian had heard enough of *Treasure Island* and was ready for a game. Mr. Killian loved games as much as Colin did, and Colin liked inventing some that Mr. K. could play without words.

"So, when you're there....do you see Mr. Killian very often?"

Colin glanced up curiously. His mom's voice had that fake smooth sound she got when she was trying to pretend a question wasn't important. Like when she said, "So, how did that geography exam go?" or "Do you ever mind that I spend so much time doing mayor stuff?"

He wondered what was important about this question. He wondered if the nurses at the home had been ratting on him. Sometimes they poked their heads in through the door and asked him to keep it down.

"Yeah," he said. He didn't want to lie if he didn't have to. His mom was pretty decent, as moms went. "I read to him almost every time. He likes exciting stories. Some of them just want me to read the newspaper. I hate that."

"Is he a nice man?"

"Yeah, he's cool. I like his family, too. Sean's cool, and his other grandson has started to come see him, too. At first I thought he was a jerk, but he got better."

His mother turned around. That surprised him. Usually, when she was cooking, their conversations were all held with him talking to her back.

She wiped her hands on a dishcloth. "You mean Jack?"

"Yeah. He said he used to know you."

She nodded. "It was a long time ago, though. I was in high school."

"Oh. Was he like your boyfriend?" Colin tried to make his own voice sound smooth and casual, and he wondered if she would recognize the trick. He looked down at his math paper so that she couldn't read his face, which she was way too good at.

She didn't answer right away. He had to work hard not to glance up and see what *her* face looked like.

"Boyfriend? I guess you could say that. Briefly." She turned back to the stovetop, where the stir-fry was sizzling and popping. She turned the burner down. "But it was a long time ago."

Yeah, she'd already mentioned that, and both times her voice had sounded funny. Sad.

Colin watched her back for a while, wondering. She

wasn't too old to be in love, and Jack was handsome. The nurses made a lot of excuses to come into the room when Jack was there.

Jack might even be rich, if the stories about the Killian gold were true. Colin would like to have a rich dad, and he wasn't ashamed to admit it. His mom worked too hard, and there were lots of things they still couldn't do.

And why shouldn't someone rich and handsome fall in love with his mom? She was the best-looking mom of all his friends, everyone said so. She had explained to Colin that she'd become a mother very young, which was unusual, and that made her younger than the other moms.

But she wouldn't explain about his dad. Not yet, she said. When he was older, she'd tell him everything, but for now he would just have to wait.

He was getting tired of waiting. She wouldn't even be specific about how *much* older, and he had a sinking feeling that she was never going to tell him.

His New Year's resolution, at the beginning of this year, had been to solve the puzzle on his own. He hadn't gotten very far because it was a tough puzzle to solve. You couldn't exactly go up to people and say "Hey, are you my real dad?"

But he'd tried to approach it scientifically. For starters, he had a list of names in a book that he hid in the floorboards of his bedroom. Names of people who might be his father. Men his mother mentioned a lot of times, or smiled at in a really girlie way. Or maybe someone would tease her about having dated someone in the past, and Colin would add that name, too.

His uncle Ethan was even on the list, though Colin

knew Uncle Ethan and his mom were like brother and sister, so he probably hadn't ever been a boyfriend. Once Colin had asked her straight out if she would ever marry Uncle Ethan, and she had laughed as if it were so funny that he knew it couldn't be true.

"Jack's pretty nice," Colin said now. He figured he could use this conversation to fish for more info. "But he's a little bossy. He asks me a lot of questions, like he's checking me out, to see if I'm good enough to hang around with his grandfather or something."

His mother grew very still. "What kind of questions?"

Colin tried to remember. He'd just said that to see how she would react. Jack's questions actually didn't bother him. It was nice to meet someone who didn't always want to talk just about themselves, someone who was interested in Colin for a change.

"Ummm…well, he wanted to know what my birthday is. And where I was born, you know, how long I've lived here and stuff. He likes to hear about you, I think. And he said he thinks Uncle Ethan sounds neat."

She turned around again. "You told him about Uncle Ethan?"

Colin realized she was holding the oven mitt so hard it was crumpling in her hand.

"Yeah," he said, feeling defensive, though he wasn't sure what about, exactly. "Is there something wrong with that? It's not like Uncle Ethan's a secret or anything. Everybody knows about him."

"No." She smiled. "No, of course not. In fact, he's arriving in a couple of days. He says your present is super this year. Now go wash up and change out of those dirty jeans. Dinner's ready."

Colin stood, glad of the excuse to go upstairs. He wanted to get out his book with the list.

There was already one Killian name on it. Sean Killian. Colin had learned about genetics in science class, and he knew you got your eyes and hair and everything from both parents. His mom had blue eyes, so that was okay, but she didn't have hair as dark as his.

Sean Killian did.

Of course, so did Tommy Newton's dad, but he was disgusting. He was fat, and he'd hit Tommy's mother once, for letting the baby fall off the bed. Colin hadn't wanted to put Mr. Newton on the list, but he had to be scientific.

If you wanted to solve a puzzle you had to look at all the clues, even the ones you didn't like.

Besides, if you looked at it logically, how great could his real dad be, if his mom had to keep him a secret? She hadn't married the guy, after all. Probably someday Colin would find out that his dad was a murderer, or a retard, or somebody who hit women, like Mr. Newton.

But just in case…tonight, he was going to add Jack Killian to the list.

WHEN THEY STOPPED to have lunch, using one of the oldest slabs in the Killian graveyard as a picnic table, Jack and Sean had been treasure hunting for almost two hours. The metal detector had led them to four chunky, rusted-out auto parts, two bent golf clubs and a gold box full of antique brass buttons.

No gold. Not even a single, washed-up coin.

To Jack's relief, Sean hadn't seemed to mind. He had been pretty excited about the buttons—his years as a junk dealer had introduced him to people who collected almost anything you could think of, and he said he could unload them for big bucks.

So, even if it was technically a failure, the morning had been a blast. While Sean had wielded the metal detector, Jack had given himself over to rediscovering Sweet Tides.

They'd tramped happily through the silver maples, mossy live oaks and ten-foot-high banks of slumbering azaleas that had been the undisputed kingdom of their youth. They'd laughed and horsed around like kids again, beginning every sentence with "Hey, remember the time…?"

When they'd reached the small, sunny hill on which the earliest Killians had been buried, they'd stopped, as planned, for lunch. Stacy had packed some sandwiches and Thermoses of tea for them, which had made Jack give Sean a quick raised eyebrow. He'd been surprised to see Sean flush.

"These are darn good," Jack said now as he made his way through his second chicken-salad sandwich. "Is there anything your amazing Stacy can't do?"

Sean grumbled. "She's not *my* Stacy," he said. "And stop with the endless winking. It's not like that. You know she's not my type."

True enough. Jack thought about tormenting Sean some more, but decided he was feeling too lazy and full of chicken.

He leaned back against the tombstone behind him. It belonged to Roderick Killian, who'd died in 1790, at twenty-six. Roderick's two-month-old son was buried beside him, but that tiny tombstone had fallen over and broken into three sad pieces more than a hundred years ago.

Roderick was the newest resident of this cemetery, which was partly why the boys had always liked coming up here to play. All the tragedies here, and there were many, had been tamed by the long, powerful whip of the centuries. Jack and Sean didn't know the men and women buried here, and neither did their parents or their parents' parents.

Since 1800, the Killians had all been buried in town, at the Presbyterian Church graveyard, where a large Killian mausoleum still had enough slots for a half dozen or so more generations.

Yawning, Jack traced the numbers carved on "baby boy" Killian's marker, the edges of which had been softened by hundreds of spring rains and winter storms.

Sean watched him. "Funny how Killians always have boys, isn't it?"

Jack nodded. He shut his eyes and tilted his face up to catch the bright sunlight that made the December chill easier to take. "Guess Killian genes just don't have any sugar and spice and everything nice. We're too ornery to make girls."

Sean tore idly at the grass. "It was a girl that time Mom miscarried, remember? I think that was really hard for her."

Jack opened one eye and squinted at his brother. He wasn't going to let this nice afternoon deteriorate into a maudlin melodrama.

"I think she really wanted a girl," Sean said.

"Yeah? Is that why she always dolled you up in those lacy dresses? Not that you didn't look adorable, but—"

Sean made a growling sound. He flung his sandwich to the side and rolled toward Jack, prepared to pummel him. Jack tensed his abdominal muscles and got ready to fight back, pleased with himself.

A good rough-and-tumble beat a self-pity hanky-fest any day.

"Jack?" The female voice just barely broke through the grunts and laughter. "Jack? I need to talk to you."

Jack held Sean off with one hand—though Sean was two years older, Jack was two inches taller, and that made all the difference—and looked up into the sun.

"Nora?"

Sean's battering stopped instantly. He looked up at the newcomer, too. "Nora?"

"Hi, Sean," she said stiffly. Jack couldn't read her expression because her back was to the sun. But if body language meant anything, she hadn't come in peace. She was as ramrod straight as the wrought-iron rails in the fence that circled the cemetery.

"Stacy told me you'd probably be here, having lunch. I'm sorry to interrupt, but I need to talk to you, and I have a meeting in twenty minutes."

For a split second, Jack tried to picture Nora hiking through the Sweet Tides acres, as they had, pushing aside low evergreen branches and stepping around fallen tree trunks. She definitely wasn't dressed for it. She wore a blue wool suit and low, ladylike pumps.

But then he remembered that most everything west of here had been sold off decades ago. This edge of the property now abutted a two-lane highway that led into town. Just about twenty yards to the west, beyond that stand of birches, cars were rolling by.

"Okay," he said. He didn't stand up, didn't brush the mulchy leaves from his sleeves, though he knew he was covered in them because Sean was. "What do you want to talk about?"

She crossed her arms over her chest, cupping both elbows in the palms of her hands. "Privately."

God, she had developed an autocratic tone. He didn't much like it.

When he didn't answer, she had the nerve to glance impatiently at her watch. That was too much. She'd sought him out, on his own private property, and she dared to cop an attitude?

"This is pretty private," he said with a smile he knew would be irritating. "No one here but me, Sean and bunch of dead Killians who couldn't care less what kind of burr you happen to have under your saddle."

This time she was the one who couldn't think of the right answer. He waited while she made small starts that went nowhere.

"So what is it, Nora? If you've got only twenty minutes, let's don't waste any of them. What do you want to talk about?"

She shifted a little, and the halo around her head disappeared. He could see her features clearly for the first time. If he'd seen that first, he might not have been so obnoxious. Under that arrogant facade, she was as nervous as hell.

"I want to talk about Colin."

Sean made a low noise. Jack covered it by sliding one knee up, scraping his foot across the papery leaves. He rested his elbow on his knee comfortably. "Okay. What about Colin?"

"I understand you have run into him at the nursing home. Several times. He tells me you've been grilling him for information."

Jack smiled again. "Grilling him? You make it sound like a police interrogation."

"I don't care what you call it. I just want you to stop doing it."

"Stop running into him? I'm afraid I can't do that. I haven't seen my grandfather in years. As long as I'm here, I'm going to—"

"No, I meant I want you to stop asking him questions." She moved closer. Her face was very intense—and, damn it, very beautiful. "He's just a child, Jack. In the future, if you have something you want to know about my son, ask me."

Jack stared at her for a minute. "Okay," he said finally. "Here's what I want to know. Who is Colin's father?"

Even Sean inhaled sharply at that one. "Wow," he said softly. "Jack."

To be honest, Jack had expected Nora to flinch. But he'd underestimated her. She stood her ground. Her long blond hair flew around a little in the wind, and her cheeks were pink from the cold, but her expression was steady, her blue eyes unblinking.

"Colin's father is none of your business," she said. "Anything else?"

Finally, he got to his feet. He took a couple of steps closer, so that they were nearly nose to nose. He could smell her perfume, and he knew she'd changed it. She no longer smelled like Confederate jasmine mixed with vanilla—homey and innocent. Now she smelled like sandalwood and spice, more mysterious, harder to understand.

Why did that surprise him? He'd changed over the past twelve years. Had he imagined that he'd left her in some hermetically sealed time capsule? Did he think she'd been floating in a magical preservative made of crushed jasmine petals, sweet red drops from her first glass of wine, and a splash of the salt water he'd kissed from her lips the night they'd gone skinny-dipping in the pond?

Of course not. Life had reshaped her, as it had reshaped him. Their bodies wouldn't fit together anymore, even if they tried.

"Yes," he said. "There's something else."

She waited.

"I don't remember much about my last night in Hawthorn Bay. I was drunk. Really drunk. I asked you to come down, but you said no. I even sent Maggie to ask you. You still said no. After that, I passed out."

He watched for any reaction, but he might as well have been talking to a wax figure in a museum. She barely seemed to be breathing.

"So here's what I want to know. I want to know whether there's anything you'd like to tell me about that night. Anything you think maybe I ought to know. Anything that it might be my *right* to know."

He wasn't even aware of Sean anymore. The moment had narrowed down to this, to the two of them, Nora and Jack, and the question that hung in the frigid air between them.

Finally she smiled, and that smile was colder than any winter day Jack had ever known.

"Yes," she said. "There is one thing I think you should know."

He held his breath.

"You should know," she said, "that I am glad, that

I have always been glad, that I didn't come to you that night. And that, if I had to do it over, I wouldn't change a thing. My answer, always and forever, would be *no*."

CHAPTER SEVEN

1880

JOE DIDN'T HAVE many breaths left, and each one he took hurt like the wrath of God. He wanted to use them well.

He wanted to use them to tell Angus about the gold.

Still, when the servants brought his son into the bedroom, as he had requested, Joe almost changed his mind. Angus looked too young, too frightened. The boy was only ten, and his mother lay dead in the front parlor, waiting for Joe to join her, so that one funeral would suffice for both corpses.

To this burden of grief, which Angus would carry for the rest of his life, how could Joe add the weight of the gold?

Yet how could he keep silent? If Angus never found the gold, then everything would have been sacrificed in vain.

Angus hesitated just inside the door, hugging his arms against his sides, clearly frightened of the dying man in the bed. They had already dressed the boy in clothes suitable for a funeral—his best jacket and fine breeches, clasped at the knee with silver buckles. Julia had wanted new clothes for her son, in the latest fashions—almost as much as she had wanted those things for herself. She had hated Joe for refusing to dig up enough gold to buy them.

Joe had not realized how virulent her hatred had become, not until she had showed up in his bedroom last night, at the stroke of midnight. He'd been surprised. It had been long since she'd come near him after dark.

This time, she'd brought only two things. Her lover and a gun.

"Come here, son." Joe tried to breathe around the bullet, which seemed to have lodged like a pebble of fire in his lungs. *Not long now, Julia,* he thought.

Angus tiptoed forward, his blue eyes watery, shining in the gaslight. His son looked like him, a sight that pleased Joe even more, now that he knew how easily the child might have resembled someone else.

"Father?" The boy's voice was very small. He sobbed suddenly. "Please don't die. I don't want you to die, too."

Joe's eyes burned as fiercely as the bullet hole, but he refused to cry. "I must," he said. "It's my time."

Angus bent over Joe's outstretched hand. Tears ran down the boy's face and into Joe's palm like rain, the soft rain that fell on Sweet Tides land and brought forth flowers.

"Why?" The boy's voice was high, thin with pain. "Why would anyone shoot you? Why would anyone shoot mother?"

Joe shut his eyes. It was so tempting, the thought of telling him the truth.

It would be Joe's chance to revenge himself on Julia.

Your mother was a faithless woman, he could tell his son now. *She brought her lover here, to steal our gold. She was going to run away with him. She was going to leave us both. But I fought him. For you, for your future, I fought.*

Joe knew the man hadn't intended to shoot. But when the gun had gone off, and Joe had fallen back, Julia's lover had turned to her, the only witness. "I'm sorry," was all he'd said. And then he'd shot her through the heart.

What an irony it was. Her lover had, in his ruthlessness, managed to reunite husband and wife for all eternity.

"He was an evil man," Joe said. "You must pray for his soul."

Angus looked up, his blue eyes bloodshot and swollen. "I won't."

"You must. We will pray together, soon. But now I want to give you something. There is a secret panel above the fireplace. You must open it, and take out what's there."

Angus frowned. "What is it?"

"A map," Joe said, though he had enough breath only to whisper the word. Angus would have to pray for the evil man alone. Joe was praying his last prayer now, asking God to give Angus wisdom—and patience.

It was too soon to dig up the gold—he didn't even dare unearth a few coins, much less the bars. Fifteen years, to these people who had lost everything to the War, was merely a heartbeat of time. Some men still spat on the street when Joe walked by. Others crossed to the other side, to avoid having to speak. One anonymous note, flung through the window of Sweet Tides attached to a stone, had warned him that the gold was cursed.

Perhaps it was. Both Joe and Julia had died for it.

As it stood, all was rumor; nothing was fact. But if

a single gold bar, a single stray coin, should surface, they would know he had been a traitor.

They would not hold little Angus to blame, surely. He hadn't even been born when Joe had buried his fortune in the dirt. But they would hate him in their hearts.

And they would confiscate the gold.

"I don't want a map," Angus said, refusing to let go of his father's hand. "A map of what?"

In the doorway now, Joe could see one of the soldiers who had haunted his dreams so long. The soldiers with the golden bones.

He was running out of time. The soldier had come for him.

"A map of what?" his son asked again.

"Sin," Joe said.

My sin, Angus, he tried to say. *Not yours.*

But there was no more breath, and there could be no more words.

THE LANGLEY GROUP had designed upscale developments all over the Carolinas, every one of which had been a financial success. To make their case for the complex they hoped to build on the Sweet Tides property, the president of the company, Jim Samoyan, was putting on quite a show.

He'd invited the members of the Hawthorn Bay city council to visit the nearest Langley Group project, the Blossoms, which had just been completed. The tour had begun with a fantastic lobster-and-wine lunch at the complex's best restaurant.

Nora had insisted that each councilman pay for his own lunch, a gesture of ethical independence that had annoyed Samoyan and made her cousin Tom laugh at her for being a prude. She didn't care. She knew what the rules were, even if Tom wanted to pretend he didn't.

Tom had indulged a bit too freely in the wine, she thought as he climbed into the limousine beside her for the next part of the show, a tour of the office complex. His breath was thick and too sweet.

She turned her head, pretending to look out the window.

It took two limousines to transport them all, but Jim Samoyan rode in theirs. As mayor, Nora technically held a position of importance, and Tom was Langley Group's best friend on the council, the driving force behind their agenda.

"We hired the very best Southern architects," Jim said as he took his seat opposite Nora and Tom. "I think you'll be impressed with how accurately they've replicated the antebellum look."

"You'd do that for the Sweet Tides complex, as well, wouldn't you?" Tom was feeding Jim the right questions, like a scripted television infomercial.

Jim nodded. "Absolutely. The condominiums would all have Doric columns, as would the office buildings. I promise you they would remain true to the flavor of the Old South."

Tom was an idiot, Nora thought to herself as she continued to stare out the window. Did he really think this was impressing her? She'd heard it all before. She'd seen the blueprints. Lots of square block structures with faux Southern geegaws attached to the facade. It would be kitschy and cheap, and trash in fifty years.

The complex was only about a mile from the restaurant. They could have walked, if Mr. Samoyan hadn't been hell-bent on showing off. The itineraries they'd been given listed four buildings to tour: the Magnolia, the Jasmine, the Gardenia and the Dogwood.

Boy, they were heaping on the Southern syrup with a big ladle. She sighed as the limo braked to a stop, then exited quickly. *Might as well get it over with.*

Once they were inside, a young woman with a Christmas-red hoop skirt and a Scarlett O'Hara accent welcomed them, handing each of them a silk magnolia. Nora accepted hers with a smile. No sense taking out her irritation on this poor girl, who probably thought the whole shtick was just as silly as Nora did.

Nora heard Tom swear under his breath. "What the hell is *he* doing here?"

"Who?"

"Jack Killian." Tom glared out the window. "If that meddling son of a bitch thinks—"

"It *is* his property you're talking about tearing down," Nora said, though she was unnerved, too. She knew how this would look—as if she were part of the whole conspiracy, as if she were letting some business-man buy her vote with lobster and limousines and artificial magnolias.

Jack had caught Jim Samoyan out on the sidewalk. Nora and Tom watched through the window as the two men talked. The other limousine drew up, and the other two councilmen, along with city attorney Bill Freeman, emerged. After a few more minutes of pantomimed discussion, they all began to move toward the building.

Samoyan entered first. He hurried up to Tom. "Mr. Killian would like to join the tour," he said quietly. "I think it's an excellent idea. He can see our quality firsthand."

Tom frowned, but Jack was now within earshot.

Samoyan turned to welcome him to the fold. "Come, Mr. Killian. We're delighted to get a chance to make our case face-to-face. I'm sure we'll win you over. To know a Langley Group project is to love it."

Jack's smile was completely neutral.

Samoyan waved his hand. "Do you know everyone?"

"I do," Jack said. "Hello, Dickson. Nora."

Tom nodded. "Killian."

Nora had to admire Tom's restraint. He hated Jack—really hated him. But he was much too smooth to show irritation openly.

Tom's poise used to impress her. About four years older than she was, he'd been blessed with physical grace, silky blond hair, intelligent brown eyes and classic features. What few imperfections he'd been born with—a minor underbite, a slight myopia—had been surgically eliminated.

Their mothers were sisters. When they were kids, Nora had naively believed that blood relatives by definition possessed the same values. And, of course, she'd been young enough to think that beauty and charm were the same thing as goodness and virtue.

Through the years she'd learned that Tom never used his many gifts for anything other than the gratification of his own appetites. Money, women, power, possessions.

And, at least in this one case, revenge.

Jim Samoyan opened his arms expansively. "Shall we go, then?"

Nora had expected the tour to be boring, but that was before Jack had joined it. Jack said almost nothing. He hung in the back, just watching, never once approaching Nora. Still, she saw everything through his eyes, and it wasn't just tacky—it was tragic. Who in his right mind would tear down Sweet Tides to put up these ridiculous boxes?

She watched the other two councilmen, wondering what they were thinking. One of them, Lon Hambrick, looked skeptical. That was a good sign. The fourth councilman, Paul Allingham, was Lon's doubles partner, and the two men frequently voted in tandem.

By the time they reached the penthouse of the Magnolia, which served as a conference room shared by all the tenants, Nora had relaxed a little.

The penthouse was a circular room, kind of like a doughnut, with a support pillar in the center that held the elevators and restrooms. The exterior walls were banks of sparkling windows, which offered a panoramic view of the town.

Everyone oohed and aahed, and then Samoyan pointed out a buffet spread of desserts, including an ice sculpture Christmas tree and petits fours sugared in the shapes of brightly wrapped presents.

The men made a beeline for the table, but Nora couldn't eat another thing. She went to the window and gradually made her way counterclockwise, until she was safely on the far side of the central column.

She could use a minute or two alone.

But she should have known that wasn't possible. When she reached the other side, she saw that Jack was already there. He was staring out the window, looking down at the roofs of houses that dated back to the early 1800s.

Nora paused, wondering if she could sneak away again without being seen.

"It's okay," Jack said without turning his head. "I was avoiding the jackals and blowhards, not you."

She smiled at his description. It couldn't have been more apt.

"Thanks for not including me among the jackals. But how do you know I'm not one of them? How do you know I don't think the Langley Group is the best thing that could possibly happen to Hawthorn Bay?"

He laughed. "Sorry, Nora. You're not a very good actress. Every time Samoyan says the word *functionality* or mentions the *Old South feel* you make a face, as if your lobster is disagreeing with you."

"Maybe it is," she said. "It was pretty rich lobster."

"I'll bet."

She went over and stood at his side, and for a moment they both stared down at the beautiful antebellum houses. She twirled her silk magnolia between her thumb and forefinger. It had been sprayed with something, and it gave off a scent that was disturbingly both flowery and chemical.

She thought about apologizing for coming on so strong the other day, when she accosted him at the Killian cemetery. But she didn't want him to get the idea that she'd changed her mind. She still didn't want him interrogating Colin.

She just wished she'd taken a more civil tone about it.

However, he seemed willing to let it go, so she decided to do the same.

"Samoyan is pretty eloquent about his projects," she said. "But even he can't explain to me why anyone needs to tear down a genuine rice plantation house with three hundred years of history in order to put up a bunch of imitations."

"It's cheaper," Jack said flatly. "Cheaper to build, cheaper to maintain, cheaper to tear down when they want to start over with some new scheme. How do you think conglomerates like Langley get rich enough to put lobster on every table and ice sculptures in every boardroom? Illusion is a hell of a lot cheaper than reality."

"I guess so." She looked at him. "I'm going to vote against it," she said. "I want you to know that. You don't have to worry about, about our past. I won't let my vote be influenced by anything…personal."

"That's more than your cousin can say."

She started to shake her head, but Jack stopped her.

"Come on, Nora. We all know what's behind this. We all know why he's salivating at the very thought of bulldozers on Sweet Tides land."

He was right, of course. Tom's motives were purely personal.

Twelve years ago, Jack Killian had almost killed him.

It had been quite a scandal. For reasons known only to the two of them, Jack had taken Tom out to one of the remote spit islands just off South Carolina's coast, beaten the hell out of him and left him there to die.

Luckily, one of Tom's friends had rescued him, so Jack hadn't quite succeeded in murder. But he had humiliated him, which, in Tom's view, was almost as bad. Jack was three years younger than Tom, and yet Jack had managed to break the older boy's arm, blacken his eyes and plant bruises up and down his torso.

Worst of all, Jack himself had come out virtually unscathed, as if Tom hadn't even managed to land a punch.

Nora had always wondered why Jack had done it. Even now, when she had accepted the truth about what a boor Tom really was, she couldn't quite understand it.

Everyone said the Killians had cruelty in their blood, but Jack had always been so gentle with her....

Of course he was, Maggie had said. *You know what he wanted, and even Killians know that some things are easier to catch with honey.*

Now, Nora realized that anything Maggie had ever said about Jack was suspect, too. Everyone, it seemed, had a hidden agenda. Apparently you had nothing to rely on in life but your own instincts.

And her instincts told her that Jack Killian was dangerous. At least to her. And to Colin.

When she'd learned that Jack didn't remember anything about the night before he'd left for the Army, she'd been so relieved she'd nearly fainted. She couldn't believe her luck, but clearly he didn't have the slightest inkling that he might have slept with Maggie that night.

He didn't remember that he had betrayed Nora.

Of course, not remembering it was not quite the same thing as not doing it in the first place. She thought she understood why he had. She had taken her cousin's side. Nora had been frightened by Jack, disgusted by the unbridled violence. She had believed his father's genes were coming out in him.

And that would be the one betrayal he couldn't endure. It must have hurt him a great deal. He must have wanted to hurt her back.

And he *had* hurt her, terribly. Unfortunately, he'd hurt Maggie, too. And the baby who was the result of that night of rage and pain.

And he had hurt himself, though he didn't know it. He'd denied himself the joy of knowing his wonderful son.

"Actually, I'm surprised you're not voting with Tom on this one," Jack said suddenly.

She started. She'd been lost so far in the past.

"Why? I've always loved Sweet Tides. I love all the old mansions. If I'd been able to go to college, I was going to be a history major, remember?"

"You might still think it would be best for the town, if you got rid of those dangerous Killians once and for all."

She looked down at her flower, wondering how to answer that. Were the Killians really so bad? Were they any worse than anyone else?

She thought of her arrogant cousin. Once, she'd heard Tom bragging to another businessman that he'd brought a project in under budget by hiring undocumented workers, then refusing to pay them, knowing that they couldn't fight back. The other man had thought it was so clever, as if honesty and fair play were things only fools would bother with.

Was everyone willing to lie and cheat, if the motive was strong enough?

She thought of her own lies, and the child who had her name, but not her blood.

"Sometimes I don't think I know what's right for anyone about anything anymore," she said.

"Don't know what's right?" He laughed. "Well, that doesn't sound like the Nora Carson I used to know."

She tried to laugh, too. She couldn't deny it. She'd been so sure of herself back then, so safe and smug inside her mansion, with her parents barring the door to anything ugly.

So quick to judge him.

"It seems so long ago. Do you think we're even the same people we were back then, Jack?"

He turned away from the window. He looked at her so intensely that she felt little nerve endings twitch beneath her skin.

"In some ways I'm nothing like that boy," he said. "And in some ways, I'm exactly the same."

Without warning, he took hold of her upper arms and pulled her into him. She shivered, feeling her balance shift. She was acutely aware of the sheer drop, ten stories down, through the window just beside her.

But as long as he held on to her, she was safe. She looked up into his eyes. They caught the afternoon light and glowed a hot, neon blue.

"I still want you, Nora," he said. "As much as I ever did."

Was he going to kiss her? She remembered how warm his kisses were. They started at her lips, but the heat didn't stop there. It slid through her, softening and warming every inch of her, inside and out.

She tilted her head back. He was so tall—he would have to bend his head to hers, and she would feel taken over, owned, safer than she'd been in so long....

She shut her eyes and waited.

After a long minute, he touched her chin with the tips of his fingers.

She opened her eyes. The light in his had gone out.

"We should go back," he said, and his voice had turned cold, too. "Before we do something we'll both regret."

CHAPTER EIGHT

COLIN'S MOM WAS finishing up a batch of jam, so Colin figured he had about an hour before she came upstairs to check on him. That wasn't enough time, really, but it would have to do.

He eased out of bed so that his springs wouldn't creak. He knelt on the floor and dragged out the cardboard box he'd pushed under it earlier this afternoon.

It was a box of junk that Mr. Killian had given him. Sean and Jack and Colin had all been visiting Mr. Killian at the same time the other day, and suddenly Mr. Killian had gotten super-excited and had begun waving his hand around and trying to talk.

It had sort of scared Colin, but Sean had decided he was talking about music. Apparently Mr. Killian's own father—Colin's mind could hardly imagine anything that far back—had been a songwriter.

"A really bad songwriter," Jack had said with a laugh. "One halfway decent Christmas song, and a bunch of hymns so saccharine you choked just trying to sing them."

Colin wondered if they could really be that bad. Probably not. That was just Jack's way, to make fun. Jack never took anything seriously.

Anyhow, it had turned out that Mr. Killian had wanted Sean and Jack to get this box of music stuff and give it to Colin. That had embarrassed Colin, for two reasons. One, he didn't want it. What the heck could he do with a bunch of smelly old sheet music and some dirty old player-piano rolls? The only player piano he'd ever even seen was at the nursing home, donated by the Killians. And, though his mom had made him take two years of piano, he could just barely read music, so it wasn't as if he could play these songs himself.

Even more important, he didn't want anybody to think he was sucking up to Mr. Killian so that he'd get presents. It hadn't even occurred to him that the old guy had anything to give.

He'd thought maybe Sean and Jack would forget about it, but they hadn't. The very next day, they'd brought the box to the nursing home and given it to Colin, which had clearly made Mr. Killian happy.

And then the weirdest thing had happened. Right after Sean and Jack had left, Mr. Killian had motioned Colin over to the bed. He had touched the box with his good hand and tried to say something. He'd tried three times before he'd gotten it right.

And then he said it. "Treasure."

So now Colin was interested. A lot.

He heard a plinking sound at his window.

Good. That meant Brad had been able to sneak out. The Butterfields' house was just three doors down, and once Mr. and Mrs. Butterfield settled into the family room to watch TV for the night, Brad could have invited the entire sixth grade over for a toga party, and no one would have noticed.

Colin went to the window of his room that opened onto the upstairs porch. Brad had already climbed the maple tree and was wriggling himself backward onto the railing. He was wearing his pajamas, a plaid bathrobe and a really dumb-looking pair of bedroom slippers with doggy faces that his mom must have picked out.

Still, he'd agreed to come, in spite of the fact that it was really cold, so Colin decided not to make fun of the shoes. At least not tonight.

Colin pulled his jacket on over the sweatsuit he slept in. Then he wedged the box through the window. When Brad landed on the porch with a soft thud—another plus for the fuzzy sippers—everything was ready and waiting.

"Hey." Brad wiped his hands on his robe to get rid of the bark dust. "Is that it?"

"Yeah." It didn't look like much, Colin knew that. But Brad was Colin's best friend because he had imagination, which most of the other boys didn't. Brad didn't think the only interesting thing in the world was which girl had or hadn't bought a bra yet.

Colin was confident that Brad would appreciate the possibilities here.

"So open it." Brad picked something out of his braces and talked around his fingers. "You said you've only got an hour. Let's get started."

For a second, when Brad saw the moldy old piano rolls, his face fell. But when Colin brought out the sheet music and announced that the great grandfather Killian had actually written the music himself, Brad's eyes lit up again.

"Awesome! Was he the one who buried the gold?"

Colin wasn't completely sure about all that, but he was doing research, and it was beginning to come clear. "I don't think so. This guy, his name was Angus, couldn't have been old enough during the Civil War. It must have been his father. But his father probably told him where he buried the gold, and this guy could have written some clues into the songs, don't you think? Maybe in code or something."

Brad sat back on his heels, staring at one of the hymns. "This is church music," he said doubtfully.

"I know. But there's a normal Christmas song, too. Sean and Jack said it was the old guy's favorite. They said their grandfather used to talk about how Angus made such a big deal about it. He thought his song was great, and it would be a big hit someday."

He stared at Brad, getting excited all over again. "He always said that they better not throw it away, that it was the song that would make the family rich."

Brad looked confused. "Well, then, that's no good. That must be what Mr. Killian meant when he said *treasure* to you, and—"

Colin shook his head. "No, no," he said, trying to remember to keep his voice down even though Brad was being so irritating. "Can't you tell what he really meant? He meant there was a clue in the song. Like a song-map."

Brad stared down at the box, obviously skeptical. "You don't know that," he said. "You dragged me out here when it's, like, fifty below, and it's just a wild goose chase?"

Colin gave Brad a dirty look. "Have a little imagination, butt head. Think. Angus knew the gold was hot. He couldn't admit straight out that they even had it. So he had to plant subtle clues."

Brad was still frowning.

"Anyhow, it's worth a try, right?" Colin raised his

eyebrows. "Or would you rather go home and watch PBS with your mom and dad?"

Brad sighed. Colin knew he wouldn't go home. Even when things seemed dull, Brad knew that Colin might at any moment dream up something cool to do, and he didn't want to miss it. Nothing interesting ever, ever happened at Brad's house, and that was just a fact.

"Okay, then. Here it is." Colin pulled out the Christmas song, which was called "The Starry Skies Sang Lullabies."

"First, you should just read it," he said.

Brad's lips moved as he studied the song, which had three verses. When he finished, he looked up and rolled his eyes.

"Brother," he said. "That's corny."

"Whatever. All songs look corny written down. It's the music that makes them sound right. But anyhow, what do you think? Do you see anything that might be a clue?"

Brad looked again.

"Not really," he said. He clearly was afraid of missing something obvious. "Do you?"

Colin shook his head. "Not right off. I've tried a bunch of stuff. Like working with every first letter of each sentence. But that doesn't spell anything at all. It's like TRALGMAT DOG."

"Dog?" Brad chewed on his fingernail, then had to work to get the sliver of nail out of his braces. "Could that mean something? Do they have a dog?"

Honestly, sometimes Brad was retarded.

"Sure," Colin said sarcastically. "They hid a fortune in gold in the collar of their *two-hundred-year-old* dog."

Brad scowled. "Okay, jerk. You got anything better?"

"I don't know. I wondered if the notes might mean something. You know how every note has a letter name? Like A, B, C? I thought maybe if we translated the notes into their letters, it might spell something."

Brad had been forced to take piano lessons, too, and he'd been even worse than Colin. At least Colin had some musical talent, even if his fingers were clumsy and always hitting the wrong keys. When Brad played, it sounded as if someone had left a drunken monkey alone in a room with a piano and a hammer.

"I guess." Brad stared at the sheet music. "But how many words can you spell with just seven letters? I mean, you can't even spell *gold* with the letters on the scale."

"I know." Colin looked over Brad's shoulder at the music. "I thought of that. And if you were worrying about spelling words instead of writing a nice melody, the song would sound lame, wouldn't it?"

"How about the lyrics?" Brad ran his finger across the words, which had been handwritten by someone with really good penmanship.

"The lyrics?"

"Wouldn't that be the easy way to do it? I mean, look, here he talks about a hill with a tree on it, and he says 'the river sings, while the Christmas bell rings, to the baby asleep in the house dark and deep.' Maybe he's describing something around Sweet Tides."

Colin's growing excitement fought with his envy that Brad had thought of the idea, not him. He was used to being smarter than his friends about puzzles.

Still… It was a really good idea.

"That's great, Brad," he said, deciding he couldn't be mean enough to deny his friend his moment of glory.

Brad narrowed his eyes. "Are you making fun of me?"

"No, really. This is a great idea. You could have found something."

Brad's smile was so wide his braces caught the moonlight and gleamed like diamonds. But he didn't get a chance to wallow in his thrill because just at that moment, the window of Colin's kitchen went black.

That meant his mother was finished with the jam and would be heading their way any minute.

Like soldiers on a dangerous but familiar sortie, they knew what to do. Silently, without even saying goodbye, Brad hoisted himself up on the railing and reached for the low-hanging maple branch. Colin scooped up all the loose sheet music and shoved it back into the box.

Then, as Brad's doggy slippers disappeared into the darkness, Colin climbed over his sill. He closed the window, tossed off his corduroy jacket, slid the Christmas song under his pillow for safekeeping and jumped back into bed.

He didn't mind going to sleep now. He would dream of trees and rivers that sang.

And the look on Mr. Killian's face when Colin was able to tell him that he, eleven-year-old Colin Carson, who lived in a tiny house, got in trouble in math class and didn't even know who his own father was, had found the Killian gold.

THE FIREPLACE IN THE gun room was about ten feet long, and it made a grand blaze that warmed even this high-ceilinged space. Jack was glad to note that Sean had sold all the old guns that used to be racked here, as well as the animal trophies—early generations of Killians had apparently loved to kill furry things.

The absence of all that death made the room a much more inviting spot, and Jack and Sean had spent a lot of time in it the past few days.

Today, Jack worked on his laptop, and Sean sorted through a small, relatively disappointing stash he'd bought from a local estate.

As the afternoon moved toward sunset, the laptop wasn't able to hold Jack's interest. He found his gaze drifting to the window. The river was like a sparkling ribbon, and the bare trees were black spiderwebs against the amber sky.

"Let's go for a walk," he said. It surprised him, this overwhelming urge to fill his lungs with damp, river air and have his feet touch the ground. He never felt that way in Kansas City. Was it really so different, if the land you walked on was your own?

His brother looked up from a heap of old clothes.

"Can't," he said. "I've got a dealer coming in a few minutes, to take this mess off my hands. I'm not through checking the pockets."

Jack closed his laptop. "For what?"

"You'd be surprised at what people leave in their pockets. Money—not just coins, but bills. Found a hundred-dollar bill one time. Receipts. Letters." He wiggled his eyebrows. "Oh, the love letters I've read. Amazing what people will sign their names to."

Jack laughed. "Anyone we know?"

"Sometimes." Sean tossed a suede coat onto the pile and picked up a black sweater. "Once, when I bought a lot of women's clothes, I found a rental receipt for a one-bedroom apartment over in the raunchy part of Chesterfield. A full year's rent, paid in advance. Clearly a love nest. Guess whose name was on the dotted line?"

"No idea."

"Tom Dickson."

Jack whistled softly. "Is that so?"

"Yep. I kept it nearly a month, dreaming about what I could do with it. Finally I decided, who gives a flip what that jerk does in bed, or who he does it with? I'll bet even his wife doesn't care. I ended up putting the receipt through the shredder."

Sean tossed the sweater aside. "Of course, that was before he started making noises about buying Sweet Tides. It might have come in handy now, as a sort of crude bargaining chip."

"I'm not sure we're going to need one," Jack said. "I saw the faces of those councilmen yesterday, and I think we're going to be okay. Except for Dickson, they didn't seem very enthusiastic. "

"Even Nora?"

"Especially Nora. She hated the Langley Group guy, Samoyan, who is a real sleaze. Definitely not her type. He couldn't sell her ice in hell."

Jack stood up and stretched. He was cramped from hunching over that computer for two hours. He really did want that walk.

"I'm going to prowl around a little." He headed for the door. "If I find any gold, I'll let you know."

Sean snorted impolitely, but Jack ignored him and kept going. He grabbed a windbreaker from the hall tree. It was too cold to stay out long in just the flannel shirt and jeans he wore indoors.

He walked toward the river, which was more muted now that the sun was sinking, but was still alive with light. The water was shallow here, where it ran alongside the back of Sweet Tides, and it burbled peacefully over rocks and fallen logs. The noise filled his mind, so that he didn't have to think at all.

For about fifteen minutes, he might as well have been alone in the world. But then, just as he reached the crest of a small hill, he saw a young boy kneeling on the ground, peering down at something.

The boy had his back to Jack, but Jack recognized the black corduroy jacket that almost matched the scruffy black curls on the bent head. It was Colin Carson.

Jack didn't want to scare the kid, so he was careful to make plenty of noise as he climbed up onto the last few feet.

As the snapping of dry leaves and twigs finally penetrated his concentration, the boy turned his head. His eyes widened, and his mouth went slack.

"Mr. Killian!"

From this angle, Jack could see everything. The heap of dirt to Colin's left, the small silver spade with the red handle, and the three-foot hole in the ground.

Correction. The three-foot *empty* hole in the ground.

Boy, did that look familiar.

"Hi, Colin. Hit gold yet?"

Colin frowned. He chewed his lower lip, clearly wondering if he could spin this scenario any other way.

Jack shook his head. "You've gotta be either digging for treasure, or disposing of a dead body. I don't see a body, so…"

Colin put down his spade. His hands were mottled with dirt, the fingernails little black crescent moons.

"I wasn't going to steal anything," he said. He rubbed his hands against his jeans. "Honestly. Even if I'd found the gold, I would have given it to Mr. Killian."

Jack sat down next to him. Here under the oak, it

must be ten degrees colder than it was in the sunshine. Jack looked into the hole, which was tangled with roots and small stones. It was pretty impressive—about three feet deep and two feet wide. Colin must have busted his butt here for hours.

"You did all this work for nothing? You're trying to tell me you don't even want the gold?"

Colin shrugged. "I just want to find it. I know it wouldn't belong to me. I just want to figure out where it is. That's different."

"Yeah," Jack agreed. "It's different, all right. Most people would—" He broke off. "Did you know that my great great grandfather was shot to death by a guy who wanted to steal this gold?"

"No." Colin looked interested. He got off his knees and sat comfortably cross-legged. "Was that Angus?"

"It was Angus's dad. Joseph Killian. He was the one who supposedly buried it in the first place. Years later, he and his wife were both killed by a robber. Everyone assumed the guy had come looking for the gold."

"That was pretty dumb. How are they going to tell him where it is if they're dead?"

Jack laughed. "That's what I always thought. The story doesn't really make sense, does it? But nothing about this gold ever has. That's why I don't believe in it. I think it's about as real as Aladdin's cave, or the pot of gold at the end of the rainbow. Nice story, but mostly baloney."

Colin knocked his spade against the edge of his shoe, dislodging the wedges of dirt. Jack couldn't read his expression because the boy stared unblinkingly into the open hole.

"You really think it's just a fairy tale? You really think there isn't any gold?"

Jack was sorry to be the Grinch who spoiled Christmas, but he knew that the sooner you stopped dreaming hopeless dreams, the better.

"I really do," he said. "There isn't any gold."

This was one tough little kid. Instead of getting tearful with disappointment, he looked up and stared at Jack a long time, his eyes narrowed. He seemed to be appraising Jack, calculating the odds that he knew what he was talking about.

Finally, he blinked. "Maybe not," he said, squaring his jaw. "But you could be wrong."

"Colin, I'm not wrong."

"You *could* be. You're that type. You don't like to just *believe* in things. Like with your grandfather. I heard you tell Sean that Mr. Killian isn't ever going to get any better. You don't know that, either. He might. You don't like to just hope. You want to be sure, or you don't want to bother."

Jack was speechless. It was an overly simplistic description, but it was pretty damn accurate. This kid was scary smart.

"Look," Jack said. "I don't care if you dig so many holes you turn Sweet Tides into Swiss cheese. If this is your idea of fun, go for it. Just don't make gold-digging your financial plan, okay? If you need money, or if your mother needs money—"

"My mother makes *plenty* of money."

"I know." Jack put out his hand. "I just meant—"

Colin stood. Leaves fell from the sagging bottom of his jeans, which were damp from the wet ground.

He stuffed the spade into his back pocket, then ran his dirty hand through his tousled hair.

"I told you, I wasn't going to steal your stupid gold. We're not poor. My mom works really hard. She is mayor of this town, and she makes the best jam in the world. Everybody buys it."

Jack hadn't been sure about Nora's financial situation—she had been born into one of Hawthorn Bay's big social families, after all. But something about having sold Heron Hill didn't quite jibe. He'd seen the cute but modest little block house they lived in today.

Now he saw that his instincts had been right. The Carson fortune was gone, and Colin knew it. He was instinctively defensive of his mom.

Jack admired that—and, at the same time, felt an ache of empathy. Jack knew what it was like to feel defensive for a mother you loved, but whose problems were bigger than a boy could fix.

Suddenly, Jack really wanted to straighten this out. "Look, I know that. I think what I was trying to say was that, if there's ever *anything* you need, or your mom needs, I would like to help. Not just money. Anything. You see, your mom and I…well, I used to—"

Oh, brother, he was getting in pretty deep.

Colin watched, his blue eyes dark and focused. He was clearly eager to hear the end of the sentence.

"It's just that we—" Jack tried to sound casual "—used to be good friends."

"How come you're not anymore?"

It didn't make sense to lie to the kid. He was intuitive, and he'd know it was a lie. But it also didn't make sense to go into too much detail.

"We had a fight, and we didn't see each other for a

long time. But I still want her to be happy, you know? I would like you to feel that you could come to me, if either of you needed anything."

Colin's jaw softened subtly, and the tension in his shoulders subsided a fraction. For a minute, Jack thought maybe the boy was going to ask for a favor.

He wondered what. Money to buy his mom a Christmas present? Jack remembered going to Patrick, one year, asking for the money to buy another of the endless glass unicorns.

Jack wondered what Nora collected. What talismans did she gather around her to ward off loneliness and fear? He wished he could see inside her house. He wondered if he could gauge her happiness by the color of her walls, the length of her curtains, the quantity of her clutter.

Colin chewed his lower lip, obviously debating with himself. He shifted from one foot to the other, and he toyed with the spade handle. He opened his mouth, then shut it.

Jack waited, unsure whether a nudge would be helpful.

"I don't really need anything right now, but—" Colin took a deep breath. "Can I ask you one thing?"

Jack nodded. "Of course. I said *anything*."

"Okay, well, when a grown-up is keeping a secret—a big secret, not just like what you're getting for Christmas, but something major…is it always something bad?"

Jack fought the urge to analyze the question, to second-guess what the boy wanted to hear and then provide it. Once again, he felt the need for honesty.

"Not always. Sometimes the secret might just be

something…very complicated. Or they might have promised someone else they wouldn't tell."

"But why would anyone ask you not to tell a good thing? I mean, if I got an A on my math exam, I wouldn't ask my teacher to promise not to tell my mom."

Why indeed? The only vow of silence Jack had ever made was to Amy Grantham.

The kid had a point.

"Sometimes it's complicated. How about what you're doing today? Does your mom know you're here?"

Colin's eyes slid away. This clearly embarrassed him. "No. She thinks I'm at Brad Butterfield's house."

"So you're keeping it a secret, right? But it's not because you're doing something bad."

Colin grimaced. "She'd think it was bad."

"Yeah, but you don't think so. But it's very complicated, so you didn't tell her. See what I mean?"

The boy's grimace turned to a small smile. "Yeah. I guess I see. Okay. Thanks."

He began buttoning his jacket. "I'd better go home now. I rode my bike, and it's getting dark. She's going to call the Butterfields pretty soon, and then I'll be busted for sure."

"How about if I give you a ride?"

"Well…" Colin looked tempted, but uncertain. "Could you let me off at the end of the block, so that she wouldn't see you?"

Jack nodded. "Absolutely. We don't have to tell her about any of this," he said. "Because, after all, it's very—"

Grinning, Colin finished the sentence with him.

"Very complicated."

CHAPTER NINE

1927

AT MIDNIGHT, ANGUS KILLIAN finished his unsavory task. It was done. He had dug up the gold and hidden it anew, so that the men who came in the night with shovels and barrows and maps could never find it.

He was sure he'd found and moved all the bars, though he'd had to leave some of the coins out there. There was just too much of it, and he was physically exhausted.

Still, he was glad the job was finished. Another generation of Killians might be led to it some day, by God or by greed. But he, Angus Killian, would never have to touch the evil things again.

The townspeople said the gold was cursed, though Angus noticed that didn't stop them from hunting for it. Angus was a religious man, and he didn't believe in curses. But he did believe in evil. He believed that some deeds were so despicable, so hateful in the eyes of the Lord, that He couldn't wait until the hereafter to mete out punishment.

Everyone in Hawthorn Bay knew that, long ago, Angus's father had lied about this gold. Old Joseph had loved money more than his brave brothers who had been fighting for their lives in the Civil War. More than his

God, whose commandments expressly demanded truth, no matter what the cost.

Joseph Killian had died for that sin. Angus would always remember the smell of his father's room as he'd lain, a bullet lodged in his lung, struggling for breath.

Blood smelled like gold, Angus had learned that night. Metallic. Hot. Unclean.

He'd smelled the blood on his mother's body, too. And he'd seen her smeared lips, from kissing the man who'd killed her. At only ten, Angus had not understood the details of that terrible night, but he understood that sin had destroyed them both.

It had terrified him, but terror had been his salvation, for he had turned onto the path of the righteous that night. It didn't make the citizens of Hawthorn Bay love the Killians any more—like the hypocrites they were, they despised his virtue as much as they'd despised his father's sin.

Now fifty-seven, Angus had few illusions left. He wasn't an easy man. His wife, Mary, had left him—and their three boys. She'd said he was cold, that he was hardly human, and that no son of his could ever learn kindness or love.

Perhaps she'd been right. James and Mark were at university now, but Angus heard the stories. They were devils. They cheated on exams, seduced maids and waitresses and drank themselves into ugly tempers every night.

And they hated him. He'd accepted that. He'd given up on them, reconciled himself to the fact that they would make a bad end. He was glad, almost, that he wouldn't be here to witness it.

It was too early to tell what Patrick, the youngest, would become. Angus didn't hold much hope. Patrick was only twelve, but he already despised his father—he called him a monster, taking his cue from his rebellious brothers.

No. He wasn't an easy man to love.

Now the doctor told Angus his heart was failing. Angus believed him. The beating lump in his chest felt as heavy as a river rock.

Angus went into the parlor, to the player piano, and sat down. He picked up the music roll. Should he insert it? He ran his hands across the metallic cylinder. He had paid a lot of money to have these rolls made, so that his songs would live after him.

Once, he had thought his music might make his fortune. Now, he could only hope that someday people would listen to his many hymns and his one beautiful Christmas ballad, and finally understand who he was.

For now, they mocked him. Patrick and his friends, those coarse young people from heathen homes, loved the rolls of jazz they had bought. But when Angus began to play his own songs they groaned and ran away. Patrick would be beaten for it later.

Angus set down the roll. He wanted to play the notes himself, though he knew that even the servants would scatter to other parts of the house. He knew what they whispered. They said he grew mad when he played.

But it wasn't madness they heard.

It was his thwarted, terrified humanity, the humanity Mary said he didn't possess, bleeding through his fingers onto the ivory keys and finally becoming melody, becoming beauty, becoming love.

JACK KNEW IT WAS a fool's game, this keeping a mental tally of things he noticed about Colin, assigning them to categories: Killian or Not Killian.

But he couldn't seem to stop himself from doing it anyhow. In theory, Jack accepted Nora's absolute denial that she'd come to him that night—primarily because he knew that Nora was a rotten liar. So the kid couldn't be a Killian.

Still, Colin intrigued him, and Jack found himself spending more and more time at the nursing home, where he could observe the boy at leisure.

Every day, though, the mystery just deepened. In addition to his coloring, an obvious match, Colin was a born devil, which fit the Killian profile. But he had a soft heart, and frequently regretted his mischief, which didn't.

He was energetic, athletic, sarcastic and stubborn. *Match*.

But he got great grades at school, apparently, and he had infinite patience with old Patrick's infirmities. *Definitely no match*.

Now, in the cold twilight, Jack settled himself on the steps of Nora's pretty, poinsettia-laden front porch, delighted with this new chance to gather details for his list.

It had been dumb luck, really. Nora, who was running late picking up a friend at the airport, had asked Stacy to bring Colin back from the nursing home. When Stacy had arrived to pick him up, Sean and Jack had been there, too, so they'd decided to tag along.

Jack knew it was pushy. Nora's feathers would definitely be ruffled when she found him here, but…well, as he'd said, Killians were born devils. He wanted a peek at the domestic setup, and he didn't intend to let a few icy glares dissuade him.

Stacy had a key, so she and Sean were already inside, helping out by getting Nora's dinner started. Colin had asked Jack to help him figure out how to play Angus's Christmas song on the guitar, so they'd camped out here, where they wouldn't be in the way.

As Jack watched Colin struggle with the guitar he'd borrowed from his friend Brad's father, he put another big checkmark on the No Match column. This kid couldn't play the guitar worth squat.

All Killians were musical, at least as far back as old Angus, who'd fancied himself a composer, and had bought one of the first player pianos, a big clunky thing they'd sent to the nursing home with Patrick.

After a couple of hopeless attempts to strum the strings, Colin made a frustrated sound. He moved closer to Jack, pushing aside a poinsettia that was in the way. He held out the guitar and the sheet music.

"I can read music, so I know what the notes are. But we don't have a piano anymore, and I can't figure this thing out. It's crazy. It's not like the piano at all."

Jack nodded. "It is hard. Somebody's got to teach you. Patrick taught me. He was really good."

Just holding the guitar reminded Jack of all the summer nights he'd spent on the back porch of Sweet Tides, listening to Patrick play. He could almost smell the Confederate jasmine and wisteria on the air, and hear the crickets sawing away. They'd stop when Patrick began to play, as if they, too, wanted to listen.

Sometimes Jack's dad had joined them, beer in hand, and started to sing along. His father might have been a beast, but he'd sung like an angel. Jack used to hold his breath when the song was over, praying that the beautiful sounds had transformed his father, like magic.

But they never had. After a couple of minutes, Kelly would tilt back his beer, swallow noisily, make some irritable comment about how the goddamn steps needed painting or the weeds needed pulling, and shuffle off to his car.

He wouldn't be seen again until morning.

Jack glanced down at the music, though he didn't really need it. He knew this song. Most of old Angus's music was sanctimonious, droning religious stuff, but this Christmas carol was kind of nice.

"I just want to know what the tune is," Colin said, looking embarrassed. "I know you don't have time to teach me how to play. I was terrible at the piano, anyhow, so I don't think I have any talent."

Jack played a chord. The guitar was so out of tune it was painful to hear. Brad's dad must be tone deaf.

He began to turn the tuning heads. "I'd be happy to teach you, if you want to learn. But I'm rusty. I don't even own a guitar anymore. I haven't played much since high school. I mostly did it to impress the girls."

Colin watched Jack's fingers carefully, as if he thought he could pick it up by osmosis. "Girls like my mom?"

Jack fought to keep his face expressionless. Nora had loved to listen to him play. A sad song with a poignant melody had been the easiest way to melt her resistance, and he'd been selfish enough to exploit it shamelessly. He'd kept his guitar in the back seat of his car for two whole years, just in case.

He decided to change the subject.

"Listen. This is how each of the strings should sound, if they're in tune."

For the next fifteen minutes, he played, and Colin watched. The kid soaked up information like a dry sponge. He might not have native talent, but he had a quick mind. Jack had a feeling that anything Colin chose to learn would get learned in a hurry.

They were so absorbed that Jack, at least, didn't hear Nora's car drive up. His first clue was when Colin turned his head and his face lit up with a toothy smile.

"Uncle Ethan!"

He vaulted off the porch steps as if he had springs in his shoes. He ran across the small plot of grass that was the front yard, and reached the car just as a tall man with brown hair and wire-rimmed glasses stepped out.

"Uncle Ethan!"

The newcomer folded Colin in with a big hug. "Hey there, High C," he said. He held Colin out to look him over. "Darn, boy. What is Nora feeding you—alligators? You're twice as big as you were this summer."

Jack set the guitar aside and stood, watching the scene curiously. "Uncle Ethan" was one of the pieces of Nora's life Jack had been eager to understand a little better. Who exactly was he? How did he fit in?

He certainly seemed to feel at home.

Nora got out, too, and beamed at the two males, clearly pleased at their camaraderie. "Colin, help Ethan with the packages in the trunk, will you? I think he's got—"

That's when she saw Jack.

She looked silly, standing there with little clouds of breath misting from her open mouth, her hand still held out, dangling the car keys toward her son.

Colin took them from her. "Mom, I told Jack and Sean it was okay if they stayed for dinner. It is, isn't it? Stacy said she would make extra pork chops. I wanted them to meet Uncle Ethan." He smiled extra hard. "It's okay, right?"

All that Carson breeding came to her rescue.

"Of course it is," she said, and if Jack hadn't known her so well he wouldn't have heard the stilted quality in her voice. "Ethan, you've never met Jack Killian, have you?"

The serious-faced man glanced at Nora, then turned and smiled at Jack.

"No," he said, moving toward Jack, his hand out-stretched, as if nothing could delight him more. "I don't think I have. It's a pleasure."

Jack put out his hand, too. But he had seen the look that had passed between "Uncle Ethan" and Nora. It had been brief, about two seconds of rapid, wordless messages, like a subliminal quick-cut montage in an action film.

Quite an interesting look.

Now Jack just had to figure out what it meant.

Nora was about to ruin the salad, her hands were so clumsy. Ethan came up behind her and took the knife out of her hands.

"Let me," he said. "You need to sit down a minute and take a deep breath."

"I'm fine," she said. But she relinquished the knife. He probably needed something to do, to take his mind off…everything.

She and Ethan had shooed everyone else out to the front porch, telling them to work on some carols together, contending that they would cook better alone. But really she'd just wanted time to talk to Ethan privately, to hear what he thought, now that he'd actually seen Jack.

They had a pretty good view of the others from the kitchen window, though they could just barely hear Jack's easy finger-picking as he played every Christmas song Colin, Stacy and Sean could think of, from "Silent Night" to "Jingle Bell Rock."

Nora noticed that Colin didn't seem to be singing. He was watching the others, wide-eyed, admiring. It made her feel skittery inside, to see him look at Jack like that.

"It's damned eerie, isn't it?" Ethan's voice was quiet. They both knew they mustn't be overheard. "When you told me you suspected Jack, I—" He tossed a handful of chopped celery into the salad bowl. "I guess I believed you, but I never thought—"

"They'd be as identical as clones?"

Ethan nodded, his deft doctor's hands dicing tomatoes perfectly, even while he stared out the window.

"Well, Colin seems to like him," he said. "They seem to get along. I guess that's a good thing. I mean, if… if…"

Nora touched his forearm. She knew this was hard for him. In a way, it brought it all back too vividly. He had changed that day, when Maggie had died in his boat, her blood pooling around her, her newborn baby crying in her arms, as if he sensed the great loss that had just come upon him.

Ethan had always been quiet, but after that he'd been painfully serious. He worked too hard and laughed too little. It was as if he lived in fear of making another mistake.

The horror of that day had changed Nora, too. But while Ethan had been alone with his grief and his guilt, Nora had had Colin. Even from infancy, Colin had been special. Rambunctious, funny, dramatic and difficult. Full of affection and warmth. So like Maggie and, Nora now knew, so like Jack, too.

A child like that had gone a long way toward restoring laughter and hope to Nora's life.

"Do you think Jack knows?" Ethan stared at the two males, with their identical dark curls and teasing smiles. He shook his head. "How could he *not* know?"

"He suspected right away. He asked me who Colin's father was. He asked me whether I had come to him that last night, when he was too drunk to remember. That's when I realized he didn't know. However it happened with Maggie that night, he truly didn't remember."

"God," Ethan breathed. "He—she—and then he forgot all about it."

Clearly Ethan couldn't imagine such a thing. He'd kissed Maggie three times, that was all.

"It was lucky that Jack phrased his question that way," she went on. "I was able to say no, I had *not* come to him. It was easier to be convincing, since I didn't have to lie."

They talked so softly they had to stand elbow to elbow in order to hear each other. And still they checked out the window every few seconds, to be sure the caroling continued.

"But how long will that story satisfy him?" Ethan gestured toward the window with the tip of the knife. "Look at the two of them! What if he asks for proof? A paternity test?"

A chill ran down Nora's back, puckering the flesh between her shoulder blades.

"He won't," she said. "He is only staying through Christmas. He'll head back to his other life soon, and he won't think about Hawthorn Bay, or Colin, or any of us, for another twelve years."

"Maybe."

Ethan didn't meet her gaze, but his profile was somber. "Do you ever think we made a mistake, Nora? Handling this the way we did?"

"No."

He put the last of the tomatoes in the salad and turned on the faucet to wash the knife. "I'm not so sure. Maybe we did. Maybe we should have gone through the conventional channels. Arranged for you to legally adopt Colin."

Nora shook her head. She'd tortured herself with this question a million times. She always came back to the same answer. They had done the only thing they could do.

"Do you really think Maggie's parents would have let me take Colin? You heard Maggie. The only thing she cared about, even when she was dying, was making sure her father couldn't get hold of her baby. We promised we wouldn't let that happen. How could we have broken that promise, Ethan?"

He placed the heels of his hands on the edge of the sink and dropped his head, as if he were tired of trying to untie this emotional knot.

"We couldn't have. But damn it, Nora, my name is on that birth certificate. My father's name is on Maggie's death certificate. *Injuries from a fall*...and I talked him into that. If the truth should come out now—"

"It won't." She squeezed his arm. "I promise. It won't. You helped Maggie, that's all you did. You and your dad, you helped her save her son. And you gave me…everything that matters. Whatever happens, I won't let you suffer for that."

He nodded. They were silent for a moment, and the sweet notes of "O Holy Night" seeped in through the edges of the window. Jack and Sean were harmonizing. The tears, which memories of Maggie always brought close, threatened to spill over.

"I loved her," Ethan said suddenly. "It's ridiculous. I only knew her for four months, and she's been gone eleven years. But I still love her. I can't seem to move beyond it."

"I know." But it startled her to hear the raw pain in his voice. It was as if Maggie had died a few months ago, instead of more than a decade. Ethan had remained a big part of Nora and Colin's lives, but they rarely discussed Maggie this openly.

Maybe he needed to get some help.

Nora blinked away the unshed tears and tried to smile. "Don't you think Maggie would want you to be happy? I know everyone says that, it's such a cliché. But you know what a firecracker Maggie was. She believed in living in the now. She put all her energy into every single minute. She would be very annoyed if she thought you were still pining away."

Nora could just imagine Maggie on the subject. She'd complain about what a waste it was. Ethan was sexy, and smart, and good-hearted—and there were too few men like that. He owed it to the world to get out there and make some living, breathing woman happy.

Ethan smiled. "Yeah, she'd be merciless, I suspect.

She hated whiners." He picked up the salad bowl and handed it to Nora. "But while we're on the subject, I don't think she'd be too happy to hear that you're still single, either."

Nora laughed. "Then she'd better send Mr. Right straight to my front door. Because I am way too busy taking care of her little rascal to go man-hunting."

Suddenly there was a knock at the kitchen window. Ethan and Nora both looked up quickly and saw two faces pressed against the glass.

It was Colin and Jack.

"Feed me," Colin mouthed and did a silly pantomime of starving, gripping his stomach and falling into Jack's waiting arms.

Ethan grinned. "Well, how about that. Could Maggie be answering you already? You request delivery of Mr. Right, and voilà!"

Nora shook her head. "No way. Maggie knows, better than anyone, that Jack Killian is Mr. Absolutely Wrong."

CHAPTER TEN

IT WAS CLEARLY TIME for them to go home.

Jack recognized the familiar tired shadows under Nora's eyes that meant she was running on empty. And no wonder. She'd fixed a wonderful dinner, but she had hardly been able to eat it. Her cell phone had never stopped ringing, either with city business or jam business.

In the end, it was Ethan who'd intervened, saying the flight in had been exhausting, and would she mind if he called it a night? Jack decided the guy might be all right.

In the flurry that followed, everyone separated. Sean and Stacy tackled the dishes, Colin showed Ethan to the guest room, and Nora went looking for an extra blanket.

Jack was dispatched to bring in Ethan's luggage, which had been forgotten in the chaos earlier. It didn't amount to much, just one black leather duffle and two professionally wrapped Christmas presents—a small square box for Nora, and a huge rectangular package for Colin. Colin's was heavy and oddly shaped.

Jack had seen that shape before, long ago, under his own Christmas tree. It might well be a guitar. If it was a halfway decent instrument, that was a pretty pricy gift, even for an "uncle."

He decided not to speculate about Nora's gift. It was a jewelry box, but Jack hadn't seen anything tonight that signaled "diamond." There was intimacy between those two, definitely. But not passion. He knew Nora well enough to be sure of that.

In fact, "Uncle Ethan" seemed like the perfect nickname. Ethan might have been Nora's protective big brother.

Jack added Ethan's gifts to the others under the tree, most of which seemed to be addressed to Colin. Then he went back out to gather up the guitar and sheet music, as well as the odd drinks and snack bowls they'd left out there earlier.

"Don't fuss with those," Nora said from the doorway. "I can get them later."

Jack continued stacking the empty glasses.

"It's the least I can do, considering how we crashed your party tonight." He smiled at her. "You were a good sport about it. Your mom would be proud."

She smiled back, the first one she'd given him directly tonight, and walked onto the porch, letting the door shut behind her.

"I hope so," she said. "Although I'm pretty sure she would be appalled at the mismatched napkins."

Jack laughed. He'd liked Angela Carson, who'd possessed something better than wealth and elegance. She'd had grit. He'd always thought that maybe, beneath the required "official" position that Jack Killian wasn't good enough for her daughter, Angela might have liked him, too.

At least up until the day they'd found Tom Dickson on that island, with Jack's fist marks all over his body.

Nora's dad, on the other hand—well, if Boss Carson hadn't lived in the civilized, modern world, he probably would have taken Jack out beyond the city walls and shot him, just for looking at his baby girl.

"I was sorry to hear you'd lost your dad," he said. "He had a heart attack, I heard. That must have been difficult."

"It was." She stood against the railing and plucked a withered leaf from one of the hanging poinsettias. "But I guess you know all about that. At least I had him until I was grown up and ready to be on my own. And my mother is still only a phone call away. You lost both parents—and you were only nineteen. I don't know how you managed."

"Very badly."

He'd been in the Army, still, when his father had wrapped his car around a tree. He'd been given a fur-lough, later that same year, to come home when his mother's cancer had finally claimed her. He'd stayed in the next town over, so that he wouldn't have to see Nora.

It wasn't until much later that he'd learned she hadn't been in town, either. She'd been in England, or Ireland, or wherever she'd met the man who'd fathered Colin.

"It's hard, whenever it happens," he said.

She nodded. She seemed softer tonight, and he wondered why. Was she just too tired to keep her antagonism fully stoked? Or was she ready to—maybe not to forgive him, but maybe to hate him a little bit less?

He wanted to say something about how gracious her little house looked tonight, and how her mother must be proud of that, too. She didn't need a mansion like Heron Hill to create grace and warmth. He wanted to tell her how lucky Colin was, to have a mother who knew how to make a home like that.

"You look beautiful tonight," he said.

Where the hell had that come from?

But it was true. Seen through the window, the multi-colored lights of her Christmas tree sparkled all around her head, like a halo of rainbows. She wasn't dressed up, but her jeans and green sweater fit her so well it made his mouth water. Her shining curls were springing loose from their red ribbon, into which someone had stuck a small sprig of holly. She wore no makeup, but her cheeks and lips glowed a light, natural pink.

"Thanks," she said awkwardly. She reached up and touched her hair, as if she knew it must be messy, as if she thought he must be joking.

He wanted to touch that hair. It would curl around his fingers like soft satin.

He knew he'd told her it would be a mistake, but damn it…he still wanted to kiss her. He knew he could make those lips burn as red as the poinsettias that bloomed at her feet.

But how could he? The house was built in a U design, with the two wings thrusting forward on either side of the small front porch. It was cozy, protected from the December wind, but it had zero privacy. Behind Jack, the kitchen window overlooked them, and behind Nora, the living room window did the same.

"Nora," he began.

"I want to ask you something," she interrupted.

He paused. "What?"

She took a deep breath. "I don't have any right to ask, I know that, but I'm going to anyway. I want to know why you hurt Tom. Why you left him on that island." She watched him carefully. "Will you tell me?"

A gust of wind came around the corner suddenly. He tightened his shoulders against it.

"No."

She flinched at the curt, unequivocal sound of the syllable. She raised her chin. "Is it because I waited too long to ask? If I had agreed to come to you that night, would you have told me then?"

He put his hands in his pockets. "No."

She stared at him a minute. Then she turned and moved toward the door.

"I see," she said.

"No, damn it, you *don't* see."

He caught her just as she reached for the knob. Grabbing her hand, he pulled her into the only square foot of darkness on the porch, in the corner formed where the front wall met the kitchen.

She gasped softly, but the sound didn't get far. He closed his lips around it, swallowing the sweet, warm cloud of her breath. She resisted for an instant, and then, as he pressed her against the wall, she yielded.

She was soft, and molded easily to him. Their bodies met at all points, from lips to feet, and created just one urgently shifting shadow.

In their private darkness, he deepened the kiss, using his tongue to coax her lips open. She moaned, and moved her hips, as if they, too, wanted to part and let him in.

It was almost more than he could bear. Every part of him throbbed, and reached mindlessly for her.

He slid his hand between her legs. Even through the denim, he could feel the heat of her response. He rubbed the thick seam of her jeans, frustrated, wanting to tear it away, wanting to reach the hot silk of the skin below.

But they could make only small, intense movements,

as if the porch light were poison, as if they'd die if any part of their body left the cocoon of darkness.

She shifted again, tossing her head silently against the wall. He felt the ribbon come free and spill to the ground. She arched, straining, and he wondered if she might come for him, might surrender here, against his hand.

He wanted that more than he'd ever wanted anything, more than he wanted his own release.

But he should have known it wouldn't be that easy. It had never been easy, not with her. Without warning, her movements changed, and her hands, which had briefly wrapped around his neck, now pushed at his chest.

"No," she said. "Stop."

Her breath was ragged. Even in the darkness, he could see her eyes shining, glazed with the desire she tried to repress.

He stepped back. Oh, this was viciously familiar.

But, in spite of how Neanderthal he'd just been, he was a thoroughly civilized man. He understood every part of the word *no*.

"I'm sorry," she said, her voice almost a whisper. "I should have stopped you sooner."

He smiled. "Not at all," he said, arching one brow. "If I recall correctly, you stopped me right on schedule."

THE NEXT MORNING was clear, but so cold the sky seemed to be made of blue ice. Nora got out her woolen coat and made her way to the Hawthorn Executive Air Field.

She'd heard Tom say he was going flying today, but if she got there before ten, she'd probably still find him on the ground.

At first, as she parked her car in the front lot, she

wondered if she could ever find anyone in this big, grassy field dotted with small planes that looked like an unruly flock of white birds.

But a young man at the front desk pointed her in the right direction, and she started walking. She was glad she'd worn sensible shoes because Tom's plane was all the way at the back.

The man must have called ahead, or else Tom recognized her as she hiked toward him, because, when she finally reached him, he didn't look at all surprised.

"I'm heading up in about ten minutes," he said, bustling around his airplane officiously, checking this and that. The plane didn't seem much larger up close, and she hoped it was safer than it looked. "Is this urgent, or can we do it when I come down?"

"It won't take long," she said.

Tom frowned. He had an annoying way of implying that his schedules were twice as important as anyone else's. Perhaps it was true—as a property developer, city councilman and amateur pilot, he stayed pretty busy. His trophy wife Jill frequently lamented that she never saw her husband. But the rumor was that Jill consoled herself with extra tennis lessons from her sexy pro, so maybe the arrangement worked.

"So?" Tom brushed his silky blond hair out of his eyes and looked down at his watch. "What can I do for you, Nora? If it's about the eminent domain—"

"It isn't." She was wearing gloves, but out here on the open field the wind cut right through the leather, so she stuffed her hands in her coat pockets. "It's about the day you said Jack Killian tried to kill you."

Tom's brows dug together like silver knives. "For

God's sake, Nora. You came all the way out here to ask me about that old—"

"Yes, I did. I want to know the truth, Tom. I want to know what really happened that day. And I want to know why."

"You know what happened. Your thug of a boyfriend decided to beat the crap out of me. He said he didn't intend to kill me, but if Buster hadn't come along and found me, that's exactly what would have happened."

"Yeah, that's the story I've always heard," she said. "But now I want the real story. Start with the *why*. Why would Jack go to all that trouble? What had you done to make him angry enough to beat you up?"

Tom shrugged. "Who knows? Maybe I'd just pissed him off by being richer, smarter, better looking. Better *period*. Whatever."

"That's a load of bull, and you know it. No one in Hawthorn Bay is better looking than the Killians, not even you, Tom. And why would he beat you up for being rich? Killians don't care about things like that."

He laughed. "Oh, yeah? What do Killians care about? I hope you aren't going to say *love,* honey, because I think that ship has sailed. I didn't notice *love* bringing that boy back to Hawthorn Bay much over the past twelve years."

She stared at her cousin, wondering exactly when their childhood friendship had withered away, leaving only the official blood tie behind. Perhaps it had been the day she'd begun to see through his surface beauty, down to the base metal beneath. After that, perhaps it had seemed a waste of time to try to charm her.

Or maybe, if she were to be even more cynical, maybe it had been when she'd sold Heron Hill. Tom respected money, and little else. A rich cousin was one thing. A poor relation quite another.

"Damn it, Tom. You're not going to bully me into backing off. I want you to be honest with me."

"You want honesty?" He came closer, and his eyes bored into hers. "Okay, sweetheart, here comes a big, sour dose of honesty. The Killians are bad people. They're coarse, and they're violent, and they don't give a damn about anybody but themselves. And if you're out here asking me questions because you've fallen for that scum again, I feel mighty sorry for you."

She looked into his eyes a long time. He didn't back down. He meant the nose-to-nose defiance to be intimidating, but suddenly she remembered how, as a child, he'd always been the most belligerent when he had something to hide.

"You're lying," she said slowly. "You did something, something so bad Jack couldn't let it go. And I'm going to find out what."

Tom shook his head. "Listen to yourself, Nora. He's getting to you all over again. Did he plant that ridiculous idea in your pretty little head? Even if that were true, would that make it right? If I did something bad, it's okay for him to break my arm and leave me for dead?"

"No, but it makes it—"

She stopped. She wasn't sure what it would change.

"It makes it less—" She tucked her coat around her chin. "Why should he take all the blame? Why should you get off scot-free?"

"The truth? Because I am a respectable member of this community. And he's a dirty son of a drunk."

She stepped back, finally. "God, Tom. When did you get to be such a snob?"

Tom pulled on his gloves, as if to say that her ten minutes were up.

"Listen, Nora. I'd leave it alone, if I were you. I don't go digging around into your past, do I? I don't go snooping around trying to find out who knocked my pretty cousin up and left her with a black-haired, blue-eyed, bad-tempered brat. And do you know why?"

She wanted to hit him. If she'd been a man, she might have. "Because it's none of your goddamn business?"

"That's right," he said. He motioned to an attendant standing a few yards away. The man came running. "And now that we're clear on that, sweetheart, I have a plane to catch."

CHAPTER ELEVEN

1936

THEY HAD NAMED the baby Lily Rose, and so naturally the funeral had been awash in lilies and roses. Even people who hated Patrick, who hated all Killians because they'd been raised to it, sent flowers. The first Killian daughter in a hundred and fifty years, born dead.

The sickeningly sweet scent had filled Patrick's nose, clogged his lungs, while the minister had droned on and on. For the rest of Patrick's life, if he smelled one of these flowers, he knew he'd have to fight back a surge of vomit and tears.

He and Virginia had been married only a year, but he had already sent her roses three times—for her birthday, for their anniversary and for Easter.

Never again. He would send daisies, or chocolate, or simply cover her in kisses.

If only God would give him the chance…

If only He would let Ginny live to see another birthday.

Please God, Patrick prayed, for once not caring whether he sounded like his father. *Please. I can't bury them both in the same week.*

"I want to die," Ginny had said as they'd walked together, stiff-backed, heavy-limbed, from the cemetery.

He had nodded, assuming that she was searching for words to express the enormity of the pain.

He hadn't imagined that she was being quite literal. When they'd returned to Sweet Tides, he'd let her go into the bathroom alone. He'd even been glad of the freedom to cry privately for a while himself.

It hadn't been until the thin line of liquid had begun to snake its way under the door that he'd grown anxious. For a confused moment, he'd tried to identify it. It was very dark, but in the light it had shone a dull red, like a rose petal long past its prime.

Now he walked back and forth outside Ginny's door, waiting for the doctor to come out. Waiting for him to tell Patrick whether enough of the rose-petal blood had remained in her body to keep her heart beating.

Her broken heart.

It didn't seem fair to pray that she should have to live, when she clearly had wanted to be released. But Ginny was only nineteen. Patrick himself was only twenty-one. There would be another baby, another little girl whose blue eyes would open, and laugh, and make her parents whole again.

Even if there were no more babies, Patrick needed Ginny. He *needed* her.

The doctor opened the door quietly. His face was somber, but he met Patrick's eyes, which gave Patrick hope.

"She'll live," he said. "But she's weak. And her mind is not well. She will need a lot of help."

"Anything," Patrick said. "Tell me what to do. The stitches—"

"The nurse will see to her stitches." The doctor looked uncomfortable. "That's not what worries me. It's her mind. She is depressed, to the point of unbalance. I can't be sure she won't try something like this again."

"I won't let her," Patrick said. "I will never leave her alone. Not for a minute."

But the doctor made him see that such a thing was not possible. Ginny didn't need a keeper to prevent her from harming herself. She needed a psychiatrist, to stop her from wanting to.

She needed professional help. It would take a long time. It would cost a lot of money.

The doctor said the last with a heavy sigh. Everyone knew that, though the Killians were not paupers, they had very little money to spare.

What there was, Patrick had inherited, as his older brothers had lived wild and died young. James had fallen from a bad-tempered horse who hadn't liked the drunken, heavy-spurred rider. Matt had tumbled out of the sky, in an airplane he couldn't afford and had barely known how to fly.

Patrick had been much younger than his reckless brothers, and in some ways had hardly known them. But the deaths had seemed to break Patrick's father, Angus. The old tyrant had died last year, leaving the house, a little money in bonds, but no real fortune.

So Patrick had the inheritance, and the little he earned from his new career as a junior accountant. That was all. Not nearly enough to pay for round-the-clock care of an invalid wife.

When the doctor left, Patrick looked in at Ginny, who was sleeping, her soft hair spread out on the pillowcase. The gauzy cuffs around her wrists looked innocent, like a child's lacy nightgown.

Patrick shut the door quietly. He went into the library

and took down the box of his father's music from the upper shelf where he'd stashed it after Angus's death.

After his first heart attack, Angus had told Patrick about the gold, about how he had dug it up and hidden it here, in the house. The key, Angus had said, was in the music. If God decided that Patrick should have the gold, he should have it. But he would have to come to it the dutiful and virtuous way—by honoring his father's creations.

How angry Patrick had been that day. Another of his father's mad lectures about the Almighty. Another of his father's egotistical power ploys, designed to bring Patrick to heel.

He didn't want the goddamn gold, he'd said. He didn't need it. He'd make his own fortune, and if he didn't, Ginny wouldn't care. She loved him, something Angus could never understand.

Angus had slapped him, for arrogance, for dishonoring his father, for taking the Lord's name in vain. For refusing to come to heel.

"I'm here now, Father," Patrick told the empty room. His voice broke, and the cracked sound echoed off the high, molded ceilings. "I'll do whatever you want. I'll sing your songs from every rooftop in Hawthorn Bay. Just give me the goddamn gold."

HAWTHORN BAY DIDN'T HAVE its own shopping mall, but it shared one with the next town over. The developers had split the distance, hoping that two small towns could combine to create one viable market, and the strategy had paid off.

Today, just five days from Christmas, it seemed to Jack that all shoppers from both towns were here, trying to find the perfect gift they should have bought a month ago.

He was as guilty of procrastination as any of them. He spent an hour at a jewelry store picking out trinkets for the three or four women he dated most frequently, and another hour at the perfume counter, choosing pretty bottles for the paralegals, secretaries and file clerks. The other partners would get wine. His postman, housekeeper, paper deliveryman and condo doorman would have to make do with cash.

"Man, you need to work at a smaller law firm," Sean said as they finally gave up and grabbed chairs at the food court. It was time for a sandwich break. "You must have bought a hundred presents this morning."

Jack refrained from pointing out that if Sean hadn't insisted that he stay in Hawthorn Bay, all this would have been accomplished with much less fuss back in Kansas City two weeks ago. And it would have saved him a small fortune in overnight shipping.

Besides, Sean had put a pretty serious dent in the mall's inventory today, himself. Jack was surprised to discover how many friends his brother had. At least twenty pals had made Santa Sean's list, in addition to the obligatory business-related gifts.

Twenty friends. That must be a world record for any Killian living in Hawthorn Bay.

"If I worked at a smaller firm, I wouldn't have the luxury to just skip out for a month," Jack observed mildly as he checked out the food court's offerings. Luckily, he wasn't a prissy eater. Hamburgers, tacos, sub sandwiches, they all sounded fine to him. He'd eaten a lot worse in the Army, and even during that last year at home, when his mother had been too sick to cook, and his father had been too drunk.

At the Desserts Galore marquee, he paused. He cocked his head. "What's the hell is a boggy bottom pie?"

"It's like a big brownie pancake, with ice cream and berries on top." Sean laughed. "It tastes a lot better than it sounds."

"It would almost have to." As Jack scanned the booths, he noticed a thin redhead standing in the pickup line at the Italian Eaterie, holding half a dozen shopping bags.

"Hey, isn't that Amy Grantham over there at the pizza place?"

Sean was studying the Burger Box menu. "You think you see Amy Grantham buying food? You gotta be hallucinating." He looked up. "Well, I'll be damned. It is Amy Grantham."

"Order me something big and greasy, okay? Extra onions." Jack patted Sean's shoulder. "I'm going to see if she wants to join us."

Sean chuckled. "Not once she hears about the onions, she won't."

But Jack was already halfway across the food court. When he reached Amy, she had just picked up her tray.

Two pieces of cheese pizza. Good for her.

"Jack!" She smiled at him. "Wow. You must have heard me thinking about you. I was just reminding myself to call you when I got home."

"Well, now you won't have to. Sean and I are getting burgers. Come sit with us."

Sean and Jack had snagged the only empty table in the whole place, so she couldn't have said no even if she wanted to. Jack watched as Amy arranged her bags. She looked good. Still too thin, still too tired, but...

He couldn't put his finger on it. She just looked more normal. More relaxed.

"Sorry about all the bags," she said, tucking one under her chair so that Jack would have enough leg room. "I've been on a real spree. That's one of the things I wanted to tell you."

"Actually, I think it's Eddie you'd better tell. It's a joint credit card, right?"

"He won't care this time," she said. She blushed a little, then ducked down and dug through one of the bags. "See?"

At first, Jack had no idea what he was looking at. Then he realized she held one of the smallest white cotton undershirts he'd ever seen in his life.

"You're—"

"Yeah." Her thin, freckled face lit up like a flashlight. "I'm going to have a baby."

He hugged her hard. "Fantastic," he said, and meant it.

"I've wanted this for so long. You remember?"

He remembered. Motherhood had been her dream for years, since way back in the Al-Anon days. But then Tom Dickson had come along and derailed all dreams.

And then the anorexia. He wondered whether that had made it difficult to conceive.

She might have been thinking the same thing. She picked up a slice of pizza and, with an air of determination, took a large bite.

"Is this why you were going to call me? To tell me about the baby?"

She nodded, chewing deliberately. "Partly." She

swallowed, and then smiled at him as if she'd done something miraculous. Which, he supposed, she had.

"But that's not all I wanted to tell you." She glanced over toward the Burger Box, where Sean was still waiting in a ridiculously long line. "I wanted to tell you that Tom Dickson came to see me yesterday."

Jack felt his shoulders tighten. "Why the hell would he do that?"

"I'm not sure. He seemed upset. Someone had clearly stirred his juices. Got him pretty riled. I thought maybe it had been you."

Jack smiled grimly. "Oh, I do hope so."

"Anyhow, I told him to get the hell out of my house before Eddie got home. But he said that he was only there to give me a warning. He said that if he ever heard that I'd been spreading lies about him, if I started saying he'd done anything nasty back in high school, he'd sue me for slander."

"What a bastard. He wouldn't dream of making it all public like that, and you know it."

"Yeah, well, he also said that if he heard I'd been talking, he'd give Eddie such an earful that he would never touch me again unless he was wearing rubber gloves."

A spurt of adrenaline shot through Jack so hard and fast he almost had to push his chair back and sprint out of the mall. Somehow, he managed not to be such an idiot. But his heart pounded in a caveman fury.

Fight or flight, my ass.

Just fight.

"Don't look like that," she said, putting her hand over his arm. "I'm not asking you to go smash him up for me."

He tried to smile. "It wouldn't be for you, Amy. It would be for the good of the planet."

"Men," she said. She took another bite of pizza. "You are so loaded up with testosterone that you can't even hear what I'm trying to tell you. I don't care about Tom Dickson anymore. When he left, I did some hard thinking. I decided that, if I'm going to be a mother, I've got to start being brave. So I sat Eddie down, and I told him everything."

Jack stared at her. "You did?"

"Yep. And you know what? He doesn't care. He said nothing that happened before he met me matters."

"He did?"

She laughed, and Jack realized that Amy's laugh was something he had heard only a very few times in his life.

"Yes, he did. So that's why I was going to call you, Jack. Because I wanted you to know how happy I am."

She folded the little white shirt carefully and returned it to the shopping bag. She didn't seem to be able to stop smiling. It made her look ten years younger.

"And here's the most important thing. In the past twenty-four hours, I've become quite a fan of honesty. So I hereby release you from your vow of silence, Jack. If you want to tell anyone what really happened that day, it's perfectly fine with me."

She squeezed his arm. "I suggest you start with Nora."

THIS WOULD BE THE last city council meeting before Christmas, and Nora expected it to be a circus. Hostility seemed inevitable. She only hoped it wouldn't come to name-calling and flying fists.

The final item on the agenda was Tom's request to raise the offer for Sweet Tides, as a last resort before filing an eminent domain claim.

The audience was crowded, unusual for any meeting, much less one held just four days before Christmas. Jack and Sean Killian were there, as was Jim Samoyan from the Langley Group. Several reporters had shown up—from the local paper, of course, but others, too, from as far away as Columbia.

The mood was restless. It was strange, Nora thought, scanning the edgy, unfriendly faces. On this issue, for once, the locals seemed to be rooting for the Killians.

Perhaps the old "traitor's gold" legend was finally losing its potency. It was about time, she thought wryly. Most of the people around here today couldn't tell you six accurate facts about the Civil War if their lives depended on it.

Or perhaps the little people of Hawthorn Bay just didn't like the idea that the city council could decide to confiscate a person's property at will.

Today the Killians…but tomorrow perhaps any one of them?

She braced herself. If the vote went for Tom, the Killian camp looked prepared to wage war. And, of course, if the vote went against Tom, he certainly knew how to make a scene.

They moved through the short agenda quickly, and finally the moment arrived.

In a bold voice, Tom moved that the council allocate the funds necessary to double the offer for the Sweet Tides property, and to set up a committee to investigate eminent domain proceedings, should the bid be rejected.

It seemed as if the entire room held its breath.

But, to Nora's amazement, the anticipated chaos never came.

The motion simply lay there.

Nora waited, then officially called for a second.

Nothing. She glanced quickly at Tom. He leaned forward, looking at his fellow councilmen one by one.

His face was ruddy with anger, his glare intimidating.

But still no one seconded the motion.

Finally Nora cleared her throat and spoke the formal words that declared the issue dead. "Since there is no second, the motion is not before this meeting."

The room broke into loud, spontaneous applause.

Obviously Nora wasn't the only person who was sick of Tom Dickson's bullying. That pleased her. It made the world feel a little less lopsided.

Tom sat back in his seat, clearly stunned.

Nora glanced at Jack. He was probably getting a special kick out of seeing Tom ambushed so thoroughly—and so publicly.

But she got another surprise. Jack hardly seemed aware of his victory. He was deep in conversation with a woman Nora didn't know, a super-thin redhead who looked sweet, but just slightly downtrodden.

Oh, well, it was none of her business, obviously. And after what had happened the other night, when he'd kissed her on the porch, she'd be smarter to avoid him, anyhow. Clearly she still had very little willpower where Jack Killian was concerned.

When the meeting adjourned, she gave a couple of quick comments to the reporters, then headed to her car. She had to pick Colin up from Stacy's house. She'd promised they'd go out for fried chicken before he went to the nursing home at three.

She'd parked out back, by the river, as usual. It made for an easier exit. But today that choice had been a mistake. In the slot right next to her sensible sedan was Jack Killian's Jaguar.

And leaning against the car's sleek, feline nose was Jack himself.

She refused to skip a beat. She moved down the sidewalk at her natural brisk pace, fishing her keys out of her purse as she walked. When she reached the cars, she smiled politely.

"I thought you'd be inside, giving interviews," she said.

"Nope. Sean's on interview duty. He's the homeboy, so it makes sense. The visiting brother doesn't really have any human-interest value."

"You don't? I would have thought the old attempted-murder story would provide extra helpings of human interest. *Bad blood, payback is hell,* don't reporters love stuff like that?"

He raised one shoulder. "They might, if they knew about it. The little girl from the local paper was probably just learning to ride a bike when all that happened. The gal from the Columbia paper isn't much older, and she's not local, so she doesn't have a clue. It's ancient history, Nora. Nobody cares anymore."

Ancient history…

Was it? Sometimes it seemed as if it had all happened yesterday. Sometimes, she felt as if she could reach back into the past and fiddle with the words. Rewrite the story.

In the new, improved version of her life, she would

throw on some clothes and run down to the park, where Jack would be waiting. She would let him make love to her, and the baby born nine months later would be her own.

Really, truly, biologically. Morally and legally her own.

But Jack was right. Twelve years was a long time. And the past was written in indelible ink. She couldn't even go back twelve minutes and change that chilly tone she'd used to greet him just now.

Oh, what was wrong with her? Surely they could be civil, couldn't they? After all these years? If she kept being so illogically hostile, he'd suspect that she had something to hide.

"Jack, about the other night—"

"Forget it. It was a mistake. My mistake. I'm sorry."

"I'm the one who's sorry," she said. "I know better than to get into a—compromising position like that. Colin was right upstairs, for heaven's sake. He could have looked out the window at any minute."

Jack smiled. "Well, I don't have children, so maybe I don't understand the rules. Does a kid turn to stone if he sees his mother kissing somebody?"

She felt herself flushing. "No, but—" She shifted her purse under her arm. "That was more than a kiss, Jack."

"Was it? Okay, then what would you call it? What exactly was happening between us?"

"Nothing." When he raised his eyebrow, she bit her lip and tried again. "Nothing significant, I mean. We've always had a lot of problems, but a lack of chemistry was never one of them. I guess the chemistry still works, but that doesn't mean anything. It's like a light burning in an empty house."

She'd pulled the image out of the air, but the minute she spoke the words she knew how true they were. Ever since Jack had left, one part of her heart had been like an empty room, hollow, and helplessly waiting.

But not for him.

Someday, she hoped, someone would fill that emptiness, but it could never be Jack. Their sins against one another were too profound.

His jaw seemed to grow subtly more square, which she recognized as a sign that he was very angry.

"Clever simile," he said. "In other words, I can come knocking, but there won't be anyone at home?"

She didn't answer. His blue eyes were glassy in the winter sunshine, and looked like ice.

"Don't worry, Nora. I don't intend to stand out there all night, banging at the door. I did that once before, remember? I learned about that cold, empty place where your heart should be, and I learned the hard way. Believe me, I've long since given up any idea of fighting my way in."

"Okay," she said numbly. She fumbled for the button to open her door. She suddenly wanted to get away. "Okay, that's fine. We understand each other, then."

"Perfectly," he said.

She struggled to get the door open. Her fingers were nearly frozen.

Then she felt him take hold of her arm. For a minute she wondered if he planned to yank her up against him again in another unstoppable kiss. Her heart skittered, frightened—and perversely excited, too.

But he didn't pull her in. He didn't want a kiss. He just held on, while his eyes bored into hers.

"There's one more thing I want to say," he said. "It's about Colin."

She couldn't breathe. She looked at him, wondering how his hand could be so hot when his eyes were so cold.

"You have to tell him the truth," he said. "About his father. The kid is going crazy, trying to figure it out."

"That's ridiculous—"

"No, it isn't. I see him almost every day. I hear things. He keeps a list, did you know that?"

She shook her head.

"I saw him scribbling in it, at the nursing home. I'm on that list, Nora. Sean is on it, too. So are Ethan, and his friend Brad's dad, and probably every man he's ever heard you mention."

"Oh, my God."

"Yeah." Jack's jaw tightened. "So tell him, damn it. I don't care how embarrassing the truth is. I don't care if his father lives in San Quentin or an insane asylum, or an igloo on the moon. I don't even care if his father could be any one of a dozen nameless black-haired boys in a Dublin pub."

He let go of her arm. She fell against the car, looking for support.

"Just tell him. He deserves to know."

CHAPTER TWELVE

EVERY CHRISTMAS, NORA DELIVERED baskets of jam, preserves, cookies and tea to their friends and neighbors. She tried to get it done at least a week before Christmas, but this year it seemed as if everything, from Colin's behavior to the eminent domain fiasco, had conspired against her.

So here she was, in her kitchen, just three days from the big event, scrambling to put the baskets together. Colin was supposed to be helping, but he couldn't tear himself away from the guitar Ethan had given him for Christmas.

Luckily, both Ethan and Stacy were pitching in, so she might make it in time. Ethan had a doctor's gift for organization and detail. Stacy had a flair for arranging the items and tying dazzling bows.

"I've got to leave early tonight," Stacy said. "Sean's entering a boat in the Christmas parade. He's asked me to help him decorate it."

Ethan and Colin both made immature *woo-hoo* noises. Even Nora grinned at Stacy, who frowned.

"Hey, I'm good at decorating." She held up a bow. "I'm helping you, too. It doesn't *mean* anything."

The males both laughed, but Nora put out her hand, calling for quiet. "You're right," she said. "All it means is that Sean's boat will be the best-looking boat in the parade."

Stacy wrinkled her nose. "I'm not sure about that. It's an ancient junker he bought in some estate sale. He's just in it for the fun. He doesn't expect to win."

He was probably right. The annual Christmas Boat Parade, which would take place tomorrow night, was an elaborate affair. Local businesses and organizations all entered fancy boats, and so did the local bigwigs.

Nora used to joke that the prizes were always awarded based on sheer wattage. They certainly didn't judge on good taste or beauty.

Nora would have to ride on the City of Hawthorn Bay boat, which meant three stultifying hours with her cousin Tom, and the other councilmen. She wasn't looking forward to it.

Ethan held up a jar of blackberry jam. "This is the one for Bill Freeman, right?" He twisted it, checking for the small tick mark Nora had added to it earlier. "He's the one who gets the sugar-free version without the sugar-free label?"

"Right." Nora reached over and pulled a box of cookies out of one of the baskets. "No, no, no! Farley Hastert never, ever gets the rum cookies."

"Oh, sorry. He's the lush?"

Colin looked up from the guitar. "Who's a lush?"

"Get back to practicing," Ethan said. "You still sound terrible."

For answer, Colin strummed the strings roughly. "Give me a break," he said. "I just got it an hour ago."

Nora smiled to herself. Colin had badgered her until she'd finally given in and allowed him to open the present early. Ethan had joined in the petition because he would be flying out again first thing in the morning, and he was eager to see whether the present had scored a hit or not.

It had.

For a whole minute, Colin had been speechless. He had picked the guitar up as gingerly as if it had been made of sugar. Then he'd simply held it, following the lovely wood grain with his fingertip, not making a sound.

That hadn't lasted long, unfortunately. The minute he touched the strings, he'd been hooked.

For the past hour, Colin had either been practicing his scales or informing them that this was how Jack had told him you should make an open G. It wasn't enough to simply murmur "um-hmm." He insisted that you look, to see how hard the finger placement was.

He seemed to be working on that Killian Christmas song, the one he and Jack had practiced the other night. But Nora couldn't be sure. For every chord he formed correctly, there were at least three dreadful ear-busters.

"Okay, out!" Nora pointed toward the living room. "We need to work in peace. Come back when you don't sound like someone strangling a cat."

Colin trotted out, clearly just as happy to be released. "Come on, Uncle Ethan," he said. "Let's go."

With a shrug to apologize for abandoning ship, Ethan tagged along. He was clearly bored with the bows and baskets, and besides, this visit had been too short, and Nora knew he wanted to spend more time with Colin.

"Do you think Colin looks tired?" She turned to Stacy when they were alone. "I wonder if he's putting in too many hours at the nursing home."

Stacy bent over a sparkling gold bow, fluffing out its many loops.

"Yeah, he looks a little tired," she said. "But if you think you can pry him away from the nursing home, think again. I hear it's become quite the *in* place this Christmas. With the Killians, anyhow."

Nora waited. An odd tone in Stacy's voice told her this was leading somewhere.

As if stalling, Stacy stepped back to judge her bow. It looked perfect, of course, and even she seemed satisfied. She placed the basket on the "finished" counter and finally gave Nora her full attention.

"Nora, look…you know I don't like to give other people advice. Heck, I've messed up my own life so bad no one would listen to me anyhow. But I'm just wondering…do you really think it's such a good idea for him to be spending so much time there?"

Naturally, Nora had already thought of that. She'd even told Colin that his punishment was over, that he was free to spend the rest of his Christmas vacation having fun. But he'd said he liked reading to the old people and they'd be disappointed if he stopped coming.

Short of forbidding him to go, which would have looked very suspicious, there wasn't much she could do.

Except…hope that Jack had believed her when she'd told him that his "lost" night had not been spent with her—and thus, couldn't have resulted in Colin.

But these were private fears, fears no one guessed at but Ethan. At least she'd thought they were.

She'd never talked about any of it with Stacy. The only person, other than Ethan, who knew the truth about Colin was Nora's mother, Angela. Nora just hadn't been able to lie to her. With her customary serenity and courage, Angela Carson had supported her daughter completely, and made sure that the entire town did the same.

Nora looked at Stacy and tried not to let her anxiety show. "Why do you say that? Why would it be a bad idea?"

Stacy was a fiddler at the best of times, and when she was nervous it was compulsive. She didn't have her glasses with her, so she toyed with a length of red ribbon flecked with metallic gold threads, wrapping it around and around her index finger.

"This is so awkward," she said. "It's just that—"

She glanced toward the living room and lowered her voice. "I've been going through old papers and things at Sweet Tides. I'm almost finished—I'll probably start writing my thesis after the new year. Anyhow, I've run across a lot of pictures."

"Pictures of what?"

"Of Killians. Killian children. Killian sons, to be precise, considering that's all they seem to have."

"Oh."

"Yeah. Anyhow, these boys. Jack, Sean. Their dad. Their granddad, and both of his brothers, too. They have a certain look, all of them." She took a deep breath. "Colin has that look."

Nora's heart was beating too fast. Obviously, this wasn't the first time she'd heard someone speculate about Colin's coloring. But usually it was some rude busybody, and she didn't mind being a little rude in response. This was her best friend. Tact was required.

Still, from the beginning, Nora had set boundaries. Some subjects were off limits.

"Yeah, well," she said. She tried a wry smile and a shrug, shooting for amused indifference. "I guess I've always had a weakness for boys with dark hair and blue eyes."

Stacy hesitated a second.

Then she nodded. "Yeah. Yeah, I know. Me, too. Zach, and now—"

She cut herself off, but Nora knew what she'd been going to say. *Zach, and now Sean Killian.*

Stacy picked up another spool of ribbon, a lovely green velvet, and rolled off a couple of yards.

Had Nora dodged the bullet? She hoped so. This conversation was a no-win situation. She couldn't be honest with Stacy, and she didn't want to hurt her friend's feelings.

Stacy started looping the bow, her head bent over her work. She looked stiff.

Darn. Were her feelings hurt?

Nora picked up a tray of freshly baked Toll House cookies and busied herself sliding them off onto a plate.

"I guess it's just a preference, like anything else," she said lightly, trying to smooth things over. "Like plain M&Ms or peanut."

"Guess so. Except more dangerous. M&M's can't break your heart." Stacy paused. "Or leave you pregnant."

Nora glanced up. "Stacy," she began, with a warning in her voice.

"I'm sorry. I know I'm over the line. You don't have to tell me anything."

"Look, I don't want you to think that—"

"It doesn't matter what I think." Stacy lowered her voice. "But you can't just ignore it forever, Nora. You've got to ask yourself the important question."

"Which is?"

"What does *Colin* think?"

JACK HAD ALWAYS LOVED to sit on the front porch on a cold December night. The grounds spreading out before him weren't as well-tended as they used to be, but Sweet Tides in winter was still one of the most peaceful places on earth.

The sky was black and starry, the air clean and still. The river slid like liquid glass over its muddy bed. Now and then an owl would hoot-hoot from its branch high in the black cypress, but mostly everything was as silent as an oil painting.

He was tired, but still he lingered, moving the porch swing with one foot and listening to the rusty hinges creak and echo down the hollow night.

Truth was, with Sean still out at the marina with Stacy, Jack had no enthusiasm for going inside.

The rooms were too crowded with memories. His bedroom was the worst. He had lain in that same bedroom a thousand nights as a boy, listening for the sound of his mother's weeping.

Once, when he'd been about six, the crying had sounded so heartbroken that he'd crawled out of bed and headed to her room, to see what was wrong.

But she hadn't been there. He could still remember the cold terror that had washed through him as he'd stood there, staring at the empty bed.

When she'd come home, an hour later, she'd found him standing, half-frozen, in the hall. She'd assumed he must have been sleepwalking, and had forced Kelly to put a motion-sensor alarm at his bedroom door. Jack had welcomed it. If he couldn't get out, he reasoned, then no one could get in.

By the time he'd turned seven, he'd toughened up. He'd told himself he'd just been dreaming that night.

There was no such thing as ghosts. The lights that played tricks in the room were merely slivers of moonlight glinting off mirrors and silver candlesticks. The restless, cracking sounds weren't bones walking toward him down the hall—they were the weary settling of a very old house. The moans and whispers were just the wind.

All that was still true.

Besides, it was getting cold out here, and he was too old to fall prey to his own imagination. He stood, stretched, yawned and headed inside. He was exhausted. The spectral weepers and moaners would have to get a megaphone if they wanted to wake him up tonight.

He thought about leaving the front door unlocked, but surely Sean had brought along his key, in case his charisma failed him at the eleventh hour.

But thirty seconds after Jack had checked every room on the first floor and started climbing the dark, twisted stairs, he heard a knock at the front door.

Great. Perfect timing.

He about-faced and headed back down. "I ought to leave you out in the cold, you lame-brain," he called out.

He threw the dead bolt and hauled the big door open. "So, Romeo strikes out, huh?"

But it wasn't Sean. Jack had to drop his gaze about a foot and a half to see the boy standing there.

It was Colin. His face was smudged with dirt, and his curly hair popped out in all directions, like crazy springs. His expression was one of barely contained panic.

"Jack?" They'd moved past the "Mr. Killian" stage days ago. "Jack, can you help me? It's an emergency."

"Of course."

It didn't occur to Jack to hedge, or to ask first what the hell the boy was doing here in the middle of the night. The mud on Colin's cheeks looked tear-streaked, and Jack knew this wasn't a wimpy kid. "What can I do?"

"I need a flashlight," Colin said. "The biggest one you have."

He held up his hands to show the size, and in the hall light Jack thought he saw blood. He took Colin's fingers. "Hey, you've cut yourself."

Colin looked at it, too. "Yeah. It's no big deal. There was a broken bottle, and I didn't see it. My flashlight sucks."

"We need to clean that hand up."

"Later," Colin said, his voice tense. "I've got to get back out there. I lost something really important, and I have to find it."

But the more Jack looked at the cut, the less he liked it. The pad of Colin's palm, just under his thumb, had been ripped open. The edges of the skin were jagged and pulled loose. The open wound was caked with dirt.

"No," Jack said. "Now. We've got to wash this and put something over it."

Colin's brows drew together, and for a minute Jack was afraid that he'd just turn and bolt back into the night.

"It won't take long," he assured the boy. "And as soon as it's clean, I promise I'll help you find your stuff. I've got a couple of lanterns so bright they look like the headlights of the mother ship. We could find a termite hiding in a tree trunk in Tennessee."

Colin smiled, finally.

"Thanks," he said. "That would be great."

As Jack walked Colin back to the kitchen, where the first-aid supplies had always been kept, he noticed that the boy's head kept swiveling, left to right, taking in everything he saw with wide eyes.

"I've never been inside this house before," Colin said. "It's awesome. I can't believe how big it is."

Jack laughed. "Sometimes it's too big," he said. "Especially when you're alone. To tell you the truth, I'm glad you showed up. Sean's not here."

"I know. He and Stacy are working on his boat. She likes him, I think."

"Yeah. I had figured that out."

They made slow progress, as Colin stopped to gawk—the high ceilings, the carved cornices and the heavy drapes that trailed along the marble floors all clearly intrigued him.

"It's awful dark," he announced finally. "That's why it feels creepy. Maybe you should break out your mother-ship flashlights."

Jack laughed. "Maybe."

"Really, I'm serious. When we lived at Heron Hill, it was big, too, but it felt nice because it was all lit up. You should get some new stuff, too. Fun stuff, like a big-screen TV and video games and those chairs that let you lie back and be all sloppy and relaxed. Invite your friends over. Then it would be fine."

Jack tried to imagine Sweet Tides like that. Lamps and friends and a Barca lounger. Would that really be enough to banish the memories?

He flicked on the kitchen lights, which were pleasantly bright. Bright enough to show Jack just what a mess Colin really was. His jeans looked black, and he left a trail of dirty sneaker prints wherever he walked.

Had the dumb kid been digging for gold all night?

Colin hopped onto the bar stool Jack dragged up to the edge of the sink. While Jack waited for the water to get hot enough to kill whatever germs had been lurking in that cold, moldy soil, Colin poked curiously at his wound.

Jack was glad to see that it didn't seem to dismay the kid too much, though it looked awful.

"Is it going to hurt?" Colin didn't sound frightened. He actually seemed to have relaxed ever since Jack had assured him they had a good flashlight.

Jack decided on honesty. "Probably. We're going to have to scrub the heck out of it before we can put on a bandage. Want me to give you a bullet to bite on?"

All Southern boys knew the Civil War stories about wounded Rebels having to undergo surgery without anesthetic. Colin smiled devilishly. "No, sir, but maybe a little whiskey would dull the pain."

"In your dreams, soldier."

He was a brave kid. He watched everything Jack did, as if he needed to store the information for the next big battle. He hissed a couple of times, when the soap stung his skin, but overall he made remarkably little fuss.

By bandage time, he was pale under the dirt, but ready to go.

"Okay," Jack said. "Now that I know you'll live, I've got some questions. First, tell me where your mom thinks you are."

"At Brad's house." Colin looked sheepish. "I'm supposed to be spending the night there. I am spending the night there, later, when I'm through here. Brad can let me back in through the window."

"So I don't need to call her? She's not likely to be having a heart attack, wondering where you are?"

"No." Colin's panic returned. "No, and even if she was, you couldn't call her until we find my ring."

"Your ring?" Jack's imagination had conjured up about a dozen things that Colin might have lost out there, from the key to his bike lock to his favorite baseball card.

A ring had not been on that list.

"Yeah." Colin frowned defensively. "It sounds girlie, but it's not. And I didn't steal it, so don't think that. It's mine, but my mom keeps it in her jewelry box. She says I'm not old enough to take care of it, so I can't have it yet."

Jack raised his eyebrow.

"I know," Colin said. "But it's mine, damn it."

Jack raised his eyebrow another inch.

"Sorry," Colin muttered. "I know I shouldn't have taken it. But, ever since I was little, she's told me how special it is. And it really is cool. I think it must have belonged to my dad. So I thought it might help to have it with me. It might make me lucky."

"Lucky about the gold?"

Colin nodded. "You think that's dumb, don't you? But there is gold out there."

He dug in his jeans pocket with his good hand and pulled out two small, ornate gold discs. Jack had seen enough of these through the years to recognize them instantly. Two pieces of Confederate gold. The same siren's lure that had kept so many men digging on Sweet Tides property for two hundred years.

Poor kid. He didn't realize that these two pieces

of gold were probably all he would ever see of the Killian gold.

"See? I found these last time," Colin said. He was excited. "I figured out the gold is buried under that tree, on the little hill by the river. The clue is in the words to the Christmas song Angus wrote."

"'The Starry Skies'?"

"Yeah. I'm going to give these to Mr. Killian for Christmas, but I was hoping to find the whole thing first. He'll be really excited. Remember when he gave me that old sheet music? I think he was trying to tell me about the clue in the song."

Jack started to laugh, but he wondered...

Could that be true?

Jack knew that Patrick's speech center had been damaged, but no one was sure how much mental clarity was still left behind the garbled words. Was it possible that Patrick had enlisted this boy to do the searching for him? Was it possible that, even from his hospital bed, Patrick was still worrying about the legendary family fortune?

Colin jumped down from the stool. He held out his hand, urging Jack to hurry. "Can you get your flashlight now? We should hurry, before anything happens to my ring."

"Okay," Jack said, trying to forget that just a few minutes ago he'd been exhausted enough to bunk down with ghosts.

He'd made a promise, and he intended to keep it.

Enough things had been lost in the past two hundred years, as people had searched for this imaginary gold. Even if it came from a gum-ball machine, Colin's lucky ring was not going to be added to that list.

THEY FOUND IT half an hour later.

Just when they'd begun to lose hope, Jack's mother-ship torchlight picked up a tiny glint of gold in the black dirt. Colin dove for it with a cry of joy.

"You found it!" He dropped his torch, the beam shooting crazily through the trees and settling on a live oak ten yards away. He knelt on the ground, brushing the earth from the ring, then shoved it on the middle finger of his right hand.

It was too big, even there.

"Thank you, Jack," he said breathlessly. He clambered to his feet and impulsively hugged Jack around the waist. "Thank you. You're the best."

Jack wanted to hug him back. It was so strong, the urge to kneel down and take the boy into his arms. But everybody knew that you couldn't get that close to other people's kids. In today's uptight world, anything could be misconstrued.

Somehow, Jack confined his reaction to a polite pat on Colin's bony shoulder.

"Well? Don't I get to see the ring? After all this tramping around hunting for it?"

Colin laughed, obviously light-headed with relief. "Sure!" He pulled it off and handed it to Jack. "It's still dirty, but you can see. It's a guy's ring. It has some Latin words carved into it."

Jack almost dropped it. All of a sudden, he couldn't feel his fingers. All the blood had rushed to his chest and set off a small, hot explosion behind his ribs.

It couldn't be.

But the weight, the color, the shape of the ring were all so familiar. He knew, without even looking, that he could take it and slide it onto his finger. It would fit perfectly.

It had been his mother's father's ring, and her grandfather's before that.

Jack's mother had given it to him, the night before he'd left for the Army. She'd meant to give it to Sean, as the firstborn. But Sean had been at college—hardly a dangerous place. Jack had needed it more.

It would keep him safe, she'd said, while he was away.

She'd said he was ready. If he was mature enough to be a soldier, he was mature enough to inherit the ring.

But she had been wrong. He had thrown this ring away, that same night, in a fit of drunken disappointment and self-pity. What did he care about being safe, if Nora didn't love him?

The next afternoon, when he'd finally pieced together enough of the night to remember what he'd done with the ring, he'd gone back to retrieve it. He'd had only about ten minutes, before his flight out of town.

But it had been gone.

He'd been miserable. The guilt was terrible because it should have been Sean's ring. He'd confessed everything to his brother, calling him at college from a pay phone on the basic-training base. He'd tried to explain. Someone must have seen it, he'd said, glimpsed it lying abandoned under the hedges. Someone must have picked it up, feeling incredibly lucky, and kept it.

Now he finally knew who that someone was.

"I can't read Latin," Colin went on, oblivious to anything but his own relief. "But my mom told me what it says. It says—"

Jack spoke the words in his head, the words that suddenly held such a terrible, indisputable irony.

It said *Fideli Certa Merces*.

Riches to the faithful.

CHAPTER THIRTEEN

THE CITY OF Hawthorn Bay's fifty-two-foot vintage mahogany sloop, which had looked so beautiful starting out, with its tall sails transformed into Christmas trees by rows of colored lights and prancing reindeer leaping and blinking off the point of the bow, was in trouble.

They'd been gliding along on motor power, the sails purely decorative tonight, when suddenly the motor began to grind and squeal. The air on deck filled with the grimy smell of dirty oil, which made the expensive champagne feel slimy in your mouth and gave the canapés a peculiar flavor.

"What?"

"What's happening?"

The elegant hum of conversation rose to a nervous buzz. The boat slowed. Smaller craft began to pass them, the plebeians in tiny day sailors and catamarans laughing and waving their beer cans at the stuffy, overdressed, becalmed politicians.

And then, just about at the halfway point of the parade, the impressive boat carrying Hawthorn Bay's elite humiliatingly came to a dead stop.

Bill Freeman, who had joined Nora along the railing to avoid the more insufferable snobs collected by the bar, sighed heavily. He peered over the side of the boat.

"Know how to swim?"

An image of Maggie, giving Ethan one last, irritated look before she dove into the green Maine water, filled Nora's mental vision. With effort, she shook it off before it could bring tears.

"Not well enough," she said with a smile. "I'm afraid we're stuck."

She looked around the deck. Several people were already on their cell phones, protesting the indignity to anyone who would listen.

As mayor, she probably ought to go mingle, assure people that everything would be fine. The city had hired a captain, and Nora was sure the man was already working on the motor, but patience was not one of the virtues this crowd possessed.

Oh, let them stew, she thought. They liked little glitches—it gave them a chance to feel superior. Tom was about twenty feet away, holding forth to some poor woman about the shoddy workmanship you found everywhere these days. Funny, Nora thought, how that bothered him only when it inconvenienced him personally. He didn't seem to mind building cheap housing and office space for other people.

She took another sip of champagne. To heck with the responsibility of being mayor. It didn't involve babysitting a bunch of spoiled grown-ups.

"I'm going to get another drink." Bill held up his empty plastic flute. "Want one?"

Nora shook her head. "No, thanks. I think I'll just enjoy the show."

And it was quite a show.

They'd lucked out with the weather. It was a cold night, but beautiful, as if the sky had decked itself out in strings of sparkling white stars for the occasion. The river, rocked by the slow wakes of a hundred boats, gave back rippling reflections of thousands of red and green and yellow and blue lights.

Even the shoreline was alive with color. The stores and houses along the river had joined in the festivity, setting out extra displays. Every roofline, gable, chimney and door was outlined in lights. On the lawns, glowing red Santas waved, white fairy-light reindeer nodded their antlers, and silver angels blew golden trumpets.

She wondered where the Butterfields' boat was. Brad's dad loved to fish, and he had a nice little cabin cruiser that they'd decorated like a giant Christmas present with a huge red bow. Colin was riding with them and would spend the night at the Butterfields' house afterward.

That would make the third night this week. She wondered whether that might account for Colin's yawns and shadowed eyes. Maybe the boys were staying up too late, playing video games.

The Butterfields were nice people, but they tended to sit in front of their TV all night and lose track of everything else.

"Hey, Nora!"

She looked around. No one on the boat seemed to be paying any attention to her. Had she imagined it?

"Hey! Mayor lady!"

Then she understood. The call had come up to her from the water below. She leaned over the railing and found Sean Killian's boat.

The small Boston whaler had obviously seen better days, but its decorations had the signature Stacy Holtsinger touch. She'd used only a few scallops of tiny blue lights, shaped like waves, to outline the boat. Then, attached to the tip of the mast, one huge white Christmas star.

Simple, but it made the other boats look tacky and overdone.

Stacy stood up and waved at Nora, smiling. "What's up with the bigwig boat? You guys run out of gas, or what?"

Sean's craft rocked, as a bigger boat went by. Sean, who was sitting on Stacy's left, reached up to steady her. Jack, who was behind the wheel, just kept watching Nora.

He looked beautiful by starlight, she thought stupidly. Even artificial starlight washed lovingly over him, dropping silver sparkles into his black curls and flattering his classic profile. She could imagine what it would do to his eyes.

No, she didn't have to imagine. She could remember.

"Our motor died," she said, forcing her thoughts back into line. "They're working on it now, but who knows?"

"Bummer," Jack said. He gave her that slow grin that had always made her stomach tingle. "Want a ride?"

She opened her mouth, surprised. Then she cast a furtive glance toward the other people on her boat. It was a crazy suggestion. She was the mayor. She couldn't just ditch the rest of the city government crowd.

Could she?

She looked back at Jack, and she knew by his saucy raised eyebrow that her indecision must be written all over her face.

"Yeah! Come on, Nora," Stacy said, laughing. "Do it. It'll be fun."

"I can't," she said, but even she could tell she didn't sound as if she meant it. The little boat looked so cozy, so simple and free. Just a few friends, a cooler of cola and the stars in your eyes…

"I can't."

"Yes, you can," Jack said. He handed the wheel to Sean, who was already standing, ready to take over. He moved to the side of the boat as Sean steered them alongside the city's yacht.

"There's a ladder right beneath you." Jack stretched out his hand, as if to show her how close they were, how easy it would be. "Make a break for it."

She put her hand down and found the first rung of the ladder. She looked at the water, which was cold and full of colors. "What if I fall in?"

Jack laughed softly. "You won't," he said. "I'm right here."

She glanced one more time at the crowd behind her. No one was looking her way.

"Come on, Nora," Jack said. He held her gaze. "Surprise me."

She couldn't really be considering it. It was absurd. Knowing it would be cold, she had worn her red-velvet Christmas dress, which was the worst possible outfit for indulging in impulsive prison breaks that required climbing ladders, jumping onto moving boats and other physical insanity.

But she did it anyhow.

She kicked off her high heels, held them by the tips of her fingers, then threw one leg over the side of the boat.

"By God, she's coming!" Stacy sounded shocked, which annoyed Nora. Was she really that prissy and predictable?

She tucked her long, full skirt into her belt, then

carefully made her way down the ladder, one bare foot after the other.

She felt ridiculous. Even worse, she felt nervous, as if she actually were an escaping prisoner, as if someone might at any moment turn a spotlight onto the side of the boat, pinning her there for all the world to see.

The bottom of the ladder was still about three feet higher than the deck of Sean's boat, a distance she hadn't appreciated from above. She hesitated, acutely aware of the movement of both boats as they reacted to the shifting water.

"This dress is velvet," she said, as if that made any difference. "It'll weigh a ton if it gets wet. If I fall in, I'll sink right to the bottom."

"Nora." She felt Jack's hands circle her waist. "Shut up and jump."

His touch was light, but it was the security she needed.

She saw Bill Freeman walking toward the spot where he'd left her, a fresh champagne flute in his hands. Their eyes met over the rim of the boat. At first Bill looked shocked, but, slowly, as the situation sank in, he began to smile.

He winked. Then he raised his hand to his forehead and gave her a crisp goodbye salute.

Okay, there was no going back now.

She shut her eyes, then pushed off gently. She dropped, landing with her back against Jack's chest. The boat dipped and wobbled under her weight, but Jack held her steady.

Stacy and Sean began to clap and whistle their approval. Nora laughed, suddenly breathless. Her head fell back against Jack's shoulder.

She felt his lips at her temple. She could tell that he was smiling.

"Welcome aboard," he said.

TWO HOURS LATER, their own motor died, but by then they'd had so much fun none of them really cared, least of all Jack.

The parade was over, and they had almost made it back to Sweet Tides anyhow. They could see the outline of the house from the river, its columns gleaming under the stars.

Jack was glad to see that Sean had at least possessed the foresight to bring oars. He wouldn't have relished the idea of jumping into the freezing water and towing the boat to shore.

Rowing wasn't difficult—the river was calm and fairly narrow here—but when they finally felt the bump as the bow hit the riverbank, the women applauded. That was how much the mood had mellowed. Even Nora seemed relaxed.

"Tell you what," Sean said as he jumped out, then held up a hand to help Stacy out, too. "Why don't you and Nora wait here with the boat, and Stacy and I can go get the tool kit?"

Nora's laid-back attitude vanished so fast it was almost laughable. She stood awkwardly, holding on to the gunwale as the boat rocked.

"It's okay," she said. "I don't mind walking. We can all go together."

Stacy turned her back on the men and looked at Nora, but not before Jack glimpsed the intense glare in her eyes.

"No, Nora," she said with slow emphasis on each

word. "You two should stay here. You don't have the right shoes for walking that far."

There followed a brief battle of wills. Jack could see only Nora's end of it, but clearly there was quite a dialogue going on with their eyes. Nora must have been very fond of Stacy because, in the end, her gaze dropped first.

She apparently had decided to sacrifice herself so that Stacy could have some private time with Sean.

"Okay," she said. She plopped back onto the cushioned seat and tried to smile, though her jaw was tight. "Take your time. We'll be fine."

They both watched as Sean and Stacy disappeared into the trees. It was probably a ten-minute walk to the stables, where Sean kept his tools, and a ten-minute walk back. But Jack had a feeling Sean wouldn't be coming back at all. When a decent interval had elapsed, Jack's cell phone would probably ring, and Sean would say that he didn't have the right tools after all, Jack should just take Nora home, they'd fix the boat tomorrow.

But in the meantime, Jack had been handed the chance he'd been waiting for. He needed to talk to Nora alone, and, for the moment at least, she was essentially a captive audience.

He didn't climb back aboard the boat. She might be more comfortable if she had at least that symbolic separation. He leaned over the gunwale and pulled another cola from the cooler.

He tilted it toward Nora. "Want one?"

She shook her head. "No, thanks," she said politely. "I've reached my limit."

He chuckled and closed the lid. "You may be over

your limit, actually," he said. "I'm not sure you would have sung 'A Hundred Bottles of Eggnog on the Wall' with us if you'd been stone-cold sober."

"Probably not," she agreed. This time her smile was more natural. "But you two do sound fantastic together. That's one thing the Killian men sure can do. They can sing."

"Why, thank you, Mayor."

He leaned against the boat, the cola open and fizzing pleasantly. This was nice. Starlight floated on the water like silver paint, and the night wind made soft sounds in the trees. He almost wished he didn't have to bring up anything serious. He would have liked to stay like this all night, just a boy and a girl flirting by the river.

But that innocent time was long gone. They were grown-ups now, and they had to start dealing with their issues maturely. Facing them squarely.

There were things that had to be said.

"I'm glad we stayed behind," he said. "I've been wanting to talk to you about something."

Funny. Now that he knew exactly what she was hiding, he could read her so much better. He knew that the slight recoil wasn't about him personally. It wasn't fear that she'd been abandoned on a dark night with a semi-homicidal Killian. It wasn't even fear that she might be unable to resist his seductions.

It was, instead, terror that he might force open her Pandora's box of secrets, and let all the dangerous truths fly into the air, changing absolutely everything.

In one way, he wondered why he didn't hate her. If everything he believed was true, she had stolen eleven years of fatherhood from him.

But he had hated Nora Carson only once in his life—

the night he'd lain there, drunk, angry, believing she had abandoned him. He never wanted to feel like that again.

So how did he feel? He wasn't sure. In the twenty-four hours since he'd seen his ring on Colin's finger, Jack's emotions had seesawed up and down, from shock to fury, from disbelief to confusion, and then to something that he couldn't quite identify.

It might have been the tentative, bewildered first stirrings of joy.

He was completely sure of only one thing. He wanted her to tell him about Colin. He wanted her to trust him enough for that.

And that meant he had to help her. He had to open the dialogue, clear the path for honesty by offering honesty of his own.

"You asked me to tell you what really happened with Tom that day," he said. "I couldn't do it then, but I'd like to tell you now."

She sat very still, her hands folded in her lap. Her blond hair caught the starlight and shone like a halo. The soft folds of her wine-velvet skirt draped around her gracefully. She might have been the Lady of Shallot, frightened as she sailed into the world outside her protected tower.

"Why now?"

"I'm not the only person involved in this story," he said. "I had given my word that I'd never tell. But the other person is ready to tell the truth. She's tired of hiding from the past."

Nora's head tilted. "She? The other person is a woman?"

He nodded.

"I always thought there might be someone else. I—"

She twined her fingers together. "I thought it might be Sean."

"No. Sean wasn't part of this. In fact, he doesn't know the whole story, either."

She looked surprised. "You didn't even tell your own brother?"

"I had promised," he said simply. "Sean didn't need to know. He trusted me."

He heard how it sounded. Sean had trusted him— Nora hadn't. But it was the truth. And tonight they were dealing only in truths.

"Anyhow, the woman involved was Amy Grantham. You probably don't know her. She still lives here, but on the wrong side of the tracks. She's just a girl I knew, a couple of years younger than we were. She was only sixteen at the time."

"No, I don't think I've ever heard of her," Nora said. "How did you—how did you know her? You must have been close, if she could make you take a vow of silence."

"We met at a meeting for children of alcoholic parents. She'd had a rough life. Their family didn't have any money—her dad drank it all, the same way mine did."

Nora nodded. "Okay." She swallowed. "Were you lovers?"

"No. But we were very close, for a while. It's the kind of thing that accelerates intimacy. You learn things about each other, things other people don't know. It's like being members of a secret family. Yes, that's how it was. She was like my secret sister."

"All right," she said. Her voice gave nothing away.

"Anyhow, she was pretty, or could have been. She had beautiful red hair, a good figure and an open, pleasant face. She had an eating disorder back then, so she was too thin, but…"

He stopped, remembering Amy chewing that pizza the way a sick person might take medicine. She'd come such a long way. He said a quick prayer that she would win the fight.

"She was mixed up, but she was a good person, deep down. The problem was, she'd fallen hard for your cousin Tom."

Nora's inhale told him she realized how dangerous that could be.

"It was kind of pathetic, everyone knew he'd never take a girl like her seriously. Everyone but Amy. She was hooked. Tom was slick as hell, you know that. I'm sure he flattered her just enough to keep her addicted, to keep her hoping."

"I can believe that," Nora said. "Every female in school thought he was gorgeous. They used to come to me, asking me to get them a date with him."

"Well, I hope you didn't do it," Jack said, "because your cousin Tom was a real sick dude."

"What do you mean?"

"I mean he was a sick son of a bitch. He started sleeping with Amy, on the sly. He'd come to her house late at night, after he took his real girlfriends home, and get her to sneak out. That went on for about a month."

Nora looked down at her hands. "I'm so sorry," she said. "Poor Amy."

"But he got bored, I guess, because then he wanted more. He told Amy that he wanted to do a threesome, with her pretty little sister as number three."

Nora lifted her head. Her wide eyes gleamed in the starlight.

"Yeah. The kicker was that her sister was only fourteen. I told you, Tom was one sick man. Anyhow, this is the part Amy was really ashamed of. This is the part she couldn't bear to let anyone know about. She agreed to bring her sister out to the spit island one day after school. She couldn't stand the thought of losing him, so she said she'd do it."

"Oh, my God. Did she?"

"No. At the last minute, she chickened out. She went to the island herself, hoping she could placate him, doing God only knows what, so that he wouldn't be so angry. But he was angry. He made her do—"

He stopped. Apparently it didn't matter how many years had elapsed. His heart still pounded with the need to teach Thomas Dickson a lesson.

"He made her do every sick, humiliating thing he could think of. He knocked her around. And then he left her there. Alone, on that island, with no way to get home except to swim. If I hadn't gone out looking for her—"

"Jack." The word was full of real horror. "Oh, Jack."

"So the next day I stole a boat and I took Tom out to that same island. I beat the hell out of him. I told him that if he ever laid another hand on Amy or her sister, I'd kill him. And I left him there."

She didn't respond, which didn't really surprise him. This story didn't exonerate him. The fact that Tom was a psycho didn't justify Jack being a thug. But she had to know the truth. Though he had no idea what the future held for them, he knew it couldn't begin with lies and secrets.

"I'll admit I was glad to do it. In a way, I was doing it for myself, too, and for all the people Tom Dickson treated like trash because they weren't as blessed or as rich as he was. But I swear to you, Nora. I had no idea I'd broken his arm. It was only about a hundred yards to shore. He was the athletic type. I assumed he'd swim home and maybe, just maybe, stop being such an asshole for a while."

Nora opened her mouth, as if she were about to speak, but she closed it again without making a sound.

She took a deep breath. And then, moving carefully so that the boat wouldn't wobble, she stood.

"Jack, I—" She paused. "Can you help me out?"

She made her way gingerly to the bow. He set his drink on the ground and met her there. He held out his arms, and she moved toward them. She put her hands on his shoulders—and though the touch was gentle it went through him like electricity.

As he lifted her above the gunwale and onto dry ground, his fingers circled her waist, pressing into the smooth velvet. Her soft hair fell forward, into his face, teasing at his lips, and it smelled of that mysterious new perfume, the dusky sandalwood and spice.

Though her balance was steady now, he found himself holding on to her. He could feel the warmth of her fragile body beneath the wine-red velvet, and it made him shiver, wanting more.

"I can't make myself let go, Nora," he said, his voice a rough whisper. "I've wanted to hold you for so long."

He felt her startled intake of breath, but she didn't pull away. She hadn't removed her hands from his shoulders, although now that they both stood on firm ground she had to lift her arms to reach him.

Her breath came shallowly, as his thumbs began to move, drifting along the lower edge of her rib cage.

"I remember you so well," he said. "I remember the shape, the feel of every inch of you."

He watched her eyes, which glistened in the starlight. If those eyes had turned cold, if she had whispered even the faintest *no,* he would have stopped.

But she didn't. She panted lightly, as if she were trying to control a primitive fear. But even when his hands rose all the way to the curve of her breasts, she didn't tell him to stop.

He cupped the graceful swell, stroked and pressed against the pebbling tips. Though the velvet was rich and thick, he could feel her heartbeat through it. He knew when its rhythm began to race.

Her hands tightened on his shoulders. She shifted, angling her body toward him. The soft warmth between her legs met the hard fire between his. He groaned, his heart a jackhammer, his whole body pounding with desire.

He could have taken her right there, in the boat, or in the river, or on the cold, hard ground. For himself, he was beyond caring how it happened, as long as it did, finally, happen. He was burning up, and he needed to quench the fire.

But somehow, for her sake, he held back. If she would let him make love to her, he wanted this time to be better.

He wanted it to be more than a drunken coupling in the scratchy winter grass. He wanted it to be soft sheets and soft words, and long stretches of foreplay that ended in explosions of pleasure. He wanted to soothe her to sleep afterward, and lie together, spooned in safety, with all the time in the world.

He wanted to offer her all the things she had always deserved, but had never been given—at least not by him.

He bent his head toward her breast.

"Jack," she whispered. "Jack, I need you to—"

His heart froze. He could feel her pulling away.

"Don't say it, Nora. *Please*. I don't think I can stand it if you tell me to stop."

She tilted her head back, so that she could look at him. The starlight found a fevered flush along her cheek and a fast-throbbing pulse in her slender neck. She threaded her hands into his hair, the way she used to do. It made him shiver now, just as it had done all those years ago.

"You didn't let me finish," she said. He heard the undercurrent of husky desire in her voice, and his heart came back to life with thick, hungry beats. "I was going to ask you to hurry."

CHAPTER FOURTEEN

HOURS LATER, NORA LAY beside Jack on the soft four-poster bed, trying to commit the entire room to memory.

The corner rosettes on the cornice above the door, the elegant tidal marsh landscape over the mantel. The ornate Chinese rug, though she could only guess at the colors in the dimness.

The slant-top desk by the window—she wondered if he'd done his homework there, as a teenager. She wondered if he had found it hard to concentrate on world history, thinking instead of her.

And of course the beautiful mahogany bed. The carved headboard she had reached up and gripped, clinging to her last shred of control. The rumpled white sheets frosted with moonlight. Soft pillows that spilled, forgotten, onto the floor.

She wanted to learn it by heart, so that for the rest of her life she could close her eyes and see him lying here, wet skin shining, black hair tossed against white cotton, eyes closed in exhausted, dreamless sleep.

As for the rest of it…

The kisses, the touches, the feel of his body, finally, *finally* inside her…

She didn't have to make a special effort to imprint those memories. They would be part of her forever.

She held her breath as he stirred in his sleep. She'd

promised herself that she would stay only a few more minutes, only until he moved. If he let go of her, that would be her sign it was time to leave.

When they had finally collapsed, shaking from the fading tremors of their last amazing climax, she had tried to roll away. But with a sleepy murmur he had reached out and pulled her up against his chest, her bottom against his belly. Settling his head above hers on the pillow, he had wrapped his arm around her waist, reaching up to cup her breast in his warm palm.

He'd fallen asleep almost instantly. His hand softened. His legs, braided with hers, relaxed heavily, and his breathing grew deep and even.

It was strange how comfortable such a tangled position could be. She'd even slept a little, herself.

He shifted again, murmuring something that might have been her name, and finally turned away, unwinding his legs.

Immediately her thighs and calves felt cold, deprived of his warmth. The large house had central heating, but the rooms were cavernous, and the chill had never completely vanished.

Except when she was in his arms.

She eased off the bed by inches, praying that he wouldn't wake. If he did, if he looked at her with eyes full of starlight and held open his strong arms, she knew she would fall right back into them. And then how would she ever find the courage to leave?

She bent and gathered her clothes from the Oriental carpet. They were scattered all the way from the door to the bed, as Jack had pulled them free. The red velvet dress had been the first to go. It was halfway out in the hall.

The bathroom was the next door down the corridor. She knew where it was because he had gone there to get the condoms, and again later, to get more. She walked softly, her bare feet silent on the glossy hardwood floor.

Before she dressed, she pulled her cell phone out of her dress pocket and called for a taxi. If the request was already placed, she'd be more likely to stick to it, even if he tried to persuade her to stay.

She tried to whisper her request, but the dispatcher sounded annoyed. "Did you say Sweet Rides? Where is that? Don't you have a regular street address?"

She finally made herself understood. Then she turned her attention to dressing. Her fair skin was pink in places, where his attentions had been concentrated. The heavy velvet felt rough against her skin, much rougher than Jack's hands had been.

She clasped her belt. Looking in the mirror, she ran her fingers through her hair to work out the worst knots, and finally just gave up. The taxi driver would assume the worst, but so what? He'd be right.

When she heard footsteps coming down the hallway, she took a deep breath and rushed to put on her last shoe. She had to be suited up and ready to go, so that nothing he said could dissuade her.

But to her surprise the footsteps seemed to be coming from the other direction. And they didn't pause at the bathroom. They went farther, stopping instead at Jack's bedroom door.

Nora peeked out. It was Sean.

She felt irrationally embarrassed. Paralyzed, the way she used to feel when she was eighteen and her dad came out to see why it was taking Nora and Jack so long to say good night.

What should she do? Announce herself?

"You sleeping alone, too? Guess we both struck out."

She stuck her head out of the bathroom cautiously. Sean stood in the bedroom doorway. He wasn't facing Jack. He had his back to the door frame, and seemed to be sliding up and down, scratching his shoulder blades on it while he talked.

He hadn't drawn a breath, even talking around a loud yawn. If Jack had tried to interrupt him, it wasn't getting through.

"And you know tonight was your last chance," he went on, "because tomorrow, when she finds out you hired a lawyer, she's more likely to shoot you than scre—"

"Sean!" Jack's voice finally pierced Sean's sleepy self-absorption. "For God's sake, shut up."

"Why?" Sean scratched his head and yawned again. "It's true. Hiring Harry is the kiss of death—"

Nora came out of the bathroom.

Sean's jaw dropped. His mouth was open wide enough to catch a baseball, and he didn't even seem aware of it. He stared at Nora with round, trapped-animal eyes.

"Holy shit," he said.

"Hi, Sean," she said. "Hired Harry for what?"

Jack must have found his clothes because suddenly he appeared in the doorway, too. He wore jeans, still unbuttoned at the waist, and nothing else.

"Nora," Jack said. "Nora, I swear. I was going to tell you."

She transferred her gaze to him. "Hired Harry for what?"

Sean cleared his throat. "Tell you what, maybe I'll

just slide on out of here, just run on to bed, what do you think?" He looked at Jack. "Good idea?"

"Excellent idea."

Sean sidled by Nora as carefully as if she were a ticking bomb. "Don't pay any attention to me," he said. "I'm an idiot. I'm sorry."

"Get out of here, Sean," Jack said. Sean nodded. He rounded the corner quickly and disappeared down the stairs.

Nora turned back to Jack and asked her question for the third time. "Hired Harry for what?"

Jack held out his hand. "Come back in, Nora. Let's sit down. We can talk this over privately, and be more comfortable."

"It's too late for privacy. And I don't want to be comfortable. I want to be answered. *Hired Harry for what?*"

Jack ran his hand through his hair, which was as big a mess as hers. "To advise me about Colin."

Suddenly she wished she had accepted his offer of a place to sit. She wasn't sure her knees would lock firmly enough to hold her up.

"Why?" She steadied her voice. "Why would you need legal advice about my son?"

"Because he's my son, too."

She started to voice some mindless, instinctive protest, but he cut her off.

"Don't," he said. "Don't lie to me anymore. I know the truth, Nora. *I know.*"

She shoved her hands in the warm, velvet pockets of her dress—not because she was cold, but so that he wouldn't see how badly they were shaking. She lifted her chin and forced her voice to come out frigid and firm.

"What exactly do you think you know?"

"I know that, somehow, later that night, you changed your mind. You came down to say goodbye to me, and we made love."

She made a dismissive noise. "You've already admitted that you were so drunk that night that you don't remember anything. Are you saying you've had a sudden, convenient recall?"

He looked as if he were wrestling with both anger and sadness.

"No, I still don't remember. I wish I did, Nora. I wish I knew what I did that night. I was drunk, and I was angry with you for not trusting me. Did I say something unforgivable? Did I do something—" He frowned sharply. "God, did I force myself on you?"

"Of course not," she said. "Don't be ridiculous. You saw how it was, just now, between us. Do you really think that, if I had come to you that night, you would have needed to *force* me to make love to you?"

"I don't know." He shook his head. "I don't know anything. All I know is that I've been a father for eleven years, and I missed every single second of it."

"Jack, there's no—"

He put up his hands. "Don't. I'm not on a fishing expedition here. I'm not trying to trick you into incriminating yourself. I tell you I *know*."

"But how could you?"

"I saw the ring. Colin's ring."

She couldn't breathe. He couldn't be making this up. He really must have seen Colin's ring, somehow. No one even knew it existed except Colin, Ethan and Nora herself.

"That doesn't prove any—"

"Yes, it does. I know that ring, Nora. It was mine."

She frowned. "That's ridiculous. I never saw—"

"You wouldn't have. My mother gave it to me on my last night at home. She'd kept it hidden for years, so that my father wouldn't sell it. It was mine for only one night. *That night*."

He waited, as if he expected her to protest again, but she couldn't think of anything to say.

"When Maggie came down to tell me that you weren't coming, I was so angry I got pretty wild. She was scared to death of me—she drove off so fast I'm surprised she didn't wreck the car. When she was gone, the last thing I remember doing was taking off that ring and hurling it into the bushes."

She still couldn't speak, though he paused to give her a chance. How had he seen it? Had he asked Colin to steal it, and show it to him?

"And now Colin has the ring." He shook his head. "You tell me, Nora. What else can that possibly mean?"

Nora knew she must be as pale as the waning moon outside. No blood was able to make its way to her face. It was all pooling miserably in her stomach, and sinking through her legs. She felt as if she might be sick.

Maggie had worn that ring, on a gold chain around her neck, every single day. Nora had caught her sometimes, just sitting, staring out the window, with one hand on her belly and the other hand wrapped around the little gold circle.

Maggie's last conscious action had been to take the ring off and give it to Nora. "For Colin," she'd said.

Her last words.

The thought of Maggie gave her courage. Nora wasn't the bad guy here. She had just spent the past eleven years trying to set straight a horrible, hopeless situation that Jack and Maggie had created.

"Why didn't you tell me about this sooner, Jack?"

She looked at his naked chest and remembered her hands there, exploring him while he did the same to her.

"Why didn't you tell me…before? Before we…"

His eyes were very dark. "I was going to," he said. "But I wanted you. I needed you. And I knew you wouldn't have—"

"You're darn right I wouldn't have." She fisted her hands inside her pockets. "Well played, Jack. A little strategic timing, and you think maybe you can walk off with everything. The woman. The child…everything. Very slick."

"Damn it, Nora. It wasn't strategy. The truth was, I couldn't think about anything but you. You were just as lost. We both forgot everything else, for a little while."

He was right. She'd certainly forgotten what a danger this man posed to her heart, her happiness, her family.

"And, frankly," he said, his voice cold, "if we're going to start accusing one another of keeping secrets…"

Her stomach tightened. She felt bruised, pummeled by her own fear and the accusations in Jack's eyes. She had to get out of here. She had to go home, where maybe she could clear her head.

She'd call Bill Freeman. He'd help her think what to do.

She heard a horn outside. It sounded like the prize-fight bell, sounding the end of this punishing round. She turned, eager to stagger to her corner, praying she could buy enough time to regroup before the match started up again, this time in earnest.

"That's my taxi," she said. "I have to go."

He grabbed her arm. "No. Stay."

She stared down at his hand, willing him to let go.

Reluctantly, he did. But he held her with his gaze. "Nora, you can't just run away. You know we need to talk."

"No, we don't," she said. "You've hired someone to represent you. I'll do the same. If there's any more talking to be done, we'll leave it to the lawyers."

CHAPTER FIFTEEN

1980

IT WAS NO kind of day to be outside. The sun was so hot it raised blisters on Kelly Killian's neck. But he hated this goddamn gazebo, and he was going to tear every last board of it down before sunset, even if it killed him.

He used the claw end of his hammer to pry out another piece of wall. How many hours had Bridey wasted out here? She said she liked the fresh air, and the roses, and the corner of the river you could glimpse behind the cedars.

But he knew what she really did out here.

She escaped. She daydreamed. She pretended that she didn't really live at Sweet Tides, that she wasn't really married to Kelly, and that she didn't really have two sons who, though they were only four and six, already looked just like their father.

Maybe she even pretended that she wasn't pregnant again, with another Killian boy.

She wanted a girl this time; she made no bones about that. She longed for a daughter, who would play Barbie dolls and unicorns with her all day long, while her sons went hungry for attention.

Just like Kelly did himself.

Just like Kelly had *always* done.

He'd grown up with a crazy mother who couldn't think about anything but the little girl baby who'd died. As if her living, breathing son was just a piece of chopped liver.

And then he'd married a crazy wife who sat around eating her heart out over not getting a daughter, too.

Well, tough. Killians didn't have girls. If Bridey wanted daughters, maybe she should have married that milksop architect she had been so in love with, back when Kelly had first met her.

He smiled as he swung his hammer. *Oh, that's right.* Mr. Milksop hadn't *wanted* to marry Bridey. He hadn't loved her. That's why, in the end, she'd settled for Kelly.

And no amount of mooning and daydreaming out here in the gazebo could change that.

Kelly ripped a board off so roughly it slapped him in the face. One of the nails gouged a hole in his cheek, missing his eye by about an inch.

"Damn it." He sat down on the gazebo bench and wiped his palm across his face. Then he wiped the blood on his jeans.

Everything was quiet out here today. Though it must be ten miles away, he could hear a train going by. He wondered where it was headed.

Now that the walls were half-gone, he could see the house. It looked like hell, and why not? It used to take a plantation full of servants to keep this monstrosity going. He had five people living with him—his whining wife, his lecturing father, his crazy mother and his two lazy sons. Not one of them would lift a finger to help him.

If only he could find that gold.

He leaned back, crossing his arms behind his head.

Bridey would be surprised to learn that she wasn't the only one who daydreamed. He thought about the gold all the time these days. If he found it, he'd be on a train to Anywhere Else so fast he'd leave his own shadow behind.

No one would miss him, and he wouldn't miss them, either. He was only forty-three, and he was so damn tired.

Tired of trying to be good enough to earn some-body's love. Tired of coming in second. Second with his own mother. Second with his own wife. Hell, even his sons, just little kids who should have idolized their dad, preferred their grandfather.

Sometimes Kelly dreamed of trains, fast-moving freight cars piled high with lumps of gold instead of coal. In the dream he was always running, running so hard his heart nearly exploded, trying to catch the handle and jump on.

He never could.

He wondered sometimes whether his father knew where the gold was, and just didn't think Kelly could be trusted with it. Patrick didn't approve of Kelly. Didn't like Kelly's drinking, he said.

Well, news flash. Kelly didn't like it, either. But no one had been able to suggest any other way to deal with a life so disappointing you couldn't hear a train go by without wanting to jump on it and run.

"Kelly? Kelly, where are you?"

It was Bridey. Come out to whine about the gazebo, no doubt. He pulled his hat down over his eyes and pre-tended to be asleep.

"Kelly, something's wrong. I need you to call the doctor."

Kelly heaved a long-suffering sigh. This woman had more aches and pains than a whole wing of a hospital. Ordinarily, she conveniently got them just about the time he came to bed, so that only a brute would insist on having sex.

"What is it now?" He tilted his hat back and looked at her through the gaping hole in the gazebo.

She stared back at him helplessly.

"I don't know," she said. "I think it's the baby. I'm bleeding…"

She dropped her arms down, stiffly, palms out, to show him. He rose slowly, trying to process what he saw.

Between her hands, her light blue cotton skirt was brightly stained with blood.

So much blood.

She was losing the baby, and he had no idea in hell how to stop it. He could call 911—he was starting even now for the house, but he could tell it was too late. It would be just one more failure that would somehow end up being his fault.

Poor Bridey, every one would say. No one would stop to think that Kelly had lost a baby, too.

No baby. No gold. No love.

No nothing.

Bridey began to cry.

And somewhere in the distance, Kelly heard the mournful sound of another swiftly moving train.

"NORA, SIT DOWN and try to relax." Bill Freeman looked up from the papers he'd spread out on the coffee table in Nora's living room. "Better yet, go upstairs and let me handle this."

Nora shook her head. "I can't. If I refuse to talk to him personally, it will just antagonize him even more. I panicked the other night, but I'm calmer now, and—"

"If this is calmer," Bill broke in, "I would hate to see what agitated looks like."

She tried to smile. "Yeah. You would."

The doorbell rang. It might as well have been electrically wired to her heart, which responded by pumping frantically in her chest.

Bill was right. She wasn't anything close to calm.

Thank goodness she'd found an excuse to get Colin out of the house. One of the big Christmas blockbuster movies had opened this week. Ordinarily, she made him wait until after the holiday—it seemed more in keeping with the season to focus on home, family and giving. He'd been ecstatic when she'd announced that, this one time, he could go early.

He never went anywhere without Brad, so Nora had recruited Stacy to take the two boys, and had asked her to make a day of it. Lunch, movie, maybe even a stop at the video arcade. Anything that would ensure they didn't come home before dark.

Stacy had accepted her mission without any questions, but her expression had been extremely curious. In a way, that was a relief. Nora wasn't sure how close Sean and Stacy had become. She'd wondered whether Sean might have spilled the gossip during pillow talk.

But apparently, bless his heart, he hadn't.

The bell rang again.

Bill stood up, adjusted his belt over his paunch and shrugged into his jacket. He looked like a teddy bear, but underneath that Southern charm she knew he was a very shrewd lawyer.

On the other hand, with a case like this, she might need a miracle worker, not an attorney. The facts simply weren't on her side.

"Ready?" Bill smiled at her. "Okay. Deep breath, and—" he put his hand on the doorknob "—showtime!"

The introductions and handshakes were a blur. Nora noticed only general impressions. Jack was blank-faced and cold. His lawyer, Harry…Harry something, she had missed his last name…was young, with smart, sharp eyes and a prominent nose that gave a rather intimidating hawkish look.

Next to this guy, Bill Freeman looked sloppy, sleepy and halfway over the hill.

Somehow they all found chairs. Bill and Harry claimed opposite sides of the coffee table. Nora sat stiff-backed in her chair, as if she were made of iron stakes instead of bones. She noticed that Jack took the seat farthest away from her.

"This shouldn't take long," Harry began politely. He seemed comfortable taking the lead, though he was on enemy ground. "In fact, I think it would be better if we don't try to get too far ahead of ourselves here. Clearly the first move is simply to arrange a paternity test."

Nora clutched the arms of her chair so hard her elbows hurt. Bill had advised her to keep quiet until he asked her to speak. That was just as well. She was so frightened, she wasn't sure she could get a word out through her iron-tight throat.

"A paternity test won't be necessary," Bill said. "Ms. Carson is willing to stipulate that Mr. Killian is the father."

Nora felt Jack's gaze whip to her, but she couldn't

meet it. She kept her eyes locked on Bill, as if he were the life rope she must cling to or sink.

With a groan as he bent over his protruding belly, Bill lifted a sheaf of legal papers from the coffee table and handed it to the other lawyer. "I've drawn up a document to that effect. I think you'll find that it's all in order."

Harry leafed through the papers without comment, without even a twitch of reaction in his face. He handed them to Jack, who scanned them quickly, as well.

Too quickly. Even Nora could tell that the men weren't really reading the document. Her heart tightened and started to drag down, down, in her chest.

"As you see," Bill said, "we've covered all contingencies. Ms. Carson—"

"I'm sorry," Harry broke in. "I'm afraid we must insist on the paternity test. In fact, Mr. Killian has arranged an appointment with a laboratory nearby, and—"

"Mr. Mathieson," Bill said genially, "I understand that you want to exercise every caution. But I assure you, Ms. Carson will not retract her admission, and even if she did—"

"No," the other lawyer said without so much as a smile to soften the categorical refusal. Nora wondered if it was always like this with lawyers, that no one let anyone else complete a sentence. "My client deserves to know definitively whether or not he's the boy's father. Surely you can appreciate that he would prefer not merely to take Ms. Carson's word for something that has such far-reaching implications."

Nora flushed. In other words, Ms. Carson had already proven herself a liar. Why would anyone believe her now?

Bill chuckled. "Come on, Mr. Mathieson. Your client is the one who told my client that he was one-hundred-percent certain the child was his. Now she agrees. Where's the problem? If we don't contest it—"

"He has moral certainty," Harry Mathieson said. Nora wondered if the man knew how to smile. "Before Mr. Killian goes any further, he would like medical certainty, as well. Surely your client can have no objection to that. It's a simple blood test. We will, of course, assume all costs."

Bill looked at Nora, and she knew what he was asking her. This was a reasonable request. Did she want him to keep fighting a losing cause?

"We've scheduled a trio test," Harry went on, clearly sensing a weakening of defenses and leaping into the breach. "Therefore, the reports would establish, both medically and legally, that your client and mine have equal rights to the child. It would protect them both, Mr. Freeman. Your client does not stand to lose by this procedure."

Bill still looked at Nora, waiting for a sign.

Harry Mathieson seemed baffled. "I'm not sure what the objection is. We can get a court order to compel the testing, but my client was hoping that wouldn't be necessary. Surely, at this preliminary stage—"

Nora finally looked at Jack.

"Don't do this to Colin," she said. Her voice was thin, threading through the unyielding column of her throat. "I will agree to any reasonable custody terms you offer. Please. Don't put him through this."

Jack hesitated. He glanced at his lawyer, who imperceptibly shook his head.

"Ms. Carson," Harry said smoothly, sounding warm

and concerned, which angered her. A minute ago he hadn't even been willing to give her a name—she had been merely "your client."

"Ms. Carson, we don't have to tell the child just yet, if you would prefer to wait for the reports. The lab will be discreet. Colin doesn't have to know what we're looking for."

Jack turned to Nora suddenly, and she was surprised to see how cold his eyes were.

"Why are you fighting this, Nora? You know this won't *put him through* anything. What a joke. He'll be relieved to know that he is finally going to get an answer. That he is finally going to get *the truth.* He certainly hasn't been able to get it from you."

"Jack—" Harry Mathieson put out one well-manicured hand.

Jack shook his head. "No. I'm through dancing around this with legalese." He stood. "The test is scheduled for the day after Christmas. At 10:00 a.m., Harry will call Bill and give him the address and the details. Be there."

She stood, too. Their gazes locked. "If you do this, Jack, I'll never forgive you."

Jack laughed. It might have been the harshest sound ever uttered in her little living room.

"Well, at least you're consistent, Nora. But you know what? I think I'll live."

CHAPTER SIXTEEN

COLIN WAS SO NERVOUS his palms were sweating, and he had to wipe them on his pants. Good thing they were corduroy because they could absorb a lot of sweat without showing it.

It was his turn, any minute now. As soon as Jack got the mechanical roll loaded properly into the player piano, Colin would have to go on.

It wasn't the singing that scared him. He knew he had a pretty good voice, and he had learned the Killian Christmas song super well. He'd practiced it endlessly on his new guitar.

What freaked him out was the thought of all these people sitting around, listening to him. There must be fifty people here. He'd never sung in front of a big audience before.

Brad had reminded him that most of the old people at the nursing home were deaf anyhow, but that didn't help. Jack and Sean were here, too. And they weren't deaf. They sang really well, and they'd know if he messed up.

His mom smiled at him from her chair in the front row. She'd been really nice to him all day, the way she was when he was sick.

In fact, when he'd asked her if he could wear his lucky ring, he hadn't even really paid attention to her answer, he'd been so sure she was going to say no, like always.

But she'd said yes, shocking the heck out of him. He'd had to ask her to repeat it, just to be sure.

"Why not," she'd said, her voice sounding strangely sad. Colin figured it might be because she had to accept that he was growing up.

Or maybe it reminded her that someday soon she'd have to tell him the truth about his dad.

She still didn't look very happy, even though she was smiling at him in that encouraging way mothers always did. Colin wondered why she wasn't sitting with Sean and Jack and Patrick. She hadn't even spoken to them when they'd come in. Colin wondered if they were having a fight.

He hoped not. He had been planning to ask her if Jack and Sean could come over after the nursing-home party, for the marshmallow roast and games and stuff they always did on Christmas eve.

Right now, she didn't look like that would be okay with her at all.

He kept clearing his throat, trying to stay ready to sing, but Jack was taking forever with the piano.

"You've gotta baby an old lady like this, Colin," Jack said with a wink, "if you want her to do anything for you."

Colin felt his throat going dry. He looked around, trying not to let his nerves get to him.

The big recreation room at the nursing home looked really pretty, with red flowers on every table, colored lights at the windows and a huge Christmas tree in the corner, twice as big as Colin's tree at home. All the residents looked nice, too. They had dressed up special, because it was Christmas Eve and this was like a party.

Some of the girls who volunteered regularly had just sung a medley of Christmas music, and, even though they didn't sound that great, the old people had clapped like crazy.

Maybe Brad was right. Maybe they were all stone deaf.

"Finally! This roll is as old as time, and Lord only knows how long it'll last, but I think it might just see us through." Jack frowned at the piano, and he didn't look very confident. He patted the piano, as if for luck. "All we can do is try. You ready, Colin?"

Colin nodded. He glanced out at Mr. Killian, also in the front row, next to Sean. Mr. Killian raised his good hand. That was the "yes" symbol, which made Colin feel better.

Yes, Mr. Killian, was saying. *Yes, this is what I wanted. You can do it.*

"I'm ready," Colin said.

Jack sat down and started the piano. He pumped the pedals slowly, and the tinny, old-fashioned music swelled out into the room.

"When the world lay in tears, men imprisoned by fears," Colin began. It was a nice melody, and it was just right for his voice, not too high and not too low. He thought he sounded pretty good. Mr. Killian was smiling, even though he could do it with only one side of his mouth.

"An angel flew down, with a star in her crown." That note was pretty high, but Colin hit it perfectly. Out of the corner of his eye, he saw that Jack was staring at him, as if it surprised him to hear Colin singing so well.

Colin's heart got big with confidence and sudden pride. See? He might be crummy at the guitar, but he wasn't a total loser.

"And promised a new joy to come."

There was a pause here, while the player piano did a beautiful trilly thing. Colin wished he could have met Angus Killian, who'd written this song. He wondered what kind of man could write music that was both sweet and sad at the same time.

Colin sang the next verse even better, now that he wasn't afraid. He stood up straighter, which made his lungs get more air, and he could hold the long notes practically forever.

When he got to the chorus, with the title line "The starry skies sang lullabies," he saw Mr. Killian's eyes fill up with tears. Colin frowned, worried, but then Mr. Killian raised his hand again and nodded, just a little.

It was okay. Mr. Killian wasn't crying, at least not sad crying. He was just happy. Embarrassingly, Colin felt a stinging behind his own eyes. He took a deep breath and started to tackle the last verses.

Suddenly something terrible happened.

The player piano, which had been doing fine so far, began to make a disgusting noise. It was as if it was playing all kinds of wrong notes, all at the same time. It sounded crazy, really loud and mixed up, like a room full of cats screeching together.

Jack immediately stopped moving the pedals, to silence the awful noise. He looked at the roll.

"Oops," he said. "The thing must have decayed more than we thought." He turned to the audience. "I'm sorry, folks. Guess that's the end of the song."

Several people groaned their disappointment. Colin's

mom looked sad, but it was Mr. Killian who reacted the most violently. He began to writhe in his wheelchair, moving every muscle that was still under his control. He began to make that babbling noise that was the only speaking he could do.

Sean stood up and tried to calm his grandfather.

"Grandfather, don't be upset," he said. "The roll is just too old. We'll get it fixed."

But Mr. Killian kept shaking his head. He seemed to be staring only at Colin, and he kept raising his hand over and over.

Colin thought he knew what the old man meant.

"It's okay, Mr. Killian," he said. "I know the song by heart. I can finish it."

He began to sing again, this time all alone.

He sang straight to Mr. Killian, as if he were the only person in the room. He sang clearly, and with all the heart he could find. He and Mr. Killian locked gazes, and gradually, as the notes rolled over him, the old man's stiff, clumsy muscles seemed to relax.

Colin wondered why he had never before realized how sad this song was. The burning behind his eyes got worse.

On the last stanza, Colin almost lost his voice. He faltered, unsure what to do. But suddenly Jack was standing beside him. He put his hand on Colin's shoulder, and then, strong again, they sang the last lines together.

"For the lost and forlorn, a promise was born. And peace flew in on angel wings, bringing joy this Christmas morn."

When the last note died away, practically everyone was crying, including Colin.

But that was okay. Because, standing here with Jack

Killian's warm hand on his shoulder, for the first time in his life Colin felt completely at peace.

ALL THE COOKIES were baked, the presents bought and wrapped, the house glowing with lights. Tomorrow's turkey was thawing in the refrigerator and the potatoes were cut and ready to mash.

Colin was finally asleep. He'd insisted on taking the Christmas song's flawed piano roll with him. He might be dreaming of that song now, of his victory today, when his voice had moved the room to tears.

But Nora hoped his dreams had brought him home again. Perhaps he was dreaming about what lay inside the colorful boxes under the tree.

It should have been the perfect Christmas eve. She should have been crawling into bed herself, exhausted but satisfied that she'd done everything she could to make tomorrow a success.

Instead, Nora sat on the edge of her bed, fully dressed, staring at the floor, fighting panic.

She had twenty-four hours to stop Jack Killian from tearing apart her life.

What could she do? How could she stop him?

She lifted her head, letting out a small gasp.

Yes. That was it.

She could run away.

She could pull out her suitcase, pack her clothes, then go into Colin's room and do the same for him. She could wake him gently and tell him they were going to Maine to surprise Uncle Ethan, to celebrate Christmas with snowmen and icicles and sleigh rides.

Later, much later, she would break it to him that they were never coming back to Hawthorn Bay.

It was possible. Of course, she would miss it all—her little house, her friends, even the nonsense involved in being the mayor of this tidal marsh town. But she could start over. She'd lost things before. She'd lost Maggie and her father, and Heron Hill.

And Jack.

She knew how to recover. She knew how to bounce back.

She'd teach Colin how to do that, too. She'd teach him that home wasn't a town or a house. It was people. It was family.

It was love.

Love.

As the word echoed in her mind, she put her head in her hands and bit back a sob of despair.

Because she couldn't run away.

For Colin, all those important things—people, family, love—were right here, in Hawthorn Bay.

She'd seen it today, when Jack and Colin had stood together, singing. Their voices had blended perfectly, and those two blue-eyed, handsome faces had matched like mirror images.

But even those touching things were merely superficial connections. Much deeper, much more important, was the glow on Colin's face.

He belonged there.

He was a Killian.

She was almost ashamed to realize how little she'd understood the meaning of those words, until today. She'd thought of being a Killian as some kind of formula, some DNA code that mattered on paper, or in a courtroom, but nowhere else.

She'd believed that, because Colin's whole life had been spent in her care, he had become a Carson.

How wrong she was! He loved her, yes. And he had learned a lot of things from her—to love animals, to play games and play fair, to laugh a lot, to eat good food straight from the earth.

But his soul was pure Killian.

From the beginning, he'd responded to Jack's affection as instinctively as a plant turned toward the light. It wasn't just that he was starved for male attention. He soaked up Ethan's friendship, too, but there was a difference.

He liked Ethan. Ethan made him smile.

But he *needed* Jack. Jack made him whole.

It wasn't exactly *love,* which was too pat and conventional a word. It was more like—*belonging.*

Finally, the panic subsided. In fact, to her surprise she felt strangely calm.

She picked up the phone and dialed Stacy's number.

"I'm sorry to ask this on Christmas eve," she said. "But could you come over and sit with Colin for a little while?"

She paused, feeling the one last frisson of fear that came right before the leap into the empty air. Right before the long, bottomless fall. "There's something I have to do."

COLIN HEARD HIS MOM whispering to Stacy. He didn't sit up because she might hear him and realize he was awake, but he listened as hard as he could, hoping to make out even a few words.

He couldn't get much. She must really be trying to keep her activities secret.

He wondered if she was heading out to pick up that cool, bright blue fourteen-speed bike he'd asked for.

Momentarily, his hopes rose, but they dropped again immediately. He didn't really think so. It was too late for the stores to be open, and besides, she had told him they couldn't afford it.

She usually didn't lie about things like that. She wasn't the kind of mom who liked to tease you, make you worry, and then pop a big surprise at the last minute.

Brad's mom did all that, and Colin had always thought it was mean. Brad went through a lot of disappointment for nothing. And by the time Brad actually got whatever he used to want, he'd talked himself out of wanting it.

Colin listened some more. This didn't actually feel like Christmas whispering, somehow. That was always happy-sounding, with giggles. This sounded…

He couldn't think of the right word.

It sounded worried. Only worse.

He thought about getting up and going out there. What would happen, he wondered, if he just came right out and asked?

But some prickly kind of instinct told him to stay put. He heard the front door close, and then the car door. He knew it wasn't Stacy leaving because he heard the muffled thrum of his mom's engine start up, then stall, as it always did when it was super cold.

She started it again.

And then everything was silent.

After a couple of minutes, he heard Stacy's footsteps on the stairs. She came to the doorway of his room and looked in. He lay as still as he could and pretended he was asleep.

Deep in, slow out. A little snort for good measure.

"You faker," Stacy said. She sounded as if she was trying not to laugh. "You are so not sleeping."

He was busted, and he knew it. He sat up in bed and smiled at her sheepishly.

"I was trying to sleep," he said. He reached out and turned on his beside lamp. "I just can't."

She came in and sat on the edge of his bed. "Nobody can sleep on Christmas eve," she said. "Not with a room full of presents downstairs, calling your name."

That wasn't really why he couldn't sleep, but he didn't say so. He was excited about the presents, of course. But mostly he was just still wired up from today.

After the singing, after they'd gotten Mr. Killian back into bed, Colin had given the old man his present, the two pieces of gold Colin had found under the tree, all wrapped up in a special box and a shiny green ribbon.

They had been the only two in the room. Colin's mother had been waiting out by the car, and Jack and Sean had been in the recreation room, helping clean up.

"I'm sorry it's only two pieces," Colin had said as he'd taken the ribbon off. Mr. Killian couldn't do it himself, of course. "I really wanted to find the real treasure. I looked for clues in the song, like you told me, but this was all I could find."

Mr. Killian had raised his hand, as if to say it was okay, he wasn't disappointed. But then he pointed to the piano roll and sheet music, which Jack had placed on the bedside table. Mr. Killian grunted.

"I know," Colin said. "I'm sorry. I guess it got broken, through the years."

Mr. Killian shook his hand sideways.

"I don't understand." Colin picked up the music, and then the roll, and suddenly Mr. Killian moved his hand up and down again.

Yes, his hand said impatiently. *Yes. Yes.*

"You want me to take this?"

Yes.

"Did I understand you right before? Do you think this has something to do with the gold? This song?"

Yes.

The nurse came in then and told Colin it was time for him to leave. Colin knew that sometimes Mr. Killian needed privacy, like for baths and the bed pan and everything, so he didn't argue. He put the piano roll under his arm, folded the sheet music into his pocket and smiled at the old man in the bed.

"Merry Christmas, Mr. Killian," Colin said. "And don't worry. I'll keep looking."

All night long, while he and his mom had played Scrabble, and had roasted marshmallows and listened to Christmas CDs, he'd really been thinking about Mr. Killian's song.

He'd promised he would keep looking, but what else could he do? He'd gone over and over every word of the song, until his head hurt. He'd already tried every kind of code he could think of.

Morse code, cryptograms, anagrams, code wheels. He'd even ironed the sheet music, like in the movies, to see if an invisible message would appear.

He'd researched codes on the Internet for so many hours that his mother had gotten nervous and had given him a lecture about visiting inappropriate sites and ex-changing e-mails with strangers—a lecture she'd al-ready given him years ago. Like he'd be that dumb.

Still, nothing panned out.

The truth was, Colin was getting tired of beating against a door that wouldn't open. Even if he found the gold, he wouldn't get any of it himself.

And neither would Mr. Killian, really. He was an old man. What difference would it make to him if they found the gold now? He couldn't go out and buy a cool new car, or fancy clothes, or a fast boat.

But for whatever reason, Mr. Killian did seem to care. And Colin hated to let him down. What if he went to the nursing home tomorrow, or the next day, and Mr. Killian had died?

Wouldn't he feel bad then, if he'd given up looking?

He frowned over at Stacy. She was nice, but he wasn't sure how good she was with puzzles. His mom would be better—except that Colin's instincts told him his mom wouldn't like it if she found out what he'd been up to.

He guessed Stacy was better than nothing. She liked history, especially Killian history. Maybe she would bring new ideas.

Maybe she'd think of something Colin had over-looked.

He reached under the covers and pulled out the piano roll and the crumpled piece of sheet music.

"Stacy," he said slowly. "Can you keep a secret?"

CHAPTER SEVENTEEN

2006

PATRICK STOOD IN THE Sweet Tides drawing room and laughed like a demon. He laughed until his chest ached, until the casement windows shimmied and threw trembling prisms onto the walls.

He was ninety years old, and he'd seen a lot of Fate's best and cruelest tricks. He'd seen the beautiful things that appeared out of nowhere, and disappeared the same way. He'd seen the vanishing money trick, the loaded dice trick, the keep-away shell game, the helpless woman who endured being sawed in half, then sawed in half again.

But this trick beat them all. This, he had to admit, was the pièce de résistance.

He looked down at the thick bar of gold bullion he held in his hands. It gleamed, as splendid as the day it had been minted. The years, which had turned Patrick's hands into weak, knot-knuckled old man's claws, had meant nothing to this bar of gold.

Six months ago, when Ginny had still been alive, when he could have bought her something beautiful to make her smile, or traveled to the Tibetan mountains to seek a magic doctor to make her mind whole again, he would have killed to find this gold.

Now it meant less than nothing.

That was Fate's final trick. Now that Patrick no longer gave a damn about it, Fate had pulled this golden rabbit out of its top hat and flourished it in his face.

And, like all the best tricks, the answer had been right in front of his eyes all the time. Right there, in his father's music. He remembered the day his father had warned him not to mock his creations, for they held the key to the family fortune.

Oh, so clever, the words that said everything—and nothing.

Angus had been Fate's smiling assistant.

Look over here, no, over there. Look until your heart breaks. Look until it's too late.

Patrick laughed again. He laughed until he cried.

He felt tired, too tired to hold the heavy bar. He set it carefully back into its secret niche, then sat down himself, in one of the silk-covered drawing room chairs. He felt dizzy suddenly, from the shock, no doubt.

And his head hurt. His laughter had been too wild, too unrestrained.

He needed to settle down. He needed to think what he should do next.

Perhaps he should tell Sean and Jack. They were good boys. When they were little, all three generations of the family had lived together at Sweet Tides. The boys had loved him. They'd sought him out, to play and laugh and cuddle. It had meant everything to him.

But Kelly had hated it. He hadn't wanted to share his sons with their grandfather. And Kelly hadn't wanted his crazy mother to be around the boys, either, though he must have known full well that Ginny had been a danger only to herself.

Still, that's what Kelly had called her, "my crazy mother."

Patrick couldn't stay after that.

It had been time to go, anyhow. Sweet Tides and the legend of the treasure had begun to dominate Ginny's nightmares. She'd imagined that there were ghosts here, ghosts of the slaves who'd worked this plantation two hundred years ago, creating the fortune in the first place. And ghosts of the Confederate soldiers who had died, needing guns and boots, for want of the Killian gold.

So he had taken her away, to a dull, safe house fifty miles inland, where she'd seemed a little better. Over the decades, even science had made strides. Patrick had found a doctor who knew about bipolar disorder, and who knew which medications to prescribe. As long as Patrick had made sure she'd taken them, things hadn't been so bad.

She'd been eighty-eight when she'd died. He'd seen her through, he'd taken care of her till the end. That was one trick he had refused to let Fate play. He had refused to let anything separate him from the gentle, beautiful girl he'd always loved.

A pain stabbed through his skull, as sharp as a blade. He felt confused. Was he dreaming the pain? He had been talking about magic tricks, and now he felt like the man in the cabinet, with the magician shoving knives into his head.

Or was there one of the ghosts in the room right now? Had he summoned it, by finally finding the gold?

Maybe Ginny hadn't been as crazy as everyone had said. Maybe she'd been the only sane one. The only one who'd known that the gold had cursed them all, right from the beginning.

Yes, he'd better tell Sean and Jack where the gold was hidden. They were good boys. They'd know what to do.

They would be back soon. He hoped they would hurry.

Patrick put his head in his hands and cried out from the pain.

He couldn't remember where the boys had gone. Maybe out hunting for tadpoles, or riding their bikes down the long, tree-lined drive.

But he knew they'd come for him. He tilted forward and felt himself hit the floor.

They would come. They were good boys.

Maybe they'd even come in time.

IT WAS AFTER eleven o'clock when Nora climbed the steps of the front porch at Sweet Tides and knocked on the door.

The Christmas moon silvered the big columns that flanked her, and winked here and there at a window, but otherwise the house looked completely dark.

Maybe Jack wasn't at home.

Surely Fate wouldn't be that cruel. Now that she'd finally found the courage to come...

She shivered and knocked again.

Finally she heard movement inside, and then the sound of a lock being turned. With a creak, the door opened.

"Nora?" Jack stood at the threshold, illuminated by a beam of moonlight. Cavernous black-and-gray shadows stretched out behind him. "What are you doing here?"

"I'm sorry to come so late," she said. "But I need to talk to you."

He hesitated, his hand on the edge of the door. He looked like a charcoal drawing, in this colorless light. His white turtleneck sweater, his black hair, his dark jeans, the silver glint as his eyes moved over her. It was all slightly unreal.

"It's cold, Jack. May I come in?"

For a second, she thought he might refuse. But he stepped away from the door and held out a hand, waving her in.

He shut the door behind her and flicked on the overhead chandelier. The hallway burst into brilliant light. She blinked, trying to adjust.

"Are you sure this is a good idea?" He leaned against the brick archway that led to the drawing room, looking darkly amused. "Wouldn't Bill Freeman have a stroke if he knew you were here?"

"Probably."

She wished Jack didn't look so distant and cynical. It made him seem like a different person, a person she barely knew at all.

"But it doesn't matter what Bill Freeman wants. I have something I need to tell you."

He shrugged. "Okay." He put out his hands. "Let me take your coat."

She turned around and let him ease the black wool coat from her shoulders. Underneath, she still wore the cheerful red skirt and sweater she'd put on for the nursing-home party. She even still wore the same dangling, tinkling earrings shaped like colorful ornaments.

She wished she'd taken those off. They were inappropriately festive, considering the story she had come here to tell.

"Do you want to sit down? There are some comfortable chairs in here. Sean's upstairs, probably asleep. We won't be disturbed."

He reached around the brick arch and found the light plate. Again, a crystal chandelier flared, and the silent gray drawing room came to life.

It was a beautiful space, she observed with some surprise—elegant and spare and well cared for.

She'd never been inside this house, until Jack had brought her here the other night—and that had hardly been a time for sightseeing. She had been entirely focused on the physical burn that had been threatening to consume them both.

Back when they were in high school, he had never invited her to Sweet Tides. She'd understood—his home life was not the kind you'd want others to witness.

He'd described it vividly enough. She could picture what Jack found here when he got home from school. More often than not, Kelly Killian would be drunk, passed out in the gun room. Bridey, Jack's mother, would be sitting alone in this drawing room, rearranging her glass unicorns, or perhaps upstairs in her bed, softly crying.

In Nora's imagination, the interior of Sweet Tides had always looked tragic, shattered, dirty and lost. But the room she saw before her now, framed by this graceful arch, was lovely, with gorgeous plasterwork around the ceiling, doorways and windows. It had only a few pieces of furniture, but each one was a thing of beauty.

She was especially struck by how peaceful the room felt. A yellow-gold silk upholstery covered the chairs, and a warm green-and-blue theme was carried out in the rugs, drapes and paintings.

He led her to one of the gold chairs. She sat obediently, though she noticed he remained standing, maintaining the dominant position.

The strategy didn't bother her. Just by coming here, she had relinquished any claim to power. And the minute she opened her mouth, Jack would realize that he held complete control of the situation in his own hands.

The question that paralyzed her with fear was a simple one.

What would he do with that power?

He seemed content to wait for her to find the words to begin. He stood by the mantel and watched her with a hooded gaze.

She began simply, as she'd promised herself she would.

"I need to tell you the truth about Colin," she said.

His brows flicked together, his first sign of impatience. "I already know the truth about Colin."

"Not all of it." She folded her hands in her lap and commanded herself not to betray her fear by wringing them, or braiding them together with white knuckles, or letting them tremble. "It's true, Colin is your son."

"Yes," he said. "I know."

"But he isn't mine."

As she'd known it would, that statement rocked him.

He stood up straighter. His frown deepened, slowly digging a heavy line between his brows as he stared at her.

He didn't say anything at all. It was as if she'd robbed him of the power to think, much less speak.

"I know you thought I was just playing games when

I asked you not to schedule a paternity test. I could tell that your lawyer was suspicious, and assumed that we were pulling some kind of trick. But I wasn't. I knew that, if you let the test go forward, you would discover that there's no way Colin could be my natural child."

"That's insane," he said finally. "How could I be the father if you're not—"

"Maggie Nicholson is Colin's mother." She had to say it quickly. She had to get it out. "Maggie. Not me."

He shook his head. "That's impossible."

"No. It's true. Maggie is his mother. She *was* his mother, I mean. She died giving birth to him. As she was dying, she asked me to take him. She was desperately afraid that her family would find out and try to get hold of him. Apparently her father—"

She broke off, swallowing hard. "Her father was abusive. I never knew that, until it was too late. But she feared for Colin's safety, if he ended up with her parents. She begged me to make sure that didn't happen. And I promised her I'd protect him. I promised her I'd bring him up as my own."

Jack moved away from the mantel. He crossed the room and stood next to her chair. He towered over her.

"What you're saying is impossible. If Maggie is Colin's mother, then I cannot be the father. I never in my life laid a hand on Maggie Nicholson."

She shook her head sadly. "Are you sure about that, Jack?"

"Of course I'm—"

But finally the truth pierced the armor of his disbelief. In the middle of his denial, his face went slack, and his eyes lost their focus as they returned, in his mind, to that night.

"Oh, my God," he said.

He reached out and grabbed the back of her chair, as if he had stumbled on something that almost brought him to his knees. "That night. It was… I made love to Maggie?"

"Yes," she said. "She and I went together to England, shortly after you left town. When we were there, she told me she was pregnant, but she always refused to discuss the father. Before we left Hawthorn Bay, she'd been seeing a married man, so I assumed he must be the one. It explained why she didn't want to tell me, so I didn't push. I never once considered the possibility that she—that you…"

She couldn't finish the sentence. Even now, years after the gut-wrenching blow of the truth, she could hardly believe it had happened.

Apparently Jack couldn't believe it, either. His eyes had narrowed.

"Nora, you're not lying to me, are you? I can't imagine how you'd think this could help your case, but… You're not making this up?"

"I wish I were, Jack. You don't know how many times I've wished I could go back and change what happened that night. If I had come down to say goodbye, I truly believe that you—you and Maggie—"

She stopped herself because she was on the edge of tears. She had vowed that she wouldn't cry while she told this story. It was melodramatic enough as it was.

And besides, in the end it wasn't her tragedy. It was Maggie's.

And it was Colin's tragedy, too. He'd lost both mother and father that terrible day.

"My god, how you must have hated me," he said.

"When you realized what I'd done…" He ran his hand through his hair. "No wonder you didn't try to get in touch with me. No wonder you didn't tell me."

"No, that wasn't because I hated you—"

"Nora." Jack looked at her with dark eyes. "We're beyond lying, aren't we? Even to ourselves?"

She held her breath. It was true, she saw that now. Deep inside, she didn't believe he deserved to have this child, not after what he'd done. He had exploited Maggie, betrayed Nora, and then he had simply disappeared. He hadn't even called.

"All right, it's true," she admitted. "I was very angry. You see, I thought you knew what you'd done. I thought it was unforgivable that you hadn't even checked on her. I understood why you didn't call me. But I thought you should have phoned Maggie. Just to be sure she was all right. Just to be sure she wasn't…"

"Yes," he said. "You believed that, because I was a two-timing heel, I had no right to know about my son."

He sounded so cold. It took her breath away.

"I didn't know he was yours at first, Jack. You have to believe that. I suspected everyone on this earth but you. I even called the man Maggie had a relationship with before, the married man. He said it couldn't be his, that he and Maggie had broken it off, and the timing just made it impossible."

"And then?"

"And then I assumed I was safe. It was years before Colin grew so like the Killians that I finally had to face the truth. By the time I did, I…I had been his mother for so long I couldn't bear the thought of losing him."

He started walking again, toward the mantel, but it

was an aimless journey. He had no purpose there—it was merely as if he was too upset to stand still.

When he got to the fireplace, he turned.

"God, what a mess," he said. "What a terrible mess."

"Yes," she said. She lifted her chin. "But it's not my mess alone, Jack. I think it took both of us to create this tangle. And it's going to take both of us to make it right."

He didn't answer. He had put up his hand and was pressing his temples hard with thumb and forefinger.

She stood. She'd done all she could do. She'd told the truth. People always told you that the truth would set you free, but that sure wasn't how it felt right now.

She felt bruised, and tired, and so vulnerable it terrified her.

She might have lost everything that mattered in her life.

The man she'd never stopped loving, and the son who was, quite simply, her heart and soul.

In the deep distance, she heard church bells ringing.

It must be midnight.

It must be Christmas.

"I'm going to go home now," she said. "Colin will be up early, eager to open his presents."

Still Jack didn't say a word.

"I know you're angry," she said. "And I don't blame you. We've hurt each other so much."

He laughed. "Is that how you'd describe it? Hurt each other? It's something of an understatement, wouldn't you say?"

"I suppose so." She tried to steady her breathing, which felt hot, with ragged edges. "But I know you, Jack. You're not a cruel person, no matter what people say. I'm not sure any of the Killians ever were as bad as people say. Sometimes human beings just get caught in situations where there's no way to keep from hurting somebody."

She moved toward the front door, pulling her keys out of her pocket. At the archway, she turned.

"Please, Jack. I know how you must hate me right now. I know how easy it would be to seize this chance for revenge. But please, please remember, I'm the only mother Colin has ever known. Don't break his heart just for the pleasure of breaking mine."

CHAPTER EIGHTEEN

JACK CAME TO with a flash of adrenaline that ran through his veins like fire along a fuse.

Nora was leaving.

And he hadn't lifted a finger to stop her. Was he insane? Was he going to let the only woman he'd ever loved walk out of this house?

He covered the drawing room in five steps, the hall in three. He caught her just as she pulled open the door.

"Nora, wait!"

She turned, and he saw that her cheeks were wet with tears.

"Oh, God, Nora," he said. He pulled her into his arms. "Don't cry, sweetheart."

Her body was stiff. She held herself away from him as if she were afraid of him, as if she wanted to run. He was such a fool, such a slow-witted fool! He'd let himself get so lost in his own bewildered thoughts that he hadn't paid attention to her anguish.

"Nora, listen to me," he said. "I don't know what to say. I don't even know what to think. I can't wrap my mind around all of this yet, but if you say Maggie is Colin's mother, then I believe you."

"It's true," she said wearily. "I've told you everything. Do the paternity test if you want it in black and white. I won't fight you."

He shook his head. "I told you, I believe you. The only question we have now is, what are we going to do about it?"

The tears started to flow again.

"Damn it," she said, brushing at the shining tracks. "I hate being so weak. I'm not weak, really. It's just that...if I lose Colin—"

"Weak?" He smiled. "After what I've just learned, I'd say you're the strongest woman I ever knew. You found out that the man you loved betrayed you with your best friend, and yet you took the child of that union and brought him up as your own. You brought him up in a home filled with love and happiness and loyalty. Not weak, Nora. Not hardly."

She frowned, as if he weren't making sense.

"What are you saying, Jack?" She blinked hard, to press away the tears. "Are you saying you can possibly forgive me for not telling you?"

"Forgive *you*?" He wiped the dampness from her cheeks gently. "Nora, listen to how absurd that is. I'm the one who sinned here. Not you. No, my love, I'm asking if you can ever forgive me."

She seemed lost, as confused as if he were speaking another language. But on some subconscious level she must have understood him because he felt her relax, just a little.

The air out here was freezing, but he was hardly aware of it. He felt only the vulnerable warmth of her body. He wanted to bring her closer, to wrap his arms around her and protect her from the cold. To protect her from everything.

But she wasn't ready for that yet.

She was still afraid of him. She was afraid of his

blood tie to Colin, of what that might mean in a courtroom.

He had so much to tell her first, so many promises to make.

He needed to make her feel safe again.

"Nora, I love you. We'll make this work, I promise. We'll find a way."

She looked hard into his eyes, her own gaze still cautious and afraid. "I need to know, Jack. Are you going to try to take him away from me?"

He shook his head slowly. "Never. How could I? It doesn't matter what the DNA says. You're his mother."

"I've tried to be," she said in a quiet voice. "I couldn't have loved him more, even if he had been my own."

"I know," he said. "Anyone can see that. So stop crying, sweetheart. You have nothing to fear from me. You are his mother, and nothing will ever change that. All I can do is ask if you'll allow me to be his father."

She caught her breath, trying to hold back a sob. "You are his father."

"Not in any way that counts. I need your permission to become his real father. Will you let me do that? Will you let me become a part of his family? Of your family?"

She nodded. Her lips trembled, but he saw that she was struggling to prevent any more tears from falling.

"Of course I will," she said. "He needs you. When I saw you singing together today, I knew. He doesn't understand it himself yet, but he knows you make him happy. You make him complete."

The enormity of it all swept over him. That spunky, amazing little boy was his own son. And he *needed* Jack.

What if he couldn't fill those needs?

What if, because he knew nothing, absolutely nothing, about being a good father, he ended up disappointing him?

It was damned terrifying.

"I don't know what to do—how to be a father," he said. "You know how rotten my role model was. My own father was just about the worst there is."

"That doesn't matter," she said. "You're nothing like your father, Jack."

"I hope you're right," he said. The confidence he saw in her eyes gave him courage. "Maybe that's a place to begin. I'll give him what I didn't get. I know what I longed for, so I can start there. Bedtime stories and baseball games and laughter and hugs. I'll be there to listen when he's sad, and I'll be there to believe in his dreams."

"Yes," she said. "That's all he needs. Just be there. Just love him."

"I will." Jack pulled Nora closer. "And, if she'll let me, I'll love his mother. I'll make my son's wonderful mother so happy she'll never regret giving me a second chance."

The relief in her face was so bright it seemed to have its own warmth, like a sun inside her.

"Never," she said softly.

"And if you will say you love me, too, Nora, that will be all I need. I'll change. I'll become the best Killian who ever walked on this earth."

She smiled, and a hint of the old, confident Nora peeked through. "According to the folks around here, that wouldn't be very hard."

He grabbed her up and swung her around. He had too much joy to stand still.

"Say it," he demanded, holding her feet just above the ground. "I know you love me. I've never deserved it, but I've always known you did. That's my miracle. That's why I won't be my father."

But she didn't get the chance to answer. Just as she looked up at him, her lips parted, a car came tearing down the drive, honking furiously.

Someone was hanging out of the window, waving and hollering.

Jack set Nora down and moved to stand in front of her. He had no idea who this was, but anyone who drove up to a stranger's house like that on Christmas eve at midnight was either drunk, or crazy, or both.

When the car screeched to a halt just in front of the steps, he finally recognized it. It was Stacy Holtsinger's blue sedan.

Nora raced down the stairs to meet them. "Stacy! Is Colin all right?"

He certainly seemed to be. His was the hollering body hanging out of the passenger's side window. He wiggled himself free and plopped onto the ground without ever opening the door.

"Mom!" He was practically screaming. He clutched a disorderly snarl of paper to his chest. "Mom, I know where the gold is!"

"Keep it down, Sherlock," Stacy said as she got out the other side, much more sedately. But Jack could tell that she, too, was excited. "You're going to wake up the entire city."

"Jack!" Ignoring Stacy, Colin raced up the porch steps, holding out the tangle of papers. "It's so cool!

You won't believe it! The answer was here all along! All that digging was just a waste of time. It was in the Christmas song!".

Nora followed, as if they were tethered. Perhaps they were, Jack thought. At the heart.

She bent down and ran her fingers through her son's tousled hair. "Colin, what are you talking about?"

Jack intervened. "Umm—Colin and I have a few things we need to confess to you, too. Apparently Patrick asked Colin to help him try to find the gold. He's been working on it...ummmm..." He looked at Colin. "In his off hours."

Nora stood and gave him a stern look. "His off hours?"

"Mom!" Colin tugged at her sleeve. "You can lecture us later. Right now we have to go inside and get the gold!"

"He's not kidding," Stacy said as she joined them on the porch. "I know it sounds crazy, but I think the kid has found an honest-to-God clue."

A light went on in one of the windows above them.

"That's one rowdy party you're having down there," Sean said, sticking his head out to grin at them. "How come I wasn't invited?"

Colin craned his neck to see Sean over the upstairs balcony. "Sean! Come down quick! We know where the gold is!"

"You do?" Sean laughed. "Hang on. I'll be right down."

Colin refused to explain anything until he had everyone gathered around. Jack had to laugh at the boy's flair for drama. Colin knew he had the grown-ups' attention, and he planned to milk it.

Jack only hoped that it didn't end in crashing disappointment.

Finally, after what seemed to Colin forever, Sean made it downstairs. He must have known that Stacy was here because, gold or no gold, he'd taken time to brush his hair and splash on some cologne.

When Sean stood next to him, Jack sniffed dramatically and rolled his eyes.

"What?" Sean grinned. "The bottle fell over when I was getting dressed. So what?"

"Hey," Colin said, scowling at the two brothers to hush them up. "Okay. First I'm going to tell you how I figured it out."

He glanced at Stacy. "I mean how *we* figured it out. Stacy helped."

Stacy curtseyed with a smile. "I just figured out how to open the music roll. The genius was all yours, Mr. Holmes."

Colin laughed. "So here's what happened. Mr. Killian gave me this box of his dad's music. He seemed really riled up about it. And when we were alone, he kept trying to say something. It sounded like the word *treasure*."

"You could understand something Patrick said?" Sean sounded incredulous.

"Yeah," Colin insisted, his chin squaring. "If you listen, you can get a lot of the words. He's getting better, whether you guys believe it or not."

Sean glanced at Jack, then subsided. They both knew how Colin clung to the hope that Patrick would recover from this stroke. He didn't seem to recognize that, at ninety-one years old, recovery was a long shot.

"So I started trying to figure out what the music

could have to do with the treasure. I tried all kinds of codes and secret messages and invisible ink and stuff like that, but I got nothing. Once, I thought I found a clue in the lyrics, so I went out to Sweet Tides and started digging—"

Nora made a sound, but Jack grabbed her hand and squeezed it reassuringly.

"Later," he promised. She gave him a quick look, but she said nothing else.

"But I still didn't find anything," Colin continued. "I was pretty discouraged. But then today, when we were singing the song at the nursing home, it began to sound really weird, really messed up. Remember, Jack?"

Jack nodded. "Absolutely. Nearly blew out my eardrums."

"Mr. Killian seemed all upset, and he nearly had a fit until I agreed to take the music home with me again. That's what made me figure out where I'd been making my mistake. You see, I'd been studying the sheet music. But really the clue was here—"

He held up the crazy wad of papers he'd been clutching. "In the roll from the player piano."

"What?" Sean sounded confused. "How?"

For the first time in his whole life, Jack felt a frisson of hope. This actually might be leading somewhere… somewhere besides the usual dead end.

The player-piano roll was about ten inches wide and, once it was unspooled, maybe about seventy-five feet long. Colin gripped one end of it and let the rest fall to the floor.

"I'll show you," he said with a flourish.

He held up the first few inches. "See how there are these little open places, these little rectangles that have been punched out of the paper? That's what makes the notes play. When the right places are cut out, the song sounds right. But if the *wrong* places are cut out…"

He paused for dramatic effect. He fed the paper through his fingers, searching for the perfect spot. He found it, about halfway through the roll.

"If the wrong pieces are cut out, it's going to sound all messed up and nasty, the way it did today. So I began to wonder, what if someone had cut out the wrong pieces deliberately? What if they did it to leave us a clue?"

They waited, transfixed.

Colin beamed, delighted at the effect he was having on his audience.

"A clue," he said, "like this!"

He lifted the paper and held it up toward the chandelier, so that the bright light from the hundreds of bulbs and crystals shone through the paper.

You couldn't miss it. For a few lines, the punched-out rectangles were sparse, and seemingly random. Then, suddenly, they came close together and clearly spelled out words.

THE GOLD

IS IN

THE ARCH

"Oh, my God," Sean said.

Stacy applauded. Nora was silent, as if she still couldn't believe what was happening.

Jack met Colin's happy smile with one of his own.

"Way to go, kiddo," he said.

"Thanks." Colin dropped the piano roll onto the floor. "Now *you* guys have to do some thinking. Where do you have an arch?"

Jack laughed. He took Colin by the shoulders and

turned him around slowly, until he was facing the one and only arch in the entire mansion.

After that it was a free-for-all. With the evidence of the piano roll staring them in the face, no one doubted that the gold had been here once—and much more recently than the Civil War.

But was it here still?

Everyone poked and prodded and knocked and tugged at the bricks, hoping to find something, anything, that would indicate that the gold had not been moved from this resting place.

Jack let Colin sit on his shoulders to explore the highest bricks. Soon Colin would grow too tall, and it wouldn't be possible to do this much longer.

He smiled to himself, realizing how lucky he was that he'd found his son just in time to make this little memory.

"Darn it," Stacy said after about five minutes. "I was so sure it would be here."

"Hey, don't lose hope already," Colin called down from his perch. "Remember what my ring says. Riches go to the faithful!"

Sean had been squatting, working on the bricks nearest the floor, but at that he glanced up, surprise in his eyes.

Jack raised one brow and shrugged. "It's a long story," he said.

Sean's gaze flicked to Colin, then back to Jack. "Can't wait to hear it," he said with a smile.

Jack had been braced for ear-piercing shrieking and screaming, if anyone should actually get lucky enough to find anything.

But when the miracle happened, it came so quietly he almost missed it.

All he knew was that suddenly, every muscle in Colin's skinny legs went taut.

"Jack," he whispered. "Jack, this one is loose."

"Okay." He held Colin's knees as the boy reached way, way up. "Be cool. Go slowly."

Jack held his breath while Colin dug around. Sure enough, one of the bricks from near the top of the arch came cleanly away in his hands.

The tiny opening was dark and deep. Like many arches of the period, it was actually several bricks thick, so that the feature would fit neatly into the thick walls.

Colin's hands were small, so he worked with excruciating slowness. He handed one brick to Jack, and then another.

"Oh," Colin said, the sound soft and awestruck.

Jack looked up. The chandelier's light finally made its way inside the empty places.

Behind the painted bricks that Colin had removed was another row of bricks.

The only difference was this row was made of gold.

CHAPTER NINETEEN

The Next Year

JACK KILLIAN WAS EXHAUSTED.

Three hours of sleep just wasn't enough, not to face a houseful of people, presents, feasting and general Killian mayhem so early on a cold Christmas morning.

But darn it, the assembly instructions for Colin's bright blue, fourteen-speed bike had been written in some kind of diabolical Martian code. Jack and Sean had still been up, cussing and banging the wrench around, when the grandfather clock in the front hall of Sweet Tides had chimed three.

And then, wouldn't you know it? Jack's head had barely hit the pillow when Virginia Lily Margaret Killian had woken up and started whimpering.

"I'll be fine. You sleep," Nora had whispered, touching his shoulder.

Yeah, right. As if he would dream of passing up the chance to watch his beautiful wife breast-feed their daughter.

Ginny wasn't, to be perfectly honest, as beautiful as her mommy yet, with her scrunched-up red face and her patchy wisps of silky black hair. She was only two months old. But when the baby opened her blue eyes and stared dreamily up at Nora while she nursed, Jack saw what was to come.

She would be lovely and smart and stubborn and sweet. And, if Jack Killian could possibly manage it, she would be the happiest little girl who ever lived.

"Dad, you're zoning out! Come on, open it! It's from Uncle Ethan!"

Jack rallied, blinking away the sleepy haze. Colin had just tossed a present in his lap, a small box covered in shiny blue paper. He peeled away the wrapping.

"Guitar picks?" He grinned up at Ethan. "You sure these aren't for Colin?"

Ethan shook his head. "Nope. They're to go with…" He reached around behind his armchair and pulled out a beautiful honey-pine acoustic guitar. "This! I figured you and Colin could start a band."

Laughing, Jack accepted the guitar and immediately began plunking out a few god-awful chords. Everyone groaned.

"I'm serious," Ethan said, pretending to be offended. "You'll become superstars, and then you can replenish the Killian coffers, which definitely need it, since you were fools enough to give the gold away."

"Not fools," Patrick said carefully. His speech was improving every day, but he still had to work at some sounds. "Smart. The gold was cursed."

Sean, who was sitting next to his grandfather, patted his shoulder approvingly. Then Sean caught Jack's eye and smiled.

They'd spent a whole lot of time trying to decide what to do with the three hundred bars of gold bullion they'd found stashed inside that arch. At first, they'd been caught up with the usual daydreams—yachts, mansions, trips around the world. Jack wanted rubies and diamonds for Nora. Sean wanted a doctorate for Stacy. They all wanted a college fund for Colin.

But in the end they'd realized they didn't need any of that. They all made decent money in their careers, and Nora had already provided a trust fund for Colin from the sale of Heron Hill.

With the help of Stacy's research, they'd pieced together the full history of the Killian men, and decided that, though there probably was no such thing as a curse, there definitely was such a thing as obsession.

And they didn't want any part of it.

They'd each kept one bar, to make one small dream come true, and they'd given the rest to charity. Everyone involved—Colin, Jack, Sean, Patrick, Nora and Stacy—had each picked their favorite cause, and the money had been divided equally among them.

Ethan, who had returned to Hawthorn Bay so that he could give away Nora at the wedding, had immediately pronounced it the dumbest move anyone had ever made. But they'd laughed at him, too, too happy to care what anyone thought.

Maybe the curse was just a myth, but there was no denying that Sweet Tides seemed lighter and healthier since the gold was gone.

Of course, that might have had something to do with the life that filled it to overflowing. Nora and Jack and Colin lived there, and so did Sean and Patrick, and the round-the-clock nurses hired to help Patrick with his therapy.

The walls rang with the noise of a big family, with singing and music and laughter. The kitchen bubbled with Nora's jams. The stables had been remodeled into a duplex that housed both Sean's estate sales and Jack's new law office—all with the unanimous permission of the Hawthorn Bay city council.

Nora fell in love with the gardens, and in the spring she'd coaxed new life out of the old wisteria and jasmine and gardenias. In the summer, the house had exploded with roses.

And in late October, when the first Killian daughter in more than two hundred years had been born, yowling her importance and waving her perfectly formed fingers and toes, even Jack had had to admit that the Killian luck had changed.

Ginny had more presents today than anyone—except maybe Colin, who had definitely cleaned up. Sean had given her a drum set and six sets of earplugs, for when the family couldn't stand the noise. Patrick had given her a framed picture of her great-grandmother, for whom she'd been named. Ethan, ever practical, had given her a certificate of deposit.

Colin had taken a long time to decide what his gift to his new baby sister should be. He and Jack had spent hours at the toy store together this past week, but it had been time well spent. Not because the final choice—a musical mobile that twirled pink-spangled ballerinas above Ginny's crib—was so inspired, but because of what Jack had learned by watching his son.

He'd learned that the damage their crazy situation had done to Colin's sense of security had not been permanent. He was going to be okay.

It hadn't been easy, this past year. Colin had been shocked when he'd learned the truth about his biological parents. He'd been ready for a new father—but the idea that Nora was not his "real" mother had unsettled him terribly.

Nora had been amazing, so patient with the boy, even through his tears and his tempers. She understood why Colin felt frightened, and she never pushed him. She just stood by, ready to resume their intimacy whenever he was.

Over the months, things had gradually calmed down. But still, Jack had secretly worried. Would the trauma leave permanent scars? Would it affect Colin's ability to trust? To love?

And would he resent the little baby girl whose entrance into the Killian fold was so uncomplicated? Would he envy Ginny's pure blood connection to Nora, and feel robbed of his mother even more?

But the tender care Colin had given the choice of Ginny's Christmas present, and the excitement with which he anticipated the family's holiday get-together had eased Jack's mind. Nora's wholehearted loving had worked its magic once again. This was a little boy who knew he was adored.

Jack had come home that night and told Nora all about it. For the first time since she'd told Colin the truth, she'd allowed herself the luxury of tears.

"Well, Daddy," she said now with a playful smile. "Don't you have anything for your little girl?"

Jack reached into his pocket and took out a small blue velvet box. He handed it to his wife, stealing a small kiss as he bent toward her. She smelled of baby powder.

Nora opened the present for the baby, who was sound asleep. Ginny seemed to have her rhythm down pat. Nap peacefully when the grown-ups were awake, scream bloody murder when they were trying to sleep.

It was a tiny golden unicorn on a thin gold chain, made from the one bar Jack had kept for himself.

Nora lifted the necklace out of the box. "Oh," she said, obviously enchanted. "It's beautiful."

He stroked his daughter's rose-petal cheek with the back of his index finger. "I hope she'll like it. Her grandmother loved unicorns."

Funny. Now that he had a daughter, Bridey's glass unicorn collection didn't seem silly at all.

He hoped Ginny loved things like that, things that stood for beauty and hope and mystery and dreams that don't ever die even though they don't ever come true.

After all the presents were open, and a heap of colorful paper and bows stood two-feet deep on the carpet, Colin asked for permission to leave.

He had his new video games to play, new sneakers to try on, a new MP3 player to load up. But what he wanted to do first of all was ride his bike, which had been the hit of the morning.

He raced out the minute he was released.

Laughing, and stepping over boxes and bows, everyone else moved the party into the kitchen, so that they could get the feast going.

Jack and Nora got there first. Ethan was bringing Ginny's basket, and he dawdled, talking baby talk to her in a ridiculously stilted way.

"That man needs a kid of his own," Jack said.

Nora laughed. "You're not going to be one of those guys, are you? Now that you've discovered the joys of fatherhood, you can't wait to recruit everyone else into your new club?"

"You bet I am," he said, unrepentant. He kissed her on the nose. "I think I'll start with Sean. Heck, if Stacy hadn't gone off to North Carolina to get her PhD, I might have had a nephew on the way by now."

"Or niece," Nora reminded him. "But I think you're wrong about that. Sean is absolutely not ready to settle down."

She glanced toward the drawing room, where Sean lingered with Patrick and the extremely pretty young nurse.

"Stacy hasn't been gone six months," Nora said, "and he's already flirting with every female who walks through the door."

Jack heard the young woman giggle as they strolled toward the kitchen. At one of Sean's favorite stock jokes, no doubt. Sean did love a fresh audience for his old routines.

Jack chuckled. "Okay. You're right. He's going to need some more work before he gets to join the club."

"What club?" Sean came through the doorway. The nurse was right behind, still smiling as she rolled Patrick along.

Jack picked up a sweet potato and tossed it at his brother. "Potato Peelers Anonymous," he said.

Sean caught it one-handed. "Not what I'd hoped, but okay. I'm in."

Jack tossed him another. "Of course you're in. You know the rules. If you plan to eat, you'd better plan to peel."

With everyone pitching in, the work went fast. They finally got everything into the oven and sat down for a few minutes of rest before the next wave of duties.

Patrick had dozed off, and Jack, who felt about

ninety-one years old himself right this minute, wondered if he might get a chance to do the same.

But the kitchen door swung open with a loud bang, and Colin came tearing in. He was absolutely filthy, his hair standing out in all directions, and smears of dirt on both cheeks.

He was holding up something long and white that looked a little like...

"Is that a *bone?*" Nora looked horrified.

"Yep!" Colin waved it around triumphantly, as if he'd done something wonderful. Little clumps of dirt fell from the white stick as it flew.

Nora held out her hand. "Get that thing away from the food! In fact, get it out of the house, period."

"I can't, Mom," Colin said apologetically. "I've got to investigate it."

"What?"

"Investigate it. You know, find out whose bone it is, and then see if I can figure out who killed them. I'd better call Brad. I'll bet there are millions of old bones on this property. I'll just have to figure out where to look."

Nora put her head in her hands.

Sean and Jack started laughing.

Just in time to catch Colin's last statement, Ethan wandered in, dangling Ginny's basket from one hand.

"That's not a human bone," he said, in his most unequivocal doctor's voice. "That's the thigh bone from some small animal. Probably a dog."

"No way." Colin stared at Ethan, then stared at the bone. "How can you be so sure?"

"I know bones," Ethan said. He picked up a deviled egg, stuffed it into his mouth all in one piece and spoke around it. "Definitely not human."

Colin scowled ferociously. At that moment, he looked exactly like his great-grandfather.

Jack looked at Patrick, to see if he'd noticed. He had. Jack and Patrick exchanged a smile and a satisfied wink.

Colin turned to Jack, appealing the unwelcome verdict. "Dad? Is he right?"

Jack couldn't help it. It still gave him a little electric thrill every time the boy called him *Dad*.

"Of course he's right," Jack said. "Uncle Ethan knows his bones."

Colin's face fell.

"Rats." He stuck the bone in the hip pocket of his jeans and headed back out the door.

In the silence left behind, Sean began to chuckle softly. Jack joined him, then Patrick. Pretty soon the kitchen was ringing with laughter.

"It's not funny," Nora said, wiping her eyes. "Ever since he found the gold, he thinks he's Indiana Jones. He's going to keep digging and hunting, and God knows what he'll find next."

"Maybe a human skull," Ethan said around another deviled egg. "With a mysterious bullet hole between the eyes."

"Or a secret document proving that Killians were British double agents during the Revolutionary War," Sean suggested, a wicked light in his eyes.

"Gentlemen!" Nora groaned. "Please. Not another Killian curse."

Jack reached across the table and took her hand.

"Don't worry, sweetheart," he said. "We've got what it takes to get rid of any curse that comes our way."

"Oh, yeah?" She smiled at him. He loved that about her. Whenever he touched her, she smiled, as if it were not a choice but a reflex. "And what exactly do we have that is so powerful?"

He brought her palm to his lips and kissed it.

"We have each other."

* * * * *

KAREN TEMPLETON

Since 1998, three-time RITA® Award winner
(*A Mother's Wish*, 2009; *Welcome Home, Cowboy*,
2011; *A Gift for All Seasons*, 2013),
Karen Templeton has been writing richly
humorous novels about real women, real
men and real life. The mother of five sons
and grandmom to yet two more little boys,
the transplanted Easterner currently calls
New Mexico home. Visit her online at
karentempleton.com.

Look for more books from Karen Templeton
in Harlequin Special Edition—the ultimate
destination for life, love and family! There are
six new Harlequin Special Edition titles available
every month. Check one out today!

HUSBAND UNDER CONSTRUCTION

Karen Templeton

To my guys who've been there for me literally
and figuratively in every way that matters.
My gratitude for all of you knows no bounds.

CHAPTER ONE

IF YOU ASKED Noah Garrett's mama to describe her son in one word, she'd immediately say, "Daredevil," accompanied by the heavy sigh of a woman who'd seen the inside of the E.R. far, far too often.

Even as an infant, the boisterous New Mexico thunderstorms that sent his older brothers diving into their parents' bed made him coo in delight. While other toddlers howled in fright if a dog licked their faces, Noah would howl with glee. As he got older, no tree or roof was too high to climb—or jump off of—no bug too big or ugly to examine, no basement too creepy to explore, no night too dark to sneak out into when he was supposed to be asleep. And woe betide the erstwhile playground bully who dared mess with Noah. Or any of his brothers.

So the churning gut as Noah said, "I'll do it," while staring his father down across the banged-up desk in the tiny, cluttered office was highly uncharacteristic.

Not to mention unsettling. Especially as that churning gut had nothing to do with his father, who, yes, made Noah crazy on a regular basis but did not frighten him in the slightest. Behind him, on the other side of the open door, power saws ripped and hammers pounded and a half dozen employees shouted to each other in Spanish over the constant noise, more secure in their jobs than they probably had any right to be. And aside from his father, nobody was more determined to give them reason for that security than Noah.

Even if it meant sacrificing his own in the process.

Rubbing his chest, Gene Garrett lowered his big-bellied self into the rickety, rolling chair behind the desk to wrestle open the perpetually stuck top drawer and rummage inside for heaven-knew-what.

"Good of you to offer," he muttered as he searched, "but Charley's *my* friend. He'll expect me to do the estimate. Not you."

"Except," Noah said, "aside from the fact that Charley's not even going to be there, I'm gathering this is going to involve a lot more than new cabinets. Not to mention you're up to your eyeballs with that order you're installing in Santa Fe next week—"

"And you've got the Jensen project," Gene grunted out as he leaned sideways, the drawer swallowing up his bulky forearm.

"Finished that up two days ago. Next objection?"

His father looked up, his thick, dark brows bouncing over his gold-rimmed glasses like a pair of goosed caterpillars. "Could be a big job."

"Not any bigger than the Cochrans', I don't imagine. And I handled that just fine."

Gene again contorted himself to peer into the depths of the drawer, then reinserted his arm. "You and *Eli* handled it just fine. So no harm in waiting a week, until I'm free."

Despite his determination not to let the old man get to him, annoyance zinged through Noah. "And you know full well it's a miracle Roxie got Charley to even think about fixing up the place," he said, over a zing of an entirely different nature. "So she probably wants to present him with the estimate as a done deal. Strike while the iron's hot. You said yourself the house is in pretty bad shape—"

"Which is why," Gene said, finally righting himself, a half-empty bottle of Tums clutched in one scarred, beefy hand, "I can't let just anybody handle it."

This honoring your father thing? Sometimes, not so easy. "I'm not 'anybody,'" Noah said patiently. "I'm your son." Even when his father shot him a pained looked that said far more than Noah wanted to hear, he refrained from pointing out exactly whose idea it had been to begin with, to branch out from woodworking into full-scale remodeling services, anyway. Instead, he simply said, "Only trying to take the load off you."

One paw straining to pry the childproof cap off the bottle, Gene flashed a frown in Noah's direction. "Don't need you or anybody else to take the load off. You still work for me, remember?"

"Like you'd ever let me forget. Give me that," Noah said, leaning across the desk to snatch away the half-strangled bottle before his father hurt himself trying to get the damn thing open. "So let me put it another way—either let me run with this, now, or risk Charley's changing his mind and we lose the job altogether."

The bottle easily—and gratefully, Noah surmised—relinquished, Gene linked his hands over his belly. "And I don't suppose Charley's pretty niece has anything to do with you wanting this job?"

Focusing *real* hard on the bottle top, Noah snorted. "Roxie? Doubt she even likes me." Which, judging from her reaction to him the few times they'd run into each other since her return to Tierra Rosa a few months back, probably wasn't that far from the truth.

Never mind that the first time Noah'd clapped eyes on her he'd felt as if somebody'd clobbered him with a telephone pole. A reaction he'd never had to another female, ever. He didn't understand it, he sure as hell didn't like it, and no way was he about to admit that after a lifetime of rushing headlong into potential danger without a second thought—or, in most cases, any thought at all—the idea of working with Roxanne Ducharme made him break out in a cold sweat.

"There some reason you get up her nose?" Gene said, in the long-suffering way of a man whose sons had more than tested the concept of unconditional love.

"Not that I can recall." Which was the truth. And you'd think her completely unexplained antipathy would at least somewhat mitigate the telephone-pole-upside-the-head thing. You'd be wrong.

"Not even back in high school?" said Mr. Dog-with-a-Bone across from him, and Noah thought, *And you're going down this road why?* They were talking a dozen years ago, for cripes' sake.

"She was only there for that one year. And ahead of me at that."

"Never mind that you lived right across the street from each other."

"Doesn't matter." Noah handed back the open bottle, thinking that even with his crazy schedule back then, working afternoons and weekends at the shop whenever he didn't have practice or a game, he must have seen her at some point. But damned if he could remember. "I doubt we exchanged two dozen words the entire time.

She's a potential client," he said, directly meeting his father's eyes. "Nothing more."

After an I-wasn't-born-yesterday look, Gene tipped the bottle into his palm, shook out a couple of antacids. "Just remember—" he popped a pill into his mouth, crunched down on it "—the past always comes back to bite us in the butt."

Meaning, Noah wearily assumed, the string of admittedly casual relationships which somehow translated in his father's mind into Noah's overall inability to commit to anything else. Like, say, the business. Noah's knowing it backward and forward—having never worked at anything else from the time he was fourteen—apparently counted for squat.

Before he could point that out, however, Gene said, "Now, if you want to get Eli in on this one, too—"

"Forget it. Eli's so sleep-deprived on account of the new baby he's liable to pass out on Charley's sofa. Dad, I can handle it. And hey—what's up with popping those things like they're candy? You okay?"

Rubbing his breastbone, Gene softly belched before palming the few valiant, light brown strands combed over an age-spotted scalp. "Other than having two weeks' worth of work left on a project due in six days? Sure, couldn't be better. That burrito I wolfed down an hour ago isn't doing me any favors, either." Then he sighed. "And your mother's about to drive me nuts. And don't you dare tell her I said that."

Aside from the fact that his parents' making each other nuts was probably the glue holding their marriage together, considering how aggravated Noah was with his father for refusing to admit he needed help, he could only imagine how his mother felt. Still, sometimes playing dumb was the smartest choice. "About what?" he asked mildly.

Gene pulled a face. "About taking some time off." Releasing another belch, he rattled the Tums. "Days like this, a guy needs his buddies. But it's not like this is the first tight deadline I've pulled off."

"And if you don't start taking better care of yourself it might be your last."

"Oh, Lord, not you, too—"

"You even remember the last time you went on vacation?"

"Sure. When we went to visit your mother's sister in Dallas. Couple years ago."

"Five. And visiting family does not count. *And* you called home a dozen times a day to check up on things."

"I did not—"

"Got the cell phone records to prove it. And anyway, whether you think you need down time or not, you ever stop to think maybe *Mom* might like to get away? With you? Alone?"

After giving Noah a "Who *are* you?" expression, Gene grunted. "Donna's never said one word to me about wanting to go anywhere."

"When does Mom ever ask for anything for herself?" Noah shot back, suddenly annoyed with both of them, for loving too much and asking too little and putting up with far more crap from their kids than any two parents should have to. At which point he wasn't sure who he was, either. "Frankly, I don't think she even remembers how. If she ever did." Emotion clogged Noah's throat. "Yeah, she's worried about you. With good reason, apparently," he said, nodding toward the Tums.

Father and son exchanged a long look before Gene said, "I had no idea you cared that much."

Honest to God. "Maybe if you looked past your own issues with me every once in a while," he said softly, "you would."

Leaning back in his chair again, Gene regarded Noah with thoughtful eyes, as a light November snow began to halfheartedly graze the grimy office window. Then, on a punched-out breath, he said, "I just don't understand—"

"I know you don't. And sometimes I'm sorry for that, I really am. Other times…well. It'd be nice if you'd find it in yourself to accept that I'm not like you. Or the others. Now," he slipped his hands into his front pockets, "what time's that appointment? At Charley's?"

After another long moment, his father said, "Two."

Noah checked his watch, then snatched his worn leather jacket off the rack by the office door, grabbed a clipboard from the table under it. "Then I'd better get going."

As he walked away, though, his father called behind him, "You call me if you've got any questions, any questions at all. You hear?"

Only, as he struck out for Charley's house—barely two blocks from the shop—the glow from the small victory rapidly faded, eclipsed by the reality of what he'd "won."

Lord, Roxie would probably laugh her head off—assuming she'd find humor in the situation at all, which was definitely not a given—if she knew Noah's brain shorted out every time he saw her.

That his good sense had apparently gone rogue on him.

Not that Noah had anything against family, or kids, or even marriage, when it came down to it, he thought as he rounded the corner and headed up the hill he and his brothers had sledded down a million times as kids. For *other people*. If his brothers and parents were besotted with wedded bliss, cool for them. As for his nieces and nephews…okay, fine, so he'd kill for the little stinkers. But since, for one thing, he'd yet to meet a gal who'd hold his interest for longer than five minutes, and for another, *he was perfectly okay with that,* his reaction to Roxanne Ducharme was off-the-charts bizarre.

God knows, he had examples aplenty of healthy, long-term relationships. Knew, too, the patience, unselfishness, dogged commitment it took to keep a marriage afloat. Thing was though, the older he got, the more convinced he became he simply didn't have it in him to do that.

To *be* that, he thought with another spurt of gut juice as he came to Charley's dingy white, 1920s-era two-story house, perched some twenty feet or so above street level at the top of a narrow, erratically terraced front yard. In the fine snow frosting the winter-bleached grass and overgrown rosebushes, it looked like a lopsided Tim Burtonesque wedding cake. Even through the snow, the house showed signs of weary neglect—flaking paint, the occasional ripped screen, cement steps that looked like something big and mean and scary had used them as a chew toy.

He could only imagine what it looked like on the inside.

Let alone what the atmosphere was likely to be.

Noah sucked in a sharp, cold breath, his cheeks puffing as he exhaled. Maybe he should've given Roxie a heads-up, he thought as he shifted the clipboard to rummage in an inside pocket, hoping he'd remembered to replenish his stash. *Yes.* Although he'd quit smoking more than five years ago, there were still times when the urge to light up was almost unbearable. This was definitely one of those times.

Thinking, *Never let 'em see you sweat,* he marched up to the front door, plastered on a grin and rang the bell.

DING-DONG.

Wrestling a dust bunny with a death grip from a particularly ornery curl, Roxie carefully set the tissue paper-smothered Lladro figurine on her uncle's coffee table and went to answer the front door…only to groan at the sight of the slouching, distorted silhouette on the other side of the frosted glass panel.

Thinking, *Road, hell, good intentions, right,* Roxie yanked open the door, getting a face full of swirling snow for her efforts. And, yep, Noah Garrett's up-to-no-good grin, glistening around flashes of what looked like a slowly-savored chocolate Tootsie Roll pop.

Eyes nearly the same color twinkled at her when Noah, a clipboard tucked under one arm, lowered the pop, oblivious to the sparkly ice bits in his short, thick hair. His dark lashes. The here-to-forever shoulders straining the black leather of his jacket—which coordinated nicely with the black Henley shirt underneath, the black cargo pants, the black work boots, sheesh— as he leaned against the door frame.

"Hey, Roxie," he rumbled, grinning harder, adding creased cheeks to the mix and making Roxie wonder if dust bunnies could be trained to attack on command.

"Dad said Charley needed some work done around the house?"

"Um…I expected your dad."

A shrug preceded, "He had other obligations. So I'm your man."

In your dreams, buddy.

Although there was no reason, really, why being within fifty feet of the man should raise every hackle she possessed. Wasn't as if there was any history between them, save for an ill-advised—and thankfully unrequited—crush in her senior year of high school, when grief had clearly addled her brain and Noah had been The Boy Every Girl Wanted. And, rumor had it, got more often than not. Well, except for Roxie.

Twelve years on, not a whole lot had changed, far as she could tell. Not on Noah's part, and—apparently—neither on hers.

Which, on all counts, was too pathetic for words.

"Kitchen first," she muttered as she turned smartly on her slipper-socked foot, keeping barely ahead of the testosterone cloud as she led Noah through the maze of crumbling boxes, bulging black bags and mountains of ancient *Good Housekeeping*s and *Family Circle*s sardined into the already overdecorated living room.

"Um…cleaning?" she heard behind her.

"Aunt Mae's…things," she said over the pang, now understanding why it had taken her uncle more than a year to deal with her aunt's vast collections. Even so, Roxie found the sorting and tossing and head shaking—i.e., a box marked "Pieces of string too small to use." Really, Aunt Mae?—hugely cathartic, a way to hang on to what little mind she had left after this latest series of implosions.

Except divesting the garage—and attic, and spare room, and shed—of forty years' worth of accumulated…stuff…also revealed the woebegone state of the house itself. Not to mention her uncle, nearly as forlorn as the threadbare, olive-green damask drapes weighing down the dining room windows. So Roxie suggested he spruce up the place before, you know, it collapsed around their heads. Amazingly, he'd agreed…to think about it.

Think about it, go for it…close enough.

However, while Roxie could wield a mean paint roller and was totally up for taking a sledgehammer to the kitchen cabinets—especially when she envisioned her ex-fiancé's face in the light-sucking varnish, thus revealing a facet to her nature she found both disturbing and exhilarating—that's as far as her refurbishing skills went. Hence, her giving Gene Garrett a jingle.

And hence, apparently, his sending the one person guaranteed to remind Roxie of her penchant for making Really Bad Decisions. Especially when she was vulnerable. And susceptible to…whatever it was Noah exuded. Which at the moment was a heady cocktail of old leather and raw wood and pine needles. And chocolate, God help her.

"Whoa," Noah said, at his first glimpse of the kaleidoscope of burnt orange and lime green and cobalt blue, all suffused with the lingering, if imagined, scents of a thousand meatloafs and tuna casseroles and roast chickens. She adored her aunt and uncle, and Mae's absence had gouged yet another hole in her heart; but to tell the truth the house's décor was intertwined with way too many sketchy memories of other sad times, of other wounds. Far as Roxie was concerned, it couldn't be banished fast enough.

"Yeah," she said. "'Some' work might be an understatement."

Just as this estimate couldn't be done fast enough, and Charley would sign off on it, and Noah or Gene or whoever would send over their worker bees to make magic happen, and Roxie would get back to what passed for her life these days—and far away from all this glittery, wood-scented temptation—and all would be well.

Or at least bearable.

The Tootsie Roll pop—and Roxie—apparently forgotten, Noah gawked at the seventies-gone-very-wrong scene in front of him, clearly focused on the job at hand. And not even remotely on her.

Well…good.

"And this is just for starters," Roxie said, and he positively *glowed,* and she thought, *Eyes on the prize, cupcake.*

And Noah Garrett was definitely not it.

DESPITE THE STERN talking-to Noah'd given himself as he hiked up all those steps about how Roxie was no different from any other female, that he'd never not been in total control of his feelings and no way in hell was he going to start now— The second she opened the door, all dusty and smudgy and glowering and hot, all he knew was if the Tootsie Roll pop hadn't been attached to a stick he would've choked on the blasted thing.

Noah'd stopped questioning a long time ago whatever it was that seemed to draw females to him like ants to sugar, it being much easier to simply accept the blessing. So if he was smart, he mused as he pretended to inspect the butt-ugly cabinets, he'd do well to consider Roxie's apparent immunity to his charm, or whatever the hell it was, a blessing of another sort. Because if she actually gave him the time of day he'd be toast.

While he was pondering all this, she'd made herself busy sorting through a couple of battered boxes on the dining table on the other side of the open kitchen—more of her aunt's stuff, he surmised—affording him ample opportunity to slide a glance in her direction now and then. Maybe the more he got used to seeing her, the sooner this craziness would wear off. Back off. Something.

Long shot though that might be.

So he looked, taking in a cobweb freeloading a ride in a cloud of soft, dark curls that were cute as all hell. The way her forehead pinched in concentration—and consternation, he was guessing—as she unloaded whatever was in those boxes. The curves barely visible underneath the baggy purple K-State sweatshirt. Then she turned her back to him, giving him a nice view of an even nicer butt, all round and womanly beneath a pair of raggedy jeans pockets.

She jerked around, as if she could read his mind, her wide eyes the prettiest shade of light green he'd ever seen, her cheeks all pink, and for a second Noah thought—hoped—the world had righted itself again. As in, pretty gal, horny guy, what's to understand? Not that he'd necessarily act on it—one-sided lust was a bummer—but at least he felt as if he'd landed back in his world, where everything was sane and familiar and logical.

Except then she picked something off the table and walked back into the kitchen. "Here, I made a list of what needs doing so I wouldn't forget," she said, handing him a sheet of lined paper and avoiding eye contact as if she'd go blind if she didn't, and suddenly her attitude bugged like an itch you can't reach.

As Noah scanned the list—written in a neat, Sharpie print that was somehow still girly, with lots of question marks and underlinings—bits and pieces of overhead conversations and whispered musings, previously ignored, suddenly popped into thought. Something about losing her job in Kansas City. And being dumped, although nobody seemed clear on the details. With that, Noah realized that grinding in his head was the sound of gears shifting, slowly but with decided purpose, shoving curiosity and a determination to get at the truth to the front of his brain…and shoving lust, if not to the back, at least off to one side.

"This goes way beyond the kitchen," he said, and she curtly nodded. And stepped away. This time Noah didn't bother hiding the sigh. She wanted to hate him? Fine. He could live with that. Heck, he'd be happy with that, given the situation. Just not without reason.

Roxie's brows dipped. "What?"

"There some unfinished business between us I'm not remembering?"

The pink turned scarlet. Huh. "Not really. Anyway," she said with a pained little smile, "the kitchen is the worst. But the whole house—"

"Not really?"

If those cheeks got any redder, the gal was gonna spontaneously combust. "Figure of speech. Of course there's nothing between us, unfinished or otherwise. Why—?"

"Because it's kind of annoying being the target for somebody else."

Dude. You had to go there.

Roxie's jaw dropped. *"Excuse me?"*

Noah crossed his arms, the list dangling from his fingers, his common sense clearly hightailing it for parts unknown. "God knows, there's women with cause to give me dirty looks. If not want my head on a platter." At her incredulous expression, he shrugged. "Misunderstandings happen, what can I say?" Then his voice softened. "And rumor has it you've got cause to be pissed. But not at me. So maybe I don't appreciate being the stand-in, you know?"

After a moment, she stomped back to the dining room to dig deep into one of the boxes, muttering, "Now I remember why I left. The way everybody's always up in everybody else's business."

"Yeah. I think that's called *caring,*" Noah said, surprised at his own defensiveness. Even more surprised when Roxie's gaze plowed into his, followed—eventually—by another tiny smile, and he felt as if his soul had been plugged into an electrical outlet. Damn.

"No, I think that's called being nosy," she said, and Noah chuckled over the *zzzzzt.*

"Around here? Same difference."

The smile stretched maybe a millimeter or two before she dropped onto a high-backed dining chair with a prissy, pressed-wood pattern along the top. "It's a bit more complicated than that, but…you're right. And I apologize. For real this time. It's not you, it's…"

She rammed a hand through her curls, grimacing when she snagged the cobweb. "This hasn't been one of my better days," she sighed, trying to disengage the clumped web from her fingers. "Sorting through my aunt's stuff and getting nowhere in my job search and thinking about…my ex—and trust me, it's not his *head* I want on a platter—" A short, hard breath left her lungs. "I feel like somebody's weed-whacked my brain. Not your fault you're the weed-whacker."

"I'd ask you to explain, but I'm thinking I don't really want to know."

"No. You don't." Once more on her feet, Roxie returned to the kitchen, leaning over the counter to scratch at something on the metallic, blue-and-green floral wallpaper over the backsplash. "I promise I'll be good from now on."

"That mean I have to be good, too?"

"Goes without saying," Roxie said, after a pause that was a hair too long, before her gaze latched onto his Tootsie Roll pop. "Got another one of those?"

Lord above. Noah had gotten tangled up with some dingbats in his time, but this one took the cake. Not even the cute butt could make up for that. Even so, this could shape up—heh—to be a pretty decent job, so he supposed he'd best be about humoring the dingbat.

"Uh…yeah. Sure." He dug a couple extras out of his pocket. "Cherry or grape?"

"Cherry," Roxie said, holding out her hand, not speaking again until it was unwrapped and in her mouth, her eyes fluttering closed for a moment in apparent ecstasy. Then, opening her eyes, she grinned sheepishly around the pop. Mumbling something that might have been "Cheap thrill," she slowly removed it, her tongue lingering on the candy's underside, her gaze unfocused as she dreamily contemplated the glistening, ruby-red candy on the end of the stick, which she gently twirled back and forth between her fingers. "Can't remember the last time I had one of these," she sighed out, then looked at him again, her pupils gradually returning to normal. "Well. Ready to see the rest of the house?"

Holy crap.

Lust run amok Noah could handle. Electric jolts he could ignore, if he really put his mind to it. But the two of them together?

This went way beyond unfamiliar territory. This, boys and girls, was an alternate universe. One he had no idea if he'd ever get out of alive.

If he even got out at all.

CHAPTER TWO

THE LONGER ROXIE trailed Noah through the house, batting away the pheromones like vines in a jungle, the easier it became to see why the man had to fight 'em off with sticks. Not that he'd ever seemed to fight too hard. His reputation was well documented. But holy moly, the dude exuded sexual confidence by the truckload. As opposed to, say, herself, who did well to summon up enough to fill a Red Rider Wagon. On a good day.

Then she mentally smacked herself for giving in to the woe-is-me's, because nobody knew better than she that the road to hell was paved in self-pity. And, um, yearnings. Reciprocated or otherwise. Especially for a man she'd likened to gardening equipment.

Anyway.

"Wow. You weren't whistling Dixie about the condition," Noah said, practically leering at the peeling wallpaper. The worn wood floor. The disintegrating window sills—ohmigod, the dude looked practically preorgasmic as he fished a penknife out of his back pocket and tested a weak spot in a sill in the living room. Years of neglect eventually took their toll.

In more ways than one, Roxie thought, savoring the last bit of her cherry-chocolate pop as she tossed the bare stick in a nearby trash can. "How bad is it?"

Noah flashed her a brief smile probably meant to be

reassuring. "Fortunately, most of it seems to be more cosmetic than structural." Now frowning at the sill, he gouged a little deeper. "I mean, this is pretty much rotted out, but…no signs of termites. Not yet, at least." A stiff breeze elbowed inside the leaking windows, nudging the ugly, heavy drapes. "Windows really need to replaced, though."

"You can do that?"

"Yep. Anything except electrical and plumbing. That, we hire out." He glanced around, frowning. "Sad, though. Charley letting the house get this bad."

Out of the blue, a sledgehammer of emotions threatened to demolish the "everything's okay" veneer she so carefully maintained. "He didn't mean to. Basically, he's fine, of course, but his arthritis gets to him more often than he'd like to admit. Then Mae got sick and he became her caregiver…." First one, then another, renegade tear slipped out, making her mad.

"He could've asked for help anytime," Noah said quietly, discreetly looking elsewhere as he snapped shut the knife and slipped it back into his pocket. "My folks, especially—they'd've been more than happy to lend a hand. If they'd known."

Swiping at her cheeks, Roxanne snorted. "Considering neither Charley nor Mae said anything to *me,* this is not a surprise."

Noah's gaze swung back to hers. "You didn't know your aunt was sick?"

"Not for a long time, no. Although, maybe if I'd shown my face, or even called more often, I might have."

"You think they would've told you if you had?"

Her mouth pulled tight. "Doubtful."

"Then stop beating yourself up," he said, and she thought, *And you, stop being nice.* A brief shadow darkened his eyes. "My folks don't tell us squat, either. And all four of us are right here in town. In fact, a few years back my brothers and I figured out they were in the middle of a financial crisis they didn't want to 'burden' us about. Had to read 'em the riot act before they finally fessed up." He half smiled. "Keeping the truth from the 'kids' is what adults do."

A bit more of the veneer curled away, letting in a surprisingly refreshing breeze. "I guess." She sighed out. "I mean, even when I came home for Thanksgiving a couple of years ago and could sense something was off, that Charley was being more solicitous toward Mae than usual—and that was going some—they both denied it. I finally browbeat him into telling me what was really going on—" she swallowed back another threat of tears "—but whenever I suggested taking a leave of absence, or even coming for the weekends to help out, he refused." A humorless laugh pushed from her throat. "*Very* emphatically."

"Don't take this the wrong way...but Dad says Charley's known for being a little, ah, on the stubborn side."

"A *little?*" She chuckled. "Why do you think it took so long before he'd let me go through Mae's things? Or even think about fixing up the house? Although, considering it had only been the two of them for so much of their marriage, I honestly think they simply didn't want anything or anybody coming between them, even at the end. Especially at the end."

After a moment's unsettling scrutiny, Noah squatted in front of a worn spot on the flooring. "And that made you feel useless as hell, right?"

"Pretty much, yeah. But how—?"

"Like I said, I've been there." He stood, his fingers crammed into his front pockets, watching her, like… like he got her. And how ridiculous was that? He didn't even know her, for heaven's sake. The logic of which didn't even slow down the tremor zapping right through her. Well, hell.

"Maybe I should've been pushier, too," Roxie said, thinking she'd take remorse over this tremor business any day. "By the time your mother called me, Mae was nearly gone. And even then, even though Charley obviously couldn't handle things by himself that last week, I still felt in the way." She backed out of Noah's path as he moved into the dining room, rapping his knuckles once on Mae's prized cherrywood dining table before crossing to the bay window, a DIY project that hadn't exactly stood the test of time. "Like I was infringing on their privacy."

"Must be scary, loving somebody that much," he said to the window, and she had the eerie feeling hers wasn't the only veneer peeling away that day.

"Yes, it is," she said carefully, although her younger self probably wouldn't have agreed with him, when she still clung to the delusion that bad things happened to other people. "Then again, maybe some people find it comforting. Knowing someone's there for you, no matter what? A lot less scary than the alternative, I'd say."

Noah craned his neck to look up at her, a frown pushing together his brows.

"Sorry," she muttered, feeling her face heat. Again. "Not sure how things got so serious. Especially for your average estimate walk-through."

Getting to his feet, Noah's crooked grin banished the

heaviness in the room like the sun burning off a fog, sending Roxie's heart careening into her rib cage. "Oh, I think *average* went out the window right around the time you compared me to a weed-whacker. Besides… this is a small town. And your aunt and uncle were friends with my folks for years. So no way is this going to be your standard contractor/client relationship." He paused, looking as if he was trying to decide what to say next. "Mom and Dad've mentioned more than once how concerned they are about Charley."

Roxie smirked. "That he's turned into a hermit since Mae's death, you mean?"

"'Closed off' was the term I believe Mom used."

"Whatever. Again, I wasn't around to see what was happening. Not that I could have been." She sighed. "Or he would have let me. He tolerated my presence for a week after the funeral, before basically telling me my 'hovering' was about to push him over the edge."

"And now you're back."

"A turn of events neither one of us is particularly thrilled about."

"You think your uncle doesn't want you here?"

Once more rattled by that dark, penetrating gaze, Roxie sidled over to a freestanding hutch, picking up, then turning over, one of her aunt's many demitasse cups.

"I think…he wants to wallow," she said, shakily replacing the cup on its saucer. "To curl up with the past and never come out. I'm not exactly down with that idea. Frankly, I think the only reason he finally agreed to let me start sorting through Mae's things was to get me off his case."

"And *you're* not happy because…?"

Roxie could practically hear the heavy doors groaning shut inside her head. Talking about her uncle was one thing. But herself? No. Not in any detail, at least. Especially with a stranger. Which, let's face it, Noah was.

"Several reasons. All of them personal."

His eyes dimmed in response, as though the door-shutting had cut off the light between them. What little of it there'd been, that is.

"So is it working?" he asked after a moment, his voice cool. "You trying to get your uncle out of his funk?"

"I have no idea. Opening up to others isn't exactly his strong suit."

A far-too-knowing smile flickered around Noah's mouth before he glanced down at the notes, then back at her. "To be honest…this is shaping up to be kinda pricey, even though I can guarantee Dad'll cut Charley a pretty sweet deal. And I haven't even seen the upstairs yet. I mean, yeah, we could paint and patch—and we'll do that, if that's what you want—but I'm not sure there'd be much point if it means having to do it all over again five years from now. But the windows should really be replaced. And the cabinets and laminate in the kitchen. We can refinish the wood floors, probably—"

"Oh, I don't think money's an issue," Roxie said, immensely grateful to get the conversation back on track. "Not that much anyway. I gather his work at Los Alamos paid very well. And he and Mae lived fairly simply. And there was her life insurance…." Another stab of pain preceded, "Anyway. Wait until you get a load of the bathroom…."

FEELING AS IF he'd gotten stuck in a weird dream, Noah followed Roxie up the stairs, the walls littered with dozens of framed photos on peeling, mustard-striped wallpaper. Mostly of Roxie as a baby, a kid, a teenager. A skinny, bright-eyed, bushy-haired teenager with braces peeking through a broad smile. Funny-looking kid, but happy.

Open.

Then her senior portrait, the bushiness tamed into recognizable curls, the teeth perfectly straight, her eyes huge and sad and damned beautiful. Almost like the ones he'd been looking at for the past half hour, except with a good dose of mess-with-me-and-you're-dead tossed into the mix.

A warning he'd do well to heed.

This was just a job, he reminded himself. And she was just a client. A pretty client with big, sad eyes. And clearly more issues than probably his past six girlfriends—although he used the term loosely—combined.

Then they reached the landing, where, on a wall facing the stairs, Roxie and her parents—she must have been eleven or twelve—smiled out at him from what he guessed was an enlarged snapshot, taken at some beach or other. Her mother had been a knockout, her bright blue eyes sparkling underneath masses of dark, wavy hair. "You look like your mom."

Roxie hmmphed through her nose. "Suck-up."

"Not at all. You've got the same cheekbones." He squinted at the fragrant cloud of curls a foot from his nose, and a series of little *pings* exploded in his brain. Like Pop Rocks. "And hair."

"Unfortunately."

"What's wrong with your hair?"

"You could hide a family of prairie dogs in it?"

If he lived to be a hundred he'd never understand what was up with women and their hair. Although then she added, "But at least I have no issues with my breasts. Or butt. I like them just fine," and the little *pop-pop-pops* become *BOOM-BOOM-BOOMS*.

Before the fireworks inside his head settled down, however, she said, "Mae and Charley really were like second parents to me. Even before…the accident. If it hadn't been for them I honestly don't know how I would've made it through that last year of school. All I wanted to do was hole myself up in my bedroom and never come out. Until Aunt Mae—she was Mom's older sister—threatened to pry me out with the Jaws of Life. So I figure the least I can do for Charley is return the favor."

"Whether he likes it or not," Noah said, even as he thought, *How do you live with that brain and not get dizzy?* Because he sure as hell was.

"As I said. And the bathroom's the second door on the right."

To get there Noah had to pass a small extra bedroom that, while tidy to a fault, still bore the hallmarks of a room done up for a teenage girl, and a prissy one at that—purple walls, floral bedspread, a stenciled border of roses meandering at the top of wall. None of which jibed with the woman standing five feet away. Except the room made him slightly woozy, too.

"You like purple?"

She snorted. "Aunt Mae wanted pink. I wanted black. Purple was our compromise. Didn't have the energy to fight about the roses."

"Somehow not picturing you as a Goth chick."

A humorless smile stretched across her mouth. "Honey, back then I made Marilyn Manson look like Shirley Temple. But…guess you didn't notice, huh?"

A long-submerged memory smacked him between the eyes, of him and his friends making fun of the clot of inky-haired, funereal girls with their raccoon eyes and chewed, black fingernails, floating somberly through the school halls like a toxic cloud. One in particular, her pale green eyes startling, furious, against her pale skin, all that black.

"Holy crap—that was you?"

To his relief, Roxie laughed. "'Twas a short-lived phase. In fact, I refuse to wear black now. Not even shoes." Grimacing, Roxie walked to her bedroom doorway, her arms crossed. "I put poor Mae and Charley through an awful lot," she said softly, looking inside. "I even covered up the roses with black construction paper. Mae never said a word. In fact, all she did was hug me. Can you imagine?"

His own childhood had been idyllic in comparison, Noah thought as a wave of shame washed over him. Man, had he been a butthead, or what? "What I can't imagine, is what hell that must've been for you. I'm sorry. For what you went through, for…all of it."

"Thanks," she said after a too-long pause.

"So you gonna paint in there or what?" Noah said, after another one.

Roxie turned, bemusement and caution tangling in her eyes. "Why? Not gonna be around long enough for it to matter, God willing. So. The bathroom?"

Yeah, about that. Nestled in a bed of yellowed, crumbling grout, the shell-pink tiles were so far out of date they were practically in again. As were the dingy hex-

agonal floor tiles. And way too many vigorous scrub-
bings had taken their toll on the almost classic pedestal
sink, the standard-issue tub bearing the telltale smudges
where a temporary bar had been installed. And removed.

There was way too much pain in this house, like a
fungus that had settled into the rotting wood, lurking
behind the peeling wallpaper, between the loose tiles.
Noah pressed two fingers into one pink square; it gave
way—probably far more easily than the bad vibes clinging to the house's inhabitants.

At least he could fix the house. The other…not his
area of expertise.

"Since the tile's crap, anyway—" He flicked another
one off. "Why don't we do one of those all-in-one tub
surrounds? Although it wouldn't be pink."

Roxie leaned against the doorjamb. "I sincerely doubt
Charley would miss the pink. Although…could we install grab bars at the same time?"

Noah got the message. "They're code now, so no
problem."

"Oh. Good." Roxie sighed. "Charley's far from de-
crepit, heaven knows, but I know he wants to live on
his own, in his own house, as long as possible. So I'd
like to make sure he can do that."

Noah looked at her. "Because you won't be around."

A dry laugh escaped her lips. "To be honest, when
I was eighteen and stuck here…oh, Lord. I thought I'd
been consigned to hell. It was one thing to come for va-
cations, but I couldn't wait to get back to the city. I love
the energy, the way there's always something going on,
the *choices*. Heck, I even like the noise. So no, I can't
see myself calling Tierra Rosa home for the long haul.

Besides, I have to go where the work is. Work in my field, I mean. And so far, I haven't even been able to find anything close by—"

"Roxie? You up there?"

Blanching, she whispered, "Crap. He wasn't supposed to be back for another hour!"

"Should I hide in the closet?"

"Believe me, it's tempting," she muttered, then pushed past Noah to call from the landing, "Up here, Charley. With…Noah Garrett."

"Noah? What the Sam Hill's he doing here?" Charley said, huffing a little as he climbed the stairs, only to release a sigh when he saw the clipboard in Noah's hand. "Ah." A bundle of bones underneath badly fitting khaki coveralls and a navy peacoat probably older than Roxie, the older man turned his narrowed gaze on his niece. "Thought you'd pull a fast one on me, eh? Guess I fooled you. No offense, Noah. But it appears the gal was getting a little ahead of herself—"

"But you agreed to let me get an estimate—"

"I *said* I'd think about it. Honestly." Again, his gaze swung to Noah, as if he expected to find an ally. "What is it with women always being in such a rush?" He glared at his niece. "Bad enough you act like you can't get rid of Mae's things fast enough, now you want to change everything in the house, too? And what's up with *you* being here and not your daddy?" he said to Noah, who was beginning to feel as if he was watching a tennis match. "You sniffing around Roxie, like you do every other female in the county?"

"For heaven's sake, Charley—!"

"I'm only here on business," Noah said, getting a real clear picture of what Roxie must be going through, dealing with her uncle every day. If it was him he'd be looking for out-of-town jobs, too. At the same time the near panic in the old man's eyes was so much like what he saw in his father's—that threat of losing control, of everything changing on you whether you want it to or not—he couldn't help but feel a little sorry for the guy. "Because Dad's tied up. And Roxie only has your best interests at heart, sir. To be honest, I'm seeing a lot of safety issues here. And the longer you put off fixing them, the worse they're going to get. And more expensive."

"Well, of course you'd say that, wouldn't you? Since it's you standing to make money off me—"

"Charley," Roxie said in a low voice, gripping his arm until, mouth agape, he swung his pale blue eyes to hers. "Listen to the man. The house needs work. A lot of work. And if you don't take care of it you're not going to be able to stay here."

Her uncle slammed his hand against the banister railing. Which was missing a couple of stiles, Noah noticed. "I'm not leaving my house, dammit! And you can't make me!"

"Then let's get it fixed," she said gently but firmly, "or you may not have any choice in the matter, because no way am I letting you stay in a pit—"

"Choice?" Her uncle yanked off his snow-frosted knit cap and slammed it to the floor, freeing a forest of thick, white hair. "What kind of *choice,*" he said, wetness sheening his eyes, "is railroading me into something before I'm r-ready?"

"Oh, Charley…" On a soft moan, she wrapped her arms around him, her tenderness in the face of his cantankerousness making Noah's breath hitch. Then she let go and said, "I know this is hard. And you *know* I know *how* hard." She ducked slightly to peer up into his averted face, thin lips set in a creased pout. "But sticking your head in the sand isn't going to solve the problem. And we can't put it off much longer, since I have no idea when a job offer's going to come through. I'm trying to *help,* Charley. We all are."

Several beats passed before her uncle finally swung his gaze back to Noah. "It's really that bad?"

Catching Roxie's exhausted sigh, Noah said, "Yes, sir. It is."

Charley held Noah's gaze for another moment or two before shuffling over to a small bench on the landing, dropping onto it like his spirit had been plumb sucked right out of him—a phenomenon he'd seen before in older clients, his own grandparents. As somebody who wasn't crazy about people telling him what to do, either, he empathized with the old man a lot more than he might've expected.

"So what's this all gonna cost me?"

Noah walked over to crouch in front of him. "Until I run the figures, I can't give you an exact estimate. But to be honest, it's not gonna be cheap." When Charley's mouth pulled down at the corners, Noah laid a hand on his forearm. "Tell you what—how about I prioritize what should be done first, and what can maybe wait for a bit? Your niece is right, a lot of this really shouldn't be put off much longer. But nobody's trying to push you into doing anything you're not ready to do. Right, Roxie?"

When he looked at her, though, she had the oddest expression on her face. Not scared, exactly, but...shook up. Like she'd seen a ghost. At her uncle's, "What do you think, Rox?" she forced her gaze from Noah's to give Charley a shaky smile.

"Sounds more than fair to me."

Nodding, Charley hoisted himself to his feet again and crossed the few steps to the bathroom, while Noah tried to snag Roxie's attention again, hoping she'd give him a clue as to what was going on. No such luck.

"Mae picked out that tile when we moved in," Charley said, then gave a little laugh. "Said the pink was kind to her complexion..." He grasped the door frame, clearly trying to pull himself together. "She would've been beside herself, though, that I'd let the place slide so much, and that's the truth of it. Should've seen to at least some of it long ago. But..."

Noah came up behind him to clamp a hand on Charley's shoulder. "But change is scary, I know. Sometimes even when you want it—"

"Charley?"

Both men turned to look at Roxie, whose smile seemed a little too bright. "What's Mae saying about this?"

Charley sighed. "That I'm being a damn fool."

"And...?" Roxie prompted.

Flummoxed, Noah watched Charley tilt his head, his eyes closed for several seconds before he opened them again. "She says to tell Noah to get going on that estimate. So I guess, since I never refused my wife anything while she was alive, no sense in starting now."

Dear Lord.

Roxie walked Noah downstairs and to the front door, her arms crossed like she was deep in thought.

"Hey. You okay?"

"What? Oh. Yes." Finally her eyes lifted to his, but

almost as if she was afraid of what she'd see there. "Thank you."

"For what?"

She smiled slightly. "For blowing my preconceived notions all to hell."

Noah mulled that over for a second or two, then said, "I guess I'll get back to you in a few days, then."

"Sounds good," she said, opening the front door to a landscape a whole lot whiter than it'd been a half hour ago. Noah stopped, shoving his hands in his pockets. "I take it you humor the old man about hearing his wife?"

That got a light laugh and a shrug. "Who am I to decide what he does and doesn't hear?" Stuffing her fists in her sweatshirt's front pouch, she squinted at the snow. "Be careful, it looks pretty slippery out there."

The door closing behind him, Noah tromped down the steps, thinking the pair of them were crazy as loons, and that was the God's honest truth.

THROUGH THE LEAKY WINDOW, Charley watched until Noah was out of sight before turning to face his niece, up to her elbows in one of the moving boxes they'd hauled out of the garage he hadn't been able to park in since 1987. The way Mae's "collections" had clearly gotten out of hand was pretty hard to swallow. That he'd become an ornery old coot who'd hung on to his wife's stuff every bit as tenaciously as she had, just because, was even harder.

However, Noah's eyeing Roxie as if she was a new item on the menu at Chili's and he hadn't eaten in a week? That was seriously annoying him. Whether she returned his interest he couldn't tell—the girl never had been inclined to share her feelings with Charley, anyway, which he'd been more than okay with until now. But as close as he was to the boy's folks, and as much as he thought the world of Gene's and Donna's other boys, his Roxie deserved far better than Noah Garrett.

"I don't imagine I have to tell you to watch out for that one."

Seated on the brick-colored, velvet sofa—definitely Mae's doing—Roxie glanced up, the space between her brows knotted. "That one?"

"Noah."

With a dry, almost sad laugh, she shook her head and dived back into the box. "No, you certainly don't."

"Because you know he's—"

"Not my type."

"Well. Yeah. Exactly."

She straightened, a tissue paper-wrapped lump in each hand and a weird half smile on her face. Her let's-pretend-everything's-fine-okay? look. "So, nothing to worry about, right?"

Charley yanked his sleeve hems down over his knuckles, the icy draft hiking up his back reminding him how much weight he'd lost this past year. Even he knew he looked like an underfed vulture, bony and stooped and sunken-cheeked. That seriously annoyed him, too.

"Glad we're on the same page, then," he muttered, winding his way through the obstacle course into the kitchen for a cup of tea—what did he care if the color scheme was "outdated," whatever the heck that meant?—thinking maybe he should get a cat or something. Or a dog, he thought, waiting for the microwave to ding. Lot to be said for a companion who didn't talk back. Besides, he'd read somewhere that pets were good for your blood pressure.

As opposed to busybody nieces, who most likely weren't.

Dunking his twice-used tea bag in the hot water, Charley watched her from the kitchen door. He loved the girl with all this heart, he really did, but being around her made him feel as if he was constantly treading in a stew of conflicting emotions. Some days, when the loneliness nearly choked him, he was actually grateful for her company; other days her energy and pushiness made him crazed.

More than that, though, he simply didn't know what to say to her, how to ease her pain while his own was still sharp enough to scrape. That'd been Mae's job, to soothe and heal. To act as a buffer between them. Not that Rox was a moper, thank goodness, but every time he looked at her, there it was, his own hurt mirrored in eyes nearly the same weird green as Mae's. And at this point the helplessness that came with that had about rubbed his nerves raw.

Especially compounded with her being constantly on his back to clear out Mae's stuff, to "move on" with his life. As if he had someplace to go. Even as a kid, Charley had never liked being told what to do, whether it was in his best interests or not. Like now. Because, truthfully? What earthly use did he have for all of Mae's collections? Yet part of him couldn't quite let go of the idea that getting rid of it all would be like saying the past forty years had never happened.

He turned back to the counter to dump three teaspoons of sugar in his tea, a squirt of juice from the plastic lemon in the fridge. Then, the mug cupped in his hands, he meandered back into the living room, where the glass-topped coffee table was practically buried underneath probably two dozen of those anemic-looking ceramic figurines Mae'd loved so much. Things looked like ghosts, if you asked him. "What'd you say that stuff was again?"

"Lladro," Roxie said, gently setting another piece on the table, next to a half dozen others. "From Spain. Mostly from the sixties and seventies." She sat back, giving him a bemused look, the spunk in those grass-colored eyes at such odds with the sadness. "Let me guess—you don't recognize them."

"Sure I do," he lied, sighing at his niece's chuckle. "I was putting in long hours at work back then, I didn't really pay much attention."

"There's probably a hundred pieces altogether."

He'd had no idea. "You're kidding?"

Her curls shivered when she shook her head. "Even though the market's pretty saturated with Lladro right now, some of the pieces could still bring a nice chunk of change from the right buyer. Mae collected some good stuff here."

"And some not so good stuff?"

She pushed a short laugh through her nose. "True. Not sure what the demand is for four decades' worth of *TV Guide* covers, or all those boxes of buttons—although some crafter might want them. Or the Happy Meal toys. But this—" She held up another unwrapped piece. "This I know. This we can sell."

Over the pang brought on by that word "sell," Charley felt a spurt of pride, too. Maybe the girl drove him bonkers, but she was damn smart. And knowledgeable, like one of those appraisers on *Antiques Roadshow*, which Charley realized he hadn't watched since Mae's passing. And for sure, Roxie's talents were wasted in some fly speck of a village in northern New Mexico. Child needed to be someplace where she could put all that education and experience to good use.

Then he could get back to living on his own, which he'd barely gotten used to when Roxie returned and tossed everything ass over teakettle.

He leaned over and picked up one of the pieces, the flawless surface smooth and cool against his hand. "Getting any messages from Mae?" Roxie asked, a smile in her voice.

Charley set the piece back down, then took a long swallow of his tea. "Do whatever you think best," he said, feeling a little piece of himself break off, like a melting iceberg.

Although the fact was, Mae had told him before she died to sell the whole shebang, put the money into an annuity. It was him who was resisting, not Mae. Who didn't really speak to him, of course. Even if he sometimes wished she did. Lord, what he'd give to hear her laughter again.

The pretense hadn't even been a conscious decision, really. Just kind of happened one day when Roxie had been bugging him about packing up Mae's clothes, and Charley, growing increasingly irritated, heard himself say, "Mae wouldn't want me to do that," and Roxie'd said, "What?" and he said, "She told me not to get rid of her things yet," and Roxie had backed right off, much to Charley's surprise.

Charley supposed it was his subconscious stumbling upon a way to make Mae the buffer again. Not that he was entirely proud of using his dead wife in this manner, but if it got Roxie off his case? Whatever worked. And that way it wasn't *him* changing his mind, it was Mae.

Long as he didn't carry things too far. Dotty was one thing, incompetent another. Fortunately the hospice social worker—who Roxie'd contacted without his say-so—had reassured her it wasn't uncommon for the surviving spouse to imagine conversations with the one who'd gone on, it was simply part of the grieving process for some people, it would eventually run its course and she shouldn't become overly concerned.

So it would. Run its course. Soon as "hearing" Mae no longer served his purpose, he'd "realize" he no longer did.

Two more pieces unwrapped and noted in that spiral notebook she carried everywhere with her, Roxie glanced up. "You okay? You're awfully quiet."

He decided not to point out he could say the same about her. And he was guessing Noah Garrett had something to do with that.

"Nothing to say, I suppose," he said as the powerless feelings once again threatened to drown him. "Need some help unwrapping?"

"Only if you want to."

He didn't. Outside, the wind picked up, the wet snow slapping against the bay window, slithering down the single-paned glass behind the flimsy plastic panels he popped into their frames every year. Simply watching the plastic "breathe" as it fought valiantly but inefficiently against the onslaught made him shiver. Roxie glanced over, then reached behind her for one of the new plush throws she'd bought at Sam's Club to replace the sorry, tattered things that had been around since the dawn of time, wordlessly handing it to him.

Charley didn't argue. Instead, he tucked it around his knees. "New windows included in that estimate Noah's gonna give us?"

Shoving a pencil into her curls, Roxie smiled. "What's Mae say about it?"

"Mae's not the one freezing her behind off," Charley snapped. "So. Am I getting new windows or not?"

Rolling her eyes, Roxie pulled her cell phone and what Charley assumed was the shop's card out of her sweatshirt's pocket and punched in a number. While she waited for somebody to pick up, she glanced over, a tiny smile on her lips. "Mae would be very proud of you, you know."

Charley grunted—only to nearly jump out of his skin when he heard, clear as day, *You want me to be proud? Fix Roxie. Then we'll talk.*

CHAPTER THREE

"THIS IS STILL way over Charley's budget, Dad," Noah said, frowning past his oldest brother, Silas's shoulder at the computer screen as the accountant ran the figures for the third time.

"Then we'll simply have to shave off some more," his father said. Silas quietly swore, then sighed.

Even though Gene insisted they'd do the work for practically cost, no matter how much they whittled, the estimate still stubbornly hovered around twice what Charley could afford, according to the figure Noah'd finally wormed out of him when he'd gone back to shore up his figures the following day. Oh, there was enough for the repairs, to get the guy some new double panes, but the bright blue daisies had probably been given a reprieve. And Roxie was not gonna like that, boy.

Not that Noah should care. It wasn't her house, and she wasn't Noah's…anything. In fact, after that little exchange between Roxie and her uncle about hearing Mae's voice…

Yeah. *That* he would do well to remember. Also, the woman's pain-in-the-butt potential was through the roof. And did he need that in his life?

He did not.

Speaking of butts…Noah pulled his head out of his when Benito, the shop foreman, called Gene out of the office and Silas pushed away from the computer with a noisy sigh, crossing his hands behind his head. Silas's involvement in the family business was limited to number crunching and filing taxes, but since the bottom line was what made the difference between success and a whole bunch of people starving to death, his input was crucial.

And now his short dark brown hair was a mess from his repeatedly ramming his hand through it over the past hour. "And you're sure Charley wasn't lowballing *his* figure?"

"Since I'm not privy to the man's bank account, I have no idea. But he's only going to spend what he's going to spend."

One side of Silas's mouth hiked up before he removed his wire-rimmed glasses to rub his eyes. "True," he said, shoving the glasses back on. "But even if you do the absolute minimum, Dad's cutting this way too close for comfort. My comfort, at least."

Straightening, Noah crammed his hands in his back pockets, frowning at the figures on the screen as if he could will them to change. "There's really no wiggle room at all, is there?"

"Nope. Meaning he'll have to eat any cost overruns."

"Then I'll just have to make sure there aren't any."

Silas snorted, then leaned forward again, apparently unaware of the SpongeBob sticker clinging to the back of his navy sweatshirt.

"I know this is your project—"

Noah snorted.

"—but can I make a suggestion?"

"Sure."

"Let's tack on another five percent to cover our backsides, in case lumber prices go up or something. Because you know what'll happen—things'll get tight, and Dad will get stressed—"

"And Mom will be all over us about how *we* let things get out of hand. Yeah, I know. And I would've suggested it if you hadn't. Except…" He cuffed the back of his neck, glowering at the screen. Or rather, the image of Roxie's sad, mad green eyes. "Adding five percent to our price isn't going to add it to his budget."

"And sometimes," Silas said quietly, "that's not our problem."

Silas was right, Noah knew he was, but… He walked around the desk to sink onto the old, dusty futon on the other side. "I did warn Roxie this might be a bigger project than she anticipated. But she's going to be pretty disappointed." A half laugh pushed through Noah's nose. "Probably more than Charley, to tell the truth. And you know Dad, he's liable to go over there himself and do it *all* for free if we're not careful. And then we're right back where we started. Having Mom mad at him. And us."

"So basically we're screwed."

"Exactly."

Silas leaned back again, taking a swig from a can of soda as he stared thoughtfully at the screen. "I suppose I could pitch in on the weekends, maybe. We could ask Jesse, too." He grinned. "Make baby brother earn his keep for once."

Noah chuckled. "Baby" brother, in charge of the business's promotion and advertising, earned his keep fine. However, homeboy was also built like an ox and not incompetent with a power saw.

"That might work—"

"Get Roxie in on the action herself, too. Why not?" Silas said to Noah's frozen expression. "No reason why she couldn't do a lot of the demo, whatever doesn't require a whole lot of expertise, save the crew for the stuff that matters." He flicked his index finger at the screen. "With enough sweat equity you might squeeze by. Think she'll go for that?"

Noah unlocked his face muscles enough to get out, "I have no idea."

"Well, I'm in," Silas said, oblivious to his brother's paralysis. "And I'm sure we can strong-arm Jesse. Might want to leave Eli out of it, though. Sleep deprivation and power tools are not a good mix."

His arms crossed, Noah grunted. "And you guys wonder why I'm perfectly happy leaving the kid raising to you."

"Uh-huh. And I suppose Jewel had to twist your arm to build that tree house for my boys?"

"And miss an opportunity to watch your brain explode? No damn way." And before Silas could pursue the topic, Noah stood, checking his watch. "I told Roxie I'd swing by with the estimate before lunch. You mind printing it out for me?"

"See that little printer icon right there?" Silas said, rising as well to slip on his denim jacket. "Click it and watch magic happen."

"Jerk," Noah muttered, plunking his butt behind the computer and hitting Print.

"By the way," Silas said, as the ancient gray monstrosity on the dinged metal table beside the desk wheezed to life. "Jewel and I set a date. April fifth."

This said with the slightly nauseating smirk of the head-over-heels in love. Not that Noah didn't like the

eccentric little midwife who'd snagged his brother's—
and his two awesome little boys'—hearts. But that left
Noah the last brother standing. Alone. Meaning his
mother could, and undoubtedly would, now focus all
her matchmaking energies on him, bless her heart. Not.

Waiting for the printer to cough up the estimates,
Noah let out an exaggerated sigh. "So you're actually
going through with it?"

"You know," Silas said after a moment's silence,
"maybe the idea of being 'stuck' with somebody for
the rest of your life gives you the heebie-jeebies, but
in case you haven't noticed, not everybody sees it that
way."

"Sorry," Noah mumbled, his face warming as he
turned back to the printer. Silas's first marriage had
sunk like a stone, followed by his ex's death in a car
crash when the boys were still babies. For so long, and
whether it was right or not, Silas had felt like a failure, Noah knew. So why was he taking potshots at his
brother's well-deserved happiness?

Fortunately single fatherhood had turned Silas—
who God knew had taken inordinate pleasure in torturing his younger brothers when they were kids—into a
model of forbearance.

"Oh, you'll get yours someday," he said, cuffing
Noah lightly on the back of his skull before heading
out the door.

When hell freezes over, he thought as he yanked on
his own jacket and scooped up the estimate, then hot-
footed it out of there before his father had a chance to
check the new figures.

Or before Noah could think too hard about what he
was about to ask of Roxie Ducharme.

FOR THREE DAYS, between temping as a receptionist for the town's only family practitioner, continuing to pound the virtual pavement looking for a "real" job and the un-ending task of sorting through her aunt's things, Roxie had kept herself so busy she'd begun to think she'd imagined the close-to-knee-buckling jolt at the end of Noah's visit earlier in the week.

Except now he was here, his forehead creased as he gently explained to her uncle why his budget was too small by half, and there was the jolt again, stronger this time, undeniable, and she found herself nearly overcome with a sudden urge to bop the man upside the head with the kitchen towel in her hand.

Or herself.

"Well. That's that, girl," Charley said, sounding al-most…disappointed. Weird. "Can't afford to do all this. So let's go with the new windows and let the rest of it ride—"

"Hold on, I'm not finished," Noah said, and Roxie's eyes flashed to his. Right there in front of her, not quite the same brown, but definitely the same kindness. The same…genuineness. That it had taken her so long to see the resemblance only proved how prejudiced she'd been. How much she'd been determined to see only what she'd wanted to see.

Her breath hitching painfully in her chest, she pro-pelled herself out of the chair and over to the fridge to pull out stuff for lunch. Cheese. Ham. Lettuce. Leftover spaghetti sauce. Cottage cheese.

"Roxie?" she heard over the roaring inside her head. "You listening?"

Sucking in a breath, Roxie shoved the streak of wetness off her cheek and turned. Both men were frowning at her.

"I'm—" She cleared her throat. Sniffed. "Sorry."

"You okay?" Noah asked, simply being nice again, and more memories surged to the surface, memories she'd assumed the spectacular implosion with Jeff had wiped out for good.

Silly her.

"Yes, fine," she said, snatching the three-page estimate off the table and leafing through it. Forcing herself to focus. Holy moly. "I'm sorry," she repeated. "If I'd realized…" Letting the papers flutter back onto the kitchen table, she crossed her arms against the sick, you-screwed-up-again feeling roiling in the pit of her stomach. It wasn't as if Noah hadn't warned her, warned both of them, how costly the project might be. But this was…

Wow.

Roxie never begged or bargained or haggled. Ever. So even though embarrassment seared her cheeks, she said, "I d-don't suppose there's any way to, um, bring down the prices…?"

"Not without jeopardizing our payroll," Noah said, his eyes even more apologetic than his voice. "But—"

"Then…I guess we'll have to stick with the windows. And maybe the front porch—?"

He chuckled. "You weren't listening, were you?"

"Um…I thought I was—"

Charley slapped the table in front of him, making both the sugar bowl and Roxie jump. "Man says if enough people pitch in to help—you know, do some of the easier stuff—Noah and his crew can handle the rest and we might be able to get everything done for the same price."

Roxie felt her forehead pinch. "I don't understand."

"Silas offered to help since things are slow, tax-wise, right now," Noah said. "Maybe Jesse, too." Noah glanced down, then back up at her with a little-boy grin. "And we figure there's a lot you could do, too. If you're amenable."

She wasn't sure what was making her heart beat faster—the grin, the eyes or the proposal. To gather her thoughts—and break the mesmeric hold Noah had on her gaze—Roxie frowned at her uncle.

"And you're okay with this?"

"Heck, yeah."

"Even though three days ago you were ready to throttle me for even thinking of changing anything in the house...oh." She sighed. "Mae?"

Her uncle's smile faltered for a second before he gave a vigorous nod. "It'll be like an old-fashioned barn raising! Or one of those HGTV shows! So whaddya say, Rox? You up for ripping off some wallpaper? Slapping on some paint?"

Roxie sighed. On the face of it, it was a brilliant plan. In some ways it could even be fun. But...working alongside Noah? Hot, sweaty, sexy, gentle-to-old-men, *major player* Noah?

Who strangely reminded her of someone who'd broken her heart ten times more than sorry-assed Jeff could even dream about?

"It won't work without you," Noah said, sounding even more reluctant about the whole idea than she. If that was possible.

Oh, boy. Part of her would rather dance naked with African bees. But as much as her uncle and she got on each other's nerves, she loved the old grouch. And she really did worry about the house falling down around his ears. So…if she sucked it up now, she could leave later with a clear conscience. Right?

Not only that, but considering what she'd put him and Mae through after her parents died? She supposed she could deal with Noah's hotness for a few weeks.

"I'd have to see what I can work out with the clinic," she said. "But sure, why not?"

Charley let out a whoop and clapped his hands, his wide grin warming her heart—even as Noah's twisted it like a wrung-out washcloth.

FAMILY DINNER NIGHTS at Noah's parents' were not for the faint of heart. Especially as his brothers' broods grew and the noise level increased exponentially. However, unless somebody's wife was giving birth or there were flu germs involved, there was no "will not be attending" option.

So here Noah slouched on the scuffed-up old leather sectional in the relatively quiet family room, his belly full of his mother's pot roast and his head full of Roxie—even though he had a date later that evening with some chick he met while working on a project in Chama—all by his lonesome. Well, except for his father's old heeler seeking refuge from way too many shrill little voices and eager little hands, and Eli's sacked-out, newborn son hunched underneath his chin.

That he was even thinking of canceling only went to show how messed up he was. Wasn't as if he'd never had more than one woman on the brain at once, for heaven's sake. Not that he'd ever two-timed anybody, exactly— he was capable of monogamy, especially once getting naked was involved, and as long as nobody was talking long-term. Except, truth be told, things went down that road a lot less often than people assumed. Having a few laughs, kicking up his heels on the dance floor, simply enjoying a pretty gal's company…that's about as far as the vast majority of his dates went. And sometimes, when things were totally casual…his mind wandered.

Or, he thought morosely as the baby squirmed and gurgled softly in his sleep—and Blue lifted his head to make sure The New One was okay—got stuck some-place it shouldn't. Tonight, much to his consternation, he couldn't blast Roxie out of his head.

"Aw—don't you two look adorable?" his sister-in-law Tess whispered, still cute as all get-out despite the bags under her deep brown eyes. He supposed she and his next older brother, Eli, qualified as high school sweet-hearts, despite the ten years of Tess's subsequent mar-riage to, and two children by, someone else. But now here they were, together again and blissfully adding to the world population. Somebody shoot him now.

At the sound of his mama's voice little Brady let out a "feed me" squawk. Smiling, the brunette carefully peeled the kid and receiving blanket off Noah's shoul-der. "You're such a good uncle."

"And don't you forget it," he said, telling himself he didn't miss the warmth, the slight weight. The trust. Knowing he didn't miss the responsibility at all.

No sooner had Tess left, however, than his dad came in, dropping with a satisfied groan into the brown La-Z-Boy recliner that had been around longer than Noah.

"Your mother will be the death of me one of these days," Gene said, his hands clamped over his stomach, "but damn, she can cook."

Noah regarded his father for a moment, thinking about how tangled his and his father's relationship was, that they could be so close and yet butt heads so often. And so hard. "I take it your stomach's okay then?"

"What? Oh. Yeah, yeah, fine. Couldn't be better."

"Glad to hear it," Noah said, leaning forward to push himself off the sofa. But his father's hand shot out.

"Hang on a minute, I want to talk to you." Grunting, he curled over the arm of the chair to dig the remote out of the pocket. The clicker found, he aimed it at the flat-screen TV, talking to the screen instead of Noah. "Why'd you jack up the figures for Charley's job?"

Sneaking a glance at his watch—it was too late to cancel now without looking like a sleazeball—Noah lowered himself again to the edge of the sofa, his hands linked between his knees. "Because you'd cut them too close," he said over some crime show he never watched. "If any of our supply prices had gone up, you'd've been screwed. And Silas agreed with me," he added before his father could protest.

"Damn repeats," his father muttered, clicking the TV off again before meeting Noah's gaze. "Except Charley doesn't have that kind of money."

"I understand that. Since I was the one who discussed the budget with him. So we all came up with a solution."

"We all?"

"Silas and me, mostly. But Roxie, too. That if a lot of the demo work got done for free, Charley's contribution would still cover materials and the crew's wages. There's like zip profit margin, but it won't take you under, either."

His father looked at him steadily for several seconds. "What about your salary?"

"I'm good for a couple of weeks. Shouldn't take any longer than that."

More staring. "Why?"

Noah knew what he was asking. "Because I know how much Charley means to you."

His father broke the connection first, shifting in his chair and turning the TV back on. "Roxie know you're doing the project gratis?"

"No. Why should she?"

The uncomfortable silence that followed was broken by Donna Garrett's hearty laugh from the dining room, where she was supervising dessert for a batch of grandchildren. "Guess that could work."

Noah knew the grudging acknowledgement was as close to a thumbs-up as Gene was going to give under the circumstances. Before he could reply, however, his father said, "I've been thinking about what you said. About how I should spend some time with your mother." He drummed his fingers on the arm of the chair. "Get away."

"Oh?"

"Except…what if I did want to go traipsing around Europe or take your mother on a cruise or something? Who'd handle things while I was gone?"

And here we go again. "Actually…probably the same people who handle things now." When his father frowned at him, Noah said, "Dad. Everybody knows you worked your butt off all those years when we were little. And that the business wouldn't be what it is today if you hadn't. But it also wouldn't be what it is if it wasn't for all of us. You gotta admit, you haven't run it on your own for some time." And it occurred to Noah that he wasn't asking for a go-ahead to take on more responsibility as much as an acknowledgement that he, and his brothers, already had.

Gene met his gaze dead on. "You telling me I'm no longer necessary?"

"Didn't say that. But it's been a long time since you were the sole decision maker—"

"Maybe so. But you all, you're…" His father made a circle with one hand, like he was searching for the right word. "Spokes of the same wheel. And a wheel's nothing without an axle."

Smiling slightly, Noah got to his feet, checking to be sure his phone was in his jeans pocket before grabbing his jacket off the seat beside him. "Axle's kind of pointless without the wheel, too, you know. This family, it's a team. We got the whole working-together-for-the-common-good thing down. Nobody's trying to put you out to pasture, okay? But I think, between us, we can keep things going for a couple of weeks while you take Mom on a second honeymoon."

"The cabinetry, though—that's still the core of the business. The biggest moneymaker. Who's gonna oversee that?"

Noah felt his good humor quickly fade. "Me. Who else?"

His father looked away. "I don't know, Noah.…"

"Okay, Dad, that's it." At Gene's startled expression, Noah hauled in a breath. "Maybe it's your prerogative that you don't agree with how I live my life. Although I would think, since I've never shown up drunk or stoned, or messed up a job, that would count for something. But whatever."

He shrugged into his jacket. "But it really chaps my hide that you apparently don't believe I'm every bit as dedicated to this business as you are. That I know it inside out. Probably better than you do at this point, since I'm the one keeping up with the technological advances and what all. I love you and I respect you, but it sure would be nice to see that respect returned, you know?

"Now if you'll excuse me, I've got a date. And no, you don't know her and probably never will, and maybe that makes me a flawed human being in your eyes." Shoving his hands in his jacket pockets, he softly said, "But that doesn't mean you can't count on me not to screw up what's really important."

His father and he did the gaze-wrestling thing for several seconds before, sighing, Noah walked away.

CHAPTER FOUR

Jumping at the duck's quacking a foot from his head, Noah grabbed for his phone off the nightstand, his brain coughing up *Who the hell changed my ring tone?* long before his bleary eyes made out the teeny, tiny numbers of the display. When he did, he jumped again, nearly dropping the phone trying to get it to his ear.

"Ma—?"

"What on earth did you say to your father last night? He's gone all mopey and won't tell me why."

Noah crashed back into his pillows, willing his heart to settle back down as he registered it was still dark. On a Saturday. "I take it you know it's not even seven yet?" he said, his eyes finally adjusting to the murky light in the bedroom. "And why are you automatically assuming I had anything to do with—?"

"Noah. Please. So what went down between the two of you?"

"I don't suppose this could wait?"

"No, it can't."

Blowing out a silent breath, Noah shoved back his black-and-tan comforter—chosen by sheer virtue of not looking like something out of either a palace or a brothel—and swung his legs over the edge to hook his abandoned jeans with one foot and kick them into his hand.

"Same old same old," he muttered around a yawn as he yanked them up one-handed, then lurched to the kitchen of his over-the-garage apartment—on the other side of town from his parents—to punch on the coffeemaker. Donna Garrett was well aware of the ongoing conflict between him and his father, no need to rehash the whole thing. Especially before coffee. "Except this time I might've put my foot down a little more. For his sake. And yours."

"Mine?"

"Yeah," Noah said, kicking on the thermostat. Dang, it was cold. "Because he told me you've been after him to take some time off. Since I agree—" although even he knew better than to bring up the Tums episode "—I had to convince him the business wouldn't fall apart if he left for a few weeks. Why are you laughing?"

"You know, sometimes I really wonder how your father and I have made it through all these years without killing each other."

"That's easy." Noah yawned again and forced his eyes open a little wider. "Neither one of you wanted to be left raising us on your own."

She laughed again. "You got that right. But the thing is…he did ask me if I wanted to get away, maybe after Christmas. A cruise."

Noah stopped in the middle of scratching his stubbled cheek. "You serious?"

"I am. And apparently he is, too. Except he practically growled the suggestion. Didn't exactly make me want to hop online to search for cruise clothes. Now, though, things are making more sense." She laughed again, more softly. "He *listened* to you, Noah. Whatever issues the two of you might have, he listened. So thank you, honey. From the bottom of my heart."

The coffee ready, Noah filled a mug already sitting on the counter, wincing when a single, grudging shaft of light pierced the kitchen blinds. The first hit of caffeine sent off to swim through his veins, he said, "It doesn't bother you that it wasn't Dad's idea?"

"Are you kidding? If left to his own devices, the man would be perfectly content going to work, coming home, eating, watching TV and sleeping. Rinse, repeat. With maturity comes the ability to be grateful for the *what,* and not worry so much about the *how.* You might have annoyed him no end, but in one conversation you pushed him further out of his comfort zone than I've been able to do in twenty years."

She rang off after that, about ten seconds before Noah's bladder exploded and a good two, three minutes before the ramifications of his father's actions sank in: that maybe, finally, Noah'd gotten through to the old man. That maybe, finally, he'd earned the old man's trust.

A smile spreading across his face, he yanked up the blinds to let in more light. His date last night had gone better than expected—enough that the prospect of meeting Roxie at Lowe's later to hash out tile and paint selection and such wasn't even bothering him—and his father *trusted* him.

Was this going to be a great day, or what?

"WHAT THE HELL do I know about any of this?" Charley barked. Loudly enough to make everybody in the tile aisle turn their heads. Roxie was briefly tempted to say, "I have no idea who this guy is, never saw him before in my life." Instead, she lugged a large square of veined slate tile off the sale pile and held it up. "This would go great with the new countertops, don't you think?"

Her uncle grunted, as cranky as a three-year-old who'd missed his nap. In theory, a field trip to Santa Fe to choose the decorative materials for the renovation had sounded like the perfect thing for a beautiful fall morning. In reality…not so much.

"Whatever you pick out is fine," Charley muttered. "I don't care. Actually, why don't I go wait in the car until you're finished?"

Replacing the tile before it somehow found itself shattered over the old man's head, Roxie sighed. "Charley. It's your house. Where you're going to be living for a long, long time. I'd think you'd want to be in on the decision making."

His face set in a mulish expression, her uncle shoved his hands in his baggy khaki pockets. At least they were an improvement over the god-awful coveralls. He'd been a good-looking dude once upon a time, when he actually took pride in his appearance.

"And why would you think that? Never did when Mae was alive, still not interested now."

Roxie opened her mouth to make him see reason, only to realize at this rate they'd be here until Christmas. Ten years from now.

"If you really don't care—"

Charley's eyes snapped to hers, full of hope. "I really don't."

"Fine. Why don't you wait in that Burger King we saw when I parked the car? I'll meet you there when I'm done. But no complaints about whatever I choose!" she called to his rapidly retreating form as she fished her ringing cell phone from her purse. Noah. She told herself the funny, fluttering sensation in her midsection was a hunger pang.

"Just walked through the door," he said, damn his bone-melting voice. "Where are you?"

"Tile. I think I found something that could work."

"Cool. Um…is that Charley headed out the exit?"

"Yep. I thought he'd like to be involved. I was wrong…." She looked up to see Noah turn into the aisle—all windblown and hunky and competent-looking—and she felt another "hunger" pang.

She dropped her phone back into her purse, pointing to the tile as Noah drew close enough for her to catch a whiff of wood-smoke-and-leather-scented stud. This time it wasn't her stomach growling. "What do you think?" she said, trying not to breathe.

He hefted a square in his hand, turned it over to give it an approving look. Hormones surged. "Good stuff," he said. "Especially at this price."

"Oh. Great."

He looked at her funny. "You have a cold?"

"What? Oh. No. I'm, um…it's the lumber smell, I guess. Tickles my nose. Anyway…so that tile for the floor. And maybe this—" she scooted down the aisle to a display of netted, one-inch tiles in coordinating shades of beige "—for the backsplash?"

"Excellent," Noah said. Grinning. But not at her, she surmised. Let alone about her.

"You seem awfully chipper this morning."

The grin broadened. "I suppose I am."

When no explanation followed—not that Roxie needed, or even wanted, one—she said, "Well. Anyway. Here's the paint samples, but I don't know how much to get—"

"Don't worry about that," he said, flipping through the samples, which she'd already marked for each room. "I'll pick it up, use my discount. So those tiles, and these, and you chose the laminate for the counter. Wanna see those tub surrounds I told you about?"

So they did, and she approved, and then they discussed schedules and things, and it was all very businesslike and professional, and little by little Roxie found herself actually becoming more impressed with Noah's expertise than his scent.

Hope. Yay.

NOAH KNEW ALL about the theory that men's brains couldn't multitask, especially when anything even vaguely resembling sex was involved. *Well, screw that,* he thought, as they walked toward the parking lot after submitting his purchase orders at the customer service desk. Because the whole time he'd done the professional contractor act with Roxie, another part of his brain kept firing off random, totally unprofessional observations.

Like how the overhead lighting made her curls all shiny.

That her top blouse button underneath her corduroy jacket stopped just short of showing any cleavage.

The way the space between her dark, natural eyebrows would pucker in concentration when he explained something, even when she was smiling.

That he was already having trouble remembering what'shertootsies from last night. Although the restaurant had been kick-ass.

"By the way," Roxie said, "I worked out my schedule with the clinic. Since Naomi's usually busier in the afternoons and evenings, anyway, I can work on the house every morning and one full day during the week. How's that?"

Huddled inside her jacket from the brisk breeze, she squinted up at him. She wasn't particularly short—sort of average, in fact—but he was tall enough for there to be an appreciable difference. A stray curl drifted across her eyes; she shoved it behind her ear, studded with a single, small gold loop. If he looked closely he could see a bunch of tiny dots from other, closed-up piercings. Funny, how he'd never even really noticed Goth Roxie, and yet he couldn't take his eyes off Real Roxie.

"Sounds good," he said. "How early you want to start?"

"I'm usually up by six. So whenever."

"I'm not, so…eight?"

She laughed. The kind of laugh that made you want to laugh back. The curl blew into her face again, but this time she let it go. "Eight's fine," she said, even as Noah decided that curl would be the undoing of him. Seriously.

He glanced out into the parking lot. "Where you parked?"

"Over there," she said, pointing. "But I have to fetch Charley first. I banished him to Burger King. Anyway," she said, turning and walking backward, her teeth chattering. "So…I'll see you Monday?"

"Actually, I could go for a hamburger myself," he said, falling into step beside her, even though the rational part of his brain screamed, *Run, fool! Run!* "If it's all the same to you."

"Suit yourself," she said, clutching her jacket collar underneath the chin.

"You're freezing."

"Wh-what w-was your f-first cl-clue?"

"Here," Noah said, placing a hand on her waist to gently shift her over. "Walk on this side, it's not as windy next to the buildings."

"Oh. Um. Yeah, you're right." Her eyes flitted to his. "Thanks."

"Anytime. That your phone?"

"What? Oh…damn," she said, digging it out of her purse. "I can never hear it when I'm outside. But let me forget to turn it off at the movies, and it sounds like a symphony…orchestra…."

As her voice faded, Noah looked over. She was still walking, but kind of like a robot. "You gonna answer it?"

"No," she said, stuffing it back into the bag as they reached the Burger King, the warm, intoxicating scent of fast food enveloping them when Noah opened the door.

"What the heck?" Roxie muttered beside him; frowning, Noah followed her gaze…to a table in the back, where Charley sat with a red-headed Shirley MacLaine look-alike, looking a lot more interested in her than his burger.

"I SWEAR, I WAS just sitting there, minding my own business, and up comes this gal, asking if the seat was taken." Charley traipsed over to the soon-to-be-history kitchen cupboard to get the box of tea bags—but with a spring in his step that reminded Roxie an awful lot of Noah. Dear God.

Her name was Eve. No, Eden. Dyed red hair, lots of jewelry. And makeup, not badly applied. Perfume, however, strong enough to overpower the fast-food fumes.

Hailed from New Jersey, lived in Santa Fe for ten years. Had immediately assumed Noah and Roxie were a couple. Not that that stopped her from flirting with him, Roxie'd noticed.

"And what's up with the attitude, anyway?" Charley said. "Thought you were so hot for me to move on?"

"Charley," Roxie said over the ten kinds of alarms going off inside her head. "You just met the woman—"

"We hit it off. Go figure. So I'm taking her to the movies tomorrow night. But could I borrow your car? The Blue Bomb's not the sort of vehicle you take a gal out in. Especially for a first date. And get this—she's crazy about action movies." Charley laughed, the sound freer than Roxie'd heard since her aunt's death. More alarms went off. At this rate, she'd be deaf before nightfall. "In fact, you should've seen the look on her face when I suggested that new Meryl Streep flick. Like she'd swallowed something nasty."

Oh, dear. Poor guy had it bad.

"Maybe…you shouldn't rush into anything."

Dunking his tea bag in the mug of hot water, her uncle shot her a reproving look from underneath his eyebrows. "I'd hardly call a movie date *rushing*. And since when are you my mother?"

"Since you started picking up chicks in Burger King?"

"Not sure which bugs me more," he said, leaning against the counter on the other side of the room. "That you don't think I'm smart enough to spot a gold digger—"

"I never said—"

"Or that I deserve to have a little fun."

"Of course I want you to have some fun! A lot of fun! As much fun as you like! It's just…"

"You think this is a rebound."

"I think I should check for the empty love potion bottle. This zero-to-sixty business is a little unnerving." When he shot her another mulish look—albeit of a much spunkier variety than the one he'd given her in the tile aisle—she said, "Charley, I know how down you've been since Mae's death, which wasn't all that long ago—"

"More than a year, Rox. And at my age, there are worse things than a rebound relationship." He shrugged. "Should it even come to that." Then his eyes found hers. "This isn't the same situation as yours, because I'm not looking for the same things. At this point, whatever happens from now on…" Another shrug. "Gravy."

One arm across her ribs, Roxie ducked her head to stare at a mystery splotch on the disgusting floor. "Maybe you're not in the same place I was…back then. But still. Acting on an attraction when you're still in love with someone else—"

"It's a *date,* Rox. That's all. Now can we drop this?"

"No. The dating scene…it's changed since you dated Mae. A lot."

"And you think I'd have a *problem* with having sex on the third date?" At her apparently appalled expression, Charley chuckled. "Your aunt and I got cozy on the second. Betcha didn't expect that, didja?"

"Geez, Charley—"

"It was the sixties. What can I say? Sex happened."

"This is supposed to be reassuring?"

"Although," he said on a sigh, "now that *I'm* in my sixties, sex probably isn't going to happen quite so much. Listen, you don't think I'm shocked, too? That one minute, I'm a lonely old man, the next, here's this pretty woman, asking if she can sit with me, and suddenly we're talking like we've known each other forever. Her dead husband, he also worked at Los Alamos. Although in a completely different department. And get this—"

"She was a teacher, too?"

"Yeah. How'd you know? Only she taught little kids, first grade. Not high school. So can I borrow your car tomorrow?"

Roxie had to admit, as the initial shock began to fade, Charley excited about going on a date with someone he barely knew was far preferable to Charley still mourning someone he'd known and loved his entire adult life. And of course he was perfectly capable of looking out for himself. No point putting her own issues on the poor man.

"Yes, Charley. You can borrow the car." Her mouth twitched. "But put gas in it. And if you're not home by midnight your car privileges are revoked."

"No problem, we're going to the afternoon show, it's cheaper that way. So how'd you and Noah get on with the selections?"

And, apparently, that was the end to that conversation.

Her issues, no. The conversation, yes.

"Fine," she said, which was the end of *that* conversation. After Charley bustled off—she assumed to confirm plans with his new "friend"—Roxie returned to the dining room to continue her unpacking, cataloguing, repacking, since everything had to be shoved back into the garage until after the reno. The better pieces she'd decided to sell on eBay, but she'd have to hold a yard sale or something for the rest of it. Although, between their being out in the boonies and winter breathing down their necks, how she was going to pull that off she had no idea.

That, however, was a worry for another day. Because today she had worries enough, between her uncle's finding love over a Whopper and fries and her insane attraction to Noah and her near heart attack when she'd seen Jeff's number on her cell phone earlier.

What on earth he wanted to say, she couldn't imagine. Certainly she had nothing to say to him. However, since he hadn't left a voice mail, she assumed it wasn't urgent. Or even important. And unless and until he did, she saw no reason to answer. Ever. Maybe he no longer had the power to hurt her—a power Roxie willingly admitted she'd given him—but allowing him renewed access to her head? So not happening.

A realization that only strengthened her resolve not to let Noah get to her, either, to not read his chivalrously moving her out of the wind, or his gracious reaction to Eden's erroneous assumption about them, as anything more than the actions of a man whose mama had brought him up right. Because she'd made the mistake before, of looking at someone through cloudy lenses, convincing herself the blurred image was what she wanted it to be, rather than what it was. Maybe, in Charley's case, that didn't matter.

But in hers? Yeah. It mattered.

Big time.

NOAH HAD TO hand it to Roxie—the woman's work ethic made him feel like a lazy slug.

Every morning for the past week, she'd already been at it for hours before he and the crew arrived at eight, stripping wallpaper or prepping walls or knocking out tiles. There was also always coffee brewing—she'd borrowed the giant pot from church—and some sort of baked goodies, usually courtesy of Silas's fiancée, Jewel, or his mother, since Roxie admitted cooking was not one of her talents. A comment which provoked a deep blush on her part, and a big grin on Noah's, right before she skittered away to her next project like one of Cinderella's little helpers.

Today, however, while the window dudes were putting in the new double panes, it was time to take a sledgehammer to the gouged, grungy kitchen floor tiles—she'd been sorely disappointed to discover they'd simply remove the cabinets, not pulverize them—a task Noah'd forbidden her to tackle when he wasn't there. He'd thought it a simple request; she, alas, saw it as his not trusting her to have at least *some* common sense, which in turn got his back up about her stubbornness, fueling a heated "discussion" that had left them both hot and panting, and, at least in Noah's case, turned on.

Yeah, the crew found that *very* entertaining.

Now, considering the gusto with which she pummeled the poor tiles, it didn't take a rocket scientist to figure out she was using it as therapy. Or imagining that the cheap ceramic she was crushing into smithereens was him. Just a guess.

"Hey, take it easy, or you're gonna be real sore tomorrow."

"Not an issue," came through the dust mask. And who knew safety goggles could be so sexy? *Wham!* "I lift weights." *Wham!* "And play tennis."

That explained a lot. "You lift weights?"

"Not barbells or anything, but when I was in middle school?" *Wham!* "We were doing gymnastics and my upper body strength was so lame I couldn't support myself on the parallel bars, so I decided to do something about it." *Wham!*

Giving him a whole new reason to be afraid of the woman, Noah thought as he raked the broken tile pieces into a pile. Gal could take him *down*. "You're not one for letting things simply happen, are you?"

Breathing heavily—God, he wished she'd stop that— she turned, swiping the back of her hand across her glistening forehead. Despite the frigid temperature, she'd removed her sweatshirt, revealing a baby blue T-shirt hugging a flat stomach, and breasts that, what they lacked in size, they made up for in charm. Especially with the heavy breathing thing.

She pushed down the mask. "What are you talking about?"

"I think it's safe to say you were a lot more motivated than your average twelve-year-old."

He thought he caught a glimpse of a smile. And her butt, when she turned back around. Covered in dusty denim, but whatever. Replacing the mask, she said, "I've never been your average anything."

Yeah, he was beginning to see that. And it wasn't making this attraction thing any easier.

"So where's Charley?"

At that, she grunted. "With his new lady love, I presume."

"That gal we met the other day?"

"The very one."

"I take it you're not exactly cool with this development?"

Her gaze flicked to his before—the sledgehammer propped against the broom closet—she navigated the loose tile floes to get to the coffeemaker and refill a mug the size of the Indian Ocean. In went an untold number of fake sugar packets and a healthy dose of half-and-half; then, stirring, she turned to lean against the counter.

"They've seen each other every day this week. And I know I should be happy for him, that he's found someone to take his mind off Mae, but..." She took a sip of coffee, then shook her head. "I can't help feeling it's too much, too fast."

Noah decided to refill his own Thermos bottle, thinking that he'd seen Charley and Roxie together enough to surmise theirs wasn't the easiest relationship, probably because they were both stubborn as mules. But if her wretched expression was any indication, she was genuinely concerned for the guy. And it got to him in ways he couldn't even define, that she cared that much. Even so...

"He is an adult, Rox," he said, his back to her as he poured.

"An adult who still hears his dead wife talk to him."

Noah turned. "So maybe Mae told him this was okay."

A frown preceded, "That doesn't bother you? That he hears dead people?"

He chose his words carefully. "Not for me to say. Long as she's not telling him to break the law, can't see the harm in it."

A brief smile touched Roxie's mouth before she

sighed again. "In any case, Mae's not here. I am. And something…just doesn't feel right. I mean, not once has Charley brought Eden here. Or suggested we all have lunch or dinner together or something—" She shook her head, one hand lifting. "Sorry, didn't mean to drag you into family business. And I've only got an hour before I have to go to the clinic, so we better get back to work, right?"

She may as well have slapped him. Noah stood there like a grade-A idiot, wanting to say…something. Anything. To plead his case…for what? The words jammed at the back of his throat, a jumbled mess he couldn't sort out to save his life.

"Yeah, whatever you say," he mumbled, thunking his mug onto the counter and grabbing a shovel.

A few minutes later, he carted the first load of tile out to the Dumpster at the bottom of the steep driveway, taking more pleasure than usual in the deafening crash when he hurled them inside. Wasn't as if he actually *enjoyed* listening to women bitch and moan, although he'd gotten better about faking it over the years, figuring it just came with the territory. So why was her dismissal ticking him off so much now?

When he returned, she was staring at her phone, her expression exactly like it'd been that Saturday outside Lowe's. Spotting Noah, she shoved it back in her pocket, clearly distressed. Clearly not sharing.

Flat-out annoyed at this point—whether that made sense or not—Noah jerked the wheelbarrow into place and began to noisily shovel in more broken tiles, even as he said, "Everything okay?"

Using a dustpan to help, Roxie added to the pile in the wheelbarrow. "Nothing I can't handle," she said, not looking at him, and Noah felt as if his gut had caught fire.

Wasn't until the third trip down the driveway that it finally hit him that he felt exactly like he had when his father wrote him off—mad that Roxie didn't feel she could trust him, either. And again, it was nuts that he should care. Was it just the challenge of "getting" something he couldn't have? Some misguided macho sense of entitlement?

Was he really as bad as all that?

He looked back up at the house, the fear swamping him all over again, that this gal was making him feel things no other woman had ever made him feel—although at the moment, mostly like a scumbag. And suddenly nothing else mattered except gaining her trust. Even though...

Even though there was no reason on earth he deserved it.

IT HAD ALREADY been dark for an hour when Naomi Johnson stuck her neatly dreadlocked head out of her office door and scanned the empty waiting room.

"We're done?"

"We are *done*," Roxie said, plopping the plastic cover over the printer and turning off the computer. Although, truth be told, the constant stream of patients—most of whom were under ten years old—had provided a welcome distraction from all the junk piling up in her brain. Even if seeing all those mamas with their little ones only threatened to add to the clutter, she thought, as she stood for the first time in an hour and her lower back let out a silent scream.

"You okay?" the doctor said, flicking off the office

lights, leaving the waiting room bathed in a ghostly glow from the reception desk light.

"Nothing a hot bath won't cure." A wince popped out when Roxie bent to retrieve her purse from the desk's bottom drawer. "And a dude named Sven who gets his jollies from pummeling ladies' backs. Word to the wise—sledgehammers are heavy suckers—"

"Not talking about your back, baby." Naomi paused, then said softly, "How's the job search going?"

"Oh, trust me, you'll be the first to know if anything happens on that front. Why?" Roxie said, smiling. "You anxious to get rid of me?"

"Not hardly. In fact—being purely selfish, here—I dread the day when you tell me you're leaving. Even though I know you will someday, because you've got way bigger fish to fry than temping behind a reception desk. But…" The doctor's eyes narrowed. "That's not it, either, is it?"

When Roxie looked over, the words "I'm fine" ready to jump out of her mouth, Naomi raised one graying eyebrow over her rimless glasses. Roxie sighed. At least Noah—and the confused, almost hurt look in his eyes— would be gone by the time she got back to the house. One less thing to fret about. But if her uncle *wasn't* there, she'd worry. Then again, if he was, she'd have to listen to "Eden said this" and "Eden said that" the rest of the evening. Gack.

And then there was Jeff.

"Just lots of stuff going on," she finally mumbled, yanking her jacket out of the closet and giving her back something else to screech about. At Naomi's pointed silence, she figured she might pick through the many bones and toss her one. "My ex keeps calling me," she said, because she didn't have the energy to discuss the Charley stuff, and she didn't understand the Noah stuff enough to talk about it with anybody.

"I see. And saying what?"

"Nothing, actually. Since I haven't answered the phone."

Her heavy sweater slipped on over her standard office attire of jeans and a baggy sweater, Naomi frowned. "Not like you to be chicken."

"Goes to show how little you know me," Roxie said with a wan smile. "And anyway, he hasn't left a message, either, so how important could it be?"

"You forgiven him yet?"

In a rare, weak moment, shortly after Roxie started working for the doctor, Roxie had told her the details behind the breakup. Because God knows she couldn't tell Charley, and having made the mistake of making her life all Jeff, all the time, she didn't even have a girlfriend to talk to. Which naturally led to her thinking about that aborted conversation with Noah earlier in the day, halted not because she didn't want to confide in him, but because she did.

And how much sense did that make?

Realizing she hadn't answered her boss, Roxie wrapped her lacy scarf around her neck and headed toward the door, and the bracing night air beyond it, which she fervently hoped would clear her addled brain.

"I think so," she finally said, after they were both outside the pseudo Territorial-style, flat-roofed building clinging to Tierra Rosa's outskirts. In the weak circle of light from the single lamp by the door, her breath puffed white in the rapidly dropping temperature.

"Meaning?" Naomi carefully prodded.

"Meaning, once I finally accepted I was with Jeff for the wrong reasons, I found my peace. Enough peace, anyway. Not that what he did was right, but after a lot of soul-searching I realized there were things I'd refused to see. That the breakup ultimately was as much my fault as his."

Her brow furrowed, Naomi reached for Roxie's ungloved hand. "Be careful where you go with that, honey. It's one thing to own up to our mistakes. Another thing entirely to own somebody else's."

Smiling, Roxie squeezed Naomi's hand, then let go to hug herself. "I'm not doing that, I promise."

"So he really can't make you unhappy anymore?"

"Nope," she said after a moment's contemplation. "He really can't."

"Then why aren't you answering his calls?"

"Because I have nothing to say to him?"

"I understand that. But maybe he has something to say to you. And maybe, if you let him do that, you'll find the rest of your peace. Just a thought," Naomi said, turning toward her SUV, parked at the other end of the small lot. Then she pivoted back. "You know you can call me, right? If you want someone to talk to, whatever. Since heaven knows my own girls don't need me anymore," she said with the laugh of a proud mom whose grown kids were doing pretty darn well for themselves, thank you.

"I know," Roxie said, even though she probably never would. "Night."

After Naomi drove off, Roxie leaned against the hood of her middle-aged Prius, staring up into the navy sky, dotted with a billion benignly twinkling stars. Even after all these months of being away from the city, it was hard to wrap her head around the absolute stillness out here, save for the whispering of a nearby stand of pines, the distant yap-yap-yap of somebody's dog—

Her phone rang; her stomach jumped. Not Jeff, though—Noah. Not exactly better.

"Everything okay?" she said, climbing behind the wheel.

"Depends on how you define that." He paused. "But thought you'd like some warning."

Her stomach fisted again. "About…?"

Noah lowered his voice. "I was about to finish up here when your uncle arrived. With Eden."

"O-oh?"

"And enough pizza for an army. Figured you probably didn't want to walk into that unprepared."

"Depends on what kind of pizza it is," she muttered, then pushed out a breath. "Thanks—"

"And Eden insisted I stay."

Roxie closed her eyes. "I see."

"Hey. If it'd been up to me, I'd've begged off, but far be it from me to break the poor gal's heart. Besides, I'll be doing you a favor. By sticking around."

"And…how is that?"

"Trust me. You do not want to face the pair of them alone."

"Bad?"

"Times ten."

Grrreeeaaaat. Her back tensing even more, Roxie drummed her fingertips on the wheel, considering her options. Which all sucked.

"I'll be there in five minutes," she said wearily as she put the car into gear, so, *so* wishing she could rewind her life to, like, the beginning.

CHAPTER FIVE

Unfortunately, Noah had not been exaggerating.

Not that Roxie had anything against bright colors, she thought as she nibbled at a mozzarella-draped mushroom across the dining room table from the happy couple. Or jewelry. Or belly laughs. Or even, in theory, crazy older ladies, who generally seemed happy enough in their own little worlds.

Except Eden Fiorelli was no sweet, dotty thing who talked to her ten cats and imagined herself the heroine of an Agatha Christie novel. *The Real Housewives of New Jersey,* maybe. If there was, you know, a postmenopausal edition.

Bad Roxie, bad, she thought, almost tilting her head in an attempt to see what her uncle saw. And heard. Because who was she to judge?

"So Charley tells me," Noah said, sitting at right angles to Roxie at the table, "you used to be on Broadway?"

"Ohmigod, a million years ago," Eden said with a blush—Roxie thought, hard to tell underneath all the makeup—and a quick hitch of her low-cut blouse. "But yeah, I was a gypsy. In the chorus," she said in explanation to whoever might not know the term. "Until I married Sal when I was twenty-one. Can you imagine? God, I was a *baby.*"

Then Roxie jumped when Eden, waving her half-eaten piece of pizza, spontaneously burst into some show number in a gutsy contralto that wouldn't have been half bad in, say, a football stadium. Noah tried to hide his grin. Sooo glad he was getting a kick out of this. Which was exactly what he was going to get if he didn't stop encouraging the woman.

Honestly, Roxie didn't know whether to laugh or cry. Whether to be grateful for Noah's presence or mad at herself for being glad he was there. To be pleased for her uncle—he certainly seemed to be having a blast, go figure—or worried that he was in way over his head.

Because Eden couldn't have been more different from Mae if she'd been from another galaxy.

The impromptu performance over—followed by applause from both males—Eden grinned at Roxie, her arm possessively linked around Charley's, her generous, albeit wrinkled, bosom so close to the man's face Roxie could tell he was seriously thinking of laying his cheek on it.

"You must think we're crazy, huh?" she said with a throaty chuckle, then planted a big kiss on said cheek without waiting for Roxie's reply. Another laugh preceded her taking a hot pink-tipped finger to the lipstick smudge. "Good thing your wife's not around," she said, "or we'd both be in *big* trouble."

Roxie nearly choked on her pepperoni—partly due to Eden's remark, partly to her uncle's guffaw in response and partly due to Noah's briefly squeezing her knee underneath the table. Her eyeballs were having an existential crisis, not knowing who to gape at first. What the hell was *wrong* with everybody?

Eden grabbed another piece of pizza—the woman

definitely did not eat like a bird—her mirror-spangled angel sleeve about to drag in the sauce.

"Oh! Your sleeve—"

Another laugh as she jerked the sleeve to safety. "Thanks, doll! I am such a slob, it's ridiculous. So whaddya think of this fabric, isn't it *gorgeous?* And I'll let you in on a secret—" the bosoms puddled on the table when she leaned forward "—it's a *drapery* remnant!"

"Oh. That's…amazing."

"I know, right? I got it for dirt cheap two, three years ago. I make all my own clothes, did Charley tell you? You should see my itty-bitty apartment, it's like the size of this room, right, Charley? One whole side of the living room—" dramatic sweep "—is nothing but shelves for my sewing and crafts and sh—stuff. Swear to God, Diva and I barely have room to *think* in there."

"Diva?"

"My Chihuahua. Sal gave her to me when we first moved out here. To help get me used to being in New Mexico, he said."

Out of the corner of her eye, Roxie saw Noah's shoulders shaking with silent laughter. Creep.

Then he cleared his throat. "So your place is small?"

"Like a postage stamp," Charley said, apparently emerging enough from his besottedness to comment. Which got a shrug from his beloved.

"Yeah," Eden said. "Couldn't afford anything bigger after Sal passed away."

Uh—boy. "When was this?"

"A year ago," Charley put in, his gaze suddenly sharp. Challenging.

"Sorry to hear that," Noah said.

"It's okay, he'd been sick a long time," Eden said,

her gaze tangling with Charley's for a long, borderline-embarrassing moment before he entwined his fingers with hers. Her eyes returned to Roxie's. "It was hard, but you gotta move on, right?"

Another pointed look from her uncle. Nothing like being hoisted on your own petard.

"Of course—"

"I'm really glad to hear you say that, since, you know—" Eden grinned at Charley. Again. "—we're gettin' kinda serious and all."

"Serious?" Roxie directed to her uncle as Noah's hand landed on her knee again. Somehow, this time, she didn't mind. "You've known each other a week!"

Charley's shoulders bumped. "And a half." At *her* pointed look, he said, sounding an awful lot like the bosomy broad beside him, "Hey. This was your idea, after all."

"*My* idea—?"

"Okay," Eden said, clearly sensing she'd gone too far. "Maybe 'serious' isn't the right word—"

"It's *exactly* the right word," Charley said, looping an arm around Eden's drapery-shirred shoulder and again lancing Roxie with his gaze, a move which definitely got him an adoring look from the redhead. Loosely interpreted though that may have been.

Then Eden tore her eyes away from Charley to face Roxie. "Maybe this isn't what you had in mind for your uncle. Rather, *I'm* not exactly what you had in mind. But us Jersey girls, we learn early how to go after what we want."

Breathe, girl. Breathe. "And why, exactly," she said evenly, "do you *want* my uncle?"

"This a trick question?" Her dyed brows lifted, Eden

seemed genuinely surprised. "Only because he's the sweetest thing going!"

"And I'm alive," Charley said with a shrug.

"Okay, that too," Eden added with another booming laugh. Then, to Roxie, "Hey, if you're not gonna eat your crust, can I have it?"

Unable to shake the sensation of tumbling head-over-heels down a steep hill, Roxie got to her feet and headed toward the kitchen, muttering, "Go right ahead, take whatever you want—"

"Where are you going?" Charley said with a steely note to his voice.

"I'm…done," she said, wishing more than anything she could shake off either the small-mindedness or protectiveness—and right now, she honestly could not tell the difference—preventing her from rejoicing in what Charley clearly saw as his unbelievably good fortune.

Or maybe that's envy, cupcake—

"Yeah, so are we," Eden said, either oblivious to Roxie's discomfort or putting her former stage skills to good use. "That flick starts in forty-five minutes, we better get going." Then she swooped around the table to give her, then Noah, hugs. "This was fun! We should do it more often!"

Just kill her now.

NOAH WATCHED ROXIE stomp around the dusty, wrecked kitchen, slamming things into the fridge, looking like she'd slam cabinet doors, too, if there'd been any to slam. Instead, she yanked a broom out of a doorless cupboard and stomped into the living room, where she came to a dead stop in front of the new picture window.

"The crew already cleaned up?"

"Yeah, I know," Noah said behind her. "Can't count on anybody these days."

She flicked him a glance and stomped back into the kitchen, swearing when the replaced broom apparently clattered onto the floor, then returned to the living room where she dropped into a squishy floral armchair, her arms tightly crossed.

"Show's over," she said through gritted teeth. "You can leave now."

Yeah, he could. Then again, it occurred to him, if he wanted people to stop treating him like a kid, he needed to start acting like an adult. And not only when it suited his purpose.

"I'm thinking…no." When she glowered up at him, the curls a blur around her thundercloud face, Noah said, "You need to vent."

"What I need is somebody, or something, to punch."

He spread his arms. "Have at it. But you'd probably hurt your hand."

On a gurgling growl, she grabbed the throw pillow beside her; Noah braced for the slam, but all she did was strangle it to her middle.

"Although," Noah said quietly, "if you really want me to go, I will."

When several seconds passed without a response, he thought, *Fine, I tried,* then returned to the kitchen to get his jacket, nearly jumping out of his skin when he turned to find Roxie standing in the doorway.

"I don't get it. Why you're here."

"I told you. Because Eden asked me—"

"Bull. If you hadn't wanted to stay, you wouldn't've. So what's in it for you?"

Irritation spiked through him. But with himself, not her. "Cynical, much?"

Her eyes burned into his. "Damn straight. Well?"

Noah felt one side of his mouth pull up. Did this gal get his juices going, or what? "Maybe I just want you to feel like—" He gave his head a sharp shake, hoping to jar loose the right words. "Like you could talk to me. Like I'd be somebody you could talk *to*."

"Why?"

"I don't *know*, dammit. Jeebus, why do women have to analyze everything to death? Something comes to me, I either roll with it or I don't. I don't pick at it until it bleeds, for god's sake."

He thought he might have seen the hint of a smile. "You want to be my…friend?"

Uncharted territory though that might have been. Noah couldn't even remember his last platonic relationship, his brothers' wives/girlfriends excepted. And yet, if he thought about it, the idea held a certain appeal, not the least of which was—since it was obvious for many reasons nothing would ever happen between them—maybe focusing on Roxie as a *friend* would finally quash the pointless sexual attraction.

Okay, maybe that was a stretch. However…

"Believe it or not, I don't have a lot of those. Brothers, yeah. Up the wazoo. But somebody I can talk to who won't go rat me out to my mother? Not really."

Her mouth twitched. "You'd trust me that much?"

Even though the barely suppressed chuckle behind her words was at his expense, warmth spread through his chest, that he'd goosed her out of her bad mood. Even if it had been unintentional. "Yeah. I would."

She seemed to consider this for a moment before

her eyes narrowed. "What about your female…companions?"

"Don't pick them for their conversational skills. And that doesn't mean what you think," he said, actually blushing when she laughed. "It means—"

"It doesn't matter," she said, clearly enjoying the heck out of his discomfort. "Really. But I still don't understand—"

"Because I *can* talk to you," he said, the truth tumbling out of nowhere, rolling right past the fear. The absurdity. "And I *like* it. That's never happened before. No, I don't suppose we have a whole lot in common—other than fathers and uncles driving us off the deep end—but for some reason, that doesn't seem to matter. And for another thing…"

Noah swung his jacket over his shoulder, shoving his other hand in his pocket. Because, yeah, maybe there was an ulterior motive. One that dovetailed nicely with that acting like a grown-up thing. "Being totally up front here…but my dad—well, everybody, frankly—expects me to come on to you. Like I wouldn't be able to help myself, or something, just because you're hot and I'm…me. Not that it's not tempting, because you *are* hot and I *am* me, but you're not…"

He pushed out a breath. "You're not the kind of gal I usually hook up with. And obviously I'm not what you're looking for, either. But I'm getting off track here. The thing is, I know Dad loves me, but I don't think he's particularly proud of me. And if I think about it from his perspective, I can sort of understand that. I don't like it, but I'm thinking maybe some changes are in order."

Skepticism shadowed her eyes, blotting out the humor. "Really?"

"Yeah. So, I got to thinking…if I could prove I'm capable of having an actual, honest-to-God friendship with a woman, it might go a long way toward convincing Dad I don't only think with my…hormones. So—whaddya say?"

Roxie stared at Noah for a long moment, thinking, *Not that it's not tempting?*

Followed by, *You think I'm hot?*

Then, finally, his "Whaddya say?" penetrated—along with the hopeful, hopeless look in those big brown eyes—and she thought, *Hell if I know.*

"Or," she said, glad she was leaning against the door frame or she might have keeled over from the dizziness, "option number two—we could keep this completely professional—"

"Nope. Won't work."

"Because…?"

"Because I like you. And for God's sake don't ask me why. I just do. And if you think that's off-the-wall from where you're standing, you should try being inside my head right now. It's like total chaos in there."

Welcome to my world, she thought, grabbing her own jacket from where she'd dumped it over the kitchen stool and shrugging into it before tugging open the back door.

"Going somewhere?"

"Fresh air helps me think," she said, fishing her scarf from her pocket and winding it twice around her neck. And God knew she needed all the help she could get right now.

"It's cold out there."

"Sure is." She started through the door, knowing Noah would follow. Which could lead to all sorts of giddy, silly feelings, if she were inclined toward such things.

The back door actually opened up to the side yard and a walk meandering around to the Machu Pichu-esque steps between the front porch and the street; Noah tagged along in silence, bless his heart, waiting for her to make the next move. Had to admit, an admirable quality in a man.

Did he have any idea how many tangled messages he'd managed to deliver in those few sentences? Although, since he was, after all, a guy, she doubted it. Roxie had no idea whether to be flattered or annoyed. Disappointed or relieved. Although what he'd said about their not being right for each other was, and always would be, true—that whole attraction confession notwithstanding—what woman wants to hear she's being used to prove something to a guy's father? Even as a sidebar.

Even though the guy thinks she's hot.

Gonna chew on that one the rest of the night, aren'tcha?

Even so—and here was the weird part—she didn't doubt his sincerity for a second. Call it intuition, call it her reaction to that whole mess with Eden—whatever. But the man now walking beside her was not the same person who'd shown up to give the estimate a couple of weeks ago. Despite his balled up, backhanded explanation, Roxie really did believe he wanted to change.

And she could use a friend right now.

They'd reached the lousy sidewalk at the bottom of the stairs. Across the street, the light from Noah's folks' TV screen eerily pulsed through the drawn family room drapes, sending another wave of envy pulsing through her.

What was wrong with *her* tonight?

Hunching against the wind, she made a left turn down the road that eventually led to what passed as the center of town.

"Christmas lights'll be up soon," Noah observed as they walked, contentment evident in his voice. A hodgepodge of three centuries' worth of architectural styles plunked down along a series of twisting roads carved out of the mountain forest, Tierra Rosa was strictly a why-would-anyone-want-to-live-here? town...except for those who couldn't imagine living anywhere else.

"Have they changed any since we were in high school?"

"Not a lot, no." Then he chuckled. "Evangelista Ortega tried to put up icicle lights instead of luminarias a few years back. You wouldn't've believed the stink. She never tried it again."

"That's actually kind of scary," Roxie said, digging a knit hat out of her other pocket and ramming it over her curls, so aware of Noah's solid presence beside her she nearly trembled with it. "Being that resistant to change."

"A lot of folks might take issue with you on that. Keeping traditions going...it's comforting in a world that isn't much inclined to be comfortable. And not to push you or anything, but if you want to talk, you might want to think about getting started before we both turn into Popsicles."

"Who says I want to talk?" Except, when Noah shrugged, she said, "Trouble is, I don't know where *to* start."

"Just pick something and run with it. See where it takes you."

"To hell, in all likelihood," she muttered, then glanced at his shadowy profile. "Since I'm not real happy with myself right now." She sighed, the earlier scene in Charley's dining room replaying in her head. Ugh. "You sure you're up for this? Could get whiny."

"I'll take my chances. So why aren't you happy with yourself?"

She clamped shut her mouth. Noah nudged her with his elbow. "Go on."

"I…" She sucked in a breath. "Okay, I hate that I'm judging Eden on surface stuff. That I'm judging her at all. She can't help who she is, and for all I know there's a really good person under there."

"But that's not what your gut's telling you, is it?"

"Yeah, well, my gut's been wrong before. Except it's just…Charley has no idea what easy pickings he is right now. And you must think I'm crazy."

"No, ma'am. I think you're a good niece who has every right to be concerned."

She snorted. "Not sure Charley sees it that way."

"Of course he doesn't. But that's not the point, is it?"

Roxie stole a glance at Noah's profile. She'd forgotten what it was like to have somebody in her corner. How good it felt.

How loath she was to trust it.

Stuffing her hands in her pockets, she muttered, "To tell the truth, I'm not sure what the point is anymore."

"Does Charley have anything worth picking, though? Besides the house? I'm sorry, I don't mean to pry—"

"No, I know you don't. You wouldn't," she said, giving him a little smile, catching one from him in return that wreaked serious havoc with her tum-tum. "And in any case, I'm talking about his heart, not his money. That...that he'll fall for her and then she'll see something sparklier over there and dump him. And he'll be devastated."

Not that she'd allow such a thing to happen to *her,* nope, havoc-wreaked tummies be damned.

Exhausted, Roxie sat on a low stone wall in front of somebody's house, ignoring the muffled yapping coming from behind a closed window. "As far as I know, Mae was Charley's only love. They met, they fell in love, they got married. No drama, no second-guessing, that was it. He has no idea what heartbreak is. Not that kind anyway."

Noah lowered himself onto the wall beside her. "And to play devil's advocate for a moment—"

"As if I haven't done that a thousand times in my own head for the past week."

"I know, but it might help to hear it outside your head. So let's see...from your standpoint, Charley's a clueless, vulnerable widower who's blinded by Eden's... vibrant personality."

"And her boobs."

"I wasn't gonna say that, but, okay, yeah. But what if we give him more credit than that? What if he knows exactly what he's doing? What if *he's* playing *her?*"

Roxie's head snapped around. "Holy schmoly," she said, valiantly fighting not to be distracted by Noah's lovely, firm mouth mere inches away. "I hadn't even considered that."

"Right? I mean, sure, he's not exactly a spring chicken, and maybe he's inexperienced, but he's still a man. Maybe this is just a fling that'll burn itself out."

"Not that you'd know anything about that."

"Me? Nah."

Then, in the feeble glow from yapping mutt's porch light, she caught the grin, and it was cocky and endearing and she felt things she had no business feeling from a *friend* in general and Noah in particular.

Well, crap.

As if on cue, her cell phone rang. Jeff. Of course. Because this night hadn't been strange enough.

"You gonna get that?" Noah asked. Since, apparently, she was staring at the phone as if she'd never seen one of these newfangled things before.

"It's my ex."

"Then you should definitely get that. Otherwise you'll end up flinching every time the phone rings."

"Which you know all too well." He shrugged. "And if you answer and tell them to stop pestering you and they don't?"

"You get a new number."

Not wanting to know how many numbers Noah had probably gone through, over the past ten or so years, Roxie thought *I can do this,* and answered the phone.

Too late to catch the call, of course. Except this time, good ol' Jeffrey had left a voice mail.

Whoopee.

NOAH DISCREETLY STOOD again to give Roxie space while she listened to her ex's message, trying not to let on that his ass was frozen solid. And that he was having some serious, not-exactly-friendly thoughts about kissing her, which weren't doing a whole lot to bolster his self-esteem.

Her phone shoved back into her pocket, she jumped

to her feet and started speed-walking down the side-walk. Noah scurried to catch up, almost missing the "He wants my address," tossed over her shoulder.

"To…see you again?"

"Have no idea." She somehow sped up, which at least got the blood in Noah's butt moving again. "Not that there's a chance in hell of that."

"He cheat on you?"

"What? Oh. No. Well, not that I know of anyway." She kept going, her breath puffing in front of her face.

"Then—"

"Why did we break up? Because I got pregnant."

Noah stopped dead in his tracks. "You have a *kid?*" he said, only to realize of course she didn't. And that she wasn't happy about that. "Oh, hell. I'm sorry."

Turning, Roxie let out a brittle half laugh. "Oddly enough, Jeff wasn't. And Charley doesn't know. So please don't say anything."

"No, of course not—"

With a sharp nod and an even sharper turn, she continued down the street, practically at a trot by now, making Noah sprint behind her.

"Dammit, Rox—" Grabbing her shoulders, he spun her around. *"Stop."* At the tears glittering in her eyes, he loosened his grip. But when she averted her gaze, clearly retreating once more into her own little safe place, he said, "You know how the tiles were coming loose in Charley's bathroom? Easiest thing would've been to simply cement 'em back into place, call it a day. Except that wouldn't've solved the problem, since the loose tiles were only a symptom. The moldy wall behind it, *that* was the problem."

She frowned up at him. "Where are you going with this?"

Hopefully not straight to your S-list. "That...there's no point in trying to fix the surface stuff without cleaning up the mess underneath. All at once. Not in bits and pieces when the mood strikes. And yes, it's messy and potentially disgusting, and even scary because you don't know exactly what you're going to find, but better that than a crap job you're only gonna have to redo at some point down the road. I'm not afraid of what's under the surface, Rox. But if you don't open up all the way, let me see the mess, I can't fix it."

Her gaze danced with his for several seconds before she said, "What makes you think you can *fix* anything?"

"What makes you so sure I can't? Rox, honey," he said when she looked away again, "it's like you keep bringing me these loose tiles, like...you want me to know they're falling off, but you won't let me see why. Like you don't trust me or something—"

"It's not that!" she said, wide, startled eyes swinging back to his. "Ohmigosh, no! It's not *you*. It's just..." She swallowed. "I'm sorry for the fits and starts, I really am. But it's just been *me* for so long...."

When she pressed her lips together, Noah exhaled. Because, by rights, that was his cue to say, *It's okay, it doesn't have to be just you anymore, I'm here.* That he couldn't made him feel like a fraud.

"But it also feels good to be pushed out of my own head," she said.

"You sure?"

"No," she said on a short, soft laugh, then sighed. "Okay. When I said earlier that Charley has no idea how vulnerable he is? That's because...that was me, three years ago when I met Jeff." At Noah's frown, a sad smile curved her mouth. "See, I was engaged before. To this amazing, funny, sweet guy…who dropped dead of a freak aneurism at twenty-eight. A month before our wedding."

"Holy hell, Rox…"

Noah pulled her close, cupping her head against his chest, for the first time in his life feeling someone else's pain like it was his own. Not a pleasant sensation, God knows, but humbling. And oddly…gratifying. After a moment, though, she slipped out of his embrace and started walking again, only at a more normal pace this time. He took her hand; she didn't object.

"How is it you're even functioning?" he asked quietly. "After everything you've been through—"

"What? I should be curled up in a corner sucking my thumb?"

"Anybody else would be."

"Not my style. Although, yeah, Mac's death hit me pretty hard. Especially after losing my parents. But you know, I figured if I could come out the other side of that, I could do the same this time. That I *had* to. So about six months after Mac died, I forced myself to start dating again. That part was good. Better, anyway. Believing I'd fallen in love with the first man who reciprocated my interest—not so much."

"And that would be this…Jeff?"

She nodded. "He was very different from Mac. But I was so lonely, and still raw, and being with him seemed to fill the void. Not that I admitted that at the time," she said with a smirk. "The being raw part, I mean. If you'd asked me, I probably would've said I refused to see myself as a victim, that putting myself out there was my way of taking back my life. But the point is, I was so intent on filling that void I'd convinced myself Jeff just wasn't *sure* about having kids. Especially since, even though he was stunned about the pregnancy—heck, so was I, I was on the pill when it happened—he did seem to come around once the shock wore off. Or at least—and again—I heard what I wanted to hear."

Several seconds passed, their footsteps echoing in the silence, until she said, very softly, "Except I miscarried at twelve weeks. And Jeff's reaction? 'Probably for the best, right?'" She let out an equally soft, but obviously bitter, laugh. "Via a text message, no less."

"You're kidding?"

"Nope. And then—"

Now she turned all the way to Noah, anger and pain and disappointment colliding in her eyes. "Then he accused me of tricking him, of getting pregnant on purpose. Why he waited until then to unleash that particular fury, I have no idea—"

"Because he was a moron?"

"Yeah, well, I was in love with that moron. Thought I was, anyway. In any case, I trusted him. Except what I trusted was all in my imagination. What I wanted him to be. Which was who I'd lost," she said, her eyes brimming again. A hand shot up to stave off whatever Noah was about to say. "No, I'm fine," she said, her voice steadier. "The thing is, what I'd forgotten in my rush to get back to 'normal' is that there's no rushing the heart. It heals when it's ready, and not a moment before. Falling in love with someone—or thinking you have—when you're not yet over whoever came before, is a really, really bad idea. And Charley doesn't get that."

Maybe not. But Noah did. At least he understood

now the sadness in Roxie's eyes, that she still mourned that first dude. And he hated the second one for *not* understanding that. For taking advantage of her.

"You have no idea," she said, the cold air snatching at her words, "how much I wanted that baby. Not that I was going to go out and get knocked up just because, I was never that far gone. But all this time the desire's been inside me, glowing like a little flame. You know?"

Ball's in your court, bud.

Uh, boy. He could be kind, or he could be honest. Although maybe, in this case, honesty was the kindest thing.

"No, actually. I don't." When Roxie tilted her head at him, he said, "Look, I would have never said to you what that butthead did. And if I'd gotten a gal pregnant, I would have dealt with it. But being a daddy has never been at the top of my list, either."

"Oh. But…" Her forehead creased. "I've seen you with your nieces and nephews—"

"Who mean the world to me, you bet. Just don't want kids of my own."

"I see," she said quietly. "Well. Thank you for being straight with me."

"One thing I've always been. So maybe you should stop blaming yourself for not hearing this Jeff when he said he didn't want kids. Because he obviously wasn't listening to you, either, when you said you did." He paused. "And by the way, if that Jeff character comes around here looking for you? He's liable to get knocked clear into next week."

Her laugh warmed him all the way through to his bones.

CHAPTER SIX

ROXIE LET HERSELF into the dark house, smacking at the switch by the front door that turned on the lamp beside the sofa, only to yelp when she saw her uncle stretched out in his recliner.

"Sorry," he mumbled, grabbing the lever to snap the chair upright. "Couldn't move fast enough to get a light on before you did."

"S'okay," she said, pressing her chest, partly because he'd scared the stuffing out of her, partly because that whole "friends" thing with Noah wasn't working. Except on an intellectual level, maybe. On a holy-smokes, it's-been-a-million-years-since-a-man-held-me level? Heh. Then she frowned. "Why are you sitting in the dark?"

"Thinking. What're you doing out this late?"

"Same thing. And it's not late, it's barely eight-thirty."

"You were out alone?"

"No, actually, Noah was with me." Since it wasn't exactly a secret or anything. She unwound her scarf, hung it over the coatrack. Played it cool. "What happened to the movie?"

"I screwed up the schedule, it was half over by the time we got there. So we decided to call it a night. And what do you mean, Noah was with you?"

Her jacket joined the scarf as heat tracked up her neck, as if she was fifteen and had been caught necking with her boyfriend on the living room couch. Honestly. "We needed to walk off the pizza. Got a problem with that?"

"Something going on between you?"

Roxie tugged down her sweater sleeve. "No," she said. Because it was true, for one thing. And for another, she wasn't a big fan of repeating her mistakes. Which their conversation had reinforced all too clearly, thank you.

"Too bad. He's a nice boy."

It took a second. Then Roxie barked out a laugh. "Less than two weeks ago you warned me away from him."

Her uncle grinned. Mischievously. "Less than two weeks ago I hadn't met Eden."

Oh, Lord. "Yes, Noah's a nice guy," she said, turning on another light, "but setting aside the fact that he's not even remotely interested in marriage, kids, all that fun stuff, we have absolutely nothing in common. You want anything?"

"Yeah. For you to like Eden."

Well. At least Noah had been booted out of the conversation. Apparently.

"Oh, Charley..." Roxie sat in the chair facing him, setting her phone on the coffee table. Trying not to squint from all the glowing across from her. "I want to. No, I really do. I just..." Crap. "Do you honestly know what you're getting into?" she said gently. "Eden's kind of...not Mae."

Chuckling softly, Charley leaned back in the sofa, cradling his probably cold tea and looking pretty much on top of the world. His face even looked fuller. "Noticed that right off, didja?"

"Kinda hard to miss."

His smile faded as his gaze sharpened. "Not looking for a clone of my dead wife, you know."

"I wasn't aware you were looking for anything."

"I wasn't. It just happened."

Let it go, girl, let it—"Are you two really serious?"

"Serious enough she wants to cook Thanksgiving dinner for us. At her place."

"Oh. Wow. And you're sure…I'm invited?"

"For God's sake, Rox—why are you being like this?"

"Because I love you and I don't want to see you hurt?"

"Not because it hurts *you* to see me happy?"

It took a second or two to get to her feet and start out of the room, although this was stupid, she had no right to take umbrage when she'd thought virtually the same thing less than an hour before….

"Rox," Charley said on a sigh. "Come back here."

Nearly to the door, she turned, hugging herself. Knowing what he was going to say. So she preempted him. "Despite what you think, this isn't about me—"

"That's right, it isn't," her uncle said, standing as well, his posture more erect, his shoulders more square than they'd been in the past several months. "You want to be cautious about your own relationships after what happened? You go right ahead. You've earned that right. But that right doesn't extend to anyone else. Especially me. And I refuse to make my decisions based on *your* fears."

For a moment she simply stood there, assaulted by a maelstrom of emotions—embarrassment, mostly, at having her face so thoroughly rubbed in the truth. But she also found herself admiring her uncle's damn-the-torpedoes courage, not only for taking on Eden, but for putting his heart out there again, period.

Didn't exactly make her feel proud of herself for dragging her feet about facing Jeff. An oversight she silently vowed to remedy ASAP.

But for now…hot *damn* she was proud of Charley. And he needed to know that.

She crossed the room, seeing surprise flash in his eyes a moment before she wrapped her arms around his waist, laying her head against his chest. "I apologize," she said, then looked up at him. "And I'm going to be pleased for you if it kills me. I am," she said at his chuckle. "Still. It's so…sudden."

Draping one skinny arm around her shoulders, Charley steered her to the sofa, where, once seated, she leaned into his side like she used to with her father when she was little. Like she'd wanted to with Charley right after her parents died, except stubbornness and pain and fear wouldn't let her.

"I have no idea where this is going, Rox," he said into her hair. "But at Edie's and my age, we don't have the luxury of taking things slowly. All I know is, we have *fun* together, and she makes me feel twenty years younger. Yes, she's crazy, but after everything I went through with your aunt…maybe a little crazy isn't such a bad thing."

She almost laughed, then sighed. "I still worry about you."

"Well, don't. I'm fine. And if I get my heart broken—" she felt him shrug "—you can tell me 'I told you so.' How's that?"

"Deal," she said, then sat up to pick her buzzing phone off the coffee table.

"So you coming to Thanksgiving or not?"

"Of course I'll come to Thanksgiving," she said, frowning at the text from the unrecognized number. Beside her, her uncle hmmphed. The man was hardly a Luddite; he'd been working with computers long before they made them small enough to fit in the palm of your hand. But he never missed an opportunity to give her grief about being attached to her phone 24/7.

"Ohmigosh," she said, blinking to make sure she'd read the message correctly.

"For heaven's sake, girl! What—"

"It's from the owner of this fabulous gallery in Atlanta! They got my resume and want me to come out for an interview! Ohmigod, Charley!" With a squeal, she lunged sideways to give him another hug. "I finally got a nibble! If this works out, I'll finally be out of your hair! Won't that be great?"

"Uh, yeah," he said. Except he didn't look nearly as thrilled about the prospect of her leaving the house, of leaving Tierra Rosa, as she might have thought.

And the kicker was, Roxie wasn't nearly as thrilled about that as she might have thought, either.

Well, hell.

NOAH TOLD HIMSELF he'd crossed the street to his parents' house for one reason, and one reason only: food. There was always something to eat there. As opposed to his place, which put Old Mother Hubbard's cupboard to shame. So sue him, he hated grocery shopping. Too damn many choices, he always came out with a bunch of junk he didn't need and usually ended up not liking, anyway.

He'd come to a standstill in his parents' small foyer, thinking that over while Blue whined and wriggled at his knees for some loving. Because some people, he mused as he idly patted the rhapsodic mutt, had no trouble knowing what they liked, what they needed, when they went into the store. If they went in for vegetables, they didn't get distracted by the donuts. Or at least they didn't get so distracted by the donuts they forgot the broccoli. Didn't feel as if they were missing something when they left, either.

Must be nice, being that focused. Knowing who you were, what you wanted….

"Hey, honey," his mother whispered, creeping toward him in her winter uniform of a loose sweatshirt, leggings and sheepskin booties, her fading red hair loose around her still-smooth face. "Blue, for heaven's sake, a person'd think you were the most neglected dog in the world. What're you doing here?" she said, accepting Noah's hug.

"Scavenging. Where's Dad?"

"Asleep," she said, following Noah and Blue into the country-style kitchen that needed updating nearly as much as Charley's. Except in Noah's opinion the blue-and-dark-red color scheme wore somewhat better than seventies bilious.

"It's barely nine."

"I know." She pulled a casserole of some kind out of the fridge. "But that project is whipping his butt. Poor guy ate dinner, watched a half hour of the sports channel and conked out in his chair. He looked so peaceful I tossed an afghan over him and left him there." Noah came up beside her to lift the foil on what looked like lasagna, while an expectantly quivering Blue planted his butt far enough away to not get stepped on, but still close enough so nobody'd forget him, either. When Donna went for a knife, though, Noah took it out of her hand.

"I came for food, not for you to wait on me."

"I wait on you today," she said, reclaiming the knife, "you change my diapers tomorrow. Fair trade. Now go sit." She cut him a big chunk of the lasagna, clunked the covered plate in the microwave. "You want some salad? It's already made."

"Sure." Noah slid into the sturdy wooden chair at the table that'd been there his entire life, the familiarity of the kitchen, his parents, even the dog, settling like a warm blanket over him. Strange, how for somebody whose longest relationship so far had lasted maybe three months, he wasn't real big on change in any other aspect of his life.

Lord, a therapist would have a field day with him, he mused as he scratched the dog's ears, the head belonging to the ears now wedged between Noah's thigh and the table.

His mother slid the plate in front of him, heaped with fragrant, gooey lasagna on one side and her everything-she-had-on-hand salad on the other. "Blue! Go! You know better than that!" The dog slunk off to collapse with a put-upon moan by the stove, biding his time until the Big Bad Woman wasn't watching to sneak right back for a handout. "So how's Charley's house reno coming along?" Donna asked, sitting opposite him with a cup of something Noah doubted he'd like.

"Pretty good, all told. Kitchen demo'll be done tomorrow, we start tiling right after. Cabinets and countertops won't be in for a few days, though."

"Your father says you're supervising the whole job? Even the cabinetry?"

"Yep."

"Lord, it's about time," Donna said on an exhale. "I've been on his case for I don't know how long about him needing to give you more responsibility."

This was news. "You have?"

She nodded. "But you know your father. Pigheaded as they come. Oh, while I'm thinking about it—why don't you invite Charley and Roxie here for family dinner on Thursday night? They don't have a *kitchen*," she said before Noah could protest. "It's the Christian thing to do. And speaking of Roxie…" Her cheek nestled in her hand, she smiled. "I hear she's been a big help."

Noah shoveled a bite of lasagna into his mouth, refusing to take his mother's bait. Never mind that he couldn't get Roxie's scent, or the feel of her in his arms, or her teary eyes when she told him about her past, out of his head. But for damn sure he wasn't about to share any of that with his mother.

So, "Yeah, she sure has," was all he offered as he got up to pour himself a glass of milk. When he returned to the table, the smile hadn't faded one bit. *Tough,* he thought, forking in a bunch of leaves and…stuff, then kicking back several swallows of milk. "Charley say anything to you guys about that gal he's dating?"

His mother's hand crashed to the table loud enough to rouse the dog. "Charley's *dating?* Who?"

"Nobody you know. Some gal from Santa Fe."

"You met her?"

"Sorta. I was still at the house tonight when they came in."

"She nice?"

"She's…different. Used to be on Broadway. Long time ago."

"Broadway? You don't say." Donna sat back in her chair with her arms crossed, as if she was trying to process all this. "Well. Good for him, I suppose. What does Roxie think?"

"Roxie's…" Twiddling his fork in his fingers, Noah weighed his words. "She's got some stuff in her past that might be coloring the way she looks at the situation."

"She doesn't like her."

"She doesn't *trust* her." At his mother's arched brow, he said, "And I've already said more than I should. So if you don't mind, can we just leave it?"

"You brought up the subject."

Yeah, desperation will do that. "I know. But…I probably should'nt've."

"Interesting," Donna said, an inscrutable smile pushing at her high cheekbones. "Roxie sharing things you can't talk about with your own mother."

"Mom. No."

Donna laughed and covered his free hand with her own. "You are so much fun to torment, you know that—?"

"Thought I heard voices," his father said, yawning as he chuffed into the kitchen. Shaking his head, he opened his eyes too wide. "Guess I passed out. There any more of that?" he said, nodding toward Noah's nearly empty plate.

"Right on the counter, help yourself," Donna said. "Although not too much, or you'll be up all night with indigestion." Behind his wife's back, Gene rolled his eyes for Noah's benefit. "And you can quit it with the eye rolling right now, Eugene Garrett!" Then, while Noah chuckled around his last bite, she twisted around to face his dad. "Did you know Charley was dating somebody?"

Getting up to help himself to a piece of apple pie on the counter, Noah listened to his parents' conversation, as soothing and predictable as always. The sound of best friends, of true partners. Again, like with the grocery shopping thing, he felt a prickle that was almost envy, not exactly for what they had as much as for who they were.

What the hell was going on with him tonight?

A little later he said his goodbyes and walked out into the night, reminding himself that right now his brothers were all probably struggling to get kids asleep in houses strewn with toys, that they couldn't simply leave when the mood struck. That in a few minutes Noah would walk into his apartment, and it would be empty and quiet, and he could walk across the floor without impaling his foot on a Lego piece or something, and he could sleep naked—hell, he could *walk around* naked if he wanted—without worrying about impressionable little minds.

Then he thought about Roxie, the pain in her eyes when she talked about her first fiancé, the baby she'd lost, about his reaction of wanting to make it better, make her better, and how that didn't jibe at all with everything, anything, he'd ever thought about himself.

And here he'd always assumed that things got clearer as you got older.

So much for that.

BY THE TIME Noah got to Charley's the next morning, Roxie had already stripped a good chunk of the stairwell wallpaper, a project that must've taken hours already.

"You even go to bed last night?" he called up the stairs, his renegade heart going *ka-thump* when she grinned down at him.

"I was up at four. Couldn't sleep."

"Meaning I was up at four, too," Charley muttered from the head of the stairs. Dressed in neatly pressed khakis, a blue button-down shirt open at the collar and a heavy brown cardigan that didn't droop from his shoulders nearly as much as it would've even a couple of weeks ago, the older man jerked his head in Roxie's direction as he passed her on the way down. "Girl's got news."

"Oh?" Noah said, his stomach crashing as he hurtled to the conclusion that The Moron and she had patched things up. What the hell?

"I might have a job! In Atlanta!"

More stomach crashing. But again…what the hell? Wasn't like he hadn't known all along she'd be blowing this joint sooner or later. Besides which, *there was nothing going on between them.*

Then she bounced downstairs, eyes sparkling, face glowing, curls bobbing, and he just thought, *Hell.* "It's for this really chi-chi gallery. They want me to come for an interview next week! So, by the way, I won't be here Friday." Man, that grin was bright. "Isn't it *wonderful?*"

Then she threw her arms around his neck and hugged him.

"Don't take it personally," Charley said. "She's hugging everything in sight."

"That's…really great," Noah finally said, trying not

to react to all that enthusiastic, sweet-smelling softness pressing against him, then setting her apart before she realized exactly how well that was not working. "You must be real excited."

Behind them, Charley grunted as Roxie bubbled, "You have no idea! And *Atlanta!*" Then she took him by the shoulders and planted a kiss on his cheek. Lord, he half expected her to twirl around and burst into song. Instead, she clasped her hands and said, "I think this calls for Evangelista's cinnamon rolls and breakfast burritos, don't you?"

"I'll go," Charley said, trekking to the front door, obviously seizing the opportunity to escape.

"Bring back enough for everybody! Silas and Jesse, too, they said they'd be here this morning!" Roxie shouted after him, then released a happy sigh. Until she must have seen something in Noah's face that made her happy to take a hike. "What's wrong?"

"Nothing. Except I *haven't* been up since four, so I'm not firing on all jets yet. So. Wow. Atlanta. That's…far."

"I know," she said dreamily, drifting back up the stairs with a goony smile on her face. "Oh, by the way…" She leaned over to look at the front door, even though they'd both heard her uncle's truck roar off. "Charley and I had a heart-to-heart last night. About Eden. And I realized…I have to let it go. That it's not up to me to protect him."

"And that maybe he doesn't need anybody protecting him?"

"That, too," she said over the sound of another swath of old wallpaper biting the dust.

"But you're still worried."

"Like you wouldn't believe. Still." She cut the air with one hand. "I'm done."

Noah leaned on the banister. "You call back your ex?"

Her eyes bounced to his, then back to the wall. "And ruin this good mood? No way."

"Rox—"

"I know, I know. And I will. I swear. But not right now."

Noah thought for a moment. Decided to spit it out anyway. "Would it help if I was around when you did?"

Big old eyes flashed to his. "No! I mean, that's very sweet, but…" Shaking her head, she slapped a wet sponge against the next piece of wallpaper. "I have to do this by myself."

"Who says?"

She frowned down at him. "Who says what?"

"That you have to deal with him on your own." *And you're setting yourself up for getting closer to the woman, why?*

"I do," she said, tossing the sponge into a bucket on the landing, then wiping her hands on a towel before sitting on the stairs a few feet above him. "Because I was the one who ran. Well, after I kicked him out of our apartment. And to be fair, I think he deserves an explanation. If not an apology."

Noah's brow knotted. "Sounds to me like he doesn't *deserve* anything. Except a swift kick in the ass, maybe."

"Already did that. Not literally, of course. But he got the message. So I'm thinking this is for me."

See, this is why female logic eluded him. "How can you apologizing to him be *for* you?"

She leaned back on her elbows, a crease digging into the space between her brows. "Because our relationship was a mistake. A mistake that would've never happened if I'd been honest with myself. And with him. If I hadn't gotten involved for the wrong reasons."

"But what he said to you—"

"Was cold and unfeeling and reprehensible. Absolutely. But even if he'd been kinder about it, things eventually would have fallen apart, anyway. And the reasons behind that were every bit as much my fault as his. That's all I'm saying."

On a sigh, Noah came to sit on the step right below hers, leaning forward so as to leave enough space between them for it not to be awkward. For her, at least. "That job offer really put you in a good mood, huh?"

Her laugh was soft. "It definitely did. But I'd already come to that conclusion about Jeff and me."

"You're something else, you know that?"

He felt her gaze on the side of his face, followed by a shrug. "Only trying to muddle through life like everybody else."

Maybe so. But clearly her muddling skills were better than most. Especially Noah's.

"So when you gonna call him?" he asked, quickly standing when his loud, chatterbox brothers walked through the door. Roxie stood as well, lightly tripping down the stairs to give them both hugs. Charley hadn't been kidding.

"Soon," Rox promised, tossing Noah a smile over her shoulder, earning him quizzical looks from both his siblings. "When it feels right."

And for a moment, assuming Jeff the Jerk wanted to

make amends, Noah almost felt sorry for him, that he was stupid enough to screw up what he'd had.

Almost.

IF NOTHING ELSE, seeing Eden every day gave Charley the perfect excuse to get out of the house, leaving Noah and Rox and the crew to the chaos. Not that he needed an excuse to visit his *girlfriend,* he thought, with what was probably a dumb grin, as he drove toward Santa Fe.

He wasn't sure, at least not yet, that what he felt for Eden was love, exactly. Not like he'd felt for Mae, that was for sure. Maybe he *was* infatuated. And maybe that's all it ever would be. But what he'd said to Rox about Eden making him happy? That was true enough. Because she made him forget the pain. Not Mae. He'd never forget her. Just the pain. And why was that a bad thing?

He pulled into Eden's apartment complex's parking lot, getting a little thrill when she waved from her balcony, her face all lit up. Although her yelling, "Yoo-hoo!" at the top of her lungs he could live without, truth be told. He could definitely understand Rox's reservations—the woman wasn't exactly a shrinking violet.

She vanished inside to greet him at her front door, giving him a big kiss on the lips, which was as far as their sex life went at this point. Not that she wasn't amenable to something more down the road, she'd said, but what with their being still newish to widowhood and all, she thought it best they wait. For what, Charley wasn't sure.

"So what do you think?" she said, spinning around in the cramped living room to show off what he assumed was one of her new creations, something that couldn't decide if it was a blouse or dress or what, worn over a pair of those skinny pants that made her feet look big. Not that he would tell her that. As usual, she'd overdone her strong, spicy perfume. Mostly it didn't bother him, but he did occasionally consider suggesting she take it down a notch—or two—only to immediately rethink that. Women rarely took kindly to what could easily be construed as criticism of their personal hygiene.

"Very nice," Charley said, smiling when Eden grinned back, even though that little Chihuahua of hers growled at Charley's feet. He'd never been a big fan of tiny dogs, but Eden was devoted to the thing, so he supposed he could get used to her.

"For goodness' sake, Diva," Eden said, scooping the little rat dog into her arms. "You act like you've never seen the man! Go on, give him some love." Thankfully, for both dog and him, she didn't actually thrust the poor creature into Charley's face—a move which would have probably resulted in Charley's losing his nose—but when she offered up her "baby" the beast did seem amenable to a quick scratch behind the ears.

"I made chicken salad inside a cranberry Jell-O mold," she said, setting the dog down and moving to her eating nook, the bistro table all set for two. "Hope that's okay, I got the recipe out of a magazine."

Still full from two burritos and a cinnamon roll earlier, Charley smiled. "Sounds perfect."

He sat while, humming to herself, Eden bustled and fussed in the kitchen, a woman apparently content in her world. Content with him, he thought on a small burst of pleasure. Her garment billowing like a benign jellyfish around her, she swept back into the living area and set the half-size serving platter in the center of the table with a "Ta-da!"

"Wow. That looks amazing," Charley said, and she flushed, pleased.

While Eden settled across from him, Charley waited to see if Mae had something to say about all of this. But no. In fact, his wife hadn't talked to him since the one time, when she'd told him to fix Rox. Not that he or anybody else could "fix" the girl any more than he'd let his niece dictate the terms of his relationship with Eden. And if she got this job, he'd be genuinely happy for her. Except there was something decidedly off about her excitement. Like it was a little too forced, maybe. And he was betting that "something" had to do with Noah—

"Everything okay?" Delicately salting her chicken salad, bracelets jangling, Eden cast a smile in his direction while the dog peered bug-eyed at Charley from her lap.

"Thinking about Roxie," he said, eagerly digging in despite his lack of appetite. Woman definitely knew her way around the kitchen, that was for sure. Although her dishes tended more toward the exotic than Mae's—there was some spice or other in here he didn't recognize—but it was pretty good.

"Is she coming for Thanksgiving?"

"She said she would."

"Willingly?"

Nodding, Charley forked in a second bite, then took a taste of the cranberry mold. Not bad. But he did not feel up to going into his and Rox's conversation the night before. "She's got a job interview next week. In Atlanta."

"Really?" Eden plucked a small, knotted roll from

the basket beside the platter, slathered on a good helping of low-fat spread. "She must be over the moon."

"She is."

"But you're not."

About to grab one of the rolls, Charley stopped, his
gaze darting to hers. "What makes you say that?"

The slippery fabric slipped off one freckled shoulder when she shrugged. "You're not exactly a closed
book, Charley." She pinched off a chunk of roll and
popped it into her mouth. "And I bet I know somebody
else who wouldn't be happy if she left," she said, waving the uneaten part of the roll at him, the dog's head
bobbing along. "That Noah."

"Noah?" Not that Charley didn't suspect the same
thing, his niece's protests that there was nothing between them notwithstanding. A blind man could see
they were attracted to each other. Because he *was* a nice
boy, despite his reputation. Good-looking, too, Charley
supposed. But after his and Rox's talk last night he'd got
to thinking, that after what she'd been through with that
Jeff, it'd take more than *nice* and *good-looking* to sweep
the gal off her feet again. "Rox'd never have him," he
said mildly. "Not her type."

"Doesn't mean she's not his."

Suddenly the very thing about Eden that had hooked
him to begin with—her boldness—wasn't sitting all that
well. But he couldn't exactly tell her she was butting
into private family business, could he? So instead, he
said, "Only because she's female, most likely. Rumor
has it boy's got more oats to sow than ten men combined. He could never make Roxie—or, I'm guessing,
any other gal—happy. At least not in the long run."

"Except you'd said yourself, when we were driving last night, that he seems to have changed in a lot of ways."

"Did I?"

"Yes, you did. So maybe he's growing up. It does happen, you know. My Sal, you should've seen him in his early twenties. Wild? You have no idea. Then suddenly he hits twenty-seven, twenty-eight, and boom! Like night and day. Thirty-five years we were married, and never once did he so much as flirt with another woman. And I know what you're thinking—how can I be sure?"

She took a sip of her iced tea. "Because these things, they never stay a secret. The guy trips up, or somebody always blabs, whatever. Especially after the funeral. That seems to be when the hitherto unknown mistresses come crawling outta the woodwork." Her head wagged. "Not with Sal. So sometimes people do change. And you know..." Her gaze averted, she picked at her gelatin. "Having her settled...well, it would take a huge load off your mind, wouldn't it?"

Charley looked up, the Jell-O quivering on his fork. "What's that supposed to mean?"

"Oh, come on, Charley! She's what, thirty? And not even your daughter! It's not right, you worrying over her like she's still a child! Or her acting like you're still one! You both deserve your own lives, don't you think?"

Funny, how thoughts that make perfect sense inside your own head sound not so perfect coming out of somebody else's mouth. Because for all Edie had virtually echoed Charley's own take on the subject, the flare of annoyance setting ablaze the chicken and gelatin in his stomach made him realize things weren't nearly that black and white.

"For one thing," he said, "it's not up to me to get her 'settled.'" *Or fix her,* he silently added to his wife, in case she was listening in. "Whether Noah really is changed or not, I have no idea. But that's for Rox to decide, not me. Or anybody else. For another, maybe she's not blood kin, but she's the closest thing to a daughter Mae and I ever had. Nor do I recall there being an age cutoff for when you stop being concerned about somebody."

Her cheeks pinker than usual, Edie leveled him with her gaze. "I'm sorry if I overstepped. I'm just afraid..." Petting the dog, she sagged back in her chair. "She doesn't like me, Charley. And my gut tells me she'll do anything she can to break us up."

"She doesn't *know* you, Edie," he said, thinking, with a start, *And obviously she's not the only one.* "Yes, we worry about each other. And it's sometimes annoying as hell. But we don't get in each other's business. I can promise you no matter what she thinks she would never interfere—"

"Maybe not overtly," Eden said, her eyes shiny. "But believe me—" she pressed one hand to her chest "—and I'm only speaking as another woman, here— if she thinks I'm bad for you she'll wear you down until you think it, too. Especially as long as she's still single herself!" At Charley's probably flummoxed expression, Edie lifted her chin. "Sorry, but I can't keep this inside. And I feel like I'm on really shaky ground here, with her."

A long moment passed before Charley folded his napkin, placing it carefully beside his plate before getting to his feet, thinking it wasn't Roxie she was on shaky ground with right now. "I like you, Edie. A lot.

But if you're convinced I can't think for myself, or tell the difference between manipulation and being cared about…that's a deal breaker. Believe *me*," he said, his eyes on hers, "I can. Thanks for lunch," he mumbled, then started for the door.

"Charley?"

When he turned she was practically on top of him, clutching her little dog and looking quite distressed. Moved—and frankly torn—Charley laid a hand on her cheek. "I don't see my niece as either a burden or an obstacle. As long as you do, however…" He took a deep breath. "If you don't trust *me,* maybe it's best if we take a break."

Then he kissed her on her soft, fragrant cheek and left, realizing with a kick to his gut that following your conscience doesn't necessarily mean you're going to be happy about it.

CHAPTER SEVEN

IN FRONT OF Roxie stood a grinning, wriggling little boy wearing well-worn blue jeans, a heavyweight hoodie and straw-colored, choir boy bangs. Beside him stood an unshaven Noah wearing well-worn jeans—black, natch—a heavyweight hoodie…and a smaller boy in plush, dinosaur-splotched footed jammies, clinging to him like a limpet.

It was a lot to take in at seven-thirty in the morning. Especially given her lack of sleep over the pending job interview, her screwing up the courage to call Jeff *and* her uncle's two-days-and-counting mopefest, which she assumed had something to with Eden but God forbid he actually talk to her or anything.

"Sorry," Noah mumbled as he ushered in his six-year-old nephew, Ollie, then gently set a still very sleepy, two years younger Tad on the sofa, along with a jumble of pint-size clothes and a largish paper bag smelling of greasy heaven. "Silas had an early appointment and Jewel's out at a birth. So I said I'd get Ollie to school by nine, and whichever one finishes up first'll swing by to collect Tad. Hope that's not a problem? Ollie!" he shouted as the boy vanished into the back of the house. "Get back here!"

"Coming!"

"Of course not," Roxie said, aching to take the sagging little boy in her arms, even as she kept an eye on his brother, darting from room to room like a pinball, his backpack going *thunkathunkathunka* between his slender shoulders, his sneakers pounding against the bare wooden floors.

First things first, though. "Hey, I called—"

"What's all that racket?" Charley called from upstairs. Blast.

"Silas's boys are here for a little while," Roxie called back up. "Come say hi!"

Slam.

Crouching in front of the wobbly kid, who was seriously listing east, Noah shot her a glance. "Still?"

"Yeah," she said on a sigh. "Um, I—"

"Tad! Wake up, buddy!"

Shaking his curly head, the little boy collapsed into a ball on the sofa cushion, hands smushed underneath his cheek. Roxie gave up. For the time being, anyway. "You want me to set out plates and stuff for the boys?"

"Nah, paper bags, fingers—we're good. Okay, Tadpole," Noah said, heaving the kid upright again, "I need to get you dressed—"

"Don'wanna," the pink-cheeked tyke said on a huge yawn, drooping forward to crumple against his uncle's chest, thumb in mouth, eyes drifting shut again.

"I know, guy," Noah said, real softly, rubbing the little back, and Roxie could actually feel her heart melting. And her knees. And…other things. "But you gotta. Aren't you hungry?"

With a slow, curl-quivering head shake, the squirt cuddled closer. Chuckling, Noah gently untangled the little arms, letting Tad slump against the back of the sofa to tug off his pj bottoms…earning himself a shriek of laughter when he tickled the soles of the little guy's feet. Meanwhile, Ollie thunked and clumped back and forth, back and forth, back and forth...

"You're good at that," Roxie said to Noah, snatching up the bag of food before the grease reached the sofa, carrying it to the one end of the dining table not covered in Mae's stuff and renovation detritus.

"What? Dressing kids?" Noah yanked a long-sleeve T-shirt over Tad's head. Not looking at her. "Line up limbs to corresponding openings in clothes, how hard could it be?" The little boy blinked, then grinned, and Roxie could practically see the jets firing, one by one. Countdown to liftoff in three...two...one...

"Shoes!" Noah boomed, grabbing Tad before he could take off after his brother. Feet rammed into a pair of SpongeBob sneakers, the little one let out a war whoop and threw his entire small self at the bigger one, igniting an instant wrestling match. In one sweet move Noah surged to his feet and yanked the two apart; Roxie tried to swallow her laughter, but a muffled snort still escaped.

"Knock it off, you two!" Noah pointed at the table. "Go, sit!"

This said with a mock stern look at the giggling boys, who flew into the dining room, chairs shimmying dangerously as they scrambled up into them, and then Noah was calmly divvying up egg sandwiches and hash browns and pint-size milk cartons between the two wiggle worms, and Roxie thought, *Yes, please, just like that,* although of course she didn't mean exactly like that, since Noah would never—

Because he wasn't—

Girl, don't even go there.

"There's plenty," Noah said to her, unwrapping his own sandwich as he sat at right angles to his nephews. "Help yourself."

Honest to Pete. Roxie plucked a bunch of napkins off the sideboard and distributed them, then pulled a still-warm sandwich out of the bag. "Mae used to make these," she said with a blissful sigh, as she settled across from the boys. "I tried once, but it was a spectacular failure."

Chewing, Noah frowned at her. "You can't make an egg sandwich?"

"I can barely make toast. I can, however, identify a piece of antique glassware down to the decade, so I'm not entirely useless. So, where'd you get these?"

"Jewel made 'em, I'm guessing. Silas sort of shoved them at me when I walked through the door. Tad, sit up, buddy, you're gonna fall out of the chair—"

"Ahmjushtryingtosee—"

"Don't talk with your mouth full."

The preschooler's arm jutted toward the window as he gulped down his bite. "That is like the *biggest* crow *ever!*"

Noah caught Oliver with one hand before the kid fell out of his chair trying to get a better look; then all three traipsed to the window, where Noah let out a long, low whistle. "Holy moly, you ain't whistling Dixie! Rox, get over here and look at this sucker!"

When she did, Noah put his hand on her waist to steer her to the right spot, and she thought, *Okay, maybe that's not such a good idea,* even before the skin-searing, hoo-hah tingling *zing!* that all too smartly reminded her exactly why celibacy sucked. Especially when it wasn't by choice. Except, as he moved away, the vivid memory of her surreal phone conversation last night reminded her that, in her experience, the alternative—as in, intimacy with the wrong person for the wrong reasons—sucked far more.

Yes, it did.

The space shuttle-size bird duly admired by all, Noah got the boys settled back in their chairs, then snapped his fingers. "I keep forgetting…Mom wants you and Charley to come over for family dinner Thursday night," he said, and Roxie's instant reaction was *Oh, heck, no,* until he added, "because you're currently kitchenless," and she remembered there'd be a million Garretts there—Noah and she probably wouldn't even see each other. And she was getting really sick of microwave dinners with mushy rice and limp broccoli—

Roxie heard Charley's floor creak overhead, then his door *eerrrk* open. And close again. Softly. As though he didn't want anyone to know he *so* wanted one of those egg sandwiches.

Sighing, she glanced at the kids, who were busy having a who-can-stuff-the-most-food-in-his-mouth contest, then said, "If I can pry Charley out of his bedroom by then, sure—"

"We're done," Ollie said, scrubbing his greasy napkin across his mouth. "C'n we go outside?"

"Yeah, c'n we?"

"I don't know, guys," Noah said, but Roxie laughed.

"The backyard's fenced. Not much harm they can do," she said.

To which Noah replied, "Remember you said that," and they were off at top speed through the kitchen and out the door.

They both took a moment to absorb the silence before she said, "All he does is sit in his room, listening to old opera recordings," while watching Noah efficiently gather the leftover debris and stuff it back into the paper bag. "I see evidence of his sneaking down to raid the fridge in the middle of the night, or going out for food while I'm at work, but other than that, he's turned into a mole."

"You think it's over?"

"Who knows? But now he's back in grump mode. I swear, it almost makes me wish Eden was still in the picture, because he's reminding me a lot of me when I was a teenager and some boy or other blew me off."

Noah gave her a look. "Like me?"

"Actually, I was thinking of Sammy Rodriquez," she lied, thinking she already had more than enough pots on the stove without stirring that one, thank you. "Speaking of former boyf—"

"Knock, knock!" came a perky female voice from the entryway, before, a moment later, Silas's windblown fiancée appeared at the dining room doorway, her little glasses fogged from coming from the cold into the heated house. "False alarm, no baby yet." A symphony of color in bright blue leggings, red high-top sneakers and a multicolored paisley jacket, Jewel glanced around.

"You lose 'em somewhere? Ah," she said as shrieks from the backyard found their way into the house. "Thanks, guy," she said to Noah, dimpling at him as she reached up to give him a quick peck on the cheek. "You're the best."

Yes, you are, dammit, Roxie thought despondently, as Jewel gathered her stepsons-to-be and herded them out to her car, around the same time the crew's assorted trucks and vans began pulling up outside, and the slamming of doors, the shouted greetings officially heralded the start of a new workday. With a grin, Noah started out of the room. "Showtime—"

"I called Jeff."

His head whipped around. "Why didn't you say something sooner?"

"I've been trying to!"

"So…what…?"

She took a deep breath. "We talked for maybe three minutes. He said, again, he wanted to see me. I said no, no point, delivered my little speech and…that was that. Except for his saying he'd found a couple of old CDs of mine mixed up with his, could he have my address so he could mail them back to me?"

Odd. If she hadn't known better, Roxie would have sworn she saw a little *"Thank you, Lord,"* flash in Noah's eyes. "Did he at least sound brokenhearted that you'd refused him?"

"Not really, no. But then, dude's got an ego like a bomb shelter."

The front door, already left ajar, burst open, followed by heavy, work-booted footfalls, more laughter, the hum of energy enveloping a half dozen men focused on what they had to do. Noah glanced toward the noise, then back at Roxie, his voice barely more than a whisper when he spoke. "You okay?"

Such a simple question, but so heartfelt it nearly brought tears to her eyes. "I think so. I'd expected… actually, I don't know what I expected, exactly. But something. Regret? Anger?" She shook her head. "It was weird. I felt absolutely…nothing. As though none of it had ever happened, really. Except for…well. You know. The baby."

Noah's gaze darkened, for barely a moment, before a slight smile curved his mouth. "Now aren't you glad you called?"

"Yeah," she said on whooshed breath. "I am."

The smile softened. "I'm real proud of you, Rox—"

"Hey, Noah—" One of his crew stuck his dark-haired head in the kitchen. "We brought the new cabinets. You installing them today?"

Ever since they'd started this project, Roxie had been all too aware of the obvious respect Noah's crew had for their boss. And he for them. Not once had she heard them talking trash about him behind his back, or seen them goof off when he wasn't there, nor had he ever complained about any of them in her presence. In fact, the more she got to know him, the more she saw the rock-solid core beneath the cocky exterior…and the more he reminded her of what she'd loved about Mac. Not personality-wise—in that respect, they couldn't have been more different—but integrity? Honesty? Fairness? They might as well have been twins.

Except, lest she carry this twin thing too far, Mac had wanted to be a father. And even she wasn't naive enough to confuse Noah's devotion to his brothers' kids for a suppressed desire to have his own. So, falling for the guy would be pointless and dumb and frustrating, especially since she'd been down that particular dead-end road once before.

Noah tore his gaze away—dear God, how long had they been staring at each other?—to nod at the baby-faced young man in a flannel shirt grinning at him. "Sure are, let's get 'em in." Then he turned to Roxie. "Ready to lend a hand?"

She blanched. Stripping wallpaper and mutilating

tile was one thing. Actually helping to install something that could fall on someone's head if she screwed up?

"I'm not sure—"

"You'll be fine, Miss Roxie," the kid said. "Mr. Noah would never let you make a mistake."

Then she met Mr. Noah's mischief-filled eyes again and thought, *I wouldn't be too sure about that.*

NOAH DIDN'T KNOW about that Miss Roxie.

Just as well she'd had to leave for work, he thought on a suppressed chuckle, as he held the next cabinet steady while Luis bolted it into place, since her carpentry talents were decidedly limited.

Not to mention for a boatload of other reasons. Like the way she'd look at him, so directly it shook him up. Probably every bit as confused as he was, too. Nothing like the coy glances he was used to. Sure, Rox would undoubtedly move mountains if necessary to achieve her own goals—rather than waiting for somebody else to do it for her, which was strangely sexy—but she wasn't the type to pout and whine in order to get her way.

Nag, yes, he thought on another chuckle as he remembered her trying to cajole her uncle into leaving his room by refusing to bring his lunch to him. She'd walked out of the house muttering something about coddling sixty-five-year-old children not being part of her game plan. Except Noah noticed she'd left sandwiches and what all for Charley in the fridge, anyway.

"What's so funny?" Luis asked, repositioning the drill.

"Nothing," Noah said as he checked the level. Dead

on. Excellent. "We should have this done by knockoff time, don't you think?"

"Easy," the young man said, hefting the next cabinet into place for Noah to hold. And kind enough to let the subject drop.

Of course, Noah guessed a good part of that directness had to do with her trying to figure him out, too. Or rather, what to do about the chemistry sizzling like acid on metal between them. Whether she'd admit it or not, he had no idea. Whether she'd be amenable to acting on it, he had even less.

Whether *he'd* be amenable to acting on it...now that was the question of the century. And wasn't that a kick in the pants, that there'd even be a question. On his part, anyway. Because, if she was leaving soon, that was perfect, right? No strings, no ties, no worries about the future....

Yeah. Perfect—if it'd been anybody but Roxie. A thought that made him feel like Luis had taken the drill to his head instead of the wall stud.

The cabinet in place and Luis called away for a minute to help with something else, Noah leaned against the counter and took a swig from the bottle of water he kept refilling from the bathroom sink, the kitchen sink being out of commission until the new laminate counters were installed. Yesterday, when the gal from the other night had called, he hadn't even hesitated to nip the whole thing in the bud. Gently, but firmly. Because somehow, when he hadn't been looking, Roxie had filled up his brain. And until that changed—probably when she left, a prospect that stung far more than it should've—he had no business dating anybody else. Even casually.

Yeah. Go figure.

"Is it safe?" came a gruff voice from a few feet away. He looked over to see Charley standing at the kitchen doorway, back in those crummy coveralls and looking like hell on a bad day, and Noah realized he'd probably never feel safe again, that the earth had shifted underneath his feet and he had no clue what to do about it.

"For the moment. Rox left your lunch in the fridge."

Grunting, Charley slogged across the kitchen, his mouth pulled down at the corners. Noah couldn't resist. "Whatever you broke, I suggest you fix it."

His hand on the refrigerator's handle, the older man swung his head around. "What the hell are you talking about?"

"The fight I'm assuming you and Eden had?"

Another grunt preceded his hauling out the plate of sandwiches, which he then clearly had no idea what to do with, since there were no counters. Noah took the plate from him and carried it out to the dining table, as Charley muttered behind him, "If I'm not gonna talk about it with Rox, I'm sure not gonna talk about it with you. And what do you care, anyway?"

"I care because Rox cares," Noah said, which surprised him nearly as much as it apparently did Charley, who came to a dead halt on his way to the table, an expression on his face like Noah'd announced he was from Neptune. "And in any case," Noah continued, once the shock subsided enough to get words out, "*talking about it* is the last thing I want. Do I *look* like a girl?"

That almost got a smile. Or at least, the grooves at the corners of Charley's mouth faded a little. He sank onto the chair where Noah'd set the plate, releasing a gusty sigh before mumbling, "Nobody talks trash about my Rox."

Noah's brows dipped. "What do you mean?"

"Okay, maybe 'trash' is a bit too strong, but…" He wagged his head. "Things kinda went sour, that's all." A bite of sandwich taken, Charley set it back on his plate, the picture of dejection. "But God, I miss her."

"So you *did* break up?"

"I didn't exactly mean to, but…yeah. I guess that's what happened. Rox was right," he said with a curt nod. "I didn't know what I was getting myself into, and now I'm paying for it." He waved Noah away. "You've got stuff to do, you don't need to stick around. I'm lousy company right now, anyway."

If the poor guy hadn't been so obviously heartsick, Noah might've found his drama queen act almost funny.

"Charley?" When Roxie's uncle lifted pain-wracked eyes to his, Noah said, "God knows, I don't claim to know everything about women, but…I've got a little experience with 'em. So if you do want a sounding board? I'm here. Okay?"

"When hell freezes over," Charley said, one side of his mouth barely tilted, "but thanks for the offer."

After a moment, Noah nodded and quietly walked away, although a sizeable chunk of the older man's misery had apparently broken off to follow Noah, doing its level best to find purchase in his gut.

BY THE TIME Thursday rolled around, Noah was so tired from pushing through on Charley's house—so he could take on another project waiting in the wings—he'd nearly forgotten that Roxie and her uncle were supposed to come to his parents' that night. Judging from

Roxie's voice over the phone, when, after his mother reminded him, he reminded *her,* she'd forgotten as well. Or hoped everyone else would.

"Oh, Lord, Noah…I've finally got Charley downstairs, but actually getting him to leave the house might be a stretch."

"Mom's insisting. In fact…" With one hand propped against the kitchen wall where he was doing the new estimate, he almost winced. "I think she might have someone for him to meet."

"Who? Charley? You're not serious."

"This is my mother we're talking about. Trust me, I'm serious—"

"Who're you talking to?" he heard in the background.

"Noah. Donna and Gene invited us for dinner tonight. I already told him you might not be up for it—"

"What're they having?"

"I have no idea." Then to Noah, as she obviously tried to hold in a laugh, "He wants to know what's on the menu."

"Beats me. Tell him to call Mom if he can't stand the suspense. So, sounds like he's recovering?"

"Apparently so. Although—" she lowered her voice "—he's still being a big old groucheroonie—"

"I heard that! And get off the phone so I can call Donna."

"I'm on my cell, use the landline! Honestly," Roxie said, chuckling aloud by this point. "I guess we'll meet you over there, then. We can't stay long, though, I've got a real early flight to Atlanta tomorrow morning."

A comment that put Noah in a funk for the rest of the day.

SHE CAME BEARING flowers and candy for his mother, who of course hugged her and told her she shouldn't have—except Noah could tell she was tickled pink, especially about the chocolate—before disappearing back into the kitchen, yelling at Noah to take the gal's coat, for heaven's sake. As if he couldn't figure that one out for himself. Charley immediately followed the sound of ESPN into the family room, where both the big screen TV and Gene resided.

"Mmm...roast pork?" Roxie said as Noah hung up her coat in the closet.

"Yep." Noah turned, fingers shoved in pockets, to admire the way her soft, white, big-collared sweater both clung to her curves and exposed her neck, flanked on either side by long, glittery earrings. "You look good."

"Well, *thank* you," she said, grinning. "Thought I'd wear this to the interview, too. With a skirt, though, not jeans. Opinions?"

"Hey. What I know about fashion can be summed up in three words—*hot* or *not*."

She laughed. "Good enough. And?"

"What do you think?" he said, leaning closer, smelling her perfume over the rich scent of roasting pig, the combination about to make his head explode, and yep, her eyes darkened and her chest rose...before she took a step backward, craning her neck to see past him.

"So. Where's this chick your mom wants to fix Charley up with?"

Got it. "Not here yet," Noah said. Frustrated. Disappointed. Grateful. "Everyone else is in the living room." A lusty newborn cry pierced the general chaos of a dozen Garretts sharing the same breathing space. "Including little Brady."

Practically shoving him aside, Roxie made a beeline for the living room, where Eli paced, trying to calm the squalling, dark-haired infant. Noah guessed his brother hadn't shaved in several days. Or, judging by the messed up hair and bags under his eyes, slept.

"Where's Tess?" Noah asked over the caterwauling.

"Home. Sleeping," Eli said, jiggling the baby, as his stepdaughter and stepson roared through the living room, Silas's two hot on their heels. He gave a slightly spacey laugh. "She actually fought me about it." He jiggled the baby again; Brady only screamed louder. "Like I couldn't handle my own son for an hour."

Rox lifted her arms. "Give him to me."

Eli shot her an are-you-nuts? look, then nearly dropped the red-faced infant into her arms. "He's fed, changed, burped and pissed about God knows what—"

"Go. Eat. You can come get him when you're done."

"You sure—?"

"We'll be fine." One hand firmly clamped around the little one's back, Rox shooed his daddy away. "Go on. Get."

Sagging with relief and gratitude, Eli blew Rox a kiss before gathering his two charges and heading into the dining room. Noah, however, followed her into the now vacated living room, where she settled with the baby in a corner of the blue-flowered sofa, plopping him on his tummy over her knees and rubbing his back. Almost immediately the infant got a lot quieter, his hollering settling into periodic screeches before, lo and behold, he passed out.

"Okay, that was spooky," Noah said from the doorway.

"Nah, just experience. I used to babysit a lot when

I was a teenager. It doesn't always work, of course, but babies pick up on when the person holding them is tense. And poor Eli looks like his brains are leaking out of his ears."

"He's taking this fatherhood thing very seriously. Tess told Mom if she wasn't breastfeeding he might not let her have the baby at all."

Roxie's soft laughter quickly dissolved into an expression that both wrecked and humbled Noah as she shifted the infant to her shoulder and leaned back into the cushions, letting the small, limp body mold to hers. He could practically *feel* her longing, her pain for the baby she'd lost. Except right at that moment she lifted her eyes to his, a slight smile touching her lips.

"Believe it or not, this doesn't make me sad."

"No?"

She shook her head. "More determined, perhaps, to have my own someday. But there's nothing better than the sweet weight of a baby in your arms."

"I know," he said, obviously startling her. "If you hadn't taken him, I would've. Don't know that I could've gotten him to crash like that, but I like holding babies, too."

"As long as you can give them back."

"You got it," he said, telling himself the words sounded hollow because his ears were still ringing from the kid's crying.

"You're a strange one, Noah Garrett." She nuzzled the baby's thick hair, like a shag rug run amok, before contorting her neck to peer down into Brady's squished little face. "I think somebody finally wore himself out."

"You want me to take him so you can eat?"

"No, we're good," she said, slouching farther into the sofa. "You go on. I'm not real hungry, anyway. Too excited about tomorrow. But save me a piece of whatever's for dessert."

"You bet," Noah said, then added, "need a ride to the airport?"

"Oh, thanks...but Charley's taking me. Besides," she said with a little smile, "when I said 'early' I wasn't kidding. I have to leave here at five in order to make it to the airport by six. And I know getting up early isn't your thing."

It could be my thing, he heard inside his head, only to then wonder who'd traded out his brain when he wasn't looking. "Yeah, you're right, that is way too early," he said, and she laughed, grabbing Brady's hands and kissing them when they shot up in his sleep. Noah stood for a moment, stealing one last glance at the pair before heading to the dining room, thinking there was a gal who deserved everything she wanted.

And for damn sure that didn't include him.

"YOU LOOK LIKE HELL," Gene said to Charley as he handed him a can of beer from the minifridge underneath the Garrett's family room bar. Dinner done, the rest of the family had crowded into the living room, knowing better than to encroach on Gene's man cave time.

Grunting, Charley dropped onto the sectional and popped off the top, took a swig. "Could say the same about you. Donna still on your case about working too hard?"

"Does the sun rise in the east?" his friend said with

a cross between a sigh and a chuckle, settling into his recliner. "What'd you think of Patty?"

That she's not Edie. "Nice enough gal, I suppose. No spark there, though, to be honest."

"Yeah, that's what I figured. But you know Donna."

"I do that."

They both sipped their beer, idly watching ESPN. Football. Charley hated football, actually, but wouldn't dream of mentioning it. Nor would Gene mention Eden unless Charley did first. That's just the way their friendship worked.

Then Gene shifted in his chair, casting a glance over Charley's head toward the other part of the house before looking at Charley and whispering, "You catch those two with Brady earlier?" and Charley didn't have to ask what Gene was talking about. Because that was another way their friendship worked.

"I certainly did."

"What's your take on it?"

Charley thought a moment, then said, "That youth is definitely wasted on the young."

"Ain't that the truth?" Gene said, settling back again, the beer propped on his stomach. "Can I say something?"

Charley braced himself. "Sure."

"That Roxie of yours turned out to be one fine gal. Smart. Sure of herself. And pretty as they come." His gaze slid to Charley's. "And you know what I think? I think she could work wonders with my boy. That she'd be real good for him. If she'd have him. Don't get me wrong, Noah's a good boy, but he needs some…fine tuning, if you know what I mean." He aimed the remote at the TV to turn up the volume. "Just thought I'd toss that out there."

Charley smiled. "Even though it's none of our business."

"Even though," Gene said with a sly smile. "Even though."

CHAPTER EIGHT

On Friday night, her head still in Atlanta—and not in a good way—Roxie and her carry-on trundled blindly down the Albuquerque Sunport concourse toward the meet-and-greet area beyond security, where Charley was supposedly waiting for her. *Supposedly* being the operative word here, she thought as, frowning, she scanned the crowd.

"Rox! Over here!"

And okay, so her heart did a little flippity-flop when she saw Noah instead. Because her heart was an idiot.

As was, apparently, the rest of her, she irritably mused as she watched him shoulder his bad, black-clad self through the mob until he reached her, panting, and irritation instantly morphed to panic.

"Ohmigod—is Charley okay—?"

"What? Yeah, yeah, he's fine. But he got tied up, so he asked if I could meet you instead. Only he didn't call until forty-five minutes ago, and I kept getting your voice mail, so I nearly busted something trying to get here in time—"

At which point her emotions did the lemmings-off-the-cliff thing, and she burst into tears. And launched herself into Noah's arms.

Like she said. *Idiot.*

"Whoa, honey…what happened?"

"I left my phone charger back here," she burbled as he wrapped his arms around her, and she thought, *Okay, so sometimes playing the distraught female has its advantages.* "Along with my pride and common sense."

"You're crying because your phone ran out of juice?"

"No, I..." She weighed the wisdom of what she was about to do, thought, *Screw it, you already threw your sobbing self into his arms, how much worse can it get?* and said, "I need a drink. And food." Then, telling herself to be brave, she pulled out of his arms to wipe her eyes, dig a tissue out of her handbag to blow her nose. "How about dinner?"

"You drink?" This said with a puzzled frown.

"I do now. Well? My treat."

"You're on," he said, which prompted her first laugh in more than twenty-four hours. Soggy though it may have been.

"You don't have a problem with a woman paying your way?"

"Oh, hell no," he said with a chuckle, steering her across miles of tile toward the glass doors, where the crisp night air dried what was left of her tears, blew some of the cobwebs from her brain. "I will, however, probably insist on reciprocating at some point. You okay with that?"

It was scary, how easily she could talk to this guy. Or, in this case, leave tear splotches all over his leather jacket—which smelled really, really good—how at ease she felt with him in so many ways, when in so many other ways they made no sense together.

"I am perfectly okay with that." A moment later they reached his truck in the parking garage and he held the door open for her and helped her in, because it was the biggest-ass truck west of the Mississippi and she was still wearing the stupid straight skirt she'd worn for the interview. And high-heel boots. When she settled into the seat, she noticed he was grinning. She sighed.

"Ogling my butt, were you?"

"It was kinda hard to miss. Because it was right in front of my face," he said, laughing when she shot him a look. And despite her disappointment and borderline humiliation, she was actually very glad to be home.

Inherent complications thereof be damned.

"So. You gonna tell me what went down?" Noah said as they drove, hoping that talking would get his mind off at least some of the crazy, explosive feelings reverberating inside his skull. Partly because he was still digesting what Charley had told him that morning about Roxie, partly because…holding her in his arms? Serious head rush.

She snorted. "Turns out they invited a *dozen* people to interview for the job. In *person*. I mean, they could have at least whittled it down to two or three, right? Because we have this thing called Skype now? But no. Twelve people had to schlep to Atlanta—except for one dude who lived there—for face time."

"Wow. That sucks."

"Tell me about it."

Noah swallowed. "I take it—?" Her eyes cut to his. "Ouch. Obviously not." And was it wrong of him to be not exactly broken up about that? Yes, of course it was. Dumb question. "I'm really sorry, Rox," he said, taking one hand off the wheel to clasp hers. When she sadly shrugged—and held on to his hand, he noticed—he said, "You gonna cry again?"

She seemed to consider this. "Nah. It's *so* nineteenth century. Mostly I'm mad. And feeling really stupid for not finding out what the deal was beforehand." Sighing, she removed her hand. "And what do you mean, Charley was tied up?"

"His words, not mine." Although he could guess. He also figured Rox had enough on her mind without getting into that right now.

Except she jumped right in anyway. "Meaning he's with Eden."

"That would be my take on it, yeah. Unless he's already found someone to replace her."

"Bite your tongue," she muttered, leaning against the passenger side window, only to immediately point to an Italian restaurant coming up on the right. "Oh! Can we eat there? I could devour my weight in shrimp scampi right now."

Noah pulled into the parking lot, taking in the faux Tuscan façade, the courtyard with a fountain. Even he could tell the place wasn't cheap, at least not by Albuquerque standards. "You sure? Might set you back a few bucks."

"You can leave the tip," Roxie said, releasing the seat belt. "How's that?"

"Deal." He got out, going around to help her down from the truck before she fell out and broke something. Except she stumbled anyway, landing smack against his chest. Never one to let an opportunity slip by, Noah hooked his hands on her waist and tugged her closer. "I'm gonna say you don't need that drink."

Rox smirked up at him. "And I'm gonna say you're wr—"

He honest to God hadn't meant to kiss her, but it

seemed like a good idea, so he thought *What the hell?* and went for it. Just followed, if not his heart, a couple other things intent on making their preferences heard. And *hel*-lo, damned if she didn't kiss him back, no holds barred, tongue and everything, right there in the halogen-lit parking lot. Kissed him as if this was the last kiss she would ever get. His hands moved from her waist to her jaw, his fingers tangling in those soft, smooth curls as he sank deeper and deeper into something he could feel picking off his brain cells, one by one by one. *Ping. Ping. Pingpingping.*

Eventually, though, common sense tapped his shoulder and cleared its throat, and he let go, only to have her grab the front of his jacket and shake her head. "You have no idea how much I needed that." Then, with a weak laugh, "Heck, *I* had no idea how much I needed that."

"I kinda guessed." He touched his forehead to hers. "Want another one? Because there's a lot more where that came from."

Then he guessed common sense tapped her shoulder, too, because he could see the focus return to her eyes. The truth of the situation. "Oh, you have no idea how much I want another one," she said softly, ruefully, taking his hands in hers. "But—"

He pressed one finger to her lips, even as that *but* walloped him upside the head. "It's okay, you don't have to explain." Stepping away, he curled his hand around hers and tugged her toward the restaurant's entrance. "It never happened, okay?"

Except it had. Because he'd let it. And thanks to following whatever the heck he'd followed he no longer had to wonder what it would be like to kiss her. Now, he knew.

Damn it.

"YOU LEAVING ALREADY?"

Buttoning his shirt, Charley looked back at Eden, still in her eyelet-smothered, four-poster bed with the covers pulled up to her chin. Still flushed from fooling around, he thought with a little thrill. Or maybe that was gratitude, that things—his, anyway—still worked. Sitting on the bed, he leaned over and pressed a quick kiss on her coral-smudged lips. "Roxie'll be back soon, she doesn't know I'm here. I don't want her to worry." Then he raised his brows, daring her to say something.

Instead, she sighed and patted his arm. "I wouldn't have called if I wasn't over all that."

"It's not a competition between the two of you—"

"I know, babe. No, really, I do." Clutching the covers, Edie settled farther into the down pillows, surprisingly modest, considering how surprisingly immodest she'd been a little bit ago. "I was just…panicked."

"Why?"

"Because I was scared I'd lose you, what else? So scared I wasn't thinking straight." She smiled. "Swear to God, I won't do it again. Promise."

"Good. Because that nearly killed me."

"Yeah. Me, too."

Edie leaned over and tugged a slithery pink robe off the nearby wing chair, somehow sliding it on without showing anything before getting out of bed, and Charley felt a surge of affection for her so strong it startled him.

They hadn't exactly talked before now, pretty much getting down to business within seconds of his walking in the door an hour earlier, with all the frantic desperation of two lonely souls who'd probably thought they'd never have that kind of connection ever again. Would they be each other's second Great Loves? Charley had no idea. But at this point he was more than willing to settle for close enough. And so, he wagered, was Eden.

"You think Roxie will be okay with this?" she now asked, watching Charley tuck his shirt into his pants, buckle his belt as she finger-combed errant red spikes back into place. Sort of.

"If she's not, she'll simply have to get over it," he said, slipping on his wool sports jacket, pocketing his keys. "Gal's not the boss of me." When, chuckling, Eden sat on the tufted pale blue velvet bench at the foot of the bed, he added, "Besides, I imagine she'll be moving to Atlanta soon, anyway. Once she gets this job."

Eden reached over to take his hand. "You don't exactly sound happy about that."

Charley met her gaze, feeling his forehead pinch. "I don't, do I?"

"Any idea why?"

He thought for a moment. "It's as if I only ever got to borrow her, you know? For a week or two in the summers, that one year she was in high school. These past few months now. I know she was never truly ours— mine—and God knows, she sometimes makes me want to pull out my hair," he said with a rueful half laugh, "but…I'm torn. Between wanting her to do whatever floats her boat and selfishly wanting her to stick around."

A half smile tilted Eden's mouth. "And you know you don't get a vote in it either way, right?"

Charley looked at her for a long moment, then said, "After your husband died, did he ever…talk to you?"

She laughed. "Only all the damn time. Especially in my dreams. Made me nuts. Why? Oh. You, too?"

He crossed his arms. "Yeah. Well, not all the time. And not for a while, actually. But a few weeks ago I got this real clear message that I was supposed to somehow 'fix' Roxie."

"Interesting. Considering the riot act you read me about you two not getting in each other's business."

"I only said I got the message. Not that I'd ever intended to act on it."

"Uh-huh." Her eyes sparkled. "So you sending Noah to pick her up…?"

"Nobody else was available," Charley said, jerking down his sleeve cuff. "He was…convenient."

"Of course he was."

"You don't see them together! The way they interact…he makes her *laugh*, Edie!"

"The maintenance guy here makes me laugh, too. Doesn't mean I want to marry him. Or even schtup him."

"I just thought—"

"Yeah, yeah, I know." She did a "Men, God," eye roll, then stood, clamping her hands around his arms. "Okay. Setting aside your one-eighty about Noah, here's where I throw your own words back in your face. Assuming Roxie's 'broken,' which I'm not all that sure about to begin with, nobody can 'fix' her except Roxie herself. Not you. Not Mae. Not Noah. Or any other man. And whether she goes or stays has nothin' to do with it, either. But considering all the crap she's had to deal with? Hell, she's stronger than you and me put together." She grinned. "Good thing, too, if she's gonna put up with me."

True enough, Charley thought, as a little more of the junk cluttering the inside of his head broke away and floated downstream. Smiling, he kissed the top of Eden's head before opening her door. Then he turned and said, "You know…I think you and I could be very good together."

Her eyes shimmered. "Funny. I was thinking the same thing," she said, and he could have *sworn* he heard Mae heave out a relieved sigh. Or maybe it was only the wind, pushing through the open door.

Charley kissed Edie again, then left, whistling quite the merry little tune as he walked down the stairs and out to his car.

ROXIE'S HEAD WAS still buzzing as she climbed the steps to the house after Noah dropped her off. Without, it should be noted, any more hanky-panky, as if they'd come to some sort of mutual unspoken agreement that as far as bad ideas went? That was the granddaddy of them all.

Never mind the electricity arcing between them during dinner, even as they pretended the kissy-face session out in the parking lot had never happened. Although she had to say, the necking definitely took the edge off losing the job. Or maybe that was the two glasses of pinot blanc with dinner. Or maybe the wine had taken the edge off knowing she would never, ever, ever kiss Noah again. Ever.

Okay, now she was making herself depressed.

She let herself inside, to find a humming Charley reloading cabinets in the newly finished kitchen, now a symphony in tans and creams and blacks. Pretty. If they'd had a kitchen table she would have definitely sat at it, since, between the flight and unwinding and the kissing and the wine she wasn't entirely sure how long she had until her knees gave out. Not to mention her brain. Which finally caught up to Charley's humming.

Ah.

"Let me guess. You and Eden are back together."

A stack of bread plates in his hands, Charley grinned over at her. "We are. At least we're going to give this thing between us a real shot, see where it goes." Then the grin melted into a frown. "You okay with that?"

"Of course," Roxie said gamely. "If she really makes you happy—"

"When we're not arguing?" The plates clattered onto the shelf. "Yeah. She does."

Okay, then. Charley had charged ahead with his life. Good for him. And God willing, the woman wouldn't drive him insane, or break his heart, or take him for every penny he had. But, hey—life was all about taking risks, right?

"And this way," he added, clunking another stack of plates on the shelf, "you don't have to worry about me being alone once you leave."

"Not an issue," she said on a sigh. Yep, Charley was striking out for distant shores, and here she was, treading water. "Not yet, anyway."

Brows drawn, Charley met her gaze again. "You didn't get the job?"

"No." She made do with the old step stool, now looking woefully out of place amidst all the Gleaming and New. "It's okay," she said with a wave of her hand, even though, now that the wine and the endorphins were wearing off, it wasn't. Drat. "The Atlanta traffic sucks anyway."

"I'm sorry, kiddo—"

"I *said,* it's okay. Any mail come while I was gone?"

"Over there, on the counter. Which looks great, by the way. It all does. Now that it's done, I'm glad you forced me into it."

"You're not just saying that?" she said, spotting the Priority Mail envelope with Jeff's return address.

"When have you ever known me to blow air up anybody's skirt? No. The old kitchen looked like Mae. This looks like me."

Never mind that he hadn't chosen so much as the paint color, Roxie thought with a half smile as she slit open the envelope, letting a half dozen CDs she had no interest in listening to, ever again, clatter onto the new laminate. To her consternation, her eyes burned, even though she knew beyond a doubt she'd been over Jeff for months. This wasn't the numbness of denial, either, but the relief of simply no longer caring.

The emotional betrayal, though, combined with lingering self-condemnation for thinking she could simply transfer all her hopes and dreams from Mac to Jeff, like switching out a bank account—that she wasn't over nearly as much as she might have thought. Or wished.

And her reaction to Noah's kisses tonight only reinforced that.

Because let's be clear, boys and girls—girlfriend was needy as hell. Emotionally, physically, the lot. But tumbling into bed with Noah—and she had no doubt the option was on the table, should she be inclined to exercise it—would solve nothing. Not for her, anyway. And right now? It was all about doing—or, in this case,

not doing—what was best for her. And what was best
for her was sticking to what was safe. What made sense.

And Noah didn't fit either of those criteria. At all.

Moving on. Great idea in theory, not so easy in practice.

ALTHOUGH NOAH HAD worked some at Charley's that
Saturday to keep the momentum going, he'd only seen
Roxie briefly as he was leaving and she was getting
home from the clinic. They exchanged pleasantries, he
caught her up on the progress, she caught him up on
Charley and Eden, they said good-night and that was
that. It hadn't seemed prudent to mention he'd slept
for crap the night before, having no idea at the time he
wouldn't sleep for crap that night or the one following, either.

So here he was on Monday, sleep-deprived as all hell,
albeit conscious enough—barely—to realize he'd never
lost sleep over a woman before. Granted, he thought
as he watched her turn the dining table into her own
branch of Ship 'n' Check, there was an outside chance
he could chalk it all up to plain old sexual frustration.
Meaning there was also an outside chance if they'd
just get it on, already, he'd be able to sleep again. And
yes, if Roxie could read minds he'd be dead right now.

Naturally she picked that moment to look up, frowning, and damned if his face didn't get hot. She picked
up a packing tape dispenser, slapping it against a box.
"You need me for anything?"

She should only know. With the morning light teasing her dark hair, her neck where she'd pulled it up save
for a bunch of little corkscrew curls around her tem-

ples, she looked nearly edible. "Just wondering what you're doing."

Roxie jerked the tape across the package. "Packing up Mae's stuff that sold on eBay so Charley won't have to worry about it. If necessary, I'll come back in the spring, hold a sale for whatever's left over."

Noah's stomach dropped. "You found a job?"

Her mouth twisted. "I wish. But you know me, ever the optimist. Obviously, if I'm still here…" He saw her chest rise with her breath. "Anyway." She rubbed her hands down the sides of her sweatshirt. "So you guys are almost finished?"

"Hope to be done and gone by Wednesday, yep."

"Charley's really pleased," she said, wrapping tissue, then bubble wrap, around a figurine of some kind. "But then he's floating on cloud nine these days, anyway. Did I tell you? He and I are going to Eden's for Thanksgiving."

"No. That should be…interesting."

"There's one word for it," she said with a low, just-Rox-being-Rox laugh, and Noah thought, *It's not gonna be the same when you're gone—*

"Noah? I know you're here, son, your truck's outside."

Roxie's head jerked up. "Your dad?"

"Yep. Said he might stop by sometime today, see how things were going."

"Checking up on you, you mean?" she whispered. "Man, that is *so* bogus."

Noah blinked at her, not sure whether to be more amused by her skateboard-dude-speak or flummoxed by her immediate defense. Flummoxed, and oddly…

pleased. Gratified. Turned on. "It's okay," he mouthed, leaving the room to meet his father in the foyer.

And even more oddly, it was. Because at some point he'd concluded that, actually, he didn't need to prove a blamed thing to his father. Or anybody else. He was hardworking, reliable and good at what he did. If his dad couldn't see that, it was his problem. Not Noah's.

Gene was already in the kitchen inspecting the cabinets, eyeballing the countertop levels, squinting at the tile floors. Arms crossed, Noah leaned against the doorjamb, watching, catching Roxie's scent as she came up behind him. His fierce little wingman, he thought with a funny twist to his midsection.

"Looks okay," Gene said, high praise for him. Only before Noah could get out his thanks, Roxie squirmed past him.

"It's a lot more than *okay*, Mr. Garrett," she said, a smile in her voice.

"Rox—"

"Hey." She wheeled on Noah, puffed up like a little bantam hen. And although she was smiling, she definitely had a *fear-me* glint in her eyes. "Am I the customer, or what? So you just hush and let me say my piece." Then she spun back to his dad. "'Okay,' my butt. It's *fantastic*. And he's ahead of schedule *and* coming in under budget."

Startled, Gene looked from Roxie to Noah—who, not about to take offense at her defense, simply shrugged—then back to Roxie. "You don't say?" his dad said, his eyes twinkling. "Well, if you're satisfied—"

"Try *thrilled*."

"Then so am I," his father said with a slight bow. "Although I take it you don't mind if I check up on some of the technical things?"

"Go right ahead. Although I can't imagine you'll find any problems."

Despite choking back a laugh, Noah was sorely tempted to pick the gal up by the back of her sweatshirt and remove her from the room before things got any more embarrassing. Especially when his father said, "Maybe you should let me be the judge of that?"

"Sure, do what you gotta do," she said with a flick of her hand, and marched out of the room, leaving Noah alone with his father. And a whole boatload of speculation, he'd wager.

"Sounds like you've got a real fan there," Gene said casually, after they'd toured the rest of the house, checking the repairs to the windows and floors before moving outside to the porch, which, under Noah's supervision, his brothers had repaired and repainted.

"Completely unsolicited, I swear."

His father let out a low chuckle. "Gal reminds me a lot of your mother when we were first dating."

"You're kidding?"

"Nope. Her passion, her honesty. Her fearlessness…" Looking over at his own house, Gene shrugged. "I remember thinking, when we first met, we'd probably knock heads at least once a day, but I'd never be bored. And I was right." He grinned. "On both counts. I never know what's gonna come out of that woman's mouth. Probably why we've never run out of things to talk about." He paused, then said, "She also told me I needed to stop being an old stick in the mud and trust you more. With the business, I mean. And on the surface, I agree with her."

"Finally," Noah muttered, but his father's hand shot up.

"Not so fast." Leaning his backside against the porch railing, he folded his arms over his heavy plaid jacket. "I'm still not exactly on board with some of your lifestyle choices."

Noah's eyes met his father's. "And I can't seriously believe you're going down this road again."

Gene's shoulders hitched. "Don't get me wrong, the house looks good. Real good. I've got no complaints about your work. But image counts for a lot more than we sometimes want to believe, whether we like it or not. How a person conducts himself carries every bit as much weight as how well he does his job. I know I can't make you into somebody you're not. That I've got no right to ask you to change, but—"

"Then stop trying," Noah said softly, his gaze swinging across the street.

"I can't help it. Just like I can't help that people naturally trust family men more. That's simply human nature, I didn't make it up—"

"Dad. For crying out loud…" On a strained half laugh, Noah faced Gene again. "You say that like being married is some sort of vaccination against never doing anything wrong again. Have you *listened* to the news lately? Plenty of married men screw up—"

"Not Garretts," his father said, as if it was an indisputable fact, then walked over to clap Noah's shoulder. "And sometimes a parent feels obligated, for his kid's own good, to point out things he knows the kid doesn't want to hear. Believe me, it would be much easier to keep my mouth shut. Except when you want that kid to be the best he can be? You don't." Gene squeezed his arm again, then started down the steps, leaving Noah to gag on the stench of his father's continued disapproval.

Despite his determination not to let the old man get to him, his stomach churned like a disturbed riverbed as he watched Gene walk out to his truck. Several deep breaths later he walked back inside to find Roxie in the living room, another box of Mae's stuff clamped in her hands and her eyes so full of sympathy he wanted to barf.

"You were eavesdropping?"

"You bet," she said mildly, setting the box on top of several others by the front door.

Anger exploded in his gut. "Coming to my defense earlier was one thing, even if it was totally unnecessary. But to blatantly listen in on a conversation that has nothing to do with you—"

"Was wrong and rotten and bad. I know." She straightened, facing him. And not the least bit repentant. "But at least it saves you the trouble of filling me in when you get over yourself enough to properly bitch about it."

"And what makes you think I need to do that?"

"Maybe because you look like you could snap nails in two with your teeth right now?"

"I'm fine."

"Bull."

Noah looked at her for a long moment, then wheeled and strode out of the room, hoping she'd get the message, that he wanted to be left alone, dammit. But no, she had to trail him like a hound dog through the house and outside to the backyard, where he slammed the palm of his hand against the trunk of an enormous, bare-limbed ash. He heard the dry grass crunch as she approached, stopping a good six or so feet away.

"For what it's worth?" she said. "You handled that with a helluva lot more restraint than I would have. That was seriously impressive."

"You're not going away, are you?"

"Nope. Just like you didn't go away the night of the pizza party. So deal. And by the way? Not sure I appreciate being made a substitute target, either."

A reluctant smile pushing at his mouth, Noah dropped his hand. Faced her. "I'd honestly thought I didn't care anymore. What he thought."

"I know," Rox said gently, and the irritation twisted into something far worse, something he had no idea how to handle. "And I swear I didn't mean to make you more angry. But I was so angry *for* you I couldn't help it." She shrugged. "Like I said. No restraint."

Right. This from the woman who had consciously chosen not to be bitter about the hand—hands—fate had dealt her. Then it registered what she'd said. "You don't agree with Dad?"

"Well," she said, perching awkwardly on the arm of an old, peeling Adirondack chair planted in the middle of the yard, "the part about people's skewed perceptions?" She let out an aggravated sigh. "Unfortunately, that's pretty much true." Snorting, Noah looked away. "But that doesn't mean I don't understand your frustration. Your crew obviously respects you. Hell, from what I can tell, they flat out worship you. Why your father can't see that, can't accept...*you*..."

He turned back to find her gripping the arms of the chair so tightly her hands looked like claws. "Ohmigod, it makes me so mad I could spit! To...to follow tradition simply because that's the way it's always been done? Especially about something as monumental as getting married? Having kids? Who gets to decide this stuff?"

Okay, color him slightly confused. "But...you're totally down with the whole marriage and kids thing."

"For *me,* yeah," Rox said, nearly toppling over when she pressed one hand to her chest. "Not for everybody. And to use marriage as some sort of yardstick to measure somebody's integrity...I can't even wrap my head around that, sorry. You have a right to live your own life, Noah, the way *you* want to live it. Not the way your father wants you to. So there."

Wow. Then, realizing she was shivering because she was probably freezing, Noah slipped out of his jacket and handed it to her, feeling another one of those funny gut twists when she practically disappeared inside it. "Thanks," she said.

Noah nodded, then smiled slightly. "Looks like there's no reason for me to bitch. Seeing as you already did it for me."

A stray, still-yellow leaf rappelled through the mostly bare branches to land in Roxie's lap. Idly, she picked it up, talking almost more to it than to him.

"Yeah, well, it hit home. See, apparently my parents had plans for me. Plans that didn't include me making a career out of telling people how much Great-Aunt Edna's eighteenth-century armoire was worth. Especially since my father had done the struggling artist thing most of their married life. Meaning Charley and Mae weren't exactly encouraging, either. We fought," she said to his questioning gaze. "A lot. Hence the Goth phase. And why I put myself through college. Out of state. That's also why I didn't come back very often to see them, because we'd get into the same argument every time I did. And it hurt, because I loved them. But it seemed the only way to ensure their happiness was to sacrifice my own."

Huh. Maybe they had more in common than he'd thought. "What did your parents want you to do?"

She smirked. "Anything that was 'stable.' As if such a thing exists in today's economy, anyway. Except maybe working for the IRS or going into undertaking," she said dryly. "They all meant well. I even knew it at the time. But we can't be who other people want us to be. Not successfully anyway." The fire flared again in her eyes. "God knows, your dad's a good man. But so are you. And it chaps my hide that he can't see that because his definition doesn't jibe with yours."

And again, her defense warmed him. However... "Rox—my reputation...that's not rumor, you know."

"Being a chick magnet doesn't automatically make you a dirtwad."

At that, he laughed out loud. "Oh, honey...if I was ever in a back alley fight? I'd definitely want you on my side."

Her eyes locked in his, she huddled more deeply into his jacket. "Same here," she said.

Then Noah said, "You're treading on real thin ice, you know that?" and her brows lifted.

"What's that supposed to mean?"

"That you have no idea how badly I want to kiss you again."

"Never mind that two minutes ago you were mad at me."

"Which would be two minutes before you blew my mind."

Then it seemed as if another two minutes passed before, on a rush of air, she said, "Okay, here's the thing—
you have no idea how much I'd like to kiss you again,
too—no, stay where you are, I'm not finished—but the
problem is, kissing has a way of leading to other things.
Which in theory is very nice. In fact, I'm a real big fan
of 'other things,' but, see…I learned the hard way that
I'm not one of those women who can fool around and
then go about my merry way. I…bond. Big time."

"As in…?"

"As in, my hormones turn to Super Glue and you'll
never get rid of me. Well, not without the words 'twenty-
to-life' being in there somewhere. And I'm thinking
that's not what you have in mind."

"Going to prison?"

Rox laughed, then sobered, a smile still lingering
on her lips. "I refuse to be anybody's jailer, Noah. Ever
again. Please don't think I'm only being a tease," she
said, concern swimming in her eyes, "because that's
not my intention. But I know who I am, what I want
and need. I don't have to defend it or make excuses for
it, but I do have to honor it. Honor myself. And I have
to honor you, too, by not letting you get into something
you don't want."

"But—"

"Sex isn't a momentary thing for me. It's a commitment. And yes, I know that makes me an oddball in this
day and age, but that's my cross to bear. So I'm going
to save both of us a lot of grief and say the subject is
now off the table."

He felt almost dizzy. "Forever?"

She got to her feet, letting his jacket slide off her
arms before she handed it back to him. "Maybe we

could make each other feel good for a little while," she said, and Noah thought, *Maybe, hell,* "but we wouldn't make each other happy. And making do simply isn't enough anymore. Not for me."

"You're still not over…what was his name? Mac?"

Instead of answering, she simply gave him one of those inscrutable smiles before walking back to the house. Swallowing hard, Noah realized he couldn't argue with her, or rise to her unspoken challenge to make her *forget* her first love. That she'd been absolutely right to walk away. That he should be grateful she'd refused to compromise his freedom.

Except, somehow he didn't think "freedom" was supposed to leave such a sour taste in your mouth.

CHAPTER NINE

GOD HELP HER, Roxie thought on Thanksgiving Day, as she listened to Charley and Eden trade good-natured barbs across the table from each other, the woman was beginning to grow on her. In much the same way one did get sucked into all those absurd reality shows, actually. Eccentric didn't even begin to cover it, she further mused when Eden bounced up from the table, one of her custom-made creations billowing around her as she floated to the kitchen to warm up the gravy, her prissy little dog clickity-clicking behind her. But she was clearly as smitten with Charley as he was with her, and jeezum, could the woman cook. So things could be a lot worse.

"So the house is all finished?" Eden now asked, settling back at the table like a swan on her nest.

Ah, yes. That. If nothing else, being here—up until this moment, at least—had diverted Roxie from thinking too hard about that last conversation with Noah. About the slightly horrified look in his eyes when she'd laid down what must have sounded like an ultimatum.

When she'd deliberately not answered that last question. Because right now, it was all about tossing out whatever obstacles came to hand, anything to slow down this runaway *thing* exploding between them.

"It sure is," Charley said, chest expanded as if he'd

done all the work himself. "And it looks terrific." Then he smiled at Roxie. "Thanks to your nagging, girl."

"Noah and his crew really did a great job," she said, poking holes in her yams, fascinated with the marsh-mallow ooze. Then, smiling for Eden, "You really need to come see the house."

Setting down her wine glass, the other woman eyed her speculatively. "You sure?"

Roxie reached out and took Eden's hand, clearly startling her. "Absolutely. You're welcome anytime." Letting go, she raised her own glass to her uncle and grinned. "Anything to get this old coot off my back!"

Eden barked out a laugh, then took up her knife and fork to resume her demolition of her turkey leg. "I like you, honey." She waved her knife in Roxie's direction. "You've got brass ones, doncha?"

Do I? she thought. Because if that were true, would she cut herself off from something she wanted so badly it made her cross-eyed, simply because she wasn't sure she could handle the aftermath?

Across the room, her phone warbled. "Sorry," she said, scooting over to get it out of her purse. "I can't imagine who it is…."

Seeing Noah's number on the readout sent a jolt through her midsection. "Noah—?"

"I'm sorry, I must be interrupting your dinner—"

"No, no, not a problem." Frowning, she shoved her hair behind her ear. "What's going on?"

She heard a rattling sigh. "Dad…he had a heart at-tack."

"Ohmigod, Noah! Is Gene…is he okay?"

"He's out of recovery after the angioplasty. So I guess so far, so good. He's still a little groggy, but def-

initely conscious. And a helluva lot calmer than the
rest of us," he said with the tense laugh of the petrified.
"And…he asked to see you."

Something close to alarm wrapped its long, bony
fingers around her neck. And squeezed. "Me? Why?"

"You'd have to ask him that. So. Will you come?"

"Of course," Roxie said, quickly, before the galloping
heart rate, the cold, sick feeling in the pit of her stomach, had a chance to fully register. After Noah told her
which hospital, she elbowed aside the panic enough to
ask, "Hey…how are *you* doing?"

"Better now than I was a few hours ago," he said on
another shaky laugh that made her ache for him, and
the panic ebbed…only to rush her from another, even
more vulnerable angle, that she could deny it 'til the
cows came home, but the fact was—big sigh, here—
she was completely, hopelessly, pointlessly in love with
the doofus.

"And your mom?" she said over the burning sensation in her eyes.

"A basket case in denial?"

"I bet," she said, then swallowed. "I'll be there in
five minutes. What's the room number?"

She found a pen in a drawer, scribbled the number
on a paper towel, then turned to find that Eden and
Charley had already put everything away and were in
their coats, ready to go, worry heavy in Charley's eyes
as he held Eden's hand.

Slipping into her coat, Roxie grabbed for her uncle's
other hand. "Hey. This is Gene we're talking about. He's
going to be fine."

Probably a lot better than I am, Roxie thought on a
sigh, as she herded the couple out to her car.

It took longer to navigate the hospital's endless corridors than it had to get there from Eden's, although the interminable marching at least gave her a chance to come to terms with her surroundings. To pat herself on the back that she hadn't walked through the glass doors, said, "Nope, can't do this," and gone tearing back out to the parking lot, a hyperventilating blur in an ivory mohair swing coat.

But she didn't. And at long last, Roxie and her mini-entourage found the coronary care waiting room, filled cheek-by-jowl with Garretts. Noah stood immediately, shaking hands with Charley and nodding to Eden before yanking Roxie against him and holding on tight. With his brothers watching, heh. But—and here was the weird thing—almost as if he were comforting *her*.

When he finally let go, searching her eyes for heaven knew what, she said, "Where's your mom?"

"In with Dad. The doctor came out a little bit ago, said if everything kept on as expected, Dad should only be in the hospital a day or so. But he's gonna be fit to be tied when the sedation wears off completely." He took her slightly aside, saying through a thick voice, "For all the man and I don't see eye to eye, I can't…"

"I know," she said, laying her hand on his arm. "I know."

At that moment, Donna Garrett emerged from the room, looking a little wan but collected—enough—in her Thanksgiving getup of a long, leaf-patterned skirt, a sweatshirt with gleefully oblivious turkeys marching across the yoke. Her sons all stood; she waved them back down. Seeing Roxie, she managed a smile, the skirt whooshing around her thighs when she sank onto the nearest seat, the adrenaline rapidly waning. She rallied enough, though, to give Charley a hug when he leaned over.

"He's dozing," she said to the room at large as she smoothed back her flyaway hair, then sagged back against the vinyl cushion, her eyes drifting closed. "He may have been the one who had the heart attack, but mine will never be the same, let me tell you." Then she opened her eyes and spotted Roxie. "Oh, my goodness…you came?"

"Well, yeah, of course." Roxie sat beside her, hugging her purse to her middle. "Because Noah said Gene asked for me?"

"About a half hour ago." Reaching for Roxie's hand, Donna gave her a gentle smile. "He wouldn't tell anybody why, but he was pretty insistent. Fair warning, though, honey—he was still pretty doped up at that point. He might not even remember asking. Hate to think you came all the way up here on a fool's errand."

"No, actually, I was already here, having dinner with Eden. But I would've come no matter what." Then, remembering her manners, Roxie introduced Eden to everyone…a moment before, unfurling her voluminous shawl, Eden plunked herself down on Donna's other side.

"I know we just met, so forgive my butting in…but I've got a pretty good idea what you're feeling right now—"

"Oh, I'll be fine in a minute—"

"Like hell." Tears glistened in Eden's mascara. "You might be brave. You might even be calm. But *fine?* No damn way. Trust me, sweetheart, I've been there. I know. Just like I know you need to let it out. And far better in front of me than your husband, right?"

Roxie could see Donna's valiant fight to hold it in—the tiny shake of her head, the tight press of her lips. But then, on a long, soft moan, she dissolved into tears, not even protesting when Eden pulled Noah's mother against her chest, making soft, crooning noises of her own.

Holy cow.

Suddenly overcome with all the emotions she'd thought she'd left back in the parking lot, Roxie stood and fled into the hall, only to hear Noah's soft, "Bringing back memories?" behind her seconds later.

She jerked around. "How did you—? Oh. You mean about the baby?"

He came closer. Wearing a brown T-shirt underneath a tan denim jacket, she noticed. Not black. "Well, that, too. But a couple of days ago, while you were at work? Charley got to talking." Compassion flooded his eyes. "Said you were at the hospital with your parents after the crash. By yourself."

Unable to speak for the tears clogging her throat, Roxie simply nodded. A second later she was once more in Noah's arms, his head nestled atop hers. "I can't imagine how awful that was for you," he whispered. "And then...the other."

"Yeah. Not a big fan of hospitals," she finally got out, pulling away. But he grabbed her hand.

"Maybe I had to tell you Dad wanted to see you, but you didn't have to say yes."

"I know. But I would've come in any case." She took a deep breath, thinking, *Fear is for wusses.* "Even if you'd only asked for yourself."

His brows lifted. "Really?"

"Really. So why didn't you?"

Still holding her hand, Noah glanced down, pushing out a sigh before meeting her gaze again. "Because I can't figure out what we are to each other. And whether whatever that is includes being able to call on you in a crisis."

"Don't make me smack you," Roxie said, and he smiled. "Look, I don't know what we are to each other, either. But I sure as heck know I hate it when we're not talking."

He gave her a crooked smile. "Me, too—"

"Rox?" Silas said from the waiting room doorway. "The nurse said Gene's asking for you."

Noah walked her to his father's door, giving her hand a brief squeeze before returning to the waiting room. But oh, dear God—the déjà vu when she stepped inside, saw Gene hooked up to all those whirring and beeping machines, was so strong she had to force herself to breathe.

Her father had passed away in the E.R. within minutes after being brought in, but her mother had hung on for almost another full day, although she never regained consciousness. Mae and Charley had gotten there as soon as they could, but Charley had told Noah the truth, that all through that long, horrible night she'd been by herself, barely seventeen and frightened out of her wits, staving off the agony of losing her father by willing her mother to stay alive. How she'd ever recovered from that, she'd never know. Let alone gone on to recover from Mac's death, from losing the baby, from Jeff's betrayal….

Noah was right, she thought with a slight smile. She was one tough little cookie.

Fortunately, Noah's dad didn't appear to be going

anywhere, thank God, even though he was still a bit loopy from the meds. But his color looked pretty good, from what she could tell, and the machines all seemed to be beeping and whirring as they should.

At Gene's indication that she should sit, Roxie silently lowered herself onto the edge of the padded chair next to the bed. "How do you feel?"

He almost smiled. "I'm gonna say like crap, although I'm not entirely sure."

"I bet." She swallowed. "You…wanted to see me?"

Gene rolled his head to look at her, grimacing at the oxygen tube in his nose. "It's funny," he said slowly. "In the back of your mind you know you don't have forever, but even further back you think you do. The doc says I'm gonna make it, but I'm not taking any chances. You sweet on my boy?"

Nothing like cutting to the chase. "Oh, Gene…if this is going where I think you're taking it…please don't—"

"I'm only asking 'cause I know he's got feelings for you." He pulled in a noisy breath. "Strong feelings. Stronger than he's probably ever had for anyone else his entire life. So before I make a damn fool of myself, I need to know if those feelings are reciprocated."

Damn. Damndamndamndamndamn. What on earth was she supposed to say? Maybe the man wasn't dying, but he wasn't exactly in optimal health, either.

"Okay, forget that," Gene said, and Roxie puffed out a sigh of relief, only to nearly choke when he said, "I'm gonna say my piece, anyway. If anybody could help that boy get his head on straight, it's you. He *needs* you, honey. Even if he's too mule-headed to see it, I do."

"Gene—"

"I know, I know…his past doesn't exactly speak in

his favor. But he's right on the cusp of changing, I can feel it. And I believe that's because of you. So if you could find it in your heart to give him a little encouragement…?"

The privacy curtain yanked back. "Okay, Mr. Garrett," said the broad-hipped, broadly smiling nurse. "We don't want you overexerting yourself now, do we?"

"But we weren't finished—"

"And there's no hurry, honey, I promise. Everything's looking good. No reason on earth why you can't continue this tomorrow when you're feeling stronger." She smiled down at Roxie. "You got a problem with waiting?"

"Me?" She practically shot to her feet. "Not at all. You have a nice, quiet night, Gene," she said, leaning over to kiss his forehead, "and…I'll see you soon, how's that—?"

He clasped her hand. "You'll think about what I said?"

As if she was going to be able to think about anything else. "I will. I promise."

"And you won't say anything to Noah?"

"He knows you asked to see me. Don't you think he's going to be the tiniest bit curious as to why?"

The nurse shot her a let's-not-upset-the-cardiac-patient-okay? look, and Roxie sighed. "I promise, I won't say anything to Noah. Do you want me to send Donna or the boys back in?"

"Donna. Please."

Naturally, Noah immediately jerked to attention when she came out of the room. Her brain going a mile a minute, Roxie delivered the message to Donna, then

walked a little apart from the others, figuring Noah
would follow.

"The nurse shooed me out before he could say very
much. And he wasn't making a whole lot of sense, really." Which was true enough. "Although…" She looked
up at him. "I think maybe this experience has made him
think differently about you."

"What's that supposed to mean? And why tell you?"

"I have no idea, and I don't think this is the best time
to look for logic."

He exhaled. "No. I guess not."

Searching for an excuse to leave, to give herself
space to figure out what the heck to do about this responsibility Gene had dumped on her, Roxie spotted her
uncle and Eden. "I hate to do this, but there's no real
reason for Charley and Eden to stay, and I drove them
here. So if it's all the same to you…"

"No, no, that's okay. We're going to try to get Mom
to go home in a little while," Noah said with a small,
tired smile, "although nobody's holding their breath on
how well that's gonna work. But thanks for coming. I'm
sure it meant a lot to Dad." He rubbed his mouth, then
crossed his arms. "And to me."

Roxie stood on tiptoe to kiss his cheek, breathing
in his scent, which ignited a sweet ohmigod-I-wanna-
make-babies-with-this-man ache in the center of her
chest, and she thought, *Biology blows.* "Tell your mom
if she needs anything, anything at all, I'm right across
the street." *For now, at least.* "And call me when you
get home. Anytime, even if it's late," she said.

He said, "Okay," even though she knew he wouldn't.

"Nothing more to do here, let's go home," she said,
waving Eden and Charley over, ignoring their puzzled

expressions as best she could as she said goodbye to the rest of the Garretts and started down the hall toward the elevators, Noah's questioning gaze burning a hole in her back the entire way.

Fortunately—deliberately?—once back in the car, Eden dragged Charley into a conversation about old movies Roxie couldn't even begin to take part in, followed by her uncle's dozing off almost immediately after they dropped Eden back at her place.

Leaving Roxie with nothing but tacky arrangements of Christmas carols on the car radio and her own thoughts to keep her company as she drove.

Blech.

"Charley? Charley!" she said after pulling up into his driveway sometime later.

"Wh— Huh?" Her uncle jerked awake, blinking like a sedated owl.

"We're home."

Well, *he* was, anyway, Roxie mused as she pulled her phone out of her purse, halfheartedly checking her Facebook page while keeping an eye on her drowsy uncle as they climbed the steps. Because hell if she knew where her home was.

Oh, joy, a friend request. Probably some friend of a friend of a friend she'd never met in her life. Yawning, she clicked on the icon, only to let out a shriek of delight when a very familiar face popped up on the tiny screen.

IT WAS WELL after midnight before Noah and his brothers finally convinced their mother to go home, get some rest, they'd bring her back as early as she wanted in the morning. Meaning, by that point, he wasn't about to call

Roxie. A good thing, all told, since he wanted to hear her voice way too much.

By the next morning, though, when they'd all trooped into Dad's room to find him sitting up and eating oatmeal and fake eggs—and moaning and groaning about it the entire time—yesterday's scare already felt like a bad dream...leaving a new reality in its wake. Because even if Dad took care of himself, lost some weight, exercised more, he couldn't keep driving himself the way he'd been.

Amazingly, Gene was the first one to admit that life as they'd all known it was never going to be the same. "I'm glad you're all here, because we need to talk about the future—"

"Dad," Silas said, his eyes bleary behind his glasses. "This can wait for five minutes."

"No, it can't. Because if you all want me to rest easy, then I need to have this settled in my head." As Donna, seated beside the bed, wrapped her hand around their father's, his eyes landed on Noah. "Well, son...you wanted more responsibility? You got it. From here on out, you're in charge."

Noah flinched. "Excuse me?"

"You heard me. You're the boss."

"What? No...the doctor said you'd probably be back at work in a week—"

"I know. But I made a promise to your mother, even after the docs give me the all clear, to cut my involvement way back. Oh, I'll still keep a hand in, retirement would drive me insane—and her, too, even if she won't admit it—but I'm turning the day-to-day stuff over to you."

Stunned, Noah looked at Eli and Jesse, standing in

almost identical, arms-crossed poses at the foot of the bed. "But you guys—"

"Come January, I'm going back to school, remember?" Jesse said, his pushed-up hoodie sleeves revealing almost solidly tattooed arms. "So I'll only be around part-time."

"And with the baby," Eli said, "I'm already behind in furniture orders as it is. I can't possibly catch up and oversee everything else."

"Besides," Gene put in, "you're right. Nobody knows the business like you do. So—it's yours. Since we're closed until Monday, anyway, we can work out the details after I get home."

Noah could imagine what some of those "details" might be. "That's…it?" he asked. Prodding. "No stipulations?"

His father regarded him in silence for a moment, then said, "Only that you remember whose standard you're bearing. And that I have the right to change my mind at any time."

"Like hell," their mother muttered, earning her a chorus of soft laughs.

"I won't let you down," Noah said.

"And I'm counting on you to keep that promise," Gene said, and Noah could still see flickers of doubt in his eyes, that while Noah may have been his only choice, he still wasn't necessarily his best.

Then his brothers said their goodbyes, with promises to stop by later, before easing back into their own lives. Their own brands of crazy. Noah was the last to give hugs, the last out of the room. And as he stopped by a water fountain to get a drink, he wondered…what did *he* have, besides new, hard-won responsibilities that came with enough entailments to sink a battleship? A sink devoid of female clutter? Nights uninterrupted by an infant's cry? The satisfaction of knowing that when he sat down to watch a movie he'd actually get to finish it?

That so-called "freedom"?

At which point, a thought that had been poking and prodding and trying to find a way into his brain showed its face in a dingy window, waving like mad to get his attention, its voice faint but insistent.

"Hey, bro," Silas said as they all piled into the elevator. "You okay?"

"Yeah, of course. Why wouldn't I be?"

Silas and Eli exchanged a glance before Eli said, "You don't exactly look happy about that conversation. Even though you've been after Dad for years to give you more authority."

"Because I'd always pictured that happening because he wanted to," he ground out. "Not because he didn't have a choice!"

The conversation died a quick death when a yakking family of five piled onto the elevator on the next floor... and when they all got off Noah strode away from his brothers, hopefully sending a clear message that he was in no mood to pick it up again. Not that they wouldn't at some point, but right now all he wanted was to be by himself.

Which wasn't exactly true, he thought, as he started back to Tierra Rosa. Right now, all he wanted was to hang out with Roxie. To somehow absorb some of that level-headedness, to hear her laughter. So when he noticed her car clinging like a mountain goat to Charley's steep driveway as he drove past, a nice little inner battle ensued as he reminded himself that what *he* wanted wasn't fair to her, that it was self-centered and childish.

And that he was better than that.

Except no sooner had he passed than he remembered it was the day after Thanksgiving. Meaning, in Garrettville, the day the Christmas decorations went up—his mom decked the halls from top to bottom, while his dad set up an outside display easily rivaling the Chevy Chase *Christmas Vacation* movie. Which, Noah thought as his eyes stung, along with *Muppets' Christmas Carol* and *It's a Wonderful Life*, they'd all watched every year.

His gut clenched. Because suddenly, he felt like a planet jettisoned from orbit, flung far, far away from its solar system.

Like hell, he thought, the brakes squealing as he made a U-turn and returned to his parents'. Twenty minutes later, a good two dozen boxes marked "Christmas—outside" sat on the porch or in the yard, along with an untold number of heavy-duty extension cords and plugs-on-a-stick.

Take that, world, he thought as he dumped out enough icicle lights to doll up the Empire State Building.

"WHAT ON EARTH is the boy doing?"

Taking a moment to let the buzzing in her brain subside, Roxie broke her gaze from her phone to see Charley standing at the brand-new, double-paned window. Around which hung motionless draperies, praise be. Eden, who'd arrived with her dog before Roxie was even up, was in the kitchen—which she'd declared "a miracle"—chopping vegetables and whatnot for stew.

And singing a tune from *Oklahoma!* Things would most definitely never be the same.

In many ways.

As if in a dream, Roxie got up to peer out the window. Across the street, Noah looked like a fly caught in a web of icicle lights, desperately struggling to break free—a sight that tickled her almost as much as it made her want to weep.

"It would appear he's putting up Christmas decorations," she said. "Trying to, anyway."

"That's Gene's job…oh. Right." Charley paused. "I'm gonna guess he has no clue what he's doing."

Roxie laughed, despite the weird, tight feeling in her chest. "I think that's a safe bet," she said, heading to the closet for her heaviest sweater-coat.

"Where you going?"

"To help. Wanna come?"

"Not on your life. Although I might dig out the Christmas wreath if the mood strikes." Her uncle settled into his overstuffed chair, grabbing his glasses and half-read mystery off the table beside it. Then he looked over the glasses at Roxie. "You gonna tell him?"

"I don't know. Because it's not settled yet," she said to Charley's raised brows.

"Sounded pretty settled to me, from what I just heard."

"Then not settled in my head. I need some time to get used to the idea myself, before I go blabbing about it to all and sundry."

"Noah's hardly all and sundry. And that didn't keep you from telling anyone who'd stand still long enough about the Atlanta thing—"

"I am capable of learning from my mistakes," Roxie

said, grabbing her mittens off the table by the front door and heading out into the cold, crisp morning, where all those mistakes she'd declared herself so capable of learning from taunted her mercilessly from the sidelines. Creeps.

Noah glanced over the minute the front door closed irrevocably behind her, and she wondered how it was possible to be this conflicted and still function.

"You look like you could use some extra hands," she called as she trooped down the steps.

He grinned the grin of the completely beleaguered, and her stomach went all disco fever on her. "Only if they're yours."

Now across the street, she forced herself to traverse his lawn, the dry, brown grass crunching underfoot as she came closer, telling herself turning tail right now would be totally lame. "How's your dad?"

"Doing pretty good, thanks. Should be home tomorrow, in fact. But…" Noah's gaze swept the house. "But ever since I can remember, the decorations went up without fail the day after Thanksgiving. And since Dad can't…" Noah cleared his throat, then looked at Roxie again, one side of his mouth lifted. "Do you remember what the yard looked like? When you were here in high school?"

"Like the mother ship had landed," she said, hating the gentleness in his voice, her susceptibility to it, as she bent over to open one of the boxes. "Wow. Inflatables?"

Noah chuckled. "We'd gone to Wal-Mart a few years back to get some replacement bulbs. I still remember the look on Dad's face when we walked through the door and spotted the display. Like a little kid, I swear. I also remember the look on *Mom's* face when we came home with not one, not two, but *three* of the damn things. There's also a lit-up train that goes around the whole yard. On tracks."

"Ohmigosh," Roxie said on another laugh. "You're kidding? No wonder he starts so early—it must take a week to get it all done!"

"Something like that, yeah. Depending on how many of us he can strong-arm into helping him." He scanned the yard, as though envisioning the scene. "Dad gets a real kick out of watching the kids when they come to see it all," he said before his eyes touched hers again. "And I know he'd be disappointed if they showed up and there was nothing to see. Here. Take this end."

He handed Roxie the plug end of the lights, slowly walking backward, patiently untangling as he went, just as he patiently dealt with his father's foibles every day…and she understood. Why he was out here freezing his butt off, why he put up with Gene's nagging, all of it. Because for all their differences, their bond was indissoluble. Although to be honest, it almost made her mad, that someone so obviously devoted to his family couldn't see his way clear to start one of his own.

"This is definitely much easier with two people," Noah said, the recalcitrant lights yielding far more quickly with four hands prying them apart.

"Most things are," she said.

His eyes cut to hers, then away. "Dad put me in charge of the business."

"Really?" He nodded. "Temporarily, or…?"

"He said from now on, but who knows?" That strand set to rights, Noah carefully laid it on the porch and dumped the next one out of its box. "Except I can tell he had…reservations. That if he hadn't had that heart attack he never would have handed over the reins, un-less…" He yanked too hard on the strand. "Unless I'd met his conditions."

"The same ones from before?"

"I imagine so. And you know what?" he said on a frosted breath. "It sucks that I'm nearly thirty and still feel like I have to fight for my father's approval. That no matter what, I still come up short in his eyes. Why the hell should it even matter?"

Okay, so maybe not *that* patient. Not that she didn't understand that, too. The closer the relationship, the more tangled it was likely to be. Like the lights.

"It matters because you love him," she said gently, even as her stomach sank, remembering what Gene had asked of her the day before. "Everybody wants their parents to be proud of them." His only reply was a grunt. "What are you going to do?"

"Work my butt off. Make sure I don't give him any reason to regret his decision. And maybe…" His eyes swung to hers, and electricity shot through her.

"What?"

He gave her a long, hard look that sent another hundred megawatts or so crackling along her skin. But instead of finishing his thought, he handed her the strand of lights. "Hang on to this while I get the ladder?"

He'd barely gotten ten feet before she blurted out, "I got a job offer."

And when he whipped around, she saw in his eyes exactly what she'd suspected he'd stopped himself from saying.

Not funny, God, she thought. *Not funny at all.*

CHAPTER TEN

"WHERE?" NOAH SAID, the only word he could squeeze past the knot in his throat.

"Austin."

"How…?"

"It was really weird, actually," Rox said, with a short, nervous laugh. "Out of the blue, my former college roommate—we lost track of each other years ago—friended me on Facebook. Turns out she's a designer now, in Austin. Which is her hometown. Anyway, long story short, we started texting, then she called me…and it turns out she also owns this funky little furniture and collectibles store, and she's looking for someone knowledgeable to take over the merchandising because she's about to have a baby. So when she found out I was looking for a job—"

"She said it was yours."

"On the spot. With the possibility of becoming a partner some day. I even get to go on shopping trips all over the world, can you imagine?"

Although she was obviously trying to soft-pedal the news, there was no keeping the excitement out of her voice. Or her eyes. "When did this happen?"

"Actually, we've been on the phone all morning, ironing out the particulars." Her nose was turning red;

she scrounged a tissue out of her pocket and wiped it. "I said I needed to give Naomi two weeks' notice."

Noah slowly lowered himself onto the cold porch steps, reminding himself they'd firmly established they didn't want the same things, that a relationship between them would have never worked. Not to mention he'd known all along she wasn't going to stick around.

Reasonable arguments, every one. And yet…

After a long pause, Roxie came and sat beside him, linking her arm through his. "This wasn't supposed to happen," she whispered, leaning her head on his shoulder. Which, because logic was clearly not his friend right now, felt inexplicably right.

"This?"

"Us."

Noah covered her hand with his. Swallowed hard. "The funny thing is, before you announced you'd found that job, I'd almost said—"

"That we should give it a shot? See where it goes?"

"Yeah," he breathed out.

"To make your father happy?"

He craned his neck to look at her. "You actually think I'd hook up with somebody just to please Dad?" She shrugged against his arm. "Honey, he's been on my case about this for years. Believe me, if all I'd wanted to do was shut him up I could've gotten hitched long ago."

"Why is that not making me feel better?" she said, and he chuckled.

"Only telling it like it is. But…even as I considered asking if you were game, I knew it wasn't fair to you. Or right." He rubbed her arm for a moment, gathering his thoughts. "The thing is…it really does feel different. With you, I mean. I actually *like* you. I like being *with* you, talking to you. And I don't doubt for a minute we'd have a lot of fun in bed. Still and all, whenever I think of the next step…I choke."

"It's okay—"

"Dammit, Rox—would you stop being so reasonable? It's not okay, it's messed up, is what it is."

"Except, it would have never worked anyway, right? I'm leaving in two weeks, you've g-got obligations here…" *Ah, hell,* he thought as she said, in a small, mad voice, "I *knew* it was stupid to let myself fall for you. Knew we'd never see eye-to-eye on certain major issues. And for damn sure I wasn't about to go through that again, not after Jeff. But it was like…knocking a glass off the counter, when you all you can do is stand there and watch it fall, knowing it's going to crash into a million pieces."

Tell me about it, Noah thought, his heart fisting in his chest. Then he slung his arm around her shoulder and pulled her to him again, rubbing his cheek in her hair. "I'm so sorry, honey."

"For what? Being who you are?" She paused, skimming one fingertip over a varnish stain on the knee of his jeans. "I was *so* sure, as long as I didn't sleep with you I'd stay in control." She made a *pfft* sound through her lips, then sighed. "But that's not *your* fault. I still could've been more careful with the glass, made sure not to leave it on the edge. And I didn't."

"Because you're still not over Mac?"

"No!" Roxie lifted her head to look at him, her gaze steady despite the crease between her brows. Then her mouth scrunched on one side. "Okay, to be honest, you do remind me of him in some ways. Or did, before I got to know you. But when I moved on from Jeff I apparently left Mac behind as well." She nestled her head on his shoulder again. "Believe me, buddy, whatever I feel for you, I feel for *you*. Not as a memory or a placeholder, but as somebody I think is amazing in his own right."

He snorted. "Amazing?"

Her soft laugh vibrated against his shoulder before she looked at him again. "It's true. Screwed up though this may be, at least I've got that part straight in my head. I'm not confusing you with anybody else. Cross my heart."

That makes one of us, Noah thought with a twist to his gut. "So...what do you want to do now?"

Roxie pushed herself to her feet, backing into the yard to look up at the porch. "Finish decorating this house, for starters."

"That's not what I'm talking about."

Her troubled gaze fell to his. "I suppose, by rights, we should call it quits now."

Noah stood as well. "Because pretending each other doesn't exist in a town the size of a peanut is going to work so well?"

"I hate this," she muttered, and he pulled her into his arms again.

"We could just play it by ear, you know," he said into her hair.

"Except—"

"Clothes will stay on. Promise."

She leaned back, frowning. "You sure you're okay with that?"

"Strangely enough, yeah." His heart hammering in his chest as he thought, *Dude, who* are *you?* "Because, you know that bonding thing? I'm thinking, in this case, you wouldn't be the only one with a problem if we fooled around."

"He said, gritting his teeth—"

"I'm serious, Rox." His hands moved to her shoulders so he could look her in the eyes. "Unless one or the other of us changes our mind about what we want, long term. And somehow I'm not seeing that happen. So," he said, releasing her, "we better get our rears in gear if we have any hope of getting this done before Dad gets home tomorrow."

Then he turned to drag the first of many reindeers and bears and such out of their oft-taped boxes, silently chewing out fate's ass.

"WHAT ARE THEY doing now?" Charley asked Eden, who, her stew on the stove, apparently had nothing better to do than stand at the window holding her little dog and watching the goings-on across the street. And report to Charley.

"Hard to tell from here—if I'd known, I would've brought my opera glasses—but after he hugged her, they talked some more and now they've gone back to decorating the house. No kissing, though. So kinda inconclusive."

Charley pushed himself out of the nice, comfy chair and joined her at the window, exchanging distrustful glances with the dog. "You think she told him?"

Eden turned her head, making the wide-neck black sweater she was wearing slide off one shoulder, exposing a bright red bra strap. "While I'm far from deaf," she said, tugging it back up, "I don't have supersonic hearing. Nor am I clairvoyant."

"Oh, I don't know about that," Charley said, thinking about that shoulder. And where it led. "You always seem to guess right when I'm about to…you know."

Eden rolled her eyes and looked back out the window, only to smile when Charley bumped his hip into hers, not even caring when the dog growled at him. "Looks like they're gonna be a while," he said, giving her moony eyes. "Wanna mess around?"

"Actually, I think we should follow their example and do some decorating ourselves." She set down the dog, who gave her a dirty look before mincing over to plop in her leopard-print bed by the fireplace. "Give the place some holiday cheer."

"I'd much rather you give *me* some holiday cheer."

"You got your holiday cheer this morning, you can wait a few hours for the next dose. So whatcha got? In the way of decorations, I mean?"

Charley pushed out a loud, pity-me sigh and started for the garage, marginally cheered when, chuckling, Eden grabbed his hand and pulled him back around to give him a compensatory kiss, and he suddenly felt so happy it nearly made him dizzy.

Then he glanced out the window one last time at his mixed-up niece, so determined to get what she wanted she couldn't see it was smack dab in front of her face. "I know it's not up to me to fix her, but it seems so… unfair."

"She's a smart girl. She'll figure it out," Eden said.

But the question was, he wondered as Donna's old Jeep Cherokee pulled into the driveway, would Noah?

HIS MOTHER GOT out of her beat-up Explorer, a big, goofy smile stretching across her face as she took in what they were doing. "I can't believe you even thought about this."

"Day after Thanksgiving means leftovers and decorating," Noah said. "Wouldn't seem right otherwise. Besides, I thought it would cheer Dad up."

"Or tick him off that he didn't get to do it himself," Donna muttered, then sighed. "To be honest, I'd totally forgotten until I overhead one of the nurses talking about setting up her tree." Then she noticed Roxie. "And how on earth did *you* get dragged into this?"

"Believe it or not, I volunteered," she said, and his mother shot him a look that plainly said, *Good Lord, she's as crazy as we are.* "How's Gene doing?"

His mother did a *you don't want to know* hand waggle, then tromped around to the back of the car and opened the hatch, the sun flashing off the silver clasp thing holding up most of her hair. "He's coming home tomorrow. If they don't kick the big pain in the patoot out sooner." Except it was perfectly obvious how scared she'd been of losing that pain in the patoot. Peering into the car, she shook her head. "Since I was in Santa Fe, anyway, I figured I may as well pick up a few things at Sam's Club. Big mistake."

Aside from the normal supplies—toilet paper and paper towels and eighteen packs of tomato and chicken noodle soup—everything else was for his father. Plaid shirts and a new pair of slippers. Hardback novels by two of his favorite writers. A treadmill. And—

"You can't be serious?" Noah hauled the boxed inflatable—an eight-foot-tall snow globe sheltering a trio of caroling polar bears—out of the depths of the truck. Behind him, Roxie giggled. "And you can just hush," he said, and she giggled harder, which only made Noah

more morose, thinking about how much he was going
to miss making her laugh.

"So you're not the only one who wants to cheer him
up," Mom said. "And anyway, when you love somebody
you give them what makes them happy." She made a
face at the inflatable's box. "Even when it hurts." Then
she looked at Roxie and smiled, and Noah heard the
Gong of Doom go off in his head. "Honey, why don't
you come inside and help me make up a couple of turkey sandwiches?"

"I'LL NEVER UNDERSTAND," Donna said, shoving up her
sweater sleeves as she regarded the inside of her refrigerator, "how I can feed so many people at Thanksgiving
and still have this many leftovers. There's ham, too, if
you like. And I suspect—" she hefted the turkey car-
cass to the counter "—you're well aware I don't need
help to make a few sandwiches."

"Yeah," Roxie said, sitting at the kitchen table, "I
kinda figured you had that down by now. So what's up?"

One eyebrow lifted. "Why don't you tell me?"

"Is this you being mama bear looking out for her
cub?"

Donna laughed. "As if I could. And anyway, the cub
is plenty able to look out for himself. Has been for some
time. Which I've been told in no uncertain terms. However, after raising a whole slew of cubs, Mama Bear
is extremely observant. And nosy." Peeling back the
foil, she cut her eyes to Roxie. "I've never seen him act
around any other gal the way he does around you. You
ask me, he's got it bad."

Heat flooding her face, Roxie lowered her eyes, worrying a little silver ring on her pinkie her mother had

given her when she turned sixteen. "I accepted a job in Austin. This morning. I start in a couple of weeks."

"Oooh." Donna's brow crinkled. "I see. Does Noah know?"

"Yeah. I just told him," she said, adding, because she'd only promised Gene she wouldn't say anything to *Noah,* "did his dad tell you why he wanted me to come to the hospital?"

"No, as a matter of fact." Donna hauled a carving knife out of a block in front of her and start shaving off slices of white meat, then glanced in Roxie's direction. "I'm not gonna like this, am I?"

"Probably not. He did everything but promise me a dowry if Noah and I got together."

"Oh, Lord, that man," Donna sighed out. The knife set down, she turned, her arms crossed under her breasts. "Although with you going to Austin, I suppose the point is moot, anyway."

"Heh," Roxie said, thinking, *So this is hell. Colder than I expected, but whatever.*

"Oh, honey…love really sucks sometimes, doesn't it?"

Figuring there was no point in denying it, Roxie got up and snatched a piece of cut turkey, cramming it into her mouth. It wasn't chocolate, but sometimes you can only work with what you're given. "I feel like I've been ambushed," she muttered, chewing.

"That's pretty much the way it goes," Donna said, handing her another piece of turkey.

"It's so unfair." With great difficulty, Roxie swallowed the dry turkey mush in her mouth. "Noah was supposed to be the same Good Time Joe he was in high school. In fact, you have no idea how much I counted on that. He wasn't supposed to have…grown up."

Donna smiled. "It does happen eventually. Even to boys."

"Except…he still doesn't see himself doing the kids-and-mortgage thing. Which doesn't make him less of a grown-up, but it does mean I could never do what Gene asked. Even if I wasn't leaving." She tried to swallow again, only to nearly choke. Donna yanked a bottle of organic milk from the fridge, pouring a glass and handing it to Roxie. She washed down the mashed turkey, then said, "Which should be a solution, right? Out of sight, out of mind? So why do I feel like I'm being ripped apart inside?"

On a soft moan, Noah's mother took Roxie into her arms, holding her tight for several seconds before releasing her to snitch her own piece of turkey. "You know… nothing ever scared that boy growing up. Nothing. And he's got the scars to prove it." She wagged the turkey at Roxie. "So why the idea of settling down, having kids of his own, rattles him so badly, I have no idea."

Sipping her milk, Roxie walked over to the window to watch Noah set up a family of lit reindeer on the front end of the lawn. "Me, either. But damn…it seems such a *waste*."

A soft chuckle preceded, "Do you trust the goofball?"

Roxie wheeled around. "You're calling your own son a goofball?"

"Oh, you have no idea some of the things I've called my boys over the years. Well?"

A second or two passed before Roxie slowly nodded. "Yes, I do. Because he's never played the player with me. He's always been totally up front about his expectations. We both have, actually."

"Then the foundation is there, believe it or not. Now all you can do is have faith that if this is meant to work out, nothing or no one can stop it."

Roxie smiled, not having it in her to disabuse the woman of her fantasies.

NOAH WALKED INTO the office and shut the door, barely muffling the noise from a half dozen power tools doing their thing. The past few days had been beyond busy. Not that Noah couldn't handle it, he was handling it all just fine—and loving it—but between his dad's return home on Saturday and his consequently needing to help his mother out, then his diving headfirst into his new duties even before the shop reopened after the holidays, he hadn't seen Roxie since the day after Thanksgiving. Meaning he felt like a game show contestant playing against a relentlessly ticking clock.

"Lunch?" he said when she answered Naomi's phone.

"Oh, um…really swamped here," she said, her voice sounding strange. And strained.

"Dinner, then? Although it might be late, I'm not getting out of here before seven these days—"

"Can't. Charley and I are going to Eden's—"

"Boss?" Benito said as he opened the door, knocking as an afterthought. "Oh, sorry—didn't realize you were on the phone."

Waving Benito inside, he said, "Tomorrow?"

"I'll call you, how's that?" she said. And hung up.

Noah frowned at the phone for a couple of seconds before clipping it back on his belt. His father's—now his—right-hand man frowned in concern.

"Everything all right?"

"Not sure," Noah said, feeling like his brain was stuffed with Silly Putty. "You need me?"

"Yeah. Thought you'd want to look over these specs for that new job before we get started."

Forcing himself back to the present, Noah considered the barrel-chested, bulbous-nosed man in front of him, who'd been working for his father since before Noah was even born. Who'd taught him even more than his father had. And who probably needed him to sign off on a project about as much as he needed Noah to teach him Spanish.

"You really think that's necessary?"

Thick, salt-and-pepper brows lifted on a weathered face. "I jus' figured, you'd want to do things like your dad."

One side of Noah's mouth lifted. "Which doesn't answer my question."

He could see the older man try to hide his smile underneath his heavy mustache, but it wasn't working. "I like to think of myself as a smart man, Mr. Noah. Smart enough to play the game however the boss man wants. No skin off my nose, you know?"

Dude was a master of diplomacy, that was for sure. "And what if I said I completely trust you to handle things on your end? Probably a lot better than I would."

Benito gave him a quizzical look. "I'm real flattered. But in this case, your daddy had the right idea, making sure at least two people know what's going on. So if it's all the same to you, I'd feel better having that second set of eyes."

"Then I'm good with whatever works for you."

The foreman nodded, then said, "Anything else?"

"Yeah. That you won't laugh too hard at my stupid questions."

"Not sure I can promise that," Benito said, his dark eyes sparkling. "Damn, it seems like yesterday when you were a baby, coming in here with your daddy an' building towers outta wood scraps over there in the corner. And now, here you are. The boss."

"*You* think that feels weird?"

Benito chuckled, then clamped his meaty hand around Noah's upper arm. "You know something, it takes a real man to admit he doesn't know it all. You're gonna make Mr. Gene real proud of you."

"That's what I'm hoping," he said, as the nonconversation with Roxie replayed in his brain, and he realized he'd never be able to fully concentrate on business until he figured out what was going on with her. Getting up to snag his barn coat off the rack by the door, he nodded in the general direction of the desk. "I need to go out for a while. Can you hold down the fort?"

"Sure thing. No problem," Benito said with a wide smile. Then he winked. "Although it might cost you."

The coat half on, Noah frowned at the other man. "How much does—did—my father pay you?"

The other man snorted. "Not enough. Not that I'm not grateful for the work—"

"Say no more." Noah hiking the coat onto his shoulders, digging in the pocket for his keys. "I'm not that familiar with the finances yet, but let me talk it over with Silas, see what we can do."

Affection gleamed in the man's dark eyes. "You know, sometimes you hear about these family businesses, the father passes it along to his kid, and the kid doesn't want it, or isn't interested, or the whole thing goes to hell in a handbasket, you know?" He shook his head, then extended his hand. "I'm proud to work for your daddy for more than thirty years. And God willing, I'm proud to work for you for thirty more."

"Same goes, Benito," Noah said, clapping the man's hand and giving it a hearty shake before heading toward the door. "I won't be long."

"Take your time, boss," he heard behind him. "Everything's under control."

In there, *maybe,* Noah thought as he stomped out to his truck. In his head, *not so much.*

CHAPTER ELEVEN

FUNNY, ROXIE THOUGHT—when she looked up from the clinic's computer to see Noah looming over her—how you think you've got your feelings about somebody all sorted out until there they are, in front of you, and suddenly you don't know squat. Especially when the sight of the looming somebody makes your mouth go dry and your stomach turn inside out, and pheromones are flitting about like frakking sugarplum fairies.

"Noah! What on earth are you doing here?"

Angling his head toward the doctor's open office door, he called out, "Hey, Naomi—you got a problem with me taking Rox out for lunch?"

"What? Now hold on just a minute—!"

"Not at all," the doctor said, coming to the door. At which point Roxie shot her a you're-not-helping glare. "Although Roxie might."

She turned the glare on Noah. "Thought I said we were busy?"

Noah glanced around the empty waiting room, prompting Naomi to say, "Yeah, I know. Slowest afternoon we've had in forever. Can't believe it myself."

"A lull," Roxie said. "It'll pick up. With appointments. And things."

"So where you taking her?" Naomi said.

"Evangelista's. Where else?"

"Oh! Bring me back a couple of cinnamon rolls, would you?" She dug in her pocket for a five-dollar bill, handed it to Noah. "And a cup of coffee?"

"Oh, see," Roxie said, banging her knee as she sprang up from behind the desk. "I need to make coffee, I can't go."

"Baby," Naomi said, "you know I adore you, but you can't make coffee to save your life."

Pocketing Naomi's five—because, you know, Roxie was just a bystander, this had nothing to do with her—Noah gave her a funny look. "You can't even make coffee? Now that's sad. Get your coat, it's freezing out there."

"I can't, I've got—" At Noah's glower, she muttered, "Fine," and trudged to the closet.

"What's this all about?" she said, once they were in Noah's truck. Black. Like a hearse. Fitting, somehow.

"You want to call it off, then call it off. Because this avoidance crap is not you."

Okay, that was her bad, hoping he'd be so busy this thing between them would simply die a natural death, and she wouldn't have to actually act on the conclusion she'd come to the moment she saw all that *hope* in his mother's eyes. "I don't want to have this discussion in the truck—"

"Or on the phone, or probably not at Ortega's, either. Well, tough. We're together for the first time in days. We're talking."

"I thought men didn't like talking."

"Never said I liked it. But you do what you gotta do. Now." He pulled the truck into the restaurant's parking lot. "We can chat out here where it's freezing, or go inside where it's warm. And where there's food. I haven't had lunch and I'm starving."

Brother.

Roxie marched through the spicy-scented restaurant to a small table at the end of a wildly colorful, primitive landscape mural and plopped down, Noah following suit. Evangelista, the mostly Mexican restaurant's bosomy owner, took one look at the pair of them, dropped menus and waddled discreetly away. Roxie smacked hers open, even though she'd memorized the damn thing in high school, only to smack it closed again. Noah was staring a hole through her. Since this wasn't going away, she said, "Noah, look. I don't know what got into us the other day, what got into *me,* but—"

"But you changed your mind."

"I came to my senses!" Leaning forward, she lowered her voice, even though the only other patrons were four cowboys from some ranch or other, laughing it up in a booth on the other side of the room. "What's the point of torturing ourselves? I'm leaving, you're staying, we still don't want the same things."

"Yeah. Got that. But I thought we were at least friends—"

"You guys ready to order?" Evangelista said, setting a basket of chips and a small bowl of salsa between them.

"Three tamale plate," Noah said, handing her the laminated menu but not taking his eyes off Roxie. "Red on the side, corn, potatoes. Oh, and two cinnamon rolls and a large coffee to go."

"Got it. And you, doll-baby?"

"Fried ice cream."

Noah frowned at her. "For lunch?"

"I'll eat my veggies tonight. Promise. And that friendship thing," she said after Evangelista waddled away again, "doesn't work for me, okay? And don't you dare give me that look, we already established things between us had gotten a little...wonky." At his continued staring, she went on. Like a runaway train, gack. "See, you're a guy, you can separate your feelings into these nice, neat compartments—friendship here, sex there, love way the heck over there somewhere. In theory, anyway. But turns out I can't really do that. At least, not with you. And *damn* you," she said, her face reddening, "for being everything I've ever wanted and everything I can't have. I mean, have you *watched* yourself with kids? With Eli's newborn?" She grabbed a chip and dunked it in the salsa, muttering, "Jerk."

Dipping his own chip, Noah glanced at her. With, to his credit, a troubled look in his eyes. "You done?"

Exhausted, Roxie sagged back against the chair as Evangelista brought their food. Roxie grabbed her spoon and gouged out her first bite so fast the woman snatched back her hand. "I think so," she said around a mouthful of hot crunch and cold, smooth sweetness.

This time Noah waited until they were alone again before saying, "Okay, you wanna know the truth? The friendship thing doesn't work for me, either."

Bent over her dessert mountain, Rox lifted her eyes to his. "Meaning you *do* want sex?"

"Was that ever even a question? You make me so hot my core temperature goes up a good five degrees every time I look at you."

"Flatterer," she said around another blissfully anesthetizing mouthful.

"Which doesn't happen as often as you might think,"

he said, and she *hmmphed*. At which point he leaned across the table and grabbed her hand, and the look in his eyes wasn't doing a blessed thing to cool her off. "Or at least not as much. That's gotta count for something."

"Yes, Noah, we have great chemistry. Still not enough. Not for what I want. Dammit," she whispered. Wiping her mouth on her paper napkin, she stared at the decimated mound of Frosted Flake-coated ice cream, angry that her eyes were stinging. "What do *you* want?"

"From you?"

"From me, for yourself…whatever."

"I want…things to be different."

At the genuine misery in his eyes, Roxie sighed around the clenched fist in her own chest. "But they're not."

"And…maybe they could be."

"Maybe? Could? Do you even hear yourself?" Jabbing her spoon into the ice cream, she crossed her arms and leaned back in the chair, her forehead pinched so tightly it hurt. "So, what? I should blow off the best job offer I've ever had in my life on the off chance that *maybe* you'll change your mind? That *maybe* I won't get my heart broken again? Holy heck, Noah—nobody knows better than I do that there are no guarantees, but there is such a thing as minimizing the risks!"

She shook her head. "I don't want an affair, Noah. I'm simply not wired that way. I thought you understood that. I guess I was wrong. And you should eat, your food's getting cold."

"Not hungry," he mumbled, signaling to Evangelista to bring a take-out box. "Finished?"

Amazingly, she was. Although she wasn't entirely sure he was talking about her "meal." His food boxed,

Noah paid at the register and picked up Naomi's bagged rolls and coffee, then walked ahead of her to his truck, yanking open the passenger side door but saying nothing, the suffocating silence cocooning them as they drove back to the clinic. Where Noah finally said, "Just so you know? I've never cared one way or the other before whether a gal stuck around or not."

"Never?" His gaze fixed out the windshield, he shook his head, and she sighed. "Still no cigar, sweet cheeks."

Tortured eyes glanced off hers, then away again. "I know."

She waited a moment, then said, very softly, "This is killing me, too, Noah. On the one hand, I already know how much it's going to hurt, leaving. On the other..." She waited until he faced her again. "I also know how much it would hurt if I stayed."

When he didn't say anything, she snatched Naomi's bag off the console, then grabbed the door handle, only to gasp when warm, strong fingers clamped around the back of her neck and brought their mouths together. And if it'd been anybody but Noah, she would've clobbered the bejeebers out of him. Instead of, you know, letting herself fall into the sweetest, hottest, deepest kiss of her life. When it was over—approximately a year later— she said, through a tear-clogged throat, "And *that's* why I'm glad I'm leaving."

When she went to open the door this time, he didn't stop her.

"...AND THAT'S ABOUT IT," Roxie said to Thea Griego, the clinic's new receptionist. "Everything's pretty straightforward, actually. Although you can call me on my cell anytime if you have questions."

Seated behind the silver garland-festooned reception desk, the pretty blonde grinned up at her. Married to a handsome rancher and mama to a rambunctious toddler boy, Thea had brought little Jonny in for a check-up when she'd heard about the job opening. Gal had jumped at it like a cat on a fly.

"Heaven knows, this is a lot easier on the back and feet than waitressing," she said with a low laugh, referring to her pre-marriage, pre-mama life. "And now that Jonny's old enough to hang out more with daddy, I figured it was time for me to spread my wings. So this is gonna be perfect."

One more thing settled, Roxie thought a few minutes later as she drove back to Charley's through a powdery, Christmas card snow. Even though it was only the middle of the afternoon, it was so dark some people had turned on their Christmas lights, and all the twinkly cheeriness was making her a little melancholy.

Okay, a lot melancholy.

Despite her best intentions, she had to admit the sleepy little town had grown on her. There was a lot of good here. A lot of love. She suspected she was going to miss it a lot more than she would have believed a few months ago, when she'd felt like a failure, having to move back. And of course there was Noah, whom she hadn't seen since the fried ice cream episode a week ago. Not sure who was avoiding whom, but he hadn't even come to his parents' family night dinner last Thursday.

And yes, she knew that because she'd looked for his truck in front of the house. So sue her.

Speaking of his parents' house…it was blazing in full Christmas glory when she pulled into Charley's driveway alongside his much more modestly decorated abode. A single string of large colored bulbs hailing from before the Moon Walk stretched along the top of the porch, a battered wreath on the door. That was it. Not even Eden had been able to convince him how sorry it looked. And Lord knows she'd tried, Roxie thought with a smile as she let herself inside to be greeted by a gleeful black-and-brown fluff ball named, of all things, Stanley.

"And you can take that mutt right back to the pound," Charley said before she'd even removed her coat, only to scoop the wriggling puppy into his arms and let him lick his chin.

"What'd he do now?"

"Only chewed up the new paperback I just bought."

"All the more reason to get an e-reader."

Charley rolled his eyes. They'd had this discussion before. "So he can chew that up instead of a seven-buck paperback? I think not. What's that?" he said, looking at the check she'd dug out of her purse and handed to him.

"From the eBay sales."

Holding the check out where the curious pup couldn't get it, Charley let out a low whistle. "Holy crap."

"Yeah. You did really well."

His eyes swung to hers. "No, *you* did really well. Okay, okay, you can get down," he said to the now yip-ping dog, who, once on the floor, tripped over himself in his haste to scramble up onto the chair in front of the window and bark at the blinking lights across the street. Charley laughed, then turned back to Roxie. "Did you take a good commission for yourself?"

"You bet."

"Seriously?"

"No. Hey, if it hadn't been for you I'd've been homeless. This was the least I could do."

Eyes watering, her uncle pulled her into a hug. "I'm gonna miss you, you big pain in the butt."

"Same goes," she said, chuckling.

Then he let her go. "Just so you know…Edie's moving in after you leave."

"As in, she's giving up her apartment?"

"Doesn't make sense to keep two places. And this way she'll finally have a room for her crafts. And yes, I know it seems fast, but—"

"Charley," Roxie said, taking hold of his arms, "you are not obligated to explain anything to me. Your life, your heart, your house. Your happiness. Go for it."

"You really mean that?"

"I really do. Besides," she said, her gaze dropping to Stanley, gnawing on something he probably wasn't supposed to have, "Diva needs to be taken down a notch or two." Then she looked at her uncle again. "Being alone—when you don't want to be—sucks." She glanced over at the fragrant Noble fir taking up a quarter of the living room, looking more like a Mardi Gras float than a Christmas tree. "Especially at Christmas."

"You'll be back for the holidays, right?"

She shook her head. "I'm going to be way busy. But it's okay, I'll be with Elise and her husband, so I won't be alone," she said, not stopping in time the memories of Christmases as a kid with her parents…the fantasy Christmases she'd always imagined she'd be having by now, with a husband and children. *Cut it out, bitterness gives you wrinkles,* she thought, grateful when Charley practically lunged at the landline when it rang.

For a moment, Roxie considered telling her uncle about losing the baby, only to decide he really didn't need to know, that it would only make things more complicated. He'd worry, is what he'd do. Or go after Jeff with a pitchfork. And heaven knew, neither of them needed that.

Leave the past in the past, cupcake, she thought, looking outside at the gentle snow, like glittering pearls in the December dusk. Perfect for taking Stanley for a walk, to hopefully exorcise both the ickies from her brain and at least some of Stanley's puppy crazies. Not that she held out much hope for either, but it might be the last time she got to walk in the snow for a while, Austin not being generally known for its winter activities.

Bundled back up, the dog turning himself inside out trying to chew his new leash, she called to Charley—who'd disappeared upstairs—"Taking the dog for a walk!" and let them both outside, where the crisp, cold air soothed her frazzled nerves. And the deep hush as they shuffled through the confectioner-sugar snow—well, she shuffled, Stanley bounced—seemed to penetrate her very being.

Now that Thea had taken the helm at the clinic, there really was no reason for her to stick around. All the eBay auctions were done and the pieces shipped, the rest of Mae's things sorted and in storage for the estate sale she'd hold in six months or so. And Charley was on the brink of starting his new life with Eden, which Roxie gratefully realized she was more happy about than not.

"Guess it's time, Stanley," she said to the dog.

Then she shrieked when Noah said, "Time for what?" right behind her.

HE HADN'T MEANT to stalk her. Exactly. But when he walked out of his parents' house and saw her and the puppy starting down the street, something—sheer idiocy, most likely—pushed him after her.

"Where on earth did you come from?" she said, blinking at him as if he'd materialized out of thin air.

"Stopped by my folks' to give Dad an update. Saw you when I came out. Guess you didn't notice me in the snow."

"Um, no." She glanced away, then back. "How's your dad doing?"

"Excellent, actually. If the docs say it's okay, he and Mom are going on a cruise, right after Christmas. To the Caribbean."

"Aw...that'll be nice."

The snow gently pinging their faces, they stood there like a couple of doofuses, Roxie apparently not knowing what to say any more than Noah. To break the awkwardness, if that was even possible, he squatted in front of the puppy, who bounded over to Noah like he'd been waiting to meet him his whole life. "Who's this?"

"Stanley. I got him for Charley. From the pound."

"Hey, guy," Noah said, laughing when the thing tried to heave himself into Noah's lap. "What is he?"

"Dog. Like one of those little sponge critters you put water on, you don't know what you've got until it's done growing."

The puppy having abandoned him to bark at the snow, Noah stood, chuckling despite the sting of seeing her again. His own damn fault, to be sure, nobody'd told him to follow her, to stir up again all those feelings he'd tried so hard to bury in work. "He'll be a good friend to Charley."

"Although he'll have to share him with Eden. She's moving in. As soon as I'm gone, apparently."

"With the rat dog?"

Roxie laughed. "I know," she said, watching Stanley chase his own tail, then fall over in the snow. "Should be interesting."

"You are so evil."

"I do what I can," she said, grinning up at him. "Anyway, Charley and Eden seem happy enough. But… would you and your folks mind keeping an eye out? Make sure he's okay?"

"You don't even have to ask, you know that."

She nodded, then they spoke together:

"So when are you going—?"

"I'm leaving tomorrow—"

Noah lost his breath. "Tomorrow? That soon?"

"Yeah, we found my replacement at the clinic. Everything's done here…there's no real reason for me to stick around." The dog yanked on the leash, nearly knocking her off balance. "Toss my clothes into a few suitcases and…head out. Rest of my stuff's in storage, I'll get it after I find my own place."

"Bet you can't wait," Noah said. Grumpily.

He thought maybe her eyes watered. "That's why I'm not," she whispered, then leaned forward, standing up on tiptoe to kiss his cheek. As she lowered herself he grabbed her hand.

"I really do wish you the best," he pushed past the

pain in his chest. "Because nobody deserves getting what she wants more than you."

A tiny smile touched her lips. "Thank you," she said, then tugged the puppy to continue their journey. A journey on which Noah was clearly not invited.

And he had nobody but himself to blame for that.

CHAPTER TWELVE

ELISE SUGIHARA-DICKSON LOOKED, dressed and sounded exactly the same as she had in college, even if her shorter hair and all-black wardrobe—velvet leggings, flats with rhinestone-studded toes and a cowl-neck sweater the size of a circus tent to cover her enormous baby bump—were definitely much spiffier than the grungy Salvation Army getups the gal used to sport back in the day.

And the store—Oh. My. God. Cozily snuggled between a trendy, upscale clothing boutique and an equally trendy Asian fusion restaurant in downtown Austin, Fly Away Home was the stuff dreams were made of. At least Roxie's dreams, she thought as she tried to take it all in at once. Lord, she'd never seen so many pretties congregated in one two-story space in her life.

"Would it sound hugely unsophisticated of me to say, 'Wow'?"

Although the store was closed on Sundays, Elise had brought Roxie to see the place without the distraction of customers and her other employees. Now she grinned. "Hell, I say pretty much the same thing every morning when I walk in," she said in her rapid-fire Southern accent. "Fun, huh?"

"Fun? It's practically a theme park."

"I know, right?" her old friend said, and they both

laughed. From the moment they'd reconnected, it was as if no time had passed at all, their easy friendship picking up exactly where they'd left off. It had been nearly three in the morning before they got to bed, after Elise's husband, Patrick, finally lumbered out of their bedroom and pointed out the time. Roxie had forgotten how good it felt to have another gal to talk to.

"So you built this up all on your own?"

"Oh, Lord, no. Although the inventory's turned over several times since I bought the place about five, six years ago, from this dude who'd decided to retire. He had some neat stuff even then, and the location is *fabulous*. So when he offered me a deal I couldn't turn down, I jumped on it. 'Course, I'll be paying him off until I'm dead," she said with a shrug, "but it's totally worth it."

Her eyes as big as a kid's in a candy store, Roxie moved through a dozen vignettes, each one done in a different period, from early nineteenth century to art nouveau to midcentury modern to contemporary. "Where do you find all this stuff?"

"Estate sales, buying trips overseas. Wherever. You like it?"

"Are you kidding? I love it. All of it." She picked up a gorgeous art deco painted glass vase. "Especially since this is so not our mothers' antique store."

"You got it. Nice to know our tastes still mesh as well as they did when we were sharing that dinky house near campus."

Roxie howled. "Ohmigosh, now I'm gonna have nightmares for a week. God, that place was ugly."

"Hey. At the time we thought we were seriously stylin'. That lime-green bathroom *rocked,* baby."

"Because it went so well with the burnt-orange shag carpet in the rest of the house."

"No, it *distracted* from the orange shag. As did the purple walls."

Roxie held up one finger. "Not purple. *Grape Mist.*"

"Thank God there's no evidence. If there'd been Facebook then, my career would be screwed—"

Elise's cell rang. She pulled it out of a hidden pocket in her sweater tent, chuckling when she checked the number. "The hubster. Suffers from heavy-duty pregnancy guilt, poor baby. Checks in at least once an hour to see how I'm doing. This won't take long. Go ahead and keep looking around."

The sting came out of nowhere. Honestly. Here she was, dream job landed, reconnected with a great friend...and about to tip over the edge from somebody else's domestic bliss? So lame.

Wasn't as if you left anything behind in Tierra Rosa, right?

If you didn't count her heart, not a thing.

She'd get over it, of course. Over Noah. Pining for what wasn't rightfully hers—and never had been—wasn't her style. God knew she was nothing if not a survivor, that for all its wounds, her heart kept on beating...and would find its way back to her, as it always had before.

Her life as a Celine Dion song. Yay, a new low.

"Rox? Hey. What's up?"

She spun around to find Elise frowning at her with don't-mess-with-me eyes. Too bad. "I think last night just caught up with me."

"Tell me about it," her friend said, yawning, then waved her toward the door. "Definitely seeing naps in

both of our near futures. Oh, by the way…" She let Rox
out first, then set the alarm before following. "Wanna
check out a couple of local estate sales this weekend?"

Roxie glanced back, her thumb jerked over her shoulder. "Because it's not crammed to the rafters already
in there?"

"Believe it or not, it doesn't stick around. If a piece
doesn't find a home with a client or sell off the floor
within three months, I eBay it. So there's always room
for more! So, you up for some shopping?"

"Bring it on," Rox said, embracing the thrill of the
hunt. That old optimism that everything she wanted
was simply waiting for her to find it. And while she
was at it? Maybe she could find a spare heart for cheap.

'Cause she needed to plug up this hole in her chest,
fast.

For as long as Noah could remember Christmas morn-
ings at his parents' house had been crazy. Factor in six
grandkids under the age of seven, and it was flat-out
insane. In the best definition of the word.

And normally Noah was right on the floor with them,
tossing wadded-up wrapping paper at his brothers and
making Blue bark and his mom go, "Noah, for pity's
sake!" at least every thirty seconds. This Christmas,
however, even though he was still on the floor, still
laughing when the kids crawled all over him, still genuinely touched by his mother's uncanny ability to give
them all exactly the right gifts whether they'd dropped
hints or not…he simply wasn't feeling the joy.

Nor was he doing a particularly good job of hiding
it, if the not-so-subtle exchanged glances between assorted adult members of the family was any indication.

At long last the Great Christmas Carnage was over, the kids had all claimed assorted corners of the family room to play with their new toys, and all the females except Tess, who was feeding the baby, had swarmed into the kitchen where his mother was hollering out who wanted bacon and who wanted sausage, and did everybody want French toast or pancakes, she could do either, it wasn't any bother.

Exactly like every Christmas since he could remember.

Only this year, Noah felt as if somebody'd ripped a hole in his heart the size of the Grand Canyon. How the morning could make him miss Roxie so much, when she'd never been a part of his family's Christmases, he had no idea. But for damn sure, he wasn't "getting over" her. If anything, every day the painful irony only got worse.

Silas plopped beside him on the beat-up sectional, lightly slapping Noah's knee before crossing his arms high on his chest, his brows dipped behind his glasses. Groaning, Noah let his head drop back on the cushions.

"Let me guess—you drew the short straw."

"Oh, they didn't even bother with straws, just pointed and said, 'You're the oldest, you go talk to him.'"

"Nothing to talk about."

"Bull. You look like a dog left behind at the pound. Come on." Silas slapped Noah's knee again as he got up. "Get your coat, we're going outside."

"And if I don't want to?"

"It's me or Mom. Choose wisely, grasshopper."

Pushing out a heavy breath, Noah heaved himself out of the nice, soft cushions, grabbed his coat off the arm of the sofa and followed his brother outside into the frigid, blue-skied morning, the sun glinting off patches of frozen snow.

"Here's a news flash, bro," Silas said before they got to the end of the walk. "It's not a crime to be in love."

Nothing like coming straight to the point. "What makes you think—?"

"You're not seriously gonna argue?"

Noah was quiet for a long moment, then said, "I honest-to-God never thought it would happen. Not to me."

"So I gathered."

Jiggling his keys in his coat pocket, Noah frowned at his brother. "Except…if this is love, how come it hurts so much?"

Silas quietly chuckled. "You remember how we used to wrestle? When we were kids?"

"Like I could forget. I've *still* got bruises."

"As does Mom, I'm sure. But do you also remember that the more you struggled after you got pinned, the more it hurt?"

"And that if I didn't I'd get creamed. Or suffocate."

"Okay, so maybe not the best analogy. Still. Love's a lot like that. Once you stop resisting, it stops hurting. So." Silas crossed his arms. "You got any idea why you're fighting so hard?"

Another several seconds passed before Noah released another, softer, "I think so, yeah."

"Care to share?"

Noah's gaze landed on Charley's house across the street, a house without Roxie, as he wrestled with himself, about whether or not to give voice to the phantom thoughts he'd kept locked up in the back of his brain for so long he'd almost stopped hearing them. Until some curly-headed gal unwittingly unlocked their cage and set them free to run amok, screaming like freaking banshees in his ear.

"What difference does it make?" he said, his voice as harsh as the wind whipping down their ice-covered street. "I'm here. She's not. I can't leave, and I sure can't ask her to come back. Especially since…"

"Go on."

Noah looked away, his breath frosting around his mouth. "Since I seriously doubt I could ever live up to the example our folks set."

Silas gawked at him. "You're kidding me, right?"

"Nope."

"Wow. Nothing like being a little hard on yourself."

"It's called being realistic. And honest. And Roxie… no way would she ever settle for something half-assed. Or should she."

Silas flipped up his jacket collar against the back of his neck, the wind ruffling his hair. "So…the feelings are mutual?"

"Yeah," Noah said, already irritated for having said as much as he had. Although the release felt good, too. Then he laughed. "All the boneheaded things I used to do without even batting an eye? This makes me feel like I'm gonna hurl. That I don't know *how* to love somebody, that I'd screw it up, that I've *already* screwed up. That…" He pushed a swallow past his constricted throat, the wind making his eyes sting. "That I've lost her."

His gaze swung to Silas, who was angled away from him with his hands shoved in his pockets and his head bent, his mouth set. His brother's "thinking hard" pose, he knew. "Before," Noah went on, his heart knocking against his ribs, "either I knew I'd succeed or it didn't matter. But this..." The frigid air scraped his lungs when he hauled in a breath. "I don't have an idea in hell whether I'd be any good at this or not. And failure's not an option."

Several beats passed before Silas released a breath, then looked at Noah again, his expression more relaxed. "For what it's worth, we've all been there. Nothing scarier than putting your heart out there."

"But you got married anyway. All of you. Even Jesse, and he was only *eighteen,* for God's sake."

"Don't discount ignorance," Silas said on a short, dry laugh. "It definitely has its uses." He glanced out at the street again. "What about kids?"

Yeah. That. Noah gave his head a sharp shake. "How one woman could turn everything I believed about myself on its head...I don't get it."

"Nobody does," Silas said, sympathetically clamping a hand on his shoulder. "Not that everyone who falls in love automatically thinks 'I wanna make babies with this person,' but it happens often enough to keep the species going." He let go to lean against the chunky stone pillar housing an old gas lantern that hadn't worked in years. "All of us go into this commitment thing blind," he said, "even when we think we've got a clue. And Mom and Dad would be the first ones to say that."

Noah frowned. "But...after Amy...?"

"How did I find the courage to try again?" He shrugged. "I don't think it's so much about finding it, as it is not ducking fast enough before it clobbers you over the head. It's just this voice that says...this is right. Along with, I suppose, a determination to *keep* it right. Of course, both people have to be on the same page

about that," he said with a slight grimace, referring—
Noah assumed—to his first wife's definite lack in that
department.

"Dad! Uncle Noah!" Sunlight glanced off Ollie's
straight blond hair when he opened the front door.
"Gramma says to tell you breakfast's ready!"

"Coming, squirt," Silas said, then looked back at
Noah. "So what are you going to do?"

"Hang myself?" Noah said, plowing his fingers
through his hair. "It's not like I can simply up and leave,
is it? All those years I've busted my buns to prove to
Dad he can count on me...what *can* I do? Tell him, after
less than a month, I've changed my mind? That some
girl is more important than the business he spent his
entire adult life building?"

"Is that all Roxie is? Some girl?"

His face heating, Noah looked away. "If she was,
we wouldn't be having this conversation." Air left his
lungs in a huge rush. "Man, am I between a rock and a
hard place, or what?"

"Sure looks like it," Silas said, not being helpful at
all. "But on the upside, at least now we all know you're
human."

"Butthead," Noah muttered at his brother's grin,
hugely tempted to cram a fistful of snow down his collar.

"YOU SURE YOU don't want me to help?" Roxie asked
Elise's husband, Patrick, as he carted off what was left
of the ham to the kitchen. Both sets of Elise's and Patrick's boisterous, energetic parents had already gone,
leaving behind a startled calm and a boatload of dirty
dishes.

The gangly, graying blonde plunked the platter on the counter dividing the living area from the kitchen in their fabulous, eclectically furnished condo overlooking the Colorado River. "Nope. Got it covered."

"But you did all the cooking, you should let me do *something*."

"What you can do," Patrick said with a wide, slightly gap-toothed smile, "is keep Her Royal Highness from waddling in here and telling me I'm not loading the dishwasher right."

"It's true," Elise said with a shrug from her perch on the tangerine-colored sofa, her puffy, fuzzy-socked feet stretched out in front of her. "I would. Because he tosses the dishes in there any old way, no respect for order at all."

Laughing, Roxie sank into the other end of the sofa, soaking in the soft glow of the colored lights on the retro silver aluminum Christmas tree and trying desperately to hang on to something that almost passed for contentment. It had been a lovely, lazy day, filled with laughter and friends and ending in the most amazing meal she'd ever eaten in her life. She absolutely loved her job. And in a week she'd be moving into her new apartment, an adorable one-bedroom in a quirky old Queen Anne not far from work.

Only then she'd have to return to Tierra Rosa to get her stuff out of storage, a thought which made the contentment go *poof*. So to distract herself she focused on Patrick's bustling about the kitchen, humming to himself as he worked.

Big mistake.

"You've got a real keeper there," she said, not even trying to keep the wistfulness out of her voice.

Elise tried to shift, winced, then sighed a happy sigh. "And don't I know it. Although I had to kiss a hella lot of frogs before I found him. Astounding, the number of losers out there...oh. Sorry," she said, grimacing as she apparently remembered Jeff. "Can I blame it on the pregnancy?"

"Sure. And it's okay. I'm more than over *him*, believe me."

Oops.

Elise nudged Roxie's thigh with her foot. "And who is it you're *not* over?"

"I have no idea what—"

"Hey." Spearing Roxie with her dark, way-too-astute gaze, Elise said, "I'm sending you to Italy next month, last thing I need is you ending up in Bulgaria by mistake because some dude keeps pulling you to La La Land. So what's going on?"

It'd been years since she'd thought of how her mother could immediately tell when something was amiss, how a simple, "What's wrong?" could reduce Roxie to tears. Fighting the suckers now, she said, "Other than managing to once again fall in love with the absolutely worst possible person for me? Not a thing."

"You really need to stop doing that," Elise said, and Roxie sputtered a laugh. "So how did this one rate on the ol' Jerk-o-meter? Assuming Jeffrey was, what? A ten?"

"Ten, hell. Try twelve. And to be honest, I'd assumed Noah was at least a seven, maybe even an eight."

Elise handed her a box of tissues off the end table. "But...?"

"But it turns out he's actually...pretty darn close to perfect. Except for one or two tiny things."

"Oh, hell…he's gay."

Roxie laughed again, even as she dabbed at her leaking eyes. "Um, no. But he is allergic to white picket fences."

"Oh, sweetie…" Elise held out her hand, wagging for Roxie to take it. "I'm so sorry," she said with a gentle squeeze. "I'd give you a hug, but bending forward ain't happening these days." Then she whispered, "Was the sex good, at least?"

"We never got that far."

"You *sure* he's not gay?"

"My decision, not his. Because I knew…" She swiped at a hot tear trickling down her cheek. "Well. It seemed like a good idea at the t-time."

With great effort, Elise slowly swung her feet off the couch to sit up, gesturing for Roxie to scoot over so she could give her that hug, at which point Patrick—who'd known Roxie for all of two weeks and had clearly heard the entire conversation—mumbled something about men being dumb as bricks, which only opened the floodgates.

Because when it came to *dumb,* Roxie had 'em all beat, hands down.

"Do you believe this snow?" Noah's father said, stomping the damn stuff off his feet as he came inside the shop, his grin broad in a face still tan from the cruise.

Plans for a new project spread out on a drafting table right inside the door, Noah grunted. Normally he greeted the first snowfall of the season like an excited little kid, champing at the bit for snowball fights and sledding parties, rubbing his hands in glee at the prospect of navigating his truck through snow-choked, winding mountain roads. But this January—the snowiest on record, for which the New Mexico ski industry was extremely grateful—it only made him grumpy as hell.

"Everything okay?" Gene asked, stuffing his gloves inside his coat pocket.

Noah pushed his mouth into a smile. "Yeah. Fine."

At least on this front it was. Apparently, Gene's forced vacation had made him look at things from a whole new angle. Including, as it happened, Noah. Not a day passed that his father didn't tell him how well he was doing, how pleased he was. In fact, whenever Noah tried to defer to his dad when the old man was around, Gene backed off, saying, "Whatever you think is best, I trust you."

Who'dathunkit?

So now he waved his father toward the back of the shop. "Go take a look at the order Benito and them are working on, it's turning out fantastic."

But as his father trundled off—whistling, for God's sake—Noah's smile quickly crumpled into a glower. Because nothing felt right anymore. Felt like home. Ever since Christmas, when he'd admitted out loud how bad he had it for Roxie, his skull had felt like a pressure cooker about to explode. And with every day that passed the discontent only grew deeper, choking out even the supreme satisfaction of proving to his father—and, okay, himself—that he was damn good at what he did. That, by making sure he had the best crew ever working with him, he could even juggle both the cabinetry and construction arms of the business.

And not drop a single ball.

By rights he should have been on top of the world.

Victorious and vindicated. Instead, he simply felt…
empty. Empty and alone and frustrated beyond belief.

The plans a blur, Noah threw down the pencil he'd
been using to make notes and roared into the office to
get his coat, still wrestling into it as he walked to his
truck through a gentle blizzard of lazily floating flakes,
as if somebody'd busted open a featherbed. The snow
was too wet to stick to the roads, although the minute
the sun went down that'd change. Now, however, it was
safe enough to take a drive, clear his head. Although
what he really wanted to do was bang that head against
the steering wheel, maybe jar something loose. Or give
himself amnesia so he'd forget about Roxie once and
for all.

He drove away from town on a sparsely populated
stretch of road that led past Garcia's Market, the Bap-
tist church, a small storage facility…nearly running the
truck off the road when he caught a glimpse of Roxie
carting a big box around to the back of a U-Haul, the
snow nearly turning her curls white.

Feeling as if King Kong was squeezing the hell out
of his chest—and having no earthly idea what he was
going to say—he drove up alongside the van and got out.

From the *Oh, crap* look on her face as he approached,
it was pretty obvious she'd hoped they wouldn't run into
each other. And if her heart was beating as hard as his
was right now, her chest probably hurt like hell, too.

"Why didn't I know your stuff was stored here?"

Typically, though, she met his gaze dead on. "It never
came up?"

"You could've asked me, I would've gladly brought
it to you. Saved you a trip." *So take that,* he thought,
as her brows lifted.

"Really?"

"Yeah. Really."

"Everything okay, Roxie?" her uncle called from a few feet away, shuffling through the snow, carrying a box.

"Yes, of course," she said with a glance in Charley's direction, then back at Noah, who could barely breathe for wanting to haul her into his arms. Get *over* the woman? In what universe?

Even through the snow he saw her cheeks redden before she cleared her throat. Behind her the van's loading door rumbled shut.

Noah slugged his hands into his coat pockets. "You sticking around for a bit?"

"No," she said on a pushed breath. "In fact, if you hadn't come along when you had, you would've missed me altogether. Hey, I hear you're doing great. With the shop and everything."

Fine. If that's the way she wanted to play, so be it. "I am." He paused. "How's the new job?"

"Everything I hoped it would be," she said, and he could tell by the way her eyes softened, she meant it. "And more. I was in Italy for a week. Going to France in the spring."

Want company? he almost said, suddenly imagining waking up in Paris with her snuggled up against him, naked and warm and smelling of faded perfume. And sex. Not that he'd ever been to Paris, but he could fill in the blanks as well as the next person. "Sounds great," he said flatly. "You seeing anybody?"

The question apparently caught her so off guard she reeled. "Um…no. Way too busy, for one thing."

His eyes trapped hers. "And for another?"

He watched probably a dozen possible responses flash behind her eyes before she finally said, "Not really interested, to tell the truth."

Noah felt the corner of his mouth tuck up. "You're not just saying that?"

Tears bulging over her lower lashes, she shook her head, and now King Kong planted his hairy butt right on Noah's chest. "No," she whispered, then swiped her mittened hand underneath her eyes, leaving snow stuck to her lashes. "How about you?"

Against his better judgment, Noah lifted a hand to brush away the tiny white clump. "You kidding?" he said softly, then turned and walked back to his truck. Yeah, just like that, like the whole thing had been a dream.

Or a nightmare.

Except, the minute he walked back inside the shop it was as if something really big and *really* loud bellowed *What the* hell *do you think you're doing?*

He stopped, looking around the shop, at what, up to that moment, he'd considered his life. The only thing he'd ever believed would be a constant in it. A second later his gaze landed on his father, joking with Benito as he showed a new hire the ropes, and he knew what he had to do. No matter how much it scared him.

Because, quite simply, if he didn't he'd die.

"Dad?" he called across the shop, waiting until his father's eyes met his before he said, "we need to talk."

GOD KNEW HOW long the banging on her front door had gone on before Roxie roused herself enough from her coma to hear it. Opening one eye, she saw it was barely eight, an unholy hour when you'd stayed up until nearly five unpacking.

She briefly considered ignoring the increasingly insistent knocking, only to decide it might be her landlady bringing her coffee cake or something equally yummy—which Mrs. Harris was prone to do, bless her seventy-something heart—and it would be rude to turn her away.

Yelling, "Just a sec!" Roxie heaved herself upright, shuddered at her Brillo-headed reflection in the mirror over the dresser, and grabbed her ratty chenille robe, yawning as she tied it closed on her way to the door. Through, she noted with disgust, stacks of boxes that had clearly multiplied during the night.

She briefly considered at least running a comb through her hair, decided Mrs. Harris wouldn't care—or see, being blind as a bat—before she yanked open the door.

And then shrieked.

Grinning around a lollypop stick, a beard-shadowed Noah straightened up from leaning against the doorjamb. "About damn time you answered the door." He pulled two Tootsie Roll pops out of his jacket pocket. "Cherry or chocolate?"

She had nothing. Speech, thought...all gone. Until, after roughly fifty years, "What...? How...?" finally screeched out, followed immediately by her realizing she looked like a haunted house reject and probably had morning breath and ohmy*god*, what was he *doing* here?

He waggled the Tootsie Roll pops. "Breakfast of champions," he said, and she took the cherry one, which she shakily unwrapped and stuck in her mouth, sucking on it like mad for several seconds before the sugar kick-started her brain enough to realize the man didn't come all the way here just to give her candy, and with a little cry, she threw herself across the threshold—nearly tripping over the doorjamb, natch—and into his arms, and then it was all about tangled tongues and knocking teeth and mixing cherry and grape and salty tears, and she grabbed his hand and yanked him inside, through the boxes and down the hall to her tornado-struck bedroom, where she proceeded to rip off his clothes, explanations could wait, she couldn't.

Apparently neither could he, praise be, and seconds later they were naked and joined, and she cried with the sheer bliss of his filling her, then cried again when he pushed her over the edge into a soaring free fall the likes of which they'd never believe down on the farm.

And when it was over, Noah gathered her close, both of them panting and sweaty, and said, "And here I was just hoping to score coffee," and she laughed so hard she started to sob, and he held her tight until she could breathe again. Could think.

Gently brushing her hair away from her temple, over and over, he whispered, "What was all that about being afraid to bond?"

"It was worth the risk," she said, then bit her lip.

And then he said, very gently, "God, I love you, Rox," and she burst into tears all over again. Jeebus.

Finally, she got out, "You're not just blowing air up my skirt?"

"That would be hard to do, seeing as you're not wearing one." And then she was laughing and crying at the same time. In his arms. Reasonably sure he was never going to let her go.

Even so…"Why?"

"Why what?"

"*Why* do you love me? If you even know, I mean—"

"Because you surprise me," he said easily. "And make me laugh. And when you smile it's like all the bad stuff in the world simply…goes away. And…" He paused, then lifted her chin to look into her eyes. "And you made me dig deeper inside myself than I ever have before. Which was scary as hell, because, man, it was like my folks' garage in there. But it's okay," he said over her chuckle, "because I know you'll never let the crap pile back up, ever again. That answer your question?"

"Very nicely, thank you," Rox said, feeling all warm and fuzzy as she laid her head back on his chest. Only to suck in an *oh, hell* breath. "Um…speaking of risks… we weren't using anything."

A long, long moment passed before Noah said, "And what's the worst that can happen? We make a baby?"

Feeling as though her curls had grown into her brain, Roxie struggled up enough to lean on Noah's chest and look down into his face. "You're not serious."

"After facing my father? And your uncle? And driving twelve straight hours to get here? Trust me, I'm serious. And if little whosits comes out with these," he said, fluffing her curls, "all the better." He kissed her, then said, "Marry me."

She stiffened. As, she noted, did he. Again. Wow. "What?"

"I can't live without you, Rox. Okay, I suppose I could, but I'd be miserable. Discovered I'm not real partial to being miserable. Or lonely. You messed with my head, lady," he said softly. Sweetly. Smiling. "Only one way to straighten it out. *Marry me.*"

Tears crowded her eyes. "I can't go back, Noah—"

"Not asking you to. I'll find work here. Or anywhere you go. Because I'm awesome," he said, and she laughed.

"But…your father," she said, sobering. "The business…?"

He tucked her head under his chin. "When I went to see your uncle to get your address—and asked for his blessing, because it seemed like the thing to do—"

"You're kidding?"

"Nope. Think he got a big kick out of it, too. *Anyway,* when I made some noise about not being sure how this was all gonna work out, he quoted some Scottish dude who'd gone on an expedition to the Himalayas in the thirties. Something about…that without commitment, there's always this temptation to turn back. To give up. But once that commitment is made, things have a way of lining up exactly the way they should."

She thought her heart would burst. "Wow. Deep."

"Hey. After the hell I went through to get to this point? No way am I gonna accept that something this good has a downside." His lips tilted. "I swear with everything I have in me, I would never hurt you. That I'm in this for the long haul. You gotta believe that."

"I do," she said, knowing beyond a shadow of a doubt she could trust this man with everything she had in her.

Looking vastly relieved, Noah tangled his fingers through her hair, then snorted. "This really is a mess, you know that?"

"And to think some fools actually pay to get this look."

Laughing again, he kissed her forehead. "Marry me?

Have my kids? Be my sparring partner for the next sixty or so years?"

She paused, skimming her knuckles across his naked chest. Oh, my. "This mean I have to learn how to cook?"

"Only if you want to, honey. Or I will. Or, hell, we'll hire someone to cook for us. Will you just answer the damn question?"

"Yes," she whispered, grinning so hard she half feared her face would freeze that way. "Yes. Yes, yes, *yes.*"

"Right answer," Noah said, kissing her again. "Now about that coffee…?" he said, and she laughed and wrapped a sheet around her to pad into the kitchen, where she soon discovered—when Noah folded her into his arms from behind as she filled the basket—exactly how much fun one can have while waiting for the coffee to brew.

Eyes on the prize, cupcake….

And here it was, right in her kitchen.

Heh.

EPILOGUE

Two days before Christmas, three years later

NOAH QUIETLY LET himself inside the new, still mostly unfurnished house on the outskirts of Austin, taking a moment to savor the soon-to-be-shattered peace before hanging his keys on a hook by the front door too high for eager little hands to reach. From the back of the house he heard his wife's low laugh, his little girl's high-pitched giggling. Contentment spreading through his chest, he shuffled through a maze of stuffed toys and board books and discarded juice cartons to peer down a hallway already adorned with jelly fingerprints and crayon graffiti. "Hey! Where're my girls?"

"Daddy! Daddy!"

Soft brown curls bouncing, Phoebe barreled toward Noah as fast as her little thunder thighs could manage, squealing when he snatched her into his arms and swung her around.

It never got old, Noah thought, his heart squeezing at her laughter, her absolute trust that he wouldn't let her fall. "Hey, Pheebs—you ready to go see Gramma and Papa? And Uncle Charley and Aunt Edie?"

Securely seated in the crook of his elbow, Phoebe nodded vigorously, her mouth puckered out in her "serious" expression. Noah quickly kissed that irresistible little mouth, then rubbed noses with his daughter. "Where's Mama?"

"Right here," Roxie said, rubbing her six-months-pregnant belly as she entered the room, lifting her face for Noah's kiss. When he pulled away far sooner than, no doubt, either of them would have liked, she arched one brow. "That the best you can do?"

"With a two-year-old in my arms? I'm thinking yes. You all packed?"

"We are, believe it or not. Even if a certain party—" she leveled a mock stern gaze at their daughter "—was determined to take *all* of her 'friends' with her. Did you talk to your folks?" she asked, anticipation twinkling in her eyes. "Is there snow?"

"They're predicting it for tomorrow, so it's looking good for a white Christmas."

"Yay!" Roxie said, taking the slightly puzzled baby into her arms and dancing around the cluttered floor with her for a moment before letting her down to go wreak even more havoc. Definitely her daddy's kid. Then Rox sighed. "Can't tell you how much I'm looking forward to this week."

"Although you do realize between my folks and yours, you might not see our daughter the entire time?"

She grinned. "As I said. So, can I have the rest of my kiss now?"

"I think that can be arranged," Noah said, pulling her as close as their gestating little boy would allow, the kiss this time nice and slow and lingering…until Phoebe decided to sing her version of "Jingle Bells" at the top of her lungs. While jumping on Roxie's cream leather sofa.

Noah laughed. "Kid's gonna fit right in."

"Which she's not going to do if we miss our flight," Rox said, pulling away.

Tugging her close again, Noah murmured, "We've got time."

Even so, he thought—through the next kiss, and the one after that—he was champing at the bit, too, to get back. Even if only for a visit. Although Austin had been damn good to both of them—Noah's fledgling renovation business was taking off, due in no small part, Noah was sure, to the advice he sought from his father on a regular basis, and Rox was still having a blast with the store—even his big city gal had to admit there really was no place like home. So for two weeks every summer and a week at Christmas, they trekked back to recharge, reconnect, remind themselves what was important. Not, Noah thought as he palmed his wife's belly, that they really needed reminding.

"Was he a good boy today?"

"You kidding? He's a Garrett. Hasn't stopped moving all day. I fully expect him to yell 'Charge!' when he comes out."

"You ready for that?"

With a sly, sexy curve of her mouth, Roxie pulled out of his arms and slowly backed away. "Hey. After breaking you in? This one'll be a piece of *cake*—! Noah, no!" she shrieked, reduced to helpless gales of laughter when he caught her and mercilessly attacked her extremely sensitive neck.

"Breaking me in?"

Breathless, still laughing, she grabbed his shoulders and grinned up at him, her curls a jumble around her face. "And what would you call it?"

"Saving my life?" he said softly, watching something melt in her eyes.

Smiling, she knuckled his cheek. "Same here," she whispered, then turned to their daughter. "Come on, sweetie," she said to their little jumping bean. "Time to go!"

"On airp'ane?"

"On airplane, yep! So let's go potty and get our coats...."

As Rox and a chattering Phoebe disappeared down the hall, Noah scanned his chronically messy living room, his gaze lighting on the big-screen TV as he tried to remember the last time he'd watched a DVD all the way through. Or been able to walk around the house naked.

Or what he thought he'd been so afraid of.

His old life? History.

But his new one?

Rox and Pheebs reappeared, Phoebe rolling a Dora the Explorer backpack behind her, and Roxie glanced over and winked at him.

A little piece of heaven.

* * * * *

This cowboy isn't so easy to catch!

Reclaiming the Cowboy
by Kathleen O'Brien

When Mitch Garwood ran away with Bonnie O'Mara, he thought he'd found forever. But all his dreams crashed the morning he woke alone. Months later, he's immune to her reappearance. Even if she's now using her real name— Annabelle Irving—and ready to tell him her secrets, he's done.

Too bad the situation is not that simple. Annabelle's willingness to leave her money and position behind so she can work at Bell River Ranch and be near him surprises Mitch. Despite his resolve, the spark of attraction flares again. The most compelling part? Her determination to win him back!

AVAILABLE OCTOBER 2014 FROM HARLEQUIN SUPERROMANCE WHEREVER BOOKS AND EBOOKS ARE SOLD.

⊕ HARLEQUIN®

super romance

More Story...More Romance
www.Harlequin.com

HTHMS1014-3

Unexpected Christmas plans...

One Frosty Night
by Janice Kay Johnson

Olivia Bowen would rather avoid this holiday season. Even her satisfaction at improving the family business doesn't make up for the loss of her beloved father and the sudden tension with her mother. Olivia questions how much longer she can live in her hometown. And her decision is further complicated by Ben Hovik.

She should keep her distance—he broke her heart years ago. Yet his compassion and their still-sizzling attraction are seductive. Could she be falling for him again? When she spends Christmas with Ben and his teenage son, she wonders if this might be the first of many more...

AVAILABLE NOVEMBER 2014 FROM HARLEQUIN SUPERROMANCE WHEREVER BOOKS AND EBOOKS ARE SOLD.

⬧HARLEQUIN®
™

super romance

More Story...More Romance

www.Harlequin.com

HTHMS1014-4

JUST CAN'T GET ENOUGH?

Join our social communities
and talk to us online.

You will have access to the latest
news on upcoming titles and special
promotions, but most importantly,
you can talk to other fans about your
favorite Harlequin reads.

Harlequin.com/Community

Facebook.com/HarlequinBooks

Twitter.com/HarlequinBooks

Pinterest.com/HarlequinBooks

HSOCIAL

HARLEQUIN®

A Romance FOR EVERY MOOD™

Save $1.00

on the purchase of any Harlequin Series book.

Available wherever books are sold, including most bookstores, supermarkets, drugstores and discount stores.

Save $1.00

on the purchase of any Harlequin Series book.

Coupon valid until December 31, 2014. Redeemable at participating retail outlets in the U.S. and Canada only. Limit one coupon per customer.

Canadian Retailers: Harlequin Enterprises Limited will pay the face value of this coupon plus 10.25¢ if submitted by customer for this product only. Any other use constitutes fraud. Coupon is nonassignable. Void if taxed, prohibited or restricted by law. Consumer must pay any government taxes. Void if copied. Millennium1 Promotional Services ("M1P") customers submit coupons and proof of sales to Harlequin Enterprises Limited, P.O. Box 3000, Saint John, NB E2L 4L3, Canada. Non-M1P retailer—for reimbursement submit coupons and proof of sales directly to Harlequin Enterprises Limited, Retail Marketing Department, 225 Duncan Mill Rd., Don Mills, Ontario M3B 3K9, Canada.

U.S. Retailers: Harlequin Enterprises Limited will pay the face value of this coupon plus 8¢ if submitted by customer for this product only. Any other use constitutes fraud. Coupon is nonassignable. Void if taxed, prohibited or restricted by law. Consumer must pay any government taxes. Void if copied. For reimbursement submit coupons and proof of sales directly to Harlequin Enterprises Limited, P.O. Box 880478, El Paso, TX 88588-0478, U.S.A. Cash value 1/100 cents.

® and TM are trademarks owned and used by the trademark owner and/or its licensee.
© 2014 Harlequin Enterprises Limited

HIINC0413COUP

HARLEQUIN®

SPECIAL EDITION

Life, Love and Family

Coming in November 2014

THE SOLDIER'S HOLIDAY HOMECOMING

by *USA TODAY* bestselling author

Judy Duarte

Sergeant Joe Wilcox is back where he never expected to be—Brighton Valley, which he left long ago. He's in town because he promised to deliver a letter for a fellow marine to Chloe Dawson, who broke his late pal's heart. But before he can do so, Joe is struck by a car and gets temporary amnesia. Joe can't remember who he is, but he's intrigued by the lovely Chloe. Can the soldier and his sweetheart find happily-ever-after just in time for Christmas?

Don't miss the latest edition of the *Return to Brighton Valley* miniseries!

Available wherever books and ebooks are sold.

www.Harlequin.com

HSE65849